Outside in the alley, Alwenna stared at the dead youth. "That's Lord Ellard's squire. His mother was so proud when he came to court."

Weaver gave a noncommittal grunt as he unbuckled the youth's knife belt and stowed it away inside his cloak.

Alwenna rounded on him. "He was so young. Have you no compassion?"

"His mother should have taught him to choose his friends more wisely." Weaver dumped the body inside with the other two, throwing straw over them before securing the door. "Come on, we've wasted enough time."

Alwenna failed to respond so he took her by the elbow. She snatched her arm from his grip. "You just butchered three men. Were their lives of no consequence?" She gripped her fallen hood with one hand, as if she'd forgotten what she meant to do with it.

"They were your enemies," he said firmly. "Now pull up that hood. We must go."

SUSAN MURRAY

The Waterborne Blade

ANGRY
ROBOT

ANGRY ROBOT
An imprint of Watkins Media Ltd.

Lace Market House,
54-56 High Pavement,
Nottingham
NG1 1HW
UK

www.angryrobotbooks.com
twitter.com/angryrobotbooks
The blade itself

An Angry Robot paperback original 2015

Cover by Paul Young
Set in Meridien by EpubServices

Distributed in the United States by Random House, Inc., New York.

ISBN 978 0 85766 436 5
Ebook ISBN 978 0 85766 437 2

Printed in the United States of America

9 8 7 6 5 4 3 2 1

To my parents, with heartfelt thanks
for the weekly trips to the library

CHAPTER ONE

By the time Weaver reached the anteroom to the king's chamber, the clammy chill of rain-soaked linen had seeped through to his very bones. The roaring fire in the grate there did little to fend it off, serving only to sting his face where it wasn't protected by several days' growth of beard. He ignored the pointed stares from the few courtiers who were about at that time in the evening. He'd sooner have paused for refreshment and dry clothing, but his orders had been clear.

The guard at the door stepped forward, blocking his path. "Halt, and state your business."

"My business is with the king and no one else."

The soldier looked taken aback, but held his ground. "The king is in session with his council and I'm to admit no one."

Another recruit from the north, still wet behind the ears. There were too many like him garrisoning the citadel at present, none of them equipped to face the challenges that lay ahead.

"Step aside, you fool. I'm Ranald Weaver, King's Man. The king and his council await my report. Will you explain to him the cause for delay?"

The soldier's jaw dropped. "I... I beg your pardon, sir."

He stepped back and fumbled the door open, announcing Weaver's arrival.

Tresilian looked up from the table where he presided over his council. The king's was the youngest face of those assembled there. "Ah, Weaver. You will excuse me for a few minutes, gentlemen." Tresilian scraped back his chair and stood.

The courtier seated to his left protested. "Sire, ought we not all hear this report without delay?" Closer to Tresilian's age than the other advisors, his elaborate sleeves trailed in wine spilled on the table next to his glass.

Tresilian stared him down. "Urgent as the situation is, Stanton, I shall hear this report through first, without interruption or cavilling."

Stanton inclined his head with an open-handed gesture of submission. "As you wish, sire. It is, of course, your prerogative."

"Prerogative be damned. Await my return here." With a glance at Weaver the king led the way to private quarters beyond the council chamber.

Servants opened and closed the door in silence, leaving the two alone together.

Tresilian looked as if he'd hardly slept in the days Weaver had been away. Small wonder, with fools like that to advise him.

Weaver bowed in formal style. "Sire–"

Tresilian raised a hand. "Never mind all that. Do you have a new name to give me?"

"No, sire. My money's still on Stanton."

Tresilian turned away to a side table and filled two pewter goblets with wine from an ornate decanter. "Dare I hope you bring proof?"

"No, sire."

Tresilian handed one goblet to Weaver, then flung himself into a chair, sprawling there irritably. "Damn the fellow, he's been pettifogging and whining all day. He's got too many supporters to risk a wrong move now." He rubbed his eyes and waved a hand towards the chair opposite. "Sit down, then. Take a drink. Tell me the rest – it's bad, isn't it?"

Weaver removed his sodden cloak and dropped it over the settle by the fire, then drew out the chair Tresilian indicated and sat. He hadn't seen his king look so defeated in a long time. Not since he'd learned of the death of his father. "It's bad. Vasic's army has crossed the river." He drew his goblet closer across the table. "Their scouts may be in the pass already. I saw campfires half a day's ride from here."

Tresilian sank his head in his hands, then looked up again. "Numbers?"

"Five, perhaps six thousand. There were regular messengers passing to and from the south, so probably more."

Tresilian swilled the wine around his goblet. "Anything else I should know?"

"He has several units of southern mercenaries."

Tresilian swore.

Weaver swallowed down several mouthfuls of wine, realising how parched his throat was.

Tresilian stretched back in his chair, easing knotted shoulders and neck. "Advice?"

"I wouldn't presume, sire."

"Horse shit. I need someone to tell me straight, Ranald. Those old women next door won't."

Weaver drew in his breath. "You'll need to recall the garrisons from the east. There's a fair chance of holding Highkell until they arrive. A better chance if you lock up Stanton and his cronies tonight."

"Ever the diplomat, eh, my friend?" For a moment Tresilian smiled. "I understand what you are saying about Stanton, I do. But there's something I must see to first."

Weaver shrugged. "Lock him up, and everyone he drinks with, games with, talks with. You are king. Don't leave it to chance." He drained his goblet.

"That would be half the court. And all on no more proof than that." Tresilian raised his hand and snapped his fingers.

Weaver lowered his eyes. He might be no diplomat, but he knew this wasn't the time to test the limits of their friendship. "What would you have me do now, sire? Take a unit east to marshal the garrisons, or deal with Stanton?" He'd need a clear head if he was setting off again in a few hours. Weaver slid his empty goblet into the middle of the table, noticing for the first time an incongruous bundle of homespun clothing sitting there.

"Neither."

Weaver looked up sharply. "Neither?"

"I'll send Teviot east with my orders."

Weaver nodded. "He's sound. What of Stanton?"

"I'll deal with him. But first I have another task for you to carry out." He paused, as if gauging Weaver's reaction. "Tonight."

What could be so urgent? Someone must have proved even less faithful than Stanton.

Tresilian emptied his own goblet and set it down with deliberation. "I want you to take Alwenna away to sanctuary at Vorrahan. She'll be safe there."

Weaver gaped at him. "But, sire, you'll need me here. Old Clarin's reliable. He'd be a better choice to escort her party. I'm a soldier, not a courtier."

"This won't be some courtly procession to draw attention. You'll travel fast, in secret. No one will even know she's gone. Not until, Goddess willing, she's safe behind the precinct walls."

"I'm not a fit escort for the lady, sire. Don't ask it of me, I beg you." A sharp pain bit behind Weaver's eyes. He knew better than to swig strong wine on an empty stomach. One day, he'd set down a goblet before it was empty. One day, but not this day.

Tresilian watched him with the sort of intensity Weaver had last seen before they were due to go into battle. "You're the only one I can trust with this. I want to put the breadth of Highground between my wife and Vasic. Must I remind you of your oath?"

A King's Man swore a lifetime's obedience to his monarch. But that was about soldiering. Not… this. "Sire, please reconsider."

"You're by far the ablest for the task. I have too much at stake to risk her safety now. Swear you'll do this." Half-rising from his chair, he planted his hands on the table and leaned over, his gaze intense. "Swear you'll keep her safe, Ranald."

Weaver lowered his head. "I swear it."

"Thank you, my friend. That's a weight off my mind." Tresilian shoved his chair back and strode over to the door at the back of the room, which opened onto the newel staircase leading up to his private chambers. A bored servant stationed there straightened up hastily.

"Summon the Lady Alwenna to my presence. Without delay."

Tresilian closed the door and returned to the table. He picked up a map scroll and pushed aside the bundle of clothing so he could open out the map, weighting the corners with the empty goblets and sliding a candle branch over to see better. "So, what will you need? My best horses are at your disposal."

Weaver stood up to study the map, rubbing the back of his neck. "If we're to avoid notice, my own remounts will be more suitable. We'd be taking poor roads, crossing hard terrain... Are you sure about this?"

A shadow crossed Tresilian's face, before he smiled tightly. "As sure as if my own life depended upon it."

CHAPTER TWO

The odour of damp wool mingled with horse sweat hit
Alwenna the moment she stepped into the king's chamber.
A sodden travelling cloak had been thrown onto the settle,
water dripping onto the flagstones beneath it. It was a
commoner's garment, yet its owner stood at the king's
side. The pair of them stooped over the table, engrossed in
discussion of a map. None of Tresilian's appointed advisors
were present. Alwenna stepped further into the room and
the servant withdrew, closing the door with a clatter.

The newcomer turned her way and bowed. "My lady."
The King's Man, Weaver. She'd have recognised him the
sooner if he'd been wearing the king's livery as normal. His
hair was wet and tangled while his face was unshaven. At
least he'd paused long enough to leave his horse outside,
if not the smell of it.

"My lord husband. Weaver. Good evening." Goddess
forfend a lady should speak what was on her mind.

Tresilian raised his head then, with no hint of his usual
smile.

"There is bad news?" As if there could be any other
reason Weaver had trailed mud into the king's presence.

Tresilian nodded. "Vasic's army has crossed the river.

The vanguard is camped two days' march away."

"So close? That's worse than you feared."

"It doesn't leave us much time." Tresilian drew a deep breath.

Alwenna knew her duty as chatelaine; now she had to prove herself competent. "There's still a good surplus from last year's harvest. Tomorrow, I must–"

"No." Tresilian turned to face her fully. "You're leaving tonight."

"What?" Not once had he suggested such a measure might be necessary. "I see no reason to do that. My place is here, at your side."

"Weaver will escort you to Father Garrad's precinct on Vorrahan." He pointed to a tiny island off the north-west coast.

"That's the furthest edge of the kingdom. Would you exile me?" She meant it as a joke, but Tresilian didn't smile.

He busied himself rolling up the map. "You'll be out of harm's way there."

"Indeed? Am I to have no say in the decision?"

"We haven't time to argue about this. Only the three of us in this room will know where you've gone."

Alwenna glanced at Weaver; his gaze was fixed on the floor.

"Why such secrecy?" For a dizzying moment she could have sworn the ground shifted beneath her feet, but her husband was speaking as if nothing untoward had happened.

"… suspected Vasic has spies at court. It's no coincidence he's made his move when I've committed so many troops to trouble in the east." Tresilian rubbed his forehead. "You'll set off after dark. This weather should at least prevent anyone seeing you leave."

"Surely this is unnecessary. It seems – so desperate."

Tresilian took her hand in his. "No one will expect this. There are factions at court who support Vasic's claim, and they will act once reinforcements are at hand. You would be their target – he needs you to legitimise his claim to the throne."

"As did you." She pulled her hand away.

Tresilian nodded. "As did I. But I'm thinking only of your safety, Alwenna."

"How can I be safer outside the citadel walls?"

"We had an informant, but last night someone inside the citadel silenced him. I will not risk you. And it will not be a wasted journey: once at Vorrahan I would have you further our cause by seeking Brother Gwydion's counsel. He is master seer there, and I will not have it said again that we slight the seers."

That put a different complexion on it. "If that is the case, I must do as you wish." The tension in Tresilian's shoulders eased; he truly believed there was danger. That shook Alwenna more than she cared to admit. "Where are the servants? I'll need to take Wynne with me, of course." From the corner of her eye Alwenna noticed Weaver turn to the fire with a gesture that might have been impatience.

"The two of you will travel faster and attract less notice without her."

Alwenna lowered her voice so only Tresilian would hear. "You would send me off on such a journey with none but Weaver? No guardsmen, no companion, no servants? Is that how you would show respect to the seers?"

"That way there will be none to betray you. I have complete trust in Weaver."

"Then you have told him everything?"   ..

"This is not the time. Tell no one as long as your condition can be hidden. No one." Tresilian picked up a bundle of clothing from the table and handed it to her. "You will travel in these."

Alwenna took the clothing from him, the homespun wool coarse beneath her fingertips. She caught a faint scent of herbs. It was vaguely familiar, though she couldn't place it. "This is madness, Tresilian."

"It's necessary." Tresilian returned to the table and gathered up the maps. "I must return to the council meeting. Be ready to leave in an hour's time."

Alwenna took half a step to the door. Was she to accept dismissal like a foolish child to the end of her days? "No. I will not go."

Tresilian leaned his hands on the table, his head lowered. "Alwenna, we have no time to discuss this."

By the fire, Weaver shifted. "Sire, if we are to leave in an hour I must–"

"Stay, Weaver." Alwenna was sure Tresilian counted on his presence to prevent her making a scene. "I know I can be frank in front of you. There are few secrets between you and my husband, after all."

Tresilian looked up sharply. Perhaps only one secret, then. How keen was he that she should not reveal it to Weaver?

"Husband, your family have long impressed upon me the importance of appropriate behaviour for my station. Imagine the outcry if it became common knowledge you had me smuggled out under cover of darkness like some wrongdoer?"

"Our whole purpose is to ensure it never will become

common knowledge." But he didn't hold her gaze for more than a few seconds.

She dropped the bundle of clothing onto the table, sending a scroll skidding off and onto the floor. "You must have arranged all this in advance. Why wait until the very last minute to tell me?"

Tresilian glanced at Weaver. "We weren't sure of Vasic's plans. And I knew you would argue. Believe me, Alwenna, I do not do this gladly."

And wasn't that typical of Tresilian, putting off an unpleasant task in the hope he might somehow avoid it entirely? Would she have agreed to set off on this journey in relative comfort days ago, accompanied by whatever retinue her husband deemed appropriate? She knew the answer to that, and felt suddenly foolish for causing a fuss.

"At the very least I must have a senior servant to accompany me and ensure propriety. And that servant will be Wynne, or I will not fall in with this mad scheme of yours."

Tresilian stooped and picked up the scroll she had knocked to the floor. "Weaver, can it be done?"

Weaver straightened up hastily. His colour was high, perhaps from standing over the fire so long. "Taking more than two horses outside the city walls would attract attention. Someone would need to ride pillion, and that would slow us down."

"Can it be done?" This time it was not a question.

Weaver bowed his head. "Yes, sire, it can be done."

"Then see to it."

CHAPTER THREE

Alwenna followed Tresilian down the winding stairs to the foot of the tower, the hood of her woollen cloak scratching against her face. Behind her she could hear the pad of Wynne's boots on the stairs. Weaver awaited them in the guardroom. Somehow he'd found time to change into dry clothing and shave off his beard. The flickering torchlight revealed a nick on his chin where the razor had slipped in his haste. The two men exchanged words in low voices; it seemed the womenfolk were not to be privy to their business. No matter. Alwenna stored up her resentment rather than give voice to it. She'd learned long ago that anger was a stronger ally than fear.

Tresilian turned to her as if he had overheard her thoughts. "This parting won't be for long."

"You ought not tempt fate, husband."

"I'll take my chance with fate, as long as you are safe. Just think, you always wanted to cross the sea. Now you shall." Tresilian reached out and pushed back her hood a fraction. Alwenna held herself aloof when he leaned in to press a hasty kiss to her lips.

"Take good care of her, Ranald. Goddess speed you all."

Weaver led the way in silence across the slick cobbles of

the inner ward to the gatehouse. Smoke from the torches
in the keep hung in the still air, acrid, catching the back of
Alwenna's throat.

The guard at the citadel gate let Weaver pass with a
respectful salute but he eyed Alwenna with undisguised
curiosity as she and Wynne followed behind him. The
rain had cleared and the moonlight was strong enough to
cast their shadows before them; every step meant placing
her foot in an uncertain pool of darkness. Each time they
passed beneath a flambeau shadows sprang up alongside
them, then sank away into the night. Wynne was a
reassuring presence at her side.

They walked in silence through the narrow streets,
boots scuffing on the cobbles. All decent folk were asleep
at this hour. Somewhere in the distance cats yowled. A
pebble clattered across the street behind them. Alwenna
glanced over her shoulder, unable to shake off the
unpleasant sensation of being watched. She turned back
to catch Weaver's attention, but he was already at her side.

Weaver took hold of her arm and steered her down
a side alley. Her feet slithered in mud and she bumped
against Wynne as Weaver pushed them into the shadow
of a low building. A stable, if Alwenna's nose were to be
trusted.

"Our spy's about to show his hand. Wait here." Weaver
strode back towards the street, shrugging his cloak back as
three men spread out across the entrance.

"Ho, Weaver! What brings you out at this time of night?
Last I heard you were south of the pass."

With relief Alwenna recognised Stanton's voice. He was
another of the King's Men: a favourite with the ladies at
court, always ready with a smile and easy conversation.

He couldn't be the spy. Weaver, on the other hand: dour to the point of morose, withdrawn in company, did he deserve Tresilian's trust?

"My business is no concern of yours, Stanton."

The courtier took a step forward, still smiling. "Is your business so urgent you have no time for civility? Come now, I have a proposition for you. Let's discuss it over a jug of ale." He gestured towards the corner where Alwenna waited. "Bring your shy companions along. I might almost think you were trying to hide them from me."

"Well I might; your looks have broken too many ladies' hearts already." Weaver set his hand on the pommel of his sword. "My gift is for breaking skulls."

"Ever the commoner." Stanton sighed. "We have you outnumbered three to one."

"I'm able to count. And I'll thank all three of you not to importune the ladies."

"But what manner of lady would keep company with the likes of you? Step clear. It's not too late for you to choose the victor's side."

Weaver remained motionless.

Was he considering the offer?

Stanton seemed to think so. "I can make it worth your while."

Alwenna caught her breath. Impossible – Tresilian trusted Weaver. But he'd trusted Stanton, too.

CHAPTER FOUR

Weaver registered the gasp from behind him; maybe now someone else would be convinced of Stanton's treachery.

"Enough talk. If you want the ladies, come and get them." He drew his sword, studying the opposition as they followed suit. Space was tight in the alley: they'd have to attack one at a time.

Stanton muttered a command and the youth on his right charged forward, sword raised for an overhead blow. Too reckless. It was easy for Weaver to deflect the blade point down and use the momentum of the blow to bring his sword around and open the lad's throat beneath the ear. He stepped away to protect his eyes from the blood which spattered over his side as the youth toppled to the ground.

Weaver drew back, raising his sword to window guard: left elbow high, point forward at eye level, right side exposed, offering the next attacker an open target he couldn't resist. The man approached more cautiously, but as he thrust for the ribs Weaver gathered the soldier's sword, pushing it out to the side as he stepped forward and plunged his own blade into the man's eye socket. Weaver drew back as his attacker fell, eyes already on Stanton.

The courtier's secret was out now. If he turned and ran he wouldn't get another chance at the girl.

Stanton's gaze flicked towards Alwenna. He raised his sword and stepped forward over the bodies of his fallen men, his approach measured. He was subtler than the other two, trained by the best swordsmen the Peninsula could offer, but he'd taken the bait. The bodies behind him would hamper his movement. Stanton hesitated.

Weaver assumed a high guard. "Come on, you pretty bastard. I've a bastard sword waiting for you."

Stanton moved in to the bind, attempting to wind his blade over the top. Weaver countered by going strong, pushing the point of his sword towards Stanton's eyes and forcing him to block the movement. Weaver closed on him and, using Stanton's sword as a fulcrum, doubled his own blade back. The courtier recognised his mistake too late: horror dawned in his eyes a split second before Weaver's sword slashed open his face. Stanton crumpled to the ground and Weaver followed up, pushing him onto his back with his foot before he plunged his blade through the man's throat.

Weaver straightened up and turned towards the women, sword still in his hand. "Open the door."

Alwenna took a hasty step back and her hood slipped down. She gaped at him, wild-eyed. "What?"

"The barn door. Beside you." She didn't have what it took for this journey. How was he to get her all the way to Vorrahan? "Open it." He stooped to clean his sword on Stanton's cloak, then sheathed it before searching the courtier's pockets.

Wynne hurried to the door and started tugging at the rusty bolt. "My lady, help me with this."

Alwenna moved to Wynne's side. "He just robbed Stanton."

Weaver took hold of Stanton's corpse by the legs and dragged it towards the stable. "He has no need of it now. Open the door. We must hide these bodies."

The bolt jerked free and Alwenna pulled the door aside. Weaver hauled Stanton's body feet-first into the shadows, the courtier's head clunking over the uneven cobbles. He dropped him next to a pile of straw.

Alwenna backed out of the way as Weaver returned for the next corpse. "I can scarce believe it. He was always so well dressed, so courteous…"

"Vermin often have the finest pelts, my lady." Weaver dragged the second body into the barn.

Outside in the alley she stared at the dead youth. "That's Lord Ellard's squire. His mother was so proud when he came to court."

Weaver gave a noncommittal grunt as he unbuckled the youth's knife belt and stowed it away inside his cloak.

Alwenna rounded on him. "He was so young. Have you no compassion?"

"His mother should have taught him to choose his friends more wisely." Weaver dumped the body inside with the other two, throwing straw over them before securing the door. "Come on, we've wasted enough time."

Alwenna failed to respond so he took her by the elbow. She snatched her arm from his grip. "We should tell Tresilian about Stanton."

He could take her back up to the keep now, let her take her chance with the rest of them in the siege. And he could get on with the work he was fitted for. But he'd given his word. "He'll find out soon enough. We have to push on – there may be others on the prowl."

"Others?"

"A man as influential as Stanton won't have been working alone." Still she hesitated. "My lady, we must hurry."

"You just butchered three men. Were their lives of no consequence?" She gripped her fallen hood with one hand, as if she'd forgotten what she meant to do with it.

"They were your enemies. Now pull up that hood. We must go."

Wynne stepped forward, setting an arm about Alwenna's shoulders. "Come, my lady. Weaver knows what he's about. Right now we must put your safety first." She whispered something in a low voice that Weaver couldn't hear. Whatever it was, it had the desired effect.

The younger woman drew up her hood. "Of course, you are both right. We must go." Her voice might have lacked conviction, but she stepped alongside Weaver, and when he took hold of her arm to guide her she didn't shake off his grip.

CHAPTER FIVE

Alwenna soon lost her sense of direction as Weaver led them through side streets and alleyways. She wanted to break away from him, run in the opposite direction and keep running until she reached the safety of the keep. What if another faction had already offered him more than Stanton? "Why are we going uphill? You're taking us further and further from the west gate."

"We're using a gate no one will be watching, my lady."

They emerged from another narrow alley into an open space where she could hear running water. The moonlight revealed the washing green at the foot of the citadel walls, fed by the spring for which Highkell was named. They kept to the shadows of the buildings alongside the green, stopping at the base of the city wall. There, Weaver unfastened his cloak and lifted a bundle from his shoulder.

"What are you doing?"

"This is the key to our gate." The bundle was a coil of rope which he looped over one arm before refastening his cloak. He began to unwind one end of the rope.

"I don't see how this will help."

Weaver leaned forward to pass the rope about her waist,

and the copper tang of blood mingled with sweat and wet wool enveloped her. He knotted the rope, adjusting it so it was a snug fit. "I'll lower you down first." Weaver secured the rope about his own waist, leaving several yards between them which he carried in a loose coil. "Then Wynne. I'll follow behind."

The citadel tower rose sheer above one side of the green while the curving city wall closed off the other. Buildings enclosed the space between them. "Down where? We're hemmed in here."

"This way." He led them across the washing green, alongside the curtain wall, and stepped down into the stream, pushing aside a clump of willow stems. There was an opening at the base of the wall, no more than shoulder height, through which the stream flowed. The opening was impossibly small, impossibly dark.

Alwenna froze. "You expect me to go in there?"

"The water's not deep." Weaver held out his hand to assist her.

She remained where she was. "I can't."

"Of course you can." He reached up and caught hold of her hand. "I've got you. Nothing can go wrong."

"No." She snatched her hand away but the bank crumbled beneath her foot and she slithered down, landing with a jolt against Weaver in the knee-deep water. The current tugged at her skirts. Weaver held the willow stems back so she could squeeze past.

"I can't. I mean it." She planted her feet, bracing one arm against the wall. "It's too narrow." Even the thought of stepping inside that constricted space was enough to make the breath fail in her lungs. The pounding of her blood filled her ears. She couldn't do it. She was dimly aware of Wynne's voice.

"Is there no other way? My lady can't bear small spaces."

"What? No." Weaver sounded exasperated. "It's only a short distance."

Alwenna drew in a deep breath, trying to calm herself, to ease the trembling that had overcome her limbs. She could master her fear. She had to. She set her hand on the inner wall of the culvert. The stone was clammy, covered in slimy growth from the lack of light. She snatched her hand back. Nearby, a man's voice shouted.

Weaver grabbed Alwenna bodily and shoved her inside the culvert, branches scraping across her face as he pressed her head down clear of the low ceiling. He clamped his hand over her mouth, stifling any protest. Instinct took over and she closed her teeth on the gloved hand, biting hard. The leather tasted rank, but she hung on until, with a muffled curse, Weaver twisted his hand free.

"Stay quiet," he hissed.

Splashing sounds announced Wynne had joined them in the culvert a split second before she bumped into them. The sound of the running water echoed off the curved ceiling and rebounded, filling Alwenna's head with noise, drowning out all but the faintest hint of voices from the green. Her limbs continued to shake, out of control.

Weaver began to edge his way through the culvert away from their pursuers, and Alwenna had no option but to go with him. One step, then another, the current tugging at her skirts, threatening to drag her feet out from under her, her senses bludgeoned by the noise of rushing water, the darkness, her fear. Then the echoing ceased and clear air caressed her face as she was able to stand up straight. She could have sobbed with relief – except Weaver still pinned her arms against her sides in a death grip. From close behind, Wynne exclaimed in horror and when Alwenna opened her eyes – she couldn't recall having shut them – she saw why.

CHAPTER SIX

They were poised on a ledge above the gorge. Moon shadows hid the depths, but many feet below them were the tops of tall trees. The stream cascaded out over a man-made ledge, falling in an arc clear of the sheer wall beneath them. The clouds shifted and the shadows below deepened, but Alwenna had seen enough. The remains of a watergate tilted out over the precipice, pushed by the flow of water fed by several days' rainfall. Weaver tied off the rope to one of the metal supports for the watergate before he eased his grip about Alwenna's waist and released her, watching her warily.

The air seemed able to fill her lungs once more and the shaking of her limbs was beginning to subside when Weaver twisted around to watch the mouth of the culvert, one hand moving to his sword hilt. They remained frozen there for what felt like half a lifetime, straining to hear any sound of pursuit over the rush of the water. Finally, Weaver's shoulders eased and he turned to face the gorge once more. "We go on. You first, my lady."

Alwenna peered into the shadows at the foot of the cliff. "Are you sure that rope will reach the ground?"

"Yes, my lady."

Anything would be better than going back through that accursed tunnel. "How do I know you won't leave me dangling halfway down?"

"I gave the king my word I'd see you safe to Vorrahan." Weaver anchored himself to the metal loop, then checked the knot was still secure about Alwenna's waist. "Turn round to face the rock and try to keep your feet against it, as if you're walking down. Don't move suddenly or you'll twist around."

"And if I do?"

"Hope you twist back again. And keep quiet." He fed the rope through so he was holding the end closest to her, then wrapped it over his shoulder and took a twist about his arm.

"Lean out over the drop. You won't fall. Try to keep your weight on your feet. And untie the rope once you're on the ground."

The tug of the rope about her waist was reassuringly firm. Alwenna leaned out over the drop, unsure what to expect. Her sodden skirts dragged down, obscuring her view of the rock face where she needed to plant her feet. A few hours ago she'd been dozing before a warm fire as the rain sheeted down the window. Now... It was better not to think too hard about it. Obey Weaver's instructions.

"I'm going to start lowering you. Just walk your feet down, keep them wide apart." He let the rope out a little and she lurched downwards, her feet suddenly uncomfortably high. She shuffled them down until she reached a balanced position, then he let more rope out. This time she kept pace with the motion. She proceeded for several feet in relative comfort, until the rock wall steepened and her foot met empty space beneath a small overhang. Her body weight swung sideways, the rope loop digging into her ribs. Her foot contacted rock again, but she'd swung too far off balance and didn't stop until her elbow crashed against the cliff. Cursing her clumsiness, she pushed herself away and managed to scramble her feet beneath her but before she could regain her balance, Weaver paid out more rope and she lost her footing entirely, spinning out of control.

Her stupid oversized hood slipped back and a squall of rain hit her full in the face. No, not rain, she'd swung towards the falling stream water. Unable to check the motion, she pitched into the waterfall. It bombarded the top of her head and ran down her neck, drenching her from head to foot. Too late she ducked, spitting out a mouthful of water as she hunched her shoulders against it. Her sodden garments grew rapidly heavier and dragged downwards, digging into her shoulders, while the rope about her waist dug ever tighter into her ribs, making it hard to draw breath. Her skirts tangled about her legs and she scrabbled for a foothold, swinging out of the downspout for a moment of blessed relief.

Weaver kept lowering the rope and she bumped and slithered her way for several feet before regaining her footing and pushing herself away from the cascading water. Then something beneath her hampered her skirts and her feet became tangled in branches. Goddess, was she stuck in a tree? She risked a look down and discovered she was close enough to set her feet on the ground, if only they weren't entangled in a scrubby thorn. Above her, Weaver paid out more rope and she landed bruisingly on her back, the rope going slack and bumping across her face as the pressure on her ribs eased. She floundered for a moment, then managed to kick her feet clear of the bush and clambered onto her knees.

The ground she knelt on was perilously steep. They had to be some forty or fifty feet below the citadel walls now. The rope dangling down the rock face above her twitched and she peered upwards, just in time to get a faceful of grit. Here in the shade of the trees it was difficult to make out what was going on, but when the rope tugged sharply at her waist she remembered she was supposed to untie it. The knot had pulled tight. She dug her fingernails into it, hands so numb with cold she could hardly tell when at last the knot loosened. She worried the loops apart, heedless of the grit that bit into her fingertips as she finally drew the end of the rope free. She tugged twice on the rope and was rewarded by another shower of grit and small pebbles from above as it snaked back up the cliff.

Then there was nothing. No movement, no sound from above. The knuckles of one hand began to sting and she discovered she'd bloodied them at some point during the descent. It crossed her mind that Weaver could just leave her down there. She would make an easy target for Tresilian's enemies. Then she glimpsed movement above: a bulky figure was being lowered down the rock face, a few feet at a time. She gathered her wits together in time to spare Wynne the ignominy of getting entangled in the same small thorn, and the pair of them began to fight with the knot about the servant's waist as the end of a wet rope slapped down against them.

A few moments later Weaver slithered down beside them. He unwrapped the rope from about his shoulder then undid the knot at Wynne's waist without any apparent effort. "Step over by that tree, so the rope won't hit you." He began pulling one end of the rope and the other vanished back up the cliff, disappearing from sight.

He kept pulling it through until a skittering sound from above and another shower of pebbles heralded the arrival of the rope on the ground.

Alwenna's clothing dragged as she moved over to the tree, weighed down from her soaking. Shivering, she perched on the steep bank and began wringing out the water. It pattered down onto the leaf mould at her feet. "W-what now?" Her fingers burned as the life returned to them.

Weaver coiled the rope hastily and draped it over one shoulder. "We get our horses."

Horses. Of course, he'd mentioned them earlier. Thank the Goddess she was not expected to walk all the way to Vorrahan.

"This way, my lady." Weaver took her elbow. "You're drenched."

This surprised him? "You just lowered me down a waterfall." It was an effort to force the words out through chattering teeth. She stood up, only to find her skirts weighed her down as heavily as before and she stooped to wring them out again.

"Let me, my lady." Wynne hurried over to help and Weaver stepped away, fixing all his attention on the gorge below them as if he expected pursuers to spring out of the river.

"That's the best I can do for now, my lady." Wynne straightened up, stretching her back.

"Thank you, Wynne." Alwenna knew a pang of guilt. The servant had agreed to accompany her on this adventure after only a moment's hesitation. At least she'd avoided a soaking as Weaver had lowered her down the cliff. He was still watching the gorge, his shoulders tight.

He probably disapproved of the delay. "Well, Weaver, where are these horses?"

"This way, my lady." He supported her weight as they scrambled over the steep ground beneath the citadel. "The walk will help you warm up. It's not—"

Weaver froze, listening. Alwenna halted, mid-stride, holding her breath. There were voices behind them – several. Had they been followed after all? Then the jingle of harness and the braying of a mule. A burst of laughter.

Weaver relaxed. "Merchants. On the road on the far side of the gorge."

They clambered out of the steep-sided gully without further incident. A few minutes' easier walking through forest brought them to the place above the citadel where two horses were tethered. Weaver tightened the girths and led one forward.

"Begging your pardon, my lady, but you're lightest, so you'd better ride behind." He didn't look for any sign of agreement, but legged Wynne up into the saddle first and helped Alwenna up behind her.

Weaver vaulted into his own saddle and turned his horse's head to the west. "We'll put a few miles between us and Highkell before we stop for the night."

When they'd climbed above the tree cover Alwenna twisted round to take one last look at the dark bulk of the citadel below them. A few dim lights showed through the patchy shroud of mist. Somewhere in there lay the bodies of Stanton and his two companions. Alwenna suppressed a shudder. Her parents had died the night she'd arrived at Highkell. Now she was leaving the same way, in the company of death and darkness.

CHAPTER SEVEN

The sound of splashing pulled Alwenna away from her old nightmare to the dank chill of early morning. It took her longer than usual to catch her breath, to convince herself she wasn't still trapped in the tumbling carriage, suffocating beneath the weight of her father's body. The twelve years that had passed since the accident had done nothing to diminish the horror. She eased herself up from the ground, her left hip protesting where a stone had been digging into it. They'd stopped by a river. Mist brooded over the sluggish water, obscuring the far bank. Nearby, Wynne was also stirring. Weaver crouched at the water's edge, refilling pear-shaped leather costrels for their journey.

Alwenna unwrapped the blanket from about her shoulders. "Is it time to move already?"

"Yes, my lady." Weaver handed her a brimming costrel.

There was a neat semi-circle of bruises coming up on his hand. Her teeth must have caused the damage when she'd panicked in the culvert. She said nothing. Instead she drank, more thirsty than she'd realised. The water still held the chill of the mountain streams that fed the river. She topped up the bottle herself, conscious of Weaver's eyes upon her as she splashed her face to chase away lingering tiredness. "So, we are to travel by daylight?"

"Until we reach open country. Then we'll rest and move on after dark."

She couldn't look at Weaver without recalling the callous way he'd dragged those bodies into the barn. Images of violent death had stalked her sleep: Stanton's bloodied head bouncing against the cobbles, moonlight glancing off Weaver's sword as he felled the men. All so she could be taken to safety. "How serious is the risk to Highkell?"

Weaver turned away to secure his blankets to his saddle; he must have saddled both horses while she and Wynne slept on. Doubtless he thought her fit for nothing more than ornamenting the high table on feast days. His dour silence irked her.

"You'd sooner be there, wouldn't you, fighting with the rest?"

"I'm sworn to do the king's bidding." He tightened both horses' girths. "We'll set off as soon as you're ready."

She gathered up her blankets and shook them, before rolling them into a bundle as he had done. Somehow her bundle was lumpier, and floppier. "You didn't answer my question. Is Highkell at risk?"

"The garrison at the citadel is under strength and Vasic has skilled mercenaries on his payroll. As long as he can pay them he's a serious threat." He took the blankets from her, rolled them up neatly and strapped them to her saddle.

"How serious?"

"If he attacks before the troops return from The Marches, the citadel will fall in a matter of days."

"Can you be so sure?"

"Soldiering's my business." He met her gaze for the first time that morning. "I deal in truth and nothing else, my lady."

Did she imagine the challenge in his eyes? "That would be when you're not dealing in death, I suppose."

"A wise man once told me that death is the ultimate truth."

"Indeed?" Weaver discussing philosophy? This was too incongruous. "And you agree with him?"

"I've seen nothing yet to convince me it could be otherwise." He stowed the last of their belongings back in his bag.

She shivered. Again she saw the image of Stanton's head bouncing as he was dragged over the rough ground, and Lord Ellard's squire, blond hair soaked with his own blood. "I suppose you've seen a lot of men die?"

"Yes, my lady. I told you – I'm a soldier."

His indifference was almost as irksome as his silence. "How many, Weaver? Do you even know?"

"I don't, my lady. Counting's for clerics. If you're ready, we'll ride on."

CHAPTER EIGHT

Weaver sat up, reaching for the hilt of his knife. Some strange sound had woken him. Not a sound of the forest, but something else. Something out of place. There it was again, a mumble, and a whimpered protest. The Lady Alwenna, uneasy in her sleep, shifted, then flung out an arm. She mumbled again, then stilled and seemed to settle. Beside her Wynne slept deeply. The older woman was everything Alwenna wasn't: solid and easygoing.

The sky in the east was lightening; it would be dawn soon enough. No point trying to catch any more sleep. He rolled up his blanket and fastened it to the back of his saddle, with another glance at the girl as she turned fretfully. For that was all she was here: not his queen, not his king's wife. But still too delicate for this journey, too fine.

Too close.

He could reach out and brush that strand of hair from her face. What was there to stop him acting on the impulse, out here, beyond the confines of citadel and court? Only his king's trust.

Tresilian could have chosen anyone else. Should have, damn him.

Another sound out of place in the forest caught his attention. Hoofbeats. Several horses, approaching, heading slowly towards the river they had crossed earlier that night. A man's voice, still too far away for the words to be distinct, but the crack of laughter in response was unmistakable. Unconcerned they might be overheard, and sounding pleased with their night's doings. And not likely to have been doing anything honourable, a group of riders abroad at this time of night.

Wynne stirred and sat up. Weaver glanced her way, holding a hand to his lips. She nodded understanding, and cautiously unwrapped the blanket from about her shoulders. Alwenna shifted again and mumbled, louder than before. If she brought that group down on them–

"Hush, my lady." Wynne set a hand on Alwenna's shoulder but the younger woman twisted away with a muffled protest, caught in the throes of some nightmare.

Weaver knelt at Alwenna's side and pressed his hand over her mouth. She threw out her arm and clawed at his face before he could catch hold of her wrist with his free hand.

"Be still, my lady. There are riders nearby."

She pulled away from him and he clamped his hand harder over her mouth, then her eyelids sprang open. She stared at him in horror, struggling to pull away until recognition dawned. She stilled.

"Riders," he hissed, inclining his head towards the track through the forest.

She blinked, then nodded as much as she was able and he lifted his hand from her mouth. She sat up abruptly and her head thudded against his chin.

"Keep quiet. You understand?"

She drew a shuddering breath in a visible effort to still the trembling of her limbs, then nodded.

Weaver twisted around to study the riders, or what little he could glimpse of them through the cover of the trees. Perhaps as many as a dozen, straggling across the forest track, unconcerned. They carried no colours to distinguish them and were too far away to be recognised, although one of the horses was a distinctive grey. The pole arms, swords and shields they carried confirmed they'd been up to no good. He was aware of the faintest sound of movement behind him as Alwenna pushed back her blanket and moved to his side.

Once the riders were out of earshot she spoke in a low voice. "Who are they? Not Vasic's men, surely? They can't have got past Highkell already, can they?"

Weaver sat back on his heels. "No. They could have been some of Stanton's men. This is – or was – his land. As well we didn't meet them on the road." Her hair was tousled, eyes heavy. In the homespun garments she looked as far removed from the untouchable queen as he could imagine. Further.

"There's blood on your face." She raised a hand towards him but checked the movement. She lowered her hand to her lap once more.

Was he relieved or disappointed? Conscious that Wynne was watching them, Weaver raised his own hand to the scratch on his cheekbone. His fingertips came away with a tiny smear of blood. "It's nothing." Relieved. She was his king's wife. Of course he was relieved.

She lowered her eyes, brushing leaf litter off the corner of her blanket. "It was another nightmare. I'm sorry."

"You've no need to apologise, my lady."

"It was so vivid. I thought I'd forgotten…" She shrugged. "Those riders – you said we would meet no one on these forest tracks."

"I said we were less likely to meet anyone."

"What do we do now? There may be others following them."

"We go carefully. They looked as if they were on the way home after riding hard through the night."

She sat up on her knees, tucking her skirts about her. "They were joking about it. So callous. I know what they'd been doing, Weaver. I know you're trying to spare me, but… Oh, never mind." She pulled a comb from her small bag and began tugging at the knots in her hair.

Wynne stepped forward. "My lady, let me do that for you."

"There's no need, Wynne. I should be able to manage this myself. You've enough to put up with as it is." Alwenna dragged the comb through her hair a few more times then fastened it back with a loop of leather.

Weaver retrieved oatcakes and dried meat from his saddlebag, and handed some out with a costrel of water. Alwenna looked doubtfully at the food but accepted it with a murmur of thanks.

"It's not what you're used to, I know, but we can't risk lighting a fire here."

Her eyes widened, a moment of startled realisation as the import of his words sank in. "No, I can see that," was all she said. She took up her meagre breakfast, tearing off a small piece of oatcake and nibbling it cautiously. She didn't say anything. She didn't need to.

Weaver left them to it while he saddled up the horses. At least the oatcakes were still fresh. Let her ladyship see how she liked them after a few more days on the road. By then they'd be so dry they'd snap.

They paused often that morning while Weaver scouted the path ahead on foot, leaving Alwenna and Wynne with the horses, hidden among the trees.

They were still backtracking the group of riders they had seen earlier. Weaver needed to know where they'd come from, if only to be sure there were no others in the vicinity. They'd been travelling thus for a couple of hours when Weaver first picked up the hint of woodsmoke on the air. Within a minute Alwenna commented on it.

"I can smell burning."

Weaver had forgotten she could speak, she'd been so quiet since they'd set off. "Stay here." Weaver slipped down from his horse and handed Alwenna the reins as before, but she hesitated.

"What is it? A forest fire?"

"With all the rain we've had lately?"

She reached out and took the reins, her face sombre. "You think it's those men we saw?"

"Their handiwork? Possibly." He turned away.

"What if some are still there? If they see you—"

"We'd hear something." Shouting. Screams. He wasn't about to spell it out for her. "They've gone."

Her expression suggested she'd guessed what he meant. "Be careful."

Fifty yards brought him to where he could hear the hiss and spit of flames. But that was all. There was no hint of commotion, of people fetching and carrying water to fight the fire. A few more yards brought him to a clearing. Smoke straggled across the open space, hanging on the still air. A wooden barn was three-parts burned, smoke rising from the collapsed roof, charred timbers jutting skywards. Beyond it low turf walls, smoking steadily, were all that remained of a farmhouse. A figure sprawled in the mud between house and barn. A lone hen scratched the ground nearby.

Weaver skirted round the clearing to the other side of the buildings, but could neither see nor hear other signs of life. No tracks left the clearing, apart from those they'd followed back from their overnight camp. Flesh of some kind burned inside the wreckage of the barn. Like the dead woman sprawled on her back in the mud, the owner of the flesh was far beyond needing his help. The only thing moving around the steading was the chicken. The attackers had probably taken the rest. He caught it and broke its neck. Her highness would enjoy one decent meal, at least. Carrying the chicken, he made his way carefully back to his original vantage point. Then he heard movement: the swish of a branch, and the thud of horses' hooves nearby. He spun around, drawing his dagger – and recognised his own horse pushing through the trees towards him, Alwenna bending over the withers to duck beneath a low branch. Wynne followed behind on the other horse.

Weaver strode over, taking his horse's bridle. "I told you to stay back there."

"You were gone so long. We thought something must have happened." Alwenna's eyes moved to the dagger in his hand, then beyond him to the burning buildings. "Was there someone there?"

"Count yourself lucky I recognised you before I threw this." He slid the dagger back into its sheath and retrieved the chicken from where he'd dropped it, tying it to his saddle.

She stared at the sorry bundle of feathers. "That's not ours to take, surely?"

"The people here have no need of it. We need to make up lost time."

Alwenna slid down from his saddle, still studying the scene.

She pointed to the woman. "I take it she's dead?"

"She is." He led his horse between her and the steading. "We need to go, my lady. There's nothing we can do here."

"We can't just leave her lying there. It's not decent."

"Believe me, her troubles are over."

"My lady, Weaver's right." Wynne spoke up firmly. "We can't risk staying here any longer. You can offer up a prayer to the Goddess at sunrise tomorrow. That would be fitting."

A crow waiting in a nearby tree flapped its wings.

Alwenna took a step back towards the horse they shared. "Shouldn't we at least cover her?"

"And announce to the world we passed this way?" Weaver set one hand on her elbow.

She frowned. "Tresilian wouldn't leave her like that."

"No, he wouldn't. He'd have enough soldiers with him to bury her in a few minutes. I haven't. His orders were to take you to safety."

"But… it's inhumane."

"It's war, my lady. Or had you forgotten?"

Alwenna shook off Weaver's grip, but made ready to mount the horse. He legged her up behind Wynne. She didn't thank him, her mouth set in a sullen line as she organised her skirts.

Weaver vaulted up into his own saddle. "Someone's stirred up trouble in these parts. The sooner we're out of this country, the better I'll like it."

CHAPTER NINE

There were still several hours of daylight remaining when they stopped that evening. Weaver kindled a fire and handed the chicken over to the women to pluck. Alwenna watched Wynne at work for a few minutes. It looked straightforward enough.

She knelt down on the ground next to the servant. "Can I help?"

"There's no need, my lady. You rest while you can. You'll need all your strength."

"I don't need to rest, Wynne. I need to be useful, instead of just being a burden to everyone."

"We all have our part to play. But if you want to try, I see no reason not to."

"I want to try."

Wynne smiled and handed over the chicken. "I shouldn't say it, but your uncle was often over-particular about his family's dignity."

"Then it's no wonder I was a sore trial to him. He was forever telling me I ought to be more grateful for my good fortune."

"He was a good man, and fond of you all, even if he wasn't prone to showing it."

Alwenna pondered Wynne's comment in silence. There was a knack to chicken-plucking, a knack she hadn't acquired yet. Several minutes' effort left her fingertips raw while the chicken clung stubbornly to its feathers.

"I suspect my uncle was always fonder of the lands I would bring to Tresilian when we married."

"Perhaps. But it's been a good match for both of you." There was a solid certainty about Wynne's statement.

"Of course. I'm not ungrateful. It's just…" There was no way to say what was on her mind without sounding ungrateful. Had Wynne been granted a choice, she would surely have preferred to remain at Highkell than come on this unpleasant journey with her mistress.

Alwenna returned her attention to the hapless chicken. Feathers clung to her clothes, adhered to the blanket she sat upon and drifted over the ground. The dead creature's head dangled over her leg, flopping back and forth each time she tugged more feathers free. She yanked at a stubborn feather, gripping it awkwardly to spare her sore fingertips, and the bird's flesh tore as it came away. The thing was repulsive. And how long had Weaver been standing watching her efforts?

His expression was deadpan. "I'll finish it off. The feathers come out easier while the bird's still warm."

"Now you tell me."

Weaver glanced her way with something that might have been a smile as he removed the last of the feathers. Alwenna was left in no doubt he'd have completed the task in a fraction of the time it had taken her.

"Have you ever been shown how to clean a chicken ready to cook?"

"No. I've never needed to do any cooking."

"You might find it useful one day, if only to make sure
your servants aren't about to poison you with bad food."
He set about removing the neck and innards. "Take care
not to burst the guts, or it'll spoil the meat. Cut here and
you remove the whole thing. Then wash out the inside
and it's ready to cook." He glanced up at her, quizzical.
"What's the matter?"

"I never saw anything so disgusting in my life."

"Have you not, my lady? Then you have been blessed
indeed." He set about cutting the meat into small pieces
and tossed them into the small pan he had set to heat over
the fire. "There are many worse sights in this world, may
the Goddess grant you never witness any."

How dare he? Face burning with embarrassment, she
jumped to her feet and made her way down to the stream
to clean her hands. To be rebuked by the churlish Weaver!
She'd done everything he'd asked: waded through
water, dangled on ropes, ridden through the night, slept
on blankets that reeked of horse, even helped pluck the
damned chicken he'd stolen from the dead woman's farm.
When she next saw Tresilian she'd have some choice
words for him, and they wouldn't involve gratitude.

The cool water had eased the raw discomfort of
Alwenna's fingertips. Now she spread her fingers wide
and lowered them to the bottom of the shallow pool. The
pebbles on the stream bed were of many different colours:
browns, greys and ochres, all intermingled, smooth to
the touch. The rippling of the water made them appear
alive as they shimmered beneath her fingers, shifting and
dancing. The rushing of the stream grew louder and her
vision blurred then cleared to reveal the citadel of Highkell
in fading light. Behind her she could hear the jingle of

harness, and the steady progress of horses' hooves on the road up to the main gate. She blinked, disorientated, and she was gazing at the pebble-strewn stream bed once more, her hands cold, still sunk to her wrists in the water. The sound of horses' hooves had gone, but she twisted round to check, nevertheless. She knelt by a stream in a forest clearing, with only Wynne and Weaver for company.

She turned back to the stream, studying the pebbles which lay innocuously beneath the surface of the water. She plunged her hands in again, spreading her fingers over the stones as before. The water was cold and wet and that was all.

Alwenna straightened up, shaking off the water, and dabbed her hands dry on her skirts. She slept so badly these days, it was no great wonder if she felt a bit lightheaded.

Weaver watched her from where he tended the fire. "Are you well, my lady?"

"Yes. My hands were sore, that's all." She returned to the fireside where the chicken now sizzled, along with some roots Weaver had added. The chicken no longer resembled the fleshy thing she'd plucked with so much difficulty. "That smells good."

"You sound surprised."

"It looked nothing like food earlier."

Wrapped in one of the oatcakes, the chicken tasted good. Delicious, in fact. But at the third mouthful Alwenna's stomach rebelled. She hurried away among the trees where she retched violently until her stomach was empty. She straightened up, shaking, relieved to find the nausea had passed. When she returned, Weaver was busy damping down the cooking fire. He made no comment about her abrupt disappearance.

Wynne was waiting for her with fresh water. "Drink this, my lady. It will help."

"Thank you." Alwenna sipped at the water before taking up her food again, this time without ill effect. It was her own stupid fault for bolting it down, of course. "You warned me how it would be. I'd almost forgotten about it." Wynne had told her how to manage the sickness. In the habit of picking at the dry oatcakes as they rode she'd begun to think the phase had passed.

Wynne glanced over towards Weaver, who was saddling up the horses, before speaking in a low voice. "It's a good sign. It means a healthy baby."

Alwenna followed the direction of Wynne's eyes. "Tresilian said I was to tell no one. Not even Weaver." The surly soldier was the last person she could imagine herself confiding in. "Why would he say that if he trusts him so completely?"

"Like as not Tresilian thought to spare him the worry. The King's Man carries burdens of his own, my lady, though he makes light of them."

This was news to Alwenna. "Burdens? What do you–" She fell silent as Weaver rejoined them.

"We'll ride on as soon as you've finished eating, my lady, in case someone saw the fire."

Alwenna gathered her feet under her and stood up. "I'm ready." She couldn't imagine Weaver making light of anything. She would ask Wynne what she meant later.

CHAPTER TEN

Weaver settled with his back against the tree trunk. There should have been another with him so they could take turns at keeping watch. Tresilian had vetoed the suggestion, as he had no idea how far Stanton's contagion had spread at Highkell. In theory the risk was minimal here in the west, now they were out of Stanton's land. But it meant a succession of near-sleepless nights for him, keeping alert for anything out of place.

And the Lady Alwenna was a restless sleeper. She didn't speak of it during the day. Mostly she didn't speak much at all. But at night, after the first hour's rest she was always uneasy, mumbling, and twisting about until she was wound up in her blanket. It was to be expected, he supposed, snatched so abruptly from everything familiar. If he'd been Tresilian he'd have kept her close. But the king had been determined, despite being so devoted to his young wife. There had to be something Tresilian hadn't told him.

Nearby, Wynne stirred and sat up, as if she too had been disturbed by Alwenna's restlessness. She set a gentle hand on Alwenna's head as the girl mumbled unintelligible words, stroking her hair until she settled again. Wynne looked over to Weaver then and smiled. She pushed herself to her feet and hobbled over to join him beneath the tree, sitting down on a fallen branch.

"This journey will be the ruin of my old body. I'm wide awake now – would you have me sit watch for a while?"

"I've had some rest. I'm used to this."

"I'm not so old I can't stay awake for an hour or two."

"And I'm still young enough I needn't ask it of you. It's a kind thought, though, for which I thank you."

Alwenna mumbled, flung out one arm then turned over before falling quiet again.

"Those night fears, she's always had them. Ever since she was a child."

Weaver glanced to where the young woman slept on. "You had the raising of her after her parents died?"

"That's right. She's the image of her mother now. Takes after her in so many ways."

"I heard she was a rare beauty." Goddess, what possessed him to say that to the old gossip?

"As if you take notice of such things, Ranald Weaver."

"I doubt there's a man in the Peninsular Kingdoms who could fail to notice."

"It's true enough." Wynne smiled at her charge fondly.

"There were other rumours…" Weaver hesitated.

"Other rumours?"

"About her mother. And… witchery." He felt foolish saying it, but Wynne's eyes were surely not sharp enough to read his expression in the shadow of the trees.

"They're of Alidreth's line, mother and daughter. The seers would have taken Alwenna as a child, you know, but her uncle wouldn't hear of it."

Then it was true. And if that was true, what about the whispers that the ill-starred queen would bring about the fall of Highkell? Old wives' tales, all of them. Tresilian had paid them no heed. Alwenna was just a young woman. A pretty young woman. Weaver was glad of the darkness to hide his thoughts.

"It's not been easy for her, you know." Wynne's eyes were focused on Alwenna, as if for a moment she'd forgotten Weaver was there. "She's never gone hungry or cold, nothing like that. But she was such a lively child. To earn her place at Highkell… it's cost her dearly. People don't realise."

"Are you saying I've been too hard on her?"

"Now why would you think that? As if I'd ever suggest such a thing."

"You've told me often enough I'm too hard on myself."

"And so you are, Ranald Weaver. So you are. But I doubt you'll pay me any more heed now than the last time I said it." Wynne pushed herself to her feet. "What I wouldn't give to find a proper garderobe among these trees." She shuffled away, leaving Weaver to his thoughts.

Alwenna mumbled a few words. Had that phrase been "Too dark"? She twisted, as if fending off invisible demons. No, Weaver thought, his own demons were the invisible ones, reaching from his past to taunt him. Who was he to say the girl's demons weren't real in the here and now? And from the way she looked at him since he had refused to bury that dead woman, he might well be one of them.

That was all it took to stop him going over to wake her. It was not his place to bring her back from a sleeping nightmare to a waking one.

Alwenna dashed across the throne room, unheeding when one of her plaits came loose, determined to win the game. She knew the perfect hiding place if she could just reach it in time. She pushed the heavy garderobe door open, then hesitated. There was a large chest set against the far wall, restricting the space where she planned to hide. The sound of footsteps running across the room behind her propelled her forward and she pushed in between the garments hanging in the alcove behind the door.

Not a moment too soon. The door creaked on its hinges and her pursuer drew near, his breathing rapid, excited. She pressed back against the wall, the folds of a heavy surcoat falling across her face, shutting out the light. She breathed in the mildewed odour and believed herself back in the fusty carriage, coming to rest at the bottom of that slope with a great weight crushing down on her, her father's woollen cloak smothering her mouth and nose, trapping her in darkness. Panic gripped her. She gasped, forgetting this was only a game, forgetting she was meant to be hiding, clawing and flailing at the heavy fabric until she fought her way clear, gulping for air as she burst into the half-light of the garderobe, startling her pursuer.

Vasic's expression transformed to a gleeful grin. "I found you! You lose, Alwenna."

Still gasping for breath, she tried to push past him through the doorway, but he blocked her path, grin broadening.

"Let me out!" She gulped at the air, which somehow seemed too thin to fill her lungs, and grabbed hold of the edge of the door.

"Not so fast. You have to pay a forfeit." With a glance over his shoulder he stepped further into the small room and started to push the door shut behind him.

She clung to the door, tugging. "No."

"I won, fair and square. And now–"

She heaved the door open. She had to get out, out of that constricted space, out where she could breathe the air, away from the musty wool, away from the crushing weight of darkness. She was dimly aware of lashing out at Vasic, shrieking, shoving him and clawing at his face until he fell back and she pelted off down the short passage back to the solar.

It was no good. After Alwenna cried out – still apparently asleep – Weaver had to step in. Even in this out-of-the-way place they couldn't afford to attract anyone's attention. Why in the name of the Goddess had he agreed to this madness?

He set a hand cautiously on her shoulder but she struck out wildly at him, landing a resounding slap against his face. He ducked back, cursing, but the contact had broken her free of the nightmare and she sat up abruptly, chest heaving as if she had been running hard.

She stared at him, her eyes wide in horror. "Did I just hit you? I did, didn't I? I'm so sorry…"

"I'll live." There was no need for her to look so stricken.

"I didn't mean… It was–"

"Another of your nightmares."

She rubbed her eyes with both hands and pushed her hair back from her face in a frustrated gesture. "Yes. No. It's not… I'm not normally like this."

Goddess, no. She wasn't about to discuss her sleeping habits with him. What was he supposed to say: how she must miss her husband? Maybe she guessed what he was thinking, because she seemed to gather her composure.

"I've been dreaming about things that happened years ago. Things I've not thought about in an age."

And none of them happy things, to judge by her expression. In another place, another time, Weaver might have offered sympathy, or even a shoulder to cry on. But this was his king's wife.

Weaver sat back on his heels, trying to summon words of reassurance, but he was never obliged to utter them as he heard footsteps hurrying through the forest towards their camp. He spun around, drawing his dagger.

Wynne appeared through the trees, gasping for breath. "Goddess spare us, there's half a dozen men camped just down the hill. I saw their fire through the trees. I think they could be following us."

CHAPTER ELEVEN

Seven men, seven horses. Weaver could see them all from his hiding place among the scrubby trees. And Wynne had been right. One of the horses was the same distinctive grey Weaver had seen the night the raiders passed by. Was this coincidence? Or had the raiders returned to the farm and picked up their trail? How, by all that was holy, was he meant to deal with this? Given a handful of men under his command, he could have ambushed this party. Single-handed, his options were limited.

He might make his way down to where the horses were tethered and release them. But the waning moon that gave him enough light to study the camp would be enough to reveal him. And where would that leave the Lady Alwenna? He might manage to remove the sentry, unseen by the others who were slouched about the fire, passing around a jug. But the sentry was in full view. If any one of them should glance up at the wrong moment...

No. His best option was to skulk away into the night with the two women, as if they were common thieves. His only option.

The women had already saddled the horses when he returned to their camp, blankets bundled up and tied in place. He could tell them how to find Vorrahan, set them on their way and double back to deal with the raiding party. If he succeeded, he'd be able to catch them up using one of the raiders' horses. If not, well, they'd be several hours down the road towards their destination before any pursuit, and he'd cut down at least some of their pursuers. And if he failed entirely he'd be spared the need to explain his actions to Tresilian. That idea was craven and foolhardy, and he knew it.

Alwenna watched him, an unspoken question in her eyes.

"Wynne's right. It's the same group of riders we saw the other night."

"So, you think we should leave now?" Her voice was tight.

"That's right." What else could they do? He couldn't abandon them on the road.

Alwenna twisted the trailing end of her belt between her fingers. "Wynne and I were talking. And we thought – if we are being followed by these men – we ought to split up. One of us could lay a false trail."

"My lady, I would gladly do that if I could leave others to guard you. But I have to see you safely to Vorrahan."

Alwenna nodded, glancing towards Wynne. "We guessed you'd say that. But… it needn't be you." Her voice tightened, as if she spoke with difficulty.

"It's out of the question. If anyone is to take that risk–"

"Begging your pardon, Weaver, but a woman can blunder about the forest on a horse just as well as any man." Wynne had been standing with her arms folded, but now she stepped forward. "You know this country. Tell me what path to take and I'll do it, while you spirit my lady away. Give me directions and I can catch up with you further down the road. You know it makes sense."

Alwenna's fingers clenched about the ornate point on her belt. Both women looked to him for an answer. He had an uneasy feeling each wanted to hear something different.

"I can't ask it of you – it's too risky. We don't even know if it'll work."

Wynne snorted disapproval. "We can be sure they'll find our campsite come morning and then cast about till they find our tracks. How long after that before they overtake us?"

"We don't even know for certain they're following us."

"So let me set a clear trail for them and we'll find out. Would you be half so reluctant if I were a man?"

Weaver shook his head. "It's my job. I swore to the king–"

"Yes, yes. We know all about that. Alwenna's as dear to me as if she'd been my own. Her life has been my life these past twelve years and there is nothing I won't do to protect her. Nothing."

"I can't ask it of you," Weaver repeated.

"You don't need to ask it of me because I'll do it anyway. Only tell me the best route to take, and let's stop wasting time."

Alwenna stepped forward. "Please, Wynne, reconsider. I fear for you if you do this."

"No, my lady. My mind's made up. You'll see one day how it is – you'll find there's nothing you won't give up for the sake of your own."

The two women embraced, with an intensity that left Weaver feeling he was intruding. A breeze picked up, stirring the trees, breaking the silence of the forest.

Wynne turned away and mounted the horse – albeit stiffly. "Well, Weaver, which way should I go? Give me the best chance of making this work."

She gave him no choice – and she was right. His misgivings had no place here. There was nothing for him to do but help her decide the best route.

After Wynne was set on her way Weaver delayed only to tie strips of blanket about his horse's hooves, to make their tracks harder to follow. He had one more strip to add when the horse snorted and raised its head. Alwenna stood at the horse's shoulder, holding the reins. She ducked down and peered beneath the horse's neck to see what it had detected. A moment later she reached over and shook Weaver's shoulder. Weaver twisted round. A man stood at the edge of the clearing, swaying slightly as he drained his bladder against a tree. A liquor jug dangled from his free hand. He hadn't noticed them at all, but if he glanced their way he could scarcely fail to see them. One shout from him and his six companions would be upon them. Even if they were all as drunk as this specimen, Weaver didn't care to take those odds.

The last strip of blanket still in his hand, Weaver left Alwenna holding the horse as he crept through the trees at the edge of the tiny clearing. The man was preoccupied in refastening his clothing and unaware of Weaver's approach until the very last minute. His jaw dropped open in surprise. Before he could utter a sound Weaver grabbed him by the throat and shoved the piece of blanket into his mouth. The drunk struggled, flailing his free hand, seemingly reluctant to damage the liquor jug. Weaver tightened his grip about his neck and crammed the cloth as far down the man's throat as he could. The man's chest convulsed as he fought for air he couldn't take in, but it was as soundless as Weaver could have hoped for. His feet scuffled on the ground, then he went limp and the jug dropped to the ground with a hollow thud. A small amount of liquor spilled out and seeped into the forest floor.

Weaver extracted the cloth from the dead man's mouth, then dragged the body over to the narrow gill and rolled it down the side. It came to rest face down in the tiny stream. With luck, the man's companions might believe he'd simply lost his footing. Weaver tossed the liquor jug after him and returned to the horse, wrapping the strip of blanket about its hoof and tying it up as he had done the others. The cloth was damp with the dead man's saliva. Alwenna held the horse's reins in silence until Weaver straightened up and took them from her. She stepped back half a pace, although she said nothing.

Weaver wasted no time in leading the horse away between the trees, its hoofbeats muffled by the strips of blanket. Alwenna ghosted along at his side as they pushed through overgrown paths a mounted rider wouldn't take. They didn't speak, not even when he paused to pull a low branch aside so Alwenna might pass more easily. If she blamed him for Wynne's decision she didn't say so. If she held him in disgust for throttling the drunken soldier she didn't say so, either. It didn't make for a companionable silence.

CHAPTER TWELVE

Alwenna was growing used to the sounds of the forest now. Small creatures scuffled in the undergrowth, scurrying away as they passed. Birds took off from branches high above them with a clatter of wings. So many things relished the cover of the trees but she found it oppressive, especially by day. Being unable to see more than a few yards in any direction troubled her; she wanted to push the trees back, clear away the canopy that masked the sky. It didn't help that her view forward was obscured by Weaver's back as she rode pillion behind him. They were far off the beaten track now, riding at a walk along a narrow path used mainly by foresters as they went about their duties – and by others like them who wished to come and go with as few witnesses as possible.

In front of her Weaver tensed. "Riders approaching. Get that hood up."

"Could it be Wynne?" Alwenna flipped the hood over her head, tugging it down so it hid her face. What if it was the raiding party?

Weaver took his reins in one hand and halted the horse, setting his right hand on his sword hilt. The first of the oncoming horses came into view: a quality animal, it carried not an ounce of fat. These were no peasant foresters. The horse's rider was tall, of lean build. Behind him plodded a string of pack ponies. A wide-brimmed hat sheltered his bearded face, while his hair was oiled and dragged tightly back in thin plaits, bleached russet by sunlight. A freemerchant. He didn't appear startled to meet them at all – instead he smiled.

He reined in his horse. "Well met, fellow travellers. May your roads be clear and the Hunter watch over your fires." His right hand moved to his left shoulder, palm downwards in the stylised gesture of greeting the freemerchants used, and he inclined his head briefly.

Weaver mirrored the gesture. "And so may your road be blessed, traveller."

The freemerchant nodded, studying Weaver for a moment before his gaze moved on to Alwenna.

"Sister, you are welcome among us." Again that gesture.

She responded in kind. She'd been taught the formal greeting long ago, but this was the first time she'd needed to use it. Freemerchants came and went at court, but their business had never involved her.

"You will always find welcome with us, sister. I am Nicholl. I give you my name that you may call on me when the need arises." Was that a hint of pity she saw in his eyes? Perhaps she imagined it. His attention returned to Weaver.

"Well met, Ranald Weaver. Much water has flowed to the sea since my father gave you his name. What news of the road?"

If Weaver was startled to hear the stranger use his name he didn't show it. They had met before, perhaps. But what an odd way to phrase it. Then again, she'd heard many strange tales of the freemerchants.

"The road is quiet, but you will find trouble as you approach Highkell. Reivers in the Stanton lands have strayed west in recent days."

"The Stanton lands? Have it as you will." The freemerchant made a moue of... disgust? Simple disagreement? "We live ever in changing times. I thank you for your warning. The road we travelled was tranquil."

"You may meet one of our party on the road: a woman on a bay horse."

"If she is in need of assistance she will not be denied it." Nicholl's eyes flicked to Alwenna once more before he took up his reins and urged his horse forward. "May the Hunter watch over you." His horse pressed past them in the narrow space between the trees and, with a creaking of harness, the string of ponies followed him. Behind them were several more men of varying ages, all with the same russet hair, then three women. Scarves wrapped about their heads hid their hair but Alwenna guessed it to be oiled back as the men's had been, for the air was heavy with the scent of the aromatic oil they used. A memory stirred, too elusive for her to pin down. She'd met that scent somewhere recently, somewhere unexpected. It was a scent she connected with the market, but she hadn't been there in recent weeks.

Weaver waited until the caravan had vanished from sight among the trees before nudging his horse forward. "We should press on."

"A coincidence to meet someone who knows you out here in the middle of nowhere."

"I've never met him before in my life." Weaver took up

his reins and kicked his horse forward.

"But he recognised you. He knew your name."

"A lucky guess, nothing more. More like he recognised you."

"Dressed like this? That would be a very lucky guess indeed."

"The freemerchants do a lively enough trade in rumour. Depend upon it I told him nothing he didn't already know."

"But how could he guess your name like that? Is it true what they say: that they have a sixth sense?"

"People say a great many things. Would you believe them all?"

"It was a perfectly reasonable question. You clearly know more of the freemerchants than I do – would it be so difficult to give a straight answer?"

"Apologies, my lady. It is not the truth that matters in this case. It suits the freemerchants to let common folk believe they could curse the ground out from beneath them if they dared cross them. It ensures the ignorant treat them with – if not respect – at least caution."

"The fact remains he knew your name. Are we compromised now? Less safe than we were?"

"The freemerchants are no threat. Nicholl gave you his name and claimed you as sister. You'd do well to remember that. They'll take no side in Peninsular issues, but you can claim their protection."

"Why would he do that? He's a total stranger – and one I'm never likely to meet again."

"My lady, your guess would be as good as mine. Like as not he wished to impress you. What man would not?" He urged his horse forward into a trot, putting an end to her questions as she sought to keep her balance. Weaver was one man who certainly had no interest in impressing her. It would have been unladylike to pull a face behind his back. And so it was. She found the tiny act of rebellion strangely satisfying.

CHAPTER THIRTEEN

The standing stones ran in a precise north-south line across the ridge. Some of the ancient stones had toppled, while others leaned at improbable angles. Weaver had ridden this road many times, but the place had an unearthly air that always made him uneasy. Their path ran alongside the stones for a short distance before dipping south-west down the flank of the ridge, traversing the lower slopes of the mountain that rose ahead of them. Their horse jogged and sidled as they neared the stones and he brought it to a halt.

"What is this place?" Alwenna slid down from where she perched behind him, looking around, eyes wide, not unlike a slack-jawed peasant on first seeing a city.

"You sense it, then?" Of course she could, he'd expected as much. There was no way she could have failed to inherit at least some of her family's witchery. In truth there were other roads he could have chosen, but this was something he'd wanted to see for himself. All his doubts might have been laid to rest if she'd ridden on by without a second look.

She turned slowly, studying the empty ridge. "Are we being watched?"

"Some say the realms of earth and sky meet here – and this is where our ancestors wait to guide the living when they need help."

"I was told those were tales for children. I used to wish so hard they might be real… Here, I feel as if they could be." She turned to Weaver. He realised he'd never seen her smile properly before, not an unguarded response like that.

Her smile faltered. "You don't believe in it?"

"I believe what I can see for myself." He dismounted. "If you look over to the west you'll see our destination."

Hills tumbled away before them, rising from a broad wooded plain punctuated with pockets of farmland and scattered settlements. Beyond that, in the distant haze, stretched a grey ribbon of apparently flat ground.

Alwenna raised one hand to shade her eyes. "Is that the sea?"

"That's right. Vorrahan's lost in the haze, but on a clear day you can see the precinct buildings."

"I'm not sure I should believe you, not by your philosophy. Not until I can take up the water in my own hands." She turned away before he could decide if she was teasing him. "There's water nearby." She walked back along the ridge, one hand still shading her eyes as she searched the sloping ground to the west. Her cloak billowed in the breeze, hinting at curved contours beneath the heavy fabric. She moved with an air of certainty, a vital being in a timeless landscape. She hadn't been like this at court. Now it was his turn to gape like a slack-jawed peasant.

Alwenna turned downhill, moving with purpose to a clump of reeds. Weaver had an uneasy sense he ought to call her back. She knelt down and reached out, parting the reeds with her hands.

"I knew it. There's a spring here." She cupped her hands and scooped up a mouthful of water.

Everything stilled: the wind dropped, even the trilling of the skylarks ceased. And, without so much as a murmur, she slumped over onto the ground.

Alwenna and Tresilian sat at the foot of the cherry tree, their backs pressed against the trunk, fallen blossom littering the ground around them.

Tresilian flung a pebble against the orchard wall. "It doesn't matter whether it's a good crop or not, I won't be here to pick them."

Alwenna paused in sifting the petals between her fingers and twisted round to look at him. "Why not?"

"I'm to go to be taught by the brethren at Vorrahan. Father told me last week."

"You didn't tell me." She scooped up another handful of the blossom.

"He said it didn't concern you."

"Because I'm a girl, or because I'm an orphan?" She threw away the blossom she held, glaring as it floated to the ground.

"He didn't say." Tresilian threw another stone after the first. It hit the wall with a sharp clack, dislodging a small shower of lime mortar. "There was something else too, but he told me not to say anything to you."

"Oh." The syllable was laden with indifference.

"I'll tell you if you want."

She shrugged. "I'm really not bothered either way."

"It's about you, so I think it's only fair you should know."

"You'd better tell me then." She sketched a circle in the

blossom with her finger. "I won't tell, promise."

"He says we're to get married."

"What?" She sat up and knelt where she could see him clearly. "That's ridiculous."

Tresilian frowned. "Not till we're older, of course. I don't think it's such a bad idea. Better than marrying some foreigner who can't speak a word of the language."

"There's more to it than that, though."

"Like what?"

"Well, having children. And things like that. It's complicated." She fixed him with a serious gaze. "I don't ever want to get married."

"I told him you'd say that." Tresilian picked up another pebble, twisting it about in his hand. "He said it's our royal duty."

"I don't care if it is." She sat back against the tree again. "I want to travel to new places, and sail across the sea."

"We could do things like that once we're married. It would be fun."

"I still don't want to."

"I thought I was your best friend?"

"You are. But most people don't marry their best friends."

"We're not most people. We're royal."

Alwenna gathered a handful of fallen blossom. "I never asked to be." She set about shredding each petal, one by one.

A gust of wind lifted the fallen blossom from the ground and sent it spinning about her, faster and faster until she could see nothing beyond it.

"You were always such an angry girl." Tresilian's voice, the adult voice she was accustomed to hearing.

Alwenna spun round, trying to find him. She thought she saw a shape through the whirling petals, but the cloud grew thicker and spun faster until she became dizzy.

"I used to think it was my fault. But I've kept my promise. You'll get to cross the sea soon enough." Tresilian coughed, a guttural, all-consuming sound that made her shudder. "I didn't think it would be... like this. But you'll see." He dragged in another pained breath, which rattled in his throat. "This parting won't be for long."

Alwenna tried to speak, to call him back, but no sound emerged from her mouth. When she tried to reach out, her limbs were leaden, unresponsive.

"Lady Alwenna, can you hear me?" The voice sounded from somewhere in the darkness. Not Tresilian's this time, but another man's.

She opened her eyes and the blur before her resolved into a face. Weaver.

"Are you hurt, my lady?" He helped her sit up.

"No. I'm fine. But... Tresilian spoke to me."

"You need to rest. I've been pushing you too hard."

"I was dreaming, and then he spoke to me. Except it wasn't a dream any more. He was in pain." She shivered.

"You fainted, that's all. You need a proper meal inside you and a good night's sleep." He began to straighten up.

Alwenna took hold of his arm. "Weaver, it wasn't a dream. It's not the first time something like this has happened."

Weaver didn't recoil immediately, but he might as well have. "You fainted, my lady. There are healers at Vorrahan–"

"There's nothing wrong with me." She clambered to

her feet, brushing away his attempts to help.

"Of course not. That was my very first thought as you keeled over."

Alwenna staggered sideways as a wave of dizziness threatened to overwhelm her. Weaver caught her by the arm and she had no option but to accept his support as they made their way back to the waiting horse in what she hoped was a dignified silence. They were perhaps three paces away from the horse when Weaver froze.

Some distance down the ridge a rider was approaching. He appeared in no great hurry, but Alwenna's gut knotted with apprehension all the same: behind him he led a riderless horse. As Alwenna's dizziness faded she could see the horse looked very much like the one Wynne had been riding when she'd set out alone from their camp.

The rider was a freemerchant youth. Alwenna recognised his face from the group they'd met in the forest. He spoke to Weaver now in an uneven voice that had only recently broken.

"My father guessed this might be your horse, with the bridle being fashioned in the northern way."

"It is indeed. Where did you come by it?" Weaver ran his hands over the horse's head and neck, checking for injuries.

"It came up to us in the forest, the day after we passed you. One stirrup was missing, and the reins were broken. We searched until daylight faded, but could find no trace of your companion." The youth glanced at Alwenna. "Except…"

Alwenna crossed over to see for herself. There on the saddle were unmistakable bloodstains. Dark and dry now, they had not been on the saddle when Wynne set off.

Alwenna folded her arms over her stomach as if she might contain the dread that curdled there. "Pray convey our gratitude to Nicholl for sending this news. And we thank you for bringing the horse to us."

The youth nodded, his expression sombre.

"Will you break bread with us?" asked Weaver.

"I thank you, but no. I must waste no time returning to the others."

"Very well. I am in your debt. May your road be clear." Weaver stepped back and the youth took up his reins.

"Wait." Alwenna found her voice at last. "What of the reivers? Did you see any sign of them?"

"We passed a camp where several horses had been kept overnight, all of them shod in Highkell style. They had been there perhaps on two separate nights. There were many tracks about the place, but the most recent led away east, and they were riding hard."

"I see. Thank you." There were proper forms of leave-taking, but her voice seemed to have lodged in her throat.

She watched as the youth rode away down the ridge. Weaver checked over the horse's legs, then ran his hands once again over its head and neck, inspecting every inch of the animal.

"The horse is uninjured," he announced eventually.

"Indeed? That's all right, then."

"Begging your pardon, my lady, but you mistake my meaning. If the horse had been injured, that might have left the marks on the saddle."

She nodded and turned away, unable to trust her voice. He had a knack of making her feel unutterably foolish.

"She made her choice. And she wouldn't have had it any other way."

"That doesn't make it any less my fault. Don't you see? I should have left her at Highkell."

"What's done is done, my lady. It does no good to dwell on it."

Easy for him to say. "There must be something we can do."

"We continue to Vorrahan, my lady."

"And what about Wynne? Do we just abandon her?"

"If she's able to follow us, then she will. That was the plan."

"It was a poor plan."

"You're still safe, my lady."

But at what cost? Guilt settled like a leaden weight in Alwenna's stomach.

CHAPTER FOURTEEN

Drew's duties at Vorrahan precinct were hardly taxing. The novice took one last look round to be sure Father Garrad's room was set in order. The flagstone floor was swept clean; the chamber was aired; a supply of ink and parchment waited at the writing desk. In the room beyond, the bedding was straight, the chamber pot in place and all his master's clean clothing stowed neatly in the oak chest.

Drew found the work a little dull if truth be told, but easy enough for one raised to the rigours of the stonemason's yard. Maybe he was better off here, away from the yard and his father's judging gaze. He'd had to work twice as hard there to overcome the limitations of his slighter build. His younger brother had been taken on as apprentice in his favour, but he was burly, like their father. Drew took after their mother, russet-haired and slight. Small wonder they called him changeling.

No, it was well enough here. Many of the brethren were misfits of one sort or another. And since the librarian had taught him his letters at Brother Gwydion's behest, a new world had opened up before him.

The clunk of the door latch alerted him to Father Garrad's arrival. Drew bowed his head in greeting, waiting apprehensively as the priest looked around the room. But he seemed pleased enough with what he saw.

"I'll have no further need of you this evening. Brother Irwyn might be glad of your help in the kitchens for an hour or two."

"Aye, father." Drew bowed his head and left, arms folded in the pious stance the brethren at Vorrahan favoured. It made it easy to blend in. As for Brother Irwyn, he might be glad of many things, but Drew was not about to gratify him.

Instead he made his way to the main gateway and stepped out through the small door that permitted easy access for the brethren as they went about their daily business. He would seek out Brother Gwydion, the master seer. Father Garrad had been at pains to keep them apart of late. Perhaps that had been a condition of his father's providing another generous donation to the precinct. Drew couldn't help being wary of Father Garrad. He sensed the eyes often said one thing, yet the man's thoughts were at variance. Brother Gwydion said such confusion was only to be expected at first: of the few who possessed the sight, fewer still could master it.

Gwydion said control would come with practice, that daily meditation was key to understanding the deeper mysteries. The seer claimed that was the reason he spent so much time in the darkness of the cavern at the source of the Holy Well. He said the peace improved the quality of his meditation. Drew suspected the old man simply found the hustle and bustle of the outside world to be too stressful. If Drew one day became Gwydion's heir, as the old man had promised, he wouldn't spend as much time sitting in the dark.

The main access to the master seer's cave followed a natural fault line in the rock. Drew knew where the floor rose sharply enough to trip the unwary, and just where to duck his head as the tunnel narrowed overhead. Brother Francis stood on guard at the end, blocking the entrance to the cavern.

"Don't disturb him. He's deep in meditation," the older monk hissed. Francis had been serving Gwydion for most of his forty years and his face had the same pallor from so many hours spent in the dark.

Torchlight glinted off still water in the cavern beyond Brother Francis. On a small island in the centre of the pool the master seer sat motionless on a robust chair, his hands resting on the wooden arms. His robes hung slack over angular knees while his eyes focused ahead on some point in the middle distance. At these moments he looked impossibly old and frail. A tremor ran through his body and he drew a sharp breath, like a man stepping into icy water, then he turned his head towards Drew.

"Ah, Drew. Brother Francis, you may leave us. It is high time you broke your fast."

"As you order, master." Francis bowed, and shuffled away down the rock passage, casting a surly glance at Drew as he left.

Gwydion waited until Francis' footsteps had retreated out of hearing range before speaking again. "You heard my call, Drew. That is excellent." He raised his hands in a gesture of benediction, executed with surprising grace for one of his advanced years. No one at Vorrahan knew for sure how old Gwydion was, but all agreed he must have been eighty if he was a day.

It was tempting to bask in the unaccustomed praise,

but in truth Drew had sensed nothing: no call, not even a whisper. "I-I don't think so, Brother Gwydion. Father Garrad dismissed me for the night, so I decided to come here."

"I'm sure he did not order you to come here." The old man smiled, as if explaining something to a child who was slow of understanding.

"No, that is true. He suggested I help in the kitchen."

"But you had a sudden inclination to come here instead?"

"Well, no..." Then he thought. He had planned to go to the library to see if the brother there could help him further with his letters. Could the old man be right? Did he have the mystical power?

"Of course, lad. That's how it works. At first you won't even notice its promptings, but as you become attuned, you'll see ever more readily. The sight will visit you more often once it has found the way." He settled his hands on the chair arms once more, and rested his head back against the wooden panel. "You have much to learn if you are to take your place as a seer. I was taught much in my time and I would pass on that knowledge. Those who possess the gift are fewer and fewer with every year. And here in the west..."

The old man lapsed into silence, his expression taking on that far-off look that Drew had come to recognise as a visitation by the sight. Gwydion's breathing slowed, and Drew watched with closer attention than usual. The notion that he too possessed the sight was an enticing one. Might he one day ascend to the rank of seer, perhaps really be heir to Gwydion's learning? Oh, yes, he watched closely as never before. Gwydion's breathing deepened, as if he took every ounce of strength from each inward breath then held that strength as he exhaled. The man's body stilled, as the breaths came further and further apart and his eyelids closed. Yet this was not some idle doze, but a state somehow attuned to the silence surrounding them. Drew settled down with his back against the cavern wall to watch and wait.

Finally Gwydion stirred. Gnarled fingers twitched in an effort to raise his hands from the arms of the chair where he had remained immobile for the past hour or more. Drew pushed himself to his feet, ready to lend assistance, but Gwydion raised one shaking hand to stop him.

"These old bones grow loath to do my bidding. Bring Brother Francis to help me, lad. I must speak with Father Garrad."

Drew did not have far to go to find Brother Francis: he was hurrying up the slope to the cave entrance, ungainly in his haste, a lantern bobbing wildly in his hand.

Drew waited by the entrance. "Brother Gwydion wishes to speak to Father Garrad. He–"

Francis gestured him out of the way. "I know what my master requires. Your gift is not as rare as you would like to think, boy. Nor as powerful." Francis pushed past Drew and ducked into the tunnel. His sandals slapped on stone as he hurried across the cavern to Gwydion's side.

"Master, you must save your strength." Francis bent low beside Gwydion, taking the frail hand in his own.

"I have a vain fancy to feel daylight on my face one last time."

"Master, you must not speak so. And besides, it is night now."

"Is it so? That is a shame. I would have preferred

sunlight." Gwydion pushed himself unsteadily to his feet. "Help me now, Francis. You, too, Drew. I need you both."

"But master, can this not wait until morning, when you are rested?" Francis supported the old man by the arm, not sparing a glance for Drew as he hurried to take his other arm.

"No, Francis, it cannot wait. I have seen the end and it is not far distant. But I have seen other things, too. Garrad must heed my words this time. He thinks me an old fool lost in the shadows, beyond reach of reason. He cannot understand the darkness as I do." With their support he shuffled towards the entrance. "And if our good father does not pay heed this time, I fear the darkness will engulf him."

CHAPTER FIFTEEN

Alwenna woke at a hand shaking her shoulder. She sat up with a start, shivering, trying to recall where they'd halted the night before. The days had merged in an exhausting round of too many hours spent in the saddle interspersed with too few hours of sleep.

"I've brewed some kopamid." Weaver held an earthenware beaker out towards her.

Of course, they'd stopped in the forest some time after dark. Weaver had been short with her since the incident on the ridge. This had to be his way of apologising.

"You lit a fire?" She rubbed her eyes, then surveyed the surrounding forest for a discreet place for her morning ablutions. Fires and hot drinks were all very well, but what she missed most on this journey was the privacy of a garderobe.

"We'll be gone soon enough. I thought you might be glad of it." Unsmiling, he pressed the hot beaker into her hands.

"Thank you." She inhaled the rich aroma, stronger than she remembered it. "I haven't tasted kopamid for a long time."

"I brought this back from The Marches. It's good for a chill morning."

She sipped at the drink, relishing the sensation of the hot fluid coursing down her throat. "I've missed this." She needn't tell Weaver her thoughts concerning garderobes. "You've been in The Marches recently? Was that–"

A rush of nausea knotted her stomach, insistent, unrelenting. She clambered to her feet and managed to dash to the cover of the trees before she was overtaken by violent retching. The sickness persisted until long after her stomach was empty, leaving her doubled over, trembling and sweating.

"Can I bring you anything?" Weaver must have followed her. And, no doubt, witnessed the whole sorry episode.

Alwenna straightened up, still shaking. "Some water?" Her voice cracked.

He handed her his costrel. She turned away as she swilled her mouth then spat away the foulness, willing him to go back to the fire and wait there.

He remained at her side. "Was it the kopamid? It didn't taste bad."

"No. It was fine." The effort of speaking abraded her throat.

"Do you have a fever?"

"No, I'm well." She rinsed and spat again. If only he'd leave her in peace. "It's never been so strong before."

He frowned. "The kopamid?"

"No..." Don't tell anyone, Tresilian had said.

"You can't afford to be taken ill now. Do you need a healer?"

"It's passed. I'll manage."

Weaver studied her, his expression sceptical. "Very well, my lady. I'll saddle the horses."

When Alwenna returned to their camp site Weaver

handed her a dry oatcake. She picked at it, aware of his covert scrutiny as he made ready to leave. The half-empty beaker, now cold, perched on the mossy ground where she'd abandoned it. She didn't dare drink it, even though her stomach had settled. Nor did she wish to offend Weaver by discarding the remains. It was the first friendly gesture he'd made in the days they'd been travelling.

As if he'd read her mind Weaver stooped and picked up the beaker, slinging the contents into the bushes before he stowed it in a saddlebag. When he'd finished, Alwenna climbed to her feet and made her way over to her horse. Without speaking, Weaver legged her up into the saddle.

"Thank you." Her voice grated in her throat. Weaver nodded curt acknowledgment, his mouth set in a grim line. This promised to be a long day.

CHAPTER SIXTEEN

Weaver glanced across at Alwenna, who sat at the foot of a smooth-trunked beech. She'd slept badly. Of course, she'd not admit it. The shadows beneath her eyes left him in no doubt, if the telling silences between her nightmares hadn't been evidence enough. She didn't speak of the horrors that stalked her sleep, but each morning she was a little paler. And she'd been too pale to start with. The sooner he could hand her over to the care of the brethren at Vorrahan, the better.

"With luck we might reach the ferry in time to cross tonight."

"I'd no idea we were so close." She took a bite of dry oatcake. "It'll be–" One hand pressed to her stomach, she jumped to her feet and hurried away between the trees.

Weaver followed a couple of paces, then stopped. He could do nothing to help, and she'd only resent his interference. She returned a few minutes later, pale and dishevelled. He offered her some water and she took it with an unsteady hand, murmuring a word of thanks.

"There's a town a few miles out of our way; we should be able to find you a healer there. I doubt Vasic's spies will have penetrated this far north."

"There's no need." She didn't meet his eyes.

"There's every need. You're eating next to nothing and losing most of that."

"I'm fine if I eat often enough." She hesitated, then seemed to reach some kind of decision. "Wynne told me what to expect. It's a good sign, she said."

"Wynne?" Realisation dawned, and with it disbelief that he had not guessed sooner. "You're carrying." Even to his ears the words sounded like an accusation.

She kept her eyes averted.

"Yet you didn't see fit to tell me? Does Tresilian know?"

"Of course." She swung round to face him, drawing herself up to her full height. "He said we must keep it secret as long as possible."

"But what if something had gone wrong? It's madness."

"Nothing has gone wrong."

"By some miracle. You should have been travelling by carriage in easy stages, resting in proper beds at night. I should have been told."

She turned her back on him and began rolling up her blanket.

"I'll get the horses ready." His words elicited no response. "Take all the time you need."

She spun round, glaring at him. "I don't need any more time than I did yesterday, or the day before, or any other day. I swear if we do reach Vorrahan tonight it won't be a moment too soon."

For once they were in total agreement. Weaver saddled the horses in silence.

CHAPTER SEVENTEEN

Alwenna's stomach churned at the sight of the waves fretting beneath a leaden sky. Through the rain squalls she could just make out grassy slopes and rocks jutting above the water across the sound. The boat waiting by the small jetty looked impossibly flimsy as the waves roiled behind it.

"We're going to cross in that tiny thing?"

It was small wonder Weaver looked surprised when she addressed him directly. They'd barely spoken since the morning's disastrous start. "There's a larger ferry a couple of hours to the north, but this way's faster."

So they'd be rid of one another the sooner. He had to be looking forward to that. She was. "What about the horses?"

"We won't need them on the island. The precinct has grazing nearby. They'll be kept there for the time being."

A boy emerged from the ferryman's hut on the shoreline and took the horses' reins. Weaver handed him a couple of coins and he led the horses away through the trees. Alwenna fought a sudden urge to follow after them. She could tell Weaver this was a mistake and order him to take her back to Highkell before it was too late.

"My lady? The boat's ready."

Wind whipped Alwenna's hair from under her hood as she clambered down from the rudimentary jetty into the rocking boat and seated herself in the very centre. She gripped the cold plank as the oarsman took his place and water slapped against the sides, splashing over and sullying her cloak with dark spots. The boat wallowed as Weaver climbed in and sat facing her, then the ferryman lowered his oars into the water and pulled back with practised ease. With a grinding of the oars against the locks they drew away from the sheltered jetty and out onto open water.

A fresh onslaught of rain all but obscured her vision as they pulled out from the shelter of the trees on the mainland; it pelted against her cheeks, stinging her eyes, weighing down her cloak. She clung there, wretched, sliding on the wooden seat as the boat pitched on the growling water. Her world dwindled until she was trapped in a limbo devoid of all sound but the buffeting of the wind and the grind, lap, slap of the oars, devoid of all sensation but the stinging rain and dull tug of nausea at the pit of her stomach.

Then, when she thought couldn't resist the heaving of her stomach another moment, the ferryman pulled them into the lee of a wooded promontory and they cut through calmer water until the bottom of the boat crunched on a shingle beach.

She clambered from the boat, leaning on the hand Weaver offered for support as her body deceived her into believing the ground still pitched beneath her feet. When she was able to pay more attention to her surroundings she saw three figures, clad in drab monastic robes, approaching the beach. The robes and hoods looked oddly familiar. She stared, unable to recall when she had seen them before.

"Is something wrong?" Weaver kept his voice low, so the boatman could not overhear.

"No." Her denial was reflexive.

"Of course not." Weaver swung their saddlebags onto his shoulders. "Forgive me if I disbelieve you, my lady." He strode away up the incline towards the robed figures without so much as looking back to see if she followed.

The centre of the three stepped forward to greet Weaver in a low voice, then bowed once Alwenna reached them. Of slight build, he moved with a suppleness that belied his age. "Lady Alwenna, we are honoured to welcome you to our house. I am Father Garrad. I regret we are not meeting in happier circumstances."

"Thank you, father. Tresilian spoke of you often. Did he send word of my arrival somehow?"

"We discussed the matter some time ago, my lady. It was Brother Gwydion who informed us you were on the way; he is eager to meet you in person, I think. But first you must recover from your journey."

Brother Gwydion? She knew that name: the master seer. Tresilian had told her to consult him. Before she could enquire further, Weaver cleared his throat.

"Father, forgive my interruption, but have you had word from Highkell in recent days?"

"None as yet. You are the first to reach our shore. I very much doubt you will be the last."

"I see." Weaver's tone was non-committal, but his eyes lingered on the priest's back as he led them towards the precinct.

Alwenna halted. "Weaver, the path is uneven, would you lend me your arm?"

"Of course, my lady." His tone didn't echo the flicker of irritation that crossed his face. He hitched the saddlebag up his shoulder out of the way and held out his arm in something approximating court style.

Alwenna set her hand on his forearm, waiting until the monks had drawn some distance ahead of them. "You disliked Father Garrad's answer, I think?"

Weaver glanced at her. "It was no answer, my lady. We've travelled by an indirect route. A messenger could have made the journey in a fraction of the time. And all the trade for the outer isles passes through the port at Vorrahan."

No prevarication, at least. She had no doubt he answered her question frankly. "Is it not possible there may simply be no news yet?"

Weaver hesitated this time. Not long, but long enough for her to suspect he was choosing his words with care. "I think it unlikely, my lady."

It was then she realised that Tresilian was the only one at Highkell likely to send an urgent message to this out-of-the-way place. No one else there knew where she was. If things went badly... She couldn't afford to dwell on that possibility. "Tresilian trusts Father Garrad; he has known him for years."

"That is so, my lady. I trust no one until they've earned it. I never met the man before today and he smiles too readily."

Once she might have suspected him of joking at her expense. "Yours is a dour philosophy."

"It serves me well enough. If you doubt me, my lady, ask yourself how often Stanton smiled."

None at court had been readier with a smile. "I must

concede you that point. By that reckoning you must be trustworthy indeed."

"I swore to protect you and so I shall, whether you choose to trust me or not."

Ahead of them the monks waited a few yards from the modest gatehouse which guarded the entrance to the precinct. Alwenna speeded her steps, digesting Weaver's words. He hadn't voiced criticism of her husband's decision to send her here, but he didn't trust Father Garrad. And he hadn't trusted Stanton. Half-remembered snatches of conversation came to mind. Tresilian had determinedly defended Stanton against his critics at court. What ought she make of that? There were surely lessons to be learned, but this wasn't the time to ponder them. She suppressed her unease that such a time might already have passed.

Sturdy walls of grey stone enclosed the heart of the precinct, although the buildings associated with it had long since spilled beyond those bounds and a settlement of sorts had formed outside the precinct gates. Alwenna was obliged to pick her way down the muddy street as best she could.

The heavy double doors were barred, but a small door set into them stood open. It was just wide enough to admit one person at a time.

Garrad stepped back, ushering Alwenna through. "I must apologise for the lodgings we have to offer you, my lady. They are not ideal for one of your station, but in the circumstances we deemed it more important to house you within the safety of our walls. I fear we cannot offer you a servant, but Brother Drew will see to all practical matters."

A gangling, red-haired novice Alwenna guessed to be sixteen or seventeen stepped forward, bowing awkwardly as Garrad took his leave. The youth led them across the cloistered courtyard and out through a door at the corner to a long, low building. He opened the first door, then hurried off to arrange hot water and food for the travellers.

Alwenna entered a modest-sized room boasting a simple table with bench seats, with the added luxury of an upholstered settle against the wall to one side of the hearth. A door to the other side of the hearth led to a smaller chamber which contained a bed frame and straw mattress. The walls were built of the same oppressive grey stone as the rest of the precinct, unrelieved by plaster or hangings. Alwenna peered out through the bedchamber's small window to see the blank wall of another building, separated from the lodging house by an alleyway. They had reached journey's end, and it could not have been more dispiriting.

Unfastening her cloak, she returned to the front room where Weaver was sorting through the bags. After a moment's hesitation she sat on the bench opposite him, setting down the cloak and leaning her arms on the table.

He glanced at her. "Is everything to your satisfaction?"

For all she'd looked forward to reaching their destination, she'd not given it much thought. She had no idea what she'd imagined awaited her in this desolate place. "It's... monastic. As I should have expected."

"It's a roof, my lady."

She told herself she imagined the reproving note in his voice. "What happens next?"

"We await word from Highkell." His expression was closed.

He'd already made it plain what he believed would happen there, and how swiftly events might move.

Alwenna pushed the thought away. Her mouth was dry, and her head ached. There was a bed in the next room; she should go through and lie down, but even that seemed like too much effort. She would, in a moment. She lowered her head onto her forearms and closed her eyes. If she'd been granted the luxury of solitude she would have wept.

CHAPTER EIGHTEEN

Torchlight flickered against stone walls, soot blackening the vaulted ceiling. The air was clammy. Alwenna shivered. A man stood with his back to her, his attention fixed on a prisoner stretched on the rack before him. All she could see of the victim were his arms, bound together above his head, the muscles spasming at intervals.

"What are you grinning at, fool?"

She knew Vasic's voice straight away. It was deeper than Tresilian's now. That must have pleased Vasic. He'd always resented that his younger cousin's voice had broken first. And with a shock of horror she knew the figure on the rack was Tresilian.

"A greater… fool… than I." Pain distorted every syllable as he forced out the words but there was no mistaking her husband's voice.

Alwenna tried to draw breath, to shout out, but somehow she couldn't move.

Vasic leaned over Tresilian, his movements measured, almost lover-like. Now Alwenna could see her husband's face, bruised and bloodied, eyes closed. She shouted out a warning, but neither man reacted.

"You begin to bore me, cousin. I cannot abide boredom."

Vasic drew an ornate dagger from his belt and set the blade against Tresilian's ribs, pressing just hard enough for the motion of his breathing to draw blood. "This is your last chance. Tell me where to find her."

Tresilian's eyes flicked open. "Just finish it."

Vasic leaned closer still, as if to whisper a confidence. "Would you like that? Would it be a kindness to you?"

"You haven't the mettle."

"You always underestimated me."

"If you only knew..." Tresilian was seized by a paroxysm of laughter.

Vasic thrust the knife between his cousin's ribs. Blood spilled over the gemstones set into the handle as he withdrew the blade, pooling on the rough timber of the rack before dripping to the stone floor beneath. So much blood. Too much.

Tresilian coughed, more blood dribbling from the corner of his mouth as he struggled to draw air into his lungs.

"No one laughs at me now, cousin." Vasic straightened up slowly. His eyes followed every heave of his cousin's ribcage and measured every choking gasp, each gagging breath harsher and more desperate than the last. Then silence fell. Vasic turned to the guards at the door, pausing to examine the congealing blood on his hands, absently rubbing his thumb against soiled fingertips. "Throw him in the pit with the rest."

His lips curled in a familiar smile as he strode past Alwenna's hiding place.

"No!" Alwenna shouted out. But no one heard. She had to do something... She leaped forward, and her knee crashed against some obstacle.

"My lady?"

Alwenna flailed against the hand that had taken hold of her arm and the grip tightened.

"Lady Alwenna?"

She knew that voice. He would help. He never smiled, but he would help.

But when she tried to speak, no sound emerged, and when she tried to open her eyes a great weight seemed to hold them pressed shut. And the same weight pressed down on her chest, her heart thundering in her ears. Trapped in the dark, she had to cry out. But to cry out she had to draw breath. And she couldn't...

"Speak to me."

Hands were pulling her free from the wreckage... And she could draw in a lungful of air, thank the Goddess.

And with the sweet air came even sweeter reason. She wasn't trapped in the dark. It was still daylight. And she was slumped over the table in that grim little room.

Weaver crouched at her side, supporting her by the shoulders, more alarmed than she had ever seen him.

"By all that's... What happened?"

"I... must have fallen asleep." She straightened up and discovered she was trembling from head to foot. "It was just a bad dream. How stupid of me."

Weaver shook his head. "But what happened? You–" He seemed to gather himself together and released her shoulders, checking her pulse at the wrist. His hand was unsteady. "You stopped breathing. I thought you were dying."

What had happened? The darkness, the pressure... "I dreamed I was back in the carriage, after the landslide. That must be what it was."

Weaver sat back on the bench next to her, their few

belongings forgotten on the table at his elbow. "You were only asleep a minute or so – two minutes at most. There was hardly time." He took her wrist again and checked her pulse a second time, as if convincing himself she was indeed alive. "Your pulse is steadier, at least." He straightened up. "You must see a healer. The journey's been too much for you."

"I'll be fine. It's the sort of thing Wynne told me to expect."

Weaver sat back, folding his arms across his chest, his expression combative. "Because you're carrying? It doesn't do that. I know what I saw, and it's not normal."

"Are you saying I'm not normal?" Alwenna rubbed her arms, trying to restore some warmth to her limbs.

Weaver jumped to his feet and picked up the cloak she'd discarded on arrival, dropping it over her shoulders without ceremony. But he didn't answer her.

"That's what you think, isn't it? I'm an abomination?"

Weaver crossed to the window, leaning there with his back to the light and arms folded. "I didn't say that."

"You were thinking it."

Weaver straightened up, unfolding his arms. "My lady–"

She raised a hand to silence him. "I wouldn't blame you if you did. I can almost believe it myself." She spoke quickly, her need to unburden herself of the scene she'd just witnessed too pressing. "Just now, when I first fell asleep, I saw – I dreamed – I was in a dungeon. Vasic was there. He had Tresilian on a rack..."

"It's only natural your fears–"

"No, let me finish. He was torturing him to find out where I was. Tresilian mocked him and Vasic... He stabbed him. I think he killed him. There was so much blood."

"My lady, in times like these when you sleep the mind brings fears to the surface. The night before a battle, I've known–" He fell silent for a moment. "It's my fault for asking about news from Highkell in your hearing."

"This was no dream. I saw everything as it happened. It was so clear."

"You're exhausted. You should consult a healer here. Maybe get a sleeping draught."

"A healer would recognise I'm... carrying." She used Weaver's phrase. "And how long then before the news reached Father Garrad? Tresilian said tell no one as long as it could be hidden."

Weaver rubbed the back of his neck. "My lady, I can clean and bind a flesh wound, splint a broken limb. But this – whatever just happened – if your health's at risk... I can't deal with this."

"Do you imagine a healer could?" The horror was fading, as if describing the scene had watered down her fear, but tremors still shook her body at intervals. Weaver's suggestion she was exhausted made so much sense. It was much easier to believe that was the cause of her nightmare. "I'm much better now," she lied. It was an attempt to convince herself as much as Weaver.

A knock at the door heralded the return of Brother Drew with servants carrying a bathtub and hot water. They set the tub in the bedchamber and hurried away to bring more water.

Weaver gathered up the few garments he had unpacked from the saddlebags. "A shame these parsimonious monks didn't think to provide a chest for your belongings."

"There's a row of hooks in the bedchamber. And I have little enough to store away."

"They should have provided a maidservant to tend to your needs at the very least. It's not right. I'll speak with Garrad."

Wynne's name hovered unspoken in the air between them.

Alwenna shrugged. "I'm not so cosseted a creature I can't manage to hang my own clothes on a few pegs."

"I never suggested such a thing. It's a slight to you, my lady."

"This way there's no one to spy on my business." None of this mattered, not really – it was simply easier to bicker about servants than contemplate the scene she'd just witnessed. But it would take a great deal of bickering to make her forget the terrible sound of Tresilian's final, choking breaths, whether real or imagined.

CHAPTER NINETEEN

Alwenna picked at her breakfast in silence, wary of bringing on another bout of sickness. The refectory at Vorrahan was every bit as unwelcoming as the spartan guest chambers: walls of the same grey stone, with cold stone slabs underfoot, and a thin draught running beneath the doors at either end of the narrow hall. Goddess knew what the place would be like in the depths of winter. Far colder, if the size of the empty hearth in the centre of one long wall was any indication.

Two female servants replenished the serving dishes on the two long tables – they were the first women she'd seen in the precinct. A low murmur of conversation filled the air as brethren came and went, their sandals slapping on the stone floor. Alwenna gave up trying to count how many monks there were. Likewise, she'd given up any pretence of eating and was debating whether she might leave Weaver to finish his breakfast and return alone to her lodgings when Father Garrad joined them at their table with an amiable greeting. As they exchanged polite small-talk she found herself inclined to agree with Weaver's criticism that Garrad smiled too readily. Weaver, on the other hand, seemed less wary this morning, and chatted readily enough with Garrad. Weaver refilled their tankards with small beer when she thought he must have been ready to take his leave, and turned the conversation towards the lack of news from Highkell.

"I confess that troubles me." Garrad's smile was replaced with an expression of concern. "It might be as well for you to return to the mainland and see what news you can glean. After all, your charge is safe here with us now."

Alwenna was certain Weaver would seize on the excuse to be on the move again, but he merely nodded and made a non-committal reply.

Garrad pushed his tankard away, making ready to stand. "You must, of course, do as you think fit. You will doubtless receive orders from the king soon enough. Now, I beg you will excuse me."

Alwenna spoke up. "Father Garrad, when we arrived you spoke of a brother who wished to meet me – the master seer? Perhaps we should consult him first?"

Garrad smiled. "Brother Gwydion's skill as seer was once unequalled, it is true, my lady. I ought to warn you he has slipped beyond reason these past years."

The fellow did smile too much. "Nevertheless he is master seer. It is a matter of simple courtesy, is it not? I would not wish to offend the Order of Seers by neglect."

Garrad pushed himself to his feet. "I doubt you will learn anything of import, my lady."

"It was my husband's specific request, Father Garrad."

"If your husband were here today he would find Gwydion much altered, and not for the better. As for the seers, they have no interest in our doings here at Vorrahan, else they would have replaced Gwydion long ago. Times have changed."

"Times may have changed, Father Garrad, but I will not permit any oversight on my part to deepen the divide with the south. I shall speak with the master seer. I trust you will make the necessary arrangements."

Garrad glanced at Weaver. "What say you, Weaver? Your scepticism is a byword – has been ever since the Battle of Vorland Pass. Would you set any store by the ramblings of an old man in his dotage?"

Weaver turned his tankard about on the table, glancing towards Alwenna before he spoke. "The king made his wishes clear when we left Highkell. It's not my place to question his orders."

Garrad inclined his head. "Very well. Brother Drew will take you to meet the master seer later today." He bowed to Alwenna. "In the meantime, I suggest you ask Weaver to tell you how he was the only one able to defeat an enemy champion steeped in dark lore."

"Vorland Pass was many years ago, father." Weaver's tone was mild enough, but the hand holding his tankard had stilled.

"But it made you the man you are today. You should tell the lady that tale, Weaver. All of it." Garrad withdrew.

Weaver waited until the priest was out of earshot. "It pains me to say it, my lady, but it might be as well to heed Garrad's advice. I've heard nothing good about this master seer."

"I shall see him. What harm can one old man do?"

"Why ask, my lady, when you have no intention of heeding my reply?"

"Father Garrad needs to learn I shan't dance to his tune." Surely he could see that, after the doubts he'd expressed about Garrad's trustworthiness? "He was too keen to dissuade me. And what was all that business about Vorland Pass?"

Weaver merely shrugged and stood, ready to leave the table.

"Wait, Weaver, what did he mean?"

"There's little enough to it. Suffice to say ever since I've been renowned for the thickness of my skull." His tone wasn't encouraging.

"In other words, you won't tell me."

"You've been close enough with your own secrets, my lady, let me keep mine."

So, he still nursed resentment that she and Tresilian had not confided in him. "I had good reason not to tell you."

"As have I, my lady." Weaver's tone made it clear the subject was closed.

CHAPTER TWENTY

Alwenna was surprised when Brother Drew, taking them to the master seer, led them out of the precinct gates and set off towards a rocky outcrop several hundred yards away. The outcrop was split from top to bottom by a gaping cave mouth.

Alwenna hesitated as they drew close enough to see the well-trodden path leading to the gash in the rock. "We must go in there?"

"That's right, my lady. It's been a hallowed site since ancient times. It is the true source of the Holy Well we passed on the way up here." The novice had a great deal more to say for himself outside the confines of the precinct.

Drew led the way inside the cave. It narrowed rapidly to form an uneven passage, forcing them to stoop. The familiar panic welled in Alwenna's chest and she stopped so abruptly that Weaver, following behind, bumped into her.

"What's wrong?"

"I can't. There's no room, no air." She backed up. "Let me out."

Weaver stood his ground. "The air's good."

"No, it's not." She twisted around, gasping for breath,

and tried to push her way past him, but he pinned her arms to her sides.

"Steady. You were set on doing this."

She was ready to lash out at him – she couldn't stay here, in the near dark. She couldn't breathe, couldn't think…

Then Brother Drew returned, carrying a lantern. "The path widens again, my lady. It's not far. Ten yards at most."

The light dispelled some of her unease. The novice set off again, more slowly, and she picked her way along the passage behind him, not so much supported by Weaver as impelled forward by him. Then they stepped out into a broad cavern and she could breathe again. She stood there, gulping air while the trembling of her limbs eased, aware that Weaver was studying her.

Two priests in the drab robes favoured by the order stepped forward to block Weaver's path. "You must wait here."

"As long as the lady doesn't leave my sight."

The priest who had spoken inclined his head to one side. "She is safe within our shrine." A cold smile flickered over his face. "If you will not trust the word of the ordained then you must trust the evidence of your own eyes. For what little that is worth."

Beyond the light from Drew's lantern the chamber was dim. As Alwenna's eyes adjusted she could make out a robed figure seated on a dais at the far side. Spluttering torches reflected on the mirror-smooth floor. Only when something small splashed into it, sending out ripples across the surface, did she realise it was water. Two torches marked a stone causeway across the pool to the dais. The cavern floor which she had to cross shifted and shivered before her.

"You may approach the master seer, my lady." The priest's voice now was respectful.

Alwenna waited for a sign of agreement from Weaver. After a moment he nodded.

She took three steps before something flipped against her foot; she froze. A frog hopped away into the shadows beyond reach of the torchlight: no ordinary frog, but a pallid creature, almost luminescent in the way its pale flesh reflected the torchlight. The floor of the cavern was covered with similar creatures, clambering over one another as they moved aside, clearing a path to the causeway. She suppressed a shudder and stepped forward with renewed caution, guessing from the tiny scufflings that the amphibians had closed in behind her.

"You have nothing to fear from my pretties, Lady Alwenna. And nothing to fear from me." The old man spoke slowly, as if the words required great effort, but she recognised his voice. She'd heard it in dreams almost as long as she could remember, ever since the night her parents died. "As for your companion, he puts all his trust in a yard of steel and will never believe what he cannot see for himself. Yet that may prove useful, sooner than you think."

The seer raised two gnarled hands and lifted clear his hood, revealing a face etched with heavy age lines, his head hairless and his skin almost as pale as the frogs that scrambled about the chamber. But most startling of all, his red-rimmed eyes were clouded. The master seer was blind.

"The human senses are remarkable. I have no need of worldly vision to see into the realms of the future; not when I see through other eyes."

"Is that why you summoned me here – to tell me the future?"

"I would help you. You have travelled far since you first arrived at Highkell as a frightened child. You need have no fear of the darkness. Alidreth's blood runs in your veins, pure and undiluted."

It was not darkness she feared, but she held her peace. Why had Tresilian told her to seek out this old man? "How would you help me now?"

"Your exile may be of greater duration than you believe, my child. That much is clear. Also..." He drew a sighing breath.

She knew why he hesitated, even as she framed her question. "You have news of Tresilian?"

"Alas, no. Tresilian has fallen into darkness. But this you already knew, had you trusted your sight."

Could she believe this strange old man? She glimpsed Weaver step forward, but one of the priests restrained him with a silent gesture. She ought to have heeded Weaver's advice in the first place.

Gwydion drew breath with difficulty. "There are things you do not yet know: by spilling the blood of his own kin in his family's stronghold, Vasic has sealed his fate. That cannot be changed. And his kin's blood will rise against him soon enough. You must prepare, for Tresilian's children will need your strength."

This was all impossible. She'd told none but Weaver of that dream. How could Gwydion know of it? The old man's head sagged forward, as if he'd dropped into a deep sleep. Behind her she heard minute shufflings and didn't need to glance over her shoulder to know the frogs moved closer.

Gwydion raised his head, eyes open. "It is time. Take my hands, Alwenna, relict of Tresilian of Highkell, true daughter descendant of the High Seer Alidreth."

Alwenna took half a step closer to his seat, then hesitated. The air resonated with tension, as if every creature present held its breath. Could she trust this old man? Should she?

"You need never fear the darkness." He smiled and reached out, palms uppermost. "Take my hands, kinswoman."

CHAPTER TWENTY-ONE

Weaver watched with foreboding as Alwenna reached for the old man's hands. Tresilian had wanted this meeting but every instinct was telling Weaver to call her away. The frogs carpeting the chamber stilled, as if of one mind. Weaver tried to step forward but the priests on either side caught him by the arms and he found himself held still by more than physical means.

The old man's fingers closed over Alwenna's.

For a moment all remained silent, then she gasped and her body stiffened. "No!"

Her scream echoed round the chamber. Weaver fought to throw off the two priests but they pinned him back against the wall.

"You mustn't interfere. The shock could kill her."

The frogs began creeping towards the edge of the pool, their attention focused on the dais where Alwenna seemed frozen in the grip of the old man. Then Gwydion released her abruptly and fell back in his seat, gasping for breath. Alwenna swayed, half turned towards Weaver, then crumpled to the ground. Weaver struggled between the two priests while she lay motionless where she had fallen.

Unnaturally still.

Then she stirred and dragged herself up onto her hands and knees.

"How could you?" Her words carried across the still water.

"No time." The old man slumped in his seat, chest rising and falling as if he had run a race. "My last gift… to you."

"A gift, you call it?" She pushed herself to her feet. "A gift?" Her voice grew shrill.

"The knowledge of ages." He drew in a harsh breath. "There is… no greater gift."

"What use is knowledge without understanding?"

"It is… your life's blood." The words cost him dear. Gwydion drew in one last rattling breath, then his head slumped to one side.

A thousand frogs scrambled forward and plunged into the dark water. Without looking back, Alwenna strode across the causeway as the priests released Weaver. She reached the main chamber as the last of the frogs disappeared underwater, leaving nothing but ripples perturbing the surface.

"Are you hurt?" Weaver reached out to support her, but she pushed him away. Drew gaped as she dashed headlong past him down the narrow passage that had caused her so much difficulty earlier. Weaver followed.

She didn't stop running until she reached the Holy Well. There she stooped over the stone basin: not to drink, but to wash her hands, over and over. Finally she sat back on the grassy bank of the stream that overflowed from the basin. Weaver went to sit beside her, but not too close.

She tucked her knees up and wrapped her arms about them, hunching forward and staring at the water. "I suppose you're going to say you told me so."

"No. But I should have stopped him."

She picked up a twig and began snapping it into short lengths. "Do you think Tresilian meant that to happen?"

This was the point to admit he had no idea what he'd just witnessed. "Garrad said Gwydion was much changed."

She shrugged. "It's done now. But I don't know what to believe. If he was telling the truth about Tresilian, then…"

"He was playing on your fears, my lady. That's what these mystics do. We've seen no proof." He'd said himself Highkell would fall swiftly, but this wasn't the time to remind her of that.

She raised a hand to her face and rubbed her eyes, then she threw the pieces of twig into the water, watching them bob away. "Proof? I suppose you heard what he had to say about you."

"I heard."

Abruptly, she jumped to her feet. "I need to walk. My mind's too full."

With a sigh Weaver stood up and followed her, warrior-turned-lapdog.

CHAPTER TWENTY-TWO

Vasic sat in the carved chair that had once been his cousin's. He scowled at the fire roaring in the hearth beneath a coat of arms that was not his own. The late evening sun burnished every detail of the elaborate fire surround. Old Brennir had loved to show off his wealth. Vasic would enjoy watching it demolished. Right now another matter was of greater importance: he may have laid claim to land and title, but his cousin's widow had eluded him.

A knock at the door announced the arrival of his steward, Hames. "Sire, a messenger has arrived from Brigholm. He brings queries from the Townsmen's Guild." Hames dropped a bundle of scrolls onto the polished oak table before Vasic.

"You don't expect me to read those, do you? That is why I employ you. What do they want?"

"There is an overriding concern for the safety of the Lady Alwenna."

"Inform the meddling fools that since she has chosen to abscond I am in no way answerable for her wellbeing."

The bearded man clasped then unclasped his hands. "Sire, they refuse to commit taxes to your administration until such time as the lady's continuing good health has been proven."

"Damn their insolence!" Vasic opened a couple of scrolls at random, then flung them aside.

"Sire, one other thing. Lord Stanton's body has been found, hidden in a stable along with two of his men. They have all been dead for some days."

"Stanton? Now that is news. He was detailed to ensure the Lady Alwenna's safety." Had Tresilian suspected Stanton after all? He'd surely have made an example of him – and disposed of the body with some measure of decency. His cousin had ever been honourable. "Hidden in a stable, you say?"

"Yes, sire, not far from the eastern gate."

Hence Stanton's failure to report before they advanced on the citadel. And the mocking smile on his cousin's face at the end took on new significance. "Damn Tresilian. She must have been long gone by the time I secured the citadel." He paced over to the window and stared out. "Despatch another search party to cover the road east. And prepare the old woman for more questioning."

"Tonight, sire?"

"Of course, tonight. No amount of sleep will render that one a beauty."

"It seems unlikely she knows anything, sire."

"I will oversee the interrogation in person."

Hames bowed and backed out of the room.

CHAPTER TWENTY-THREE

Alwenna woke with a scream dying on her lips. She sat up in her bed, rigid with horror. Not Wynne. How could he? There was a hammering against her door.

"What is it? Are you hurt?" Weaver.

"No." She tried to gather her wits. "I'm fine. Just a minute." She drew a blanket over her shoulders, pulling it round to cover her shift, and padded barefoot to the door. The flagstones struck chill against her feet as she made her way across the unfamiliar room. She slid back the bolt and peered out.

Glowing embers in the dying fire gave off just enough light to see Weaver standing there in his shirtsleeves, fastening the ties of his leggings about his waist. "What happened? Another nightmare?"

"No."

Weaver moved over to the hearth. "I'll kindle the fire, else you'll catch a chill." He stirred the embers into life and added wood, setting the kettle over it.

Alwenna crossed the room and perched on the end of the table nearest the fire, resting her feet on the bench. "I think it was the sight."

"You're no stranger to nightmares, my lady. Why would

this time be any different?" He straightened up and faced her once more, his expression guarded.

"Nightmares never make sense. But this… I saw Wynne. Vasic was torturing her, he…" She shivered.

Weaver folded his arms. "My lady–"

"This was real. You heard Gwydion – he knew what I'd already seen. Did you tell him? That I saw Vasic kill Tresilian?"

"Of course not. I heard Gwydion: those were the ravings of a crazy old man."

"How can you speak so of the dead?"

"My lady, if you'd seen as many men die as I have you'd set less store by their last words."

It was clear he still thought her a cosseted fool. "Disbelieve me if you will. Vasic's torturing Wynne to find out where I am. There must be something we can do."

"Would you have me besiege the citadel single-handed? She'd be beyond help long before I could reach Highkell."

"We shouldn't have let her go off alone."

"She made her own choice."

"You are so callous." The man was impossible. "What if it's a vision of the future? We might be able to save her."

Weaver took a couple of steps. "You'd have me ride all that way because you had a bad dream? I swore I'd see you safely through this. That comes first."

"Very fine, I'm sure, to hide behind your duty."

Weaver planted both hands on the table beside her, leaning face to face with her. "I'm sorry, my lady, if you're not best pleased by our situation, but right now we must play a waiting game. Goddess knows I've no appetite for such work."

Alwenna resisted the urge to draw back. "Do you

imagine I have? None of this is my choosing – trailing all the way out here with you, leaving Highkell, leaving Wynne – none of it. I know what duty is. Even my marriage wasn't my choice."

"You don't seem to have managed the business so ill, my lady."

"And in your eyes even that is a fault. It's time you found work more to your liking, Weaver."

His scowl deepened. "You sound as if you mean that."

"And why not, when you disapprove of every word I say and doubtless every thought I carry in my head as well?"

Weaver withdrew to the fireside. "If I do it's no fault of yours."

"Then I haven't been imagining it?"

"It's time you knew." Weaver drew a weary breath. "The man I fought at Vorland Pass was a kinsman of yours. He was my commanding officer before he turned coat and joined the Marcher rebellion. I served with him for several years." His gaze moved to her face. "Sometimes I see his likeness in you."

"And? I remember nothing of my family there."

"Then be thankful." He hesitated. "Most of them were lost in dark mysteries, though none could match Stian's appetite for evil."

She'd heard that said often enough at Highkell. If she were to believe what she'd been told, every fault on her part was a result of her father's family's influence. "This was what Garrad meant you should tell me?"

Silence stretched between them. Weaver's expression told her she'd said something wrong. "Garrad doesn't know the half of it." Weaver straightened up and walked over to the door that led out to the cloister. He snatched it open, pausing with his hand on the latch. "While he was still my commanding officer, your kinsman... He was the man who killed my wife and our unborn child." The latch dropped back into place with a sharp clatter as the door closed behind him.

CHAPTER TWENTY-FOUR

The ashes in the hearth were grey and cold by morning. Weaver hadn't returned. It was possible he didn't mean to return – she'd told him to leave, after all. Alwenna set about kindling a new fire with the few sticks that remained. His flint and steel lay where he'd set them down the night before. He must mean to come back at some point, then. Nausea dulled her movements as she stooped over the dry kindling, working to strike a strong enough spark from the flint. She'd watched Weaver do this enough times – surely it wasn't beyond her.

She heard footsteps outside and behind her the door opened. She twisted round. Weaver stood there, pale and heavy-eyed.

"My lady, you shouldn't be doing that." His voice was hoarse.

"I need to learn how." The realisation that she was unable to complete even so simple a task was humiliating in the extreme.

Weaver pushed the door shut and crossed the room, kneeling beside her. The smell of the brewhouse hit her in a wave of stale beer. No need to ask how he'd spent the night. She battled another rush of nausea and won.

"You hold the flint like this." He set the flint down on the hearth so it presented an edge to the steel. His hands shook as he fumbled to position the flint just so. Her father's hands had been prone to shaking that way. Was Weaver another such? She'd begun to think him something more.

"Keep the edge uppermost, that brings the best spark, and strike fast with the steel, like this." Weaver's words called her back to the present.

Alwenna sat back on her heels to watch as he demonstrated; his second attempt produced a shower of sparks.

"Set the charcloth here to catch the sparks, and keep some dry tinder ready in your hand." The shaking of his hands did not seem to interfere with the process as he struck another burst of sparks that set the charcloth smouldering, cupping it in his hands until the tinder began to burn, transferring the smoking handful to the kindling she had set in the grate. To Alwenna's disgust, smoke began to curl from the kindling within a matter of seconds.

"As simple as that." If she reached her hand out she'd be able to touch him. Instead she pushed herself to her feet and moved over to the table, brushing fireside dust from her skirts. Weaver was every bit as rough as he looked this morning: a beer-soaked, unshaven commoner who killed without compunction; who killed with an athletic grace that at once repelled and fascinated her; who had every reason in the world to hate her.

Weaver added sticks to the fire. "It just takes practice. And dry tinder." He straightened up. "I'm sorry, my lady, I should have been here to do that before now."

She brushed off the apology with a shrug. "You're not my nursemaid, why ever should you?" She wasn't about to tell him how stupidly relieved she was that he'd returned at all.

"I swore to Tresilian I'd–"

It was as if he sought to stand Tresilian between them. And well he might. "Yes, we went through all that last night."

Weaver stood up. He looked faintly ill. Good. It was self-inflicted, after all. "My lady, I said things then that I ought not have."

"Why not? You spoke honestly. In all conscience I cannot claim your loyalty in these circumstances. I am dismayed that Tresilian could require it of you. He must have known."

"He knew. It all happened years ago, my lady."

She'd expected him to seize on the excuse to leave. "He told me he trusted you above all others; I confess at the time I was surprised by his choice."

"And now?" There was a sudden intensity in Weaver's gaze. Just for a moment. Damped down faster than an unwanted campfire; damped down so fast she doubted she'd seen it at all.

"Now? I realise Tresilian's judgement was sounder than I guessed."

"I am honoured, my lady."

This was no way to convince him to leave.

A knock sounded at the door.

Weaver spun round with a scowl, his hand moving to the hilt of his dagger. "Who is it?"

"Father Garrad." The latch lifted and the priest stepped inside. "Good morning." Garrad's eyes darted between the two of them and he smiled knowingly.

Alwenna felt heat rising in her face. She picked up an

empty tankard from the table and turned away to set it by the stone basin in the corner, recovering her composure as Weaver spoke.

"Good morning, father. What can we do for you? Or dare we hope you bring us news from Highkell?"

"Alas no, I have no news for you. But perhaps the two of you have news for me?"

Alwenna faced him again. The priest smiled, but the semblance of warmth did not reach his eyes.

Weaver stepped between them. "What news could we possibly have, cooped up here as we are, father? Will you take a drink with us? Let me make you some kopamid." Weaver's manner was all smooth ease now, his annoyance at the interruption vanished. Or so well concealed that Alwenna would have been fooled into thinking she had imagined the flash of irritation. "The Lady Alwenna has determined to master the art of kindling fires." He glanced at Alwenna. "She makes good progress."

Alwenna suspected Father Garrad was drawing his own conclusions about the pair of them – highly inaccurate ones.

Father Garrad took a seat at the table as Weaver set the kettle over the fire to boil.

"I heard you had a lively night in the brewhouse, Weaver. What was the celebration? Surely not marking old Gwydion's passing?"

"I may have drunk a pint or two to set him on his way. But does a man need a reason to drink, father? I never have."

"So I have heard, Weaver. Your reputation precedes you."

Weaver smiled. "People love to talk." His tone reminded

Alwenna of the way he had spoken to Stanton that night in the alley. "And most people, when they're talking, they're not thinking."

"And some would say the same about drinkers." Garrad smiled. "What say you, Lady Alwenna?"

"About what? Talking or drinking?" Alwenna returned smile for smile as she sat down at the far end of the table from Father Garrad. "Too much of either can cause a sore head. Or so I've been led to believe."

"There are certainly a few sore heads in the refectory this morning, whatever the cause." Garrad leaned back against the wall, setting one arm on the window sill, very much at ease.

Alwenna smiled her court smile. "I confess I was surprised to learn the brethren keep such a large brewhouse here, father."

"Perhaps you did not know, my lady, that Vorrahan is a safe haven for all travellers to and from the Outer Isles. The founding brethren were granted the land where our precinct now stands on condition they provided appropriate hospitality."

"A safe haven for which I am most grateful." She resisted the temptation to cast a meaningful glance around their meagre lodgings. "And I'm sure Weaver is especially appreciative of your hospitality this morning."

Weaver nodded. "It is as the lady says, father. But with all the travellers who pass through Vorrahan, this lack of news from the east worries me. I am loath to make decisions founded on nothing more substantial than Gwydion's ramblings."

"Indeed, it is troubling. But what decisions are to be made? The Lady Alwenna is safe here. You may leave her in our care with a clear conscience; we will ensure she wants for nothing."

Weaver didn't reply. Instead he turned to remove the kettle from the heat, then set about brewing the aromatic kopamid.

Alwenna's stomach clenched at the memory of the scene in the forest when she'd last tasted the spiced drink, but she managed to control her nausea. It was no longer as severe as before. She was aware of a glance from Weaver as he joined them at the table. So, she suspected, was Father Garrad. The priest missed nothing: he was weighing every look, every smile. Did he suspect a liaison between them? Or was he simply interested in his visitors? Gwydion had not trusted the man, but they'd been at odds for many years, and the master seer's judgement had been questionable at best. Weaver had called him a crazy old man and now she was inclined to agree.

Garrad took up the drink Weaver set before him. "Have you no other trade than the sword, Weaver? Something you may work at here on Vorrahan?"

"I'm the son of a ploughman, father. Blades are all I know."

"We have little use for ploughs here, not when we can sell wool to meet most of our needs. You must be resourceful enough to turn your hand to other skills, elsewise you would not have been made King's Man."

"Tresilian and I chanced to be side by side in battle one day, that is all. A happy chance for me. I'd never been so well clothed or fed before that day."

Garrad sipped his drink. "Lady Alwenna, he does himself an injustice. I suggest you don't believe a word he says." The priest did not remain long after that. He took his leave of them, still smiling, leaving most of his drink untouched.

After the door had closed behind their visitor, Alwenna voiced the thought uppermost in her mind. "All those questions – what was he after?"

"To hide his purpose in coming here, I imagine." Weaver swallowed a mouthful of his drink. "And that purpose – I think – was to find out why I was drowning my sorrows last night. I let you down badly there, my lady. It won't happen again."

She shrugged off the apology. "Then he's learned nothing he didn't already know."

"My lady, I think he sees our situation more clearly than we do ourselves." Weaver twisted the earthenware beaker in his hands.

"Indeed? What do you imagine he sees?"

"Two people with more than enough time on their hands to get up to no good. And that gives us all the more reason to be wary."

"That's nonsense."

"I'm serious, my lady. I suspect where you are concerned he hopes if I'm given enough rope I'll hang myself and save him the trouble of building a scaffold."

"Surely not?"

"It would be no great challenge to find a servant to act as chaperone. Men such as Garrad do nothing without a reason. I shan't oblige him, have no fear. There's too much at stake."

Alwenna felt her face redden. "You presume a great deal, Weaver."

"Is it not better to speak plainly about the risks we face?"

He was right, of course. "Ought we remain here if

Father Garrad intends to play cat-and-mouse games with us?"

"I can't drag you round the country indefinitely, not in your condition. It wouldn't be right." Weaver hesitated. "But I'll admit I'd feel easier knowing the news from Highkell. I suspect Garrad is not being entirely frank about that. Ferries are coming and going across the sound several times a day."

"But local farmers bringing tithes to the brethren, what would they know of war so far from their own fields?"

"More than Father Garrad is telling us: strangers passing through by night, soldiers on scouting missions, dozens of tiny things have meaning. Even a foolish man-at-arms wasting his pay on ale in the brewhouse." Weaver stood up. "Forgive me for inflicting myself on you in this condition, my lady. It's high time I rendered myself presentable." He took up the empty log basket and left Alwenna with her thoughts.

Could Tresilian have been mistaken in entrusting her safety to Father Garrad? It had been Tresilian who insisted she should seek out Gwydion in the first place. Had that been wise? And what had become of her husband: should she be grieving for him? She wouldn't. Not until rumour confirmed her sight. Until then she could hope she'd been mistaken; that Gwydion had misled her at every turn; that her fears for Wynne were nothing more than nightmares. And until then she could keep the burden of unwanted knowledge Gwydion had bestowed on her in check. If once she believed her sight told her the truth, then so much more would follow in its wake.

CHAPTER TWENTY-FIVE

Gwydion's burial took place at sunrise on the third day after his death, according to tradition. The cemetery had been sited on the wind-scoured slope to the north of the precinct, where few trees grew to interrupt the view east over the sound to the mainland.

Alwenna felt lightheaded as she watched the rough coffin being lowered into the ground. At times, the sense that her mind was too full became overpowering. This was one of those times, made worse by a deep unease: funerals changed things. A dozen years had passed since she stood with Wynne on the battlements at Highkell, watching her parents' coffins being lowered into the ground. Eight year-old girls didn't belong at the graveside, however tragic the circumstances. She and Tresilian had hidden at the foot of the stairs afterwards, listening to the grown-ups deciding her future. Their future.

And later another ceremony honouring Tresilian's father, after he'd fallen in battle in The Marches. Tresilian had been overburdened with grief. He'd insisted she attend at his side. And she'd set her hand on his arm, trying to ease some of his pain and understood then, finally, why she had to agree to their marriage. The state was fragile, but between them they could strengthen it.

Now the master seer was committed to the ground, leaving her his gift: a cacophony of half-seen, impossible-to-understand fragments. Even when she was awake unfamiliar voices tugged at the back of her mind, half-resolved images ghosted through her consciousness, crowding in if she let her attention wander. A thousand open graves gaped before her. Some contained rudimentary coffins, others corpses wrapped only in winding sheets. Some were pits into which fallen soldiers were flung without ceremony, without rites to ease their passing. So many fallen, taking countless secrets with them...

Alwenna shook her head to dispel the flood of unwelcome images. Once more she was on the hillside above the precinct with Garrad intoning rites over Gwydion's coffin. His words of regret were hollow. He was glad the seer was gone. Did he know of the seer's gift to her? She thought not. According to Drew the two priests who had served Gwydion had taken a vow of silence to mark their respect. A convenient way to sidestep Garrad's questioning, without doubt. And if they were not about to tell Garrad of Gwydion's so-called gift to her, she assuredly would not.

After the ceremony was complete she turned away from the graveside to find Weaver waiting nearby, dour as ever. He'd been careful to spend little time in her company since Garrad's morning visit. She could understand it, but nevertheless it hurt. Weaver was the last thread connecting her to her old life. And her sight told her he was about to leave.

Weaver walked over to join her. "I spoke to Father Garrad this morning. He agrees I should find out what's happening at Highkell."

That much was no surprise. "When will you leave?" Again, that rush of unease. Funerals changed things. Ought she stop him?

Weaver shifted his weight from one foot to the other. "Today."

So soon. "Are you sure it is wise?"

"Garrad has found a maidservant to assist you. There's no need for me to stay any longer." He glanced at her, then lowered his eyes.

He didn't mean to come back. "So, you will return to Highkell?"

"That depends on what I learn. I'll send word as soon as I have news."

They were still within earshot of the other mourners. He was deliberately giving her this news with others about. Perhaps he didn't trust himself. Or perhaps he didn't trust her.

"Will you walk with me for a minute or two?"

"Of course, my lady."

They set off along the path back towards the precinct. Weaver didn't offer her his arm. He was doing his best to be correct, and had been ever since he'd sobered up.

"Don't worry, I shan't attempt to talk you out of leaving."

"It is for the best, my lady."

"Undoubtedly." She almost believed it. "You say you discussed it with Father Garrad. Have you some reason to be more kindly disposed towards him now?"

"He hasn't bought me, if that's what you're asking." Weaver's tone was clipped.

She stopped in her tracks. Did that mean Garrad had tried to bribe the King's Man? "I'd never believe that of you."

"You should trust no one. Every man has his price."

"I learned that long ago. And I think I know yours." She ventured a smile.

He stepped back half a pace. "I must catch the tide, my lady. I cannot play at riddles with you all day."

She shrugged: a courtly gesture of indifference, fake to the core. "Before you leave I would know your opinion. Ought I continue to be guarded in what I tell Father Garrad?"

"Yes, my lady. Perhaps I should have said: trust no one, particularly the good father."

"Yet you still sought his advice on leaving?"

"My road will be easier if he believes I trust him."

How foolish of her not to guess that. She began walking again. Weaver fell into step beside her as they climbed the slope leading towards the Holy Well, matching his pace to hers.

"Will you try to learn more about Father Garrad as you are seeking news, Weaver? And send me word if you learn anything of import?"

"I will, my lady. I swore to your husband I would protect you."

They had reached the Holy Well. There, a sudden impulse seized her. "Swear it to me, Weaver, now, over this water. Swear what you once swore to Tresilian." She dipped her hand in the small pool, and, cupping the water in her palm, held it out towards Weaver. After a moment's hesitation he closed his own hand over it, clasping hers. "I will do everything in my power to keep you from harm, my lady. All my allegiance is yours." His hand tightened over hers for a moment, then he released it.

If she begged him not to leave, would he stay? She

could convince him. "Then nothing remains but for me to wish you a safe journey."

"Thank you, my lady." Weaver swept a courtly bow, then turned and strode away. Every sure stride took him further away from her.

Alwenna didn't need the sight to know he would never return to Vorrahan.

"Well, Tresilian, is this what you planned when you sent me here?"

There was no answer but the mournful keening of seagulls.

CHAPTER TWENTY-SIX

Alwenna had no wish to remain in her lodgings while the silent maidservant went about her work. Instead she made her way to the precinct gates. At this time of the morning the cloister was bustling as the brethren went about their duties. Some had become friendly faces and smiled as she passed. Others averted their eyes. It was one of the latter who stepped forward as she was about to push open the wooden door.

"I beg your pardon, but Father Garrad has instructed that you must not venture out without a suitable escort."

"I only want to walk up to the Holy Well." She doubted he'd be swayed by learning of her need to seek out the tranquillity of the place. "I won't even be out of sight of the gate."

"I am sorry, my lady, Father Garrad's instructions were precise. Please be so kind as to remain within the precinct walls." The priest stepped in front of the doorway, even as she smiled and tried to sidestep him.

"Surely he cannot have meant..." Of course Garrad had meant this. But for him to play his hand so swiftly following Weaver's departure was troubling. "There must be someone who could walk the short distance with me?

We could gather a few herbs along the way, to make it worthwhile."

The priest returned her smile with a steely gaze. "The brethren cannot neglect their duties on a whim. I shall enquire of Father Garrad when it might be convenient, if you wish?"

"You need not trouble him, brother." She turned away from the gate, burning with embarrassment at once again being treated like some errant child. Father Garrad was approaching, smiling as ever.

"Good day to you, Lady Alwenna. I hope you are well."

"Yes, I thank you, father. I hoped to walk up to the Holy Well, but your gatekeeper tells me you have left orders not to allow me outside."

"My apologies. I meant to discuss this with you earlier but it slipped my mind." He smiled, too smooth this time.

"Indeed?" She made no attempt to hide her displeasure.

Garrad's smile did not falter. "Weaver and I agreed it would be best while he is away. None of our brethren here are as well qualified as he to protect you. It will be safer for you to remain within our walls until he has returned."

Garrad's face faded before her, as if seen through a veil of mist. The mist strengthened, altering colour as the sky darkened and took on an amber glow. Her view of the main precinct building was occluded by flames and smoke billowing from the roof. The cuprous taste of blood filled her mouth which was dry, so dry and parched...

"My lady? Are you unwell?" Garrad's voice broke through the roar of flames and her surroundings twisted back into focus. The sky was light and clear, the air free of any hint of smoke.

Alwenna blinked. "I believe the sun is perhaps too hot

to venture out onto the hillside in any event. I have a slight headache. I shall seek shade in the library instead."

"A wise choice, Lady Alwenna." Did she imagine a note of relief that he'd prevailed upon her stay within the walls?

She returned his smile, mirroring his for emptiness. He didn't appear to notice.

In the cool of the library the librarian bent over his table, scrolls and ancient tomes spread before him. He raised his head at Alwenna's approach and smiled. This was a true smile. As well, since instinct told her the question she was about to ask was important.

"I wonder, brother, if I might find such a thing as a history of the seers and their lore somewhere on your shelves?"

He straightened up from the manuscript he had been copying, painstakingly setting down his quill. "Indeed you may, my lady. The seers have had a safe haven here at Vorrahan some four centuries and more. We have works concerning their lore dating back to their earliest days here, but they are kept in a storeroom. I will send my assistant to retrieve them for you, if you can wait until tomorrow. In the meantime, there is a simple history you might find interesting."

She lifted down the tome he indicated and knew in that instant it did not contain whatever it was she sought, but she sat for an hour in the library leafing through the descriptions of the building of the precinct at Vorrahan. She lingered for some time over a diagram showing the layout of the precinct. It indicated the position of a shore gate she'd not noticed while walking through the precinct. She replaced the book and thanked the librarian, promising to return the next day. He nodded and smiled, the greater part of his attention on the work he was copying so meticulously. She left him in the silence of his domain, determined to see if the gate was still there.

CHAPTER TWENTY-SEVEN

Weaver let his horse pick its way through the forest. The tree canopy shaded out much of the moon's light, but there was still enough to continue his journey. It was good to be on the move again: easier to take action than sit at Vorrahan waiting. And watching. The further he travelled from the Lady Alwenna the better it would be for both of them. But before he was too far from the island he had discreet enquiries to make about Father Garrad. The priest was playing some kind of double game. Tresilian's faith in Garrad had been unshakable, yet Tresilian now lay in a mass grave of his cousin's providing – if Alwenna's sight could be trusted.

But Weaver would be wise not to trust anything about Alwenna, tainted as she was by her father's blood. She claimed to know nothing of her dark legacy, but it made her anathema nonetheless. Soft-skinned, warm-curved anathema. She might already have worked her wiles on him. Since Tresilian had first led his bride-to-be to the top table at Highkell her ill-starred beauty had drawn Weaver like a moth to her flame. Tresilian had finally introduced Weaver to her when they'd just finished a training bout. She'd looked over him with that cool green gaze and he'd known she saw a smelly commoner with no wit or charm to offer her – a misfit among the courtiers. And in case he'd been left in any doubt, Stanton had leaned to whisper some joke in her ear, drawing a smile from her. No, the further Weaver travelled from his king's wife, the better. Her allure remained as potent as–

Something smashed against the side of his skull. His horse spun around, pitching him towards the ground. Head ringing, Weaver dropped his shoulder as he fell, rolling the moment he hit the ground and reaching for his knife as he regained his feet. A veil of sparks clouded his vision as he faced his still-mounted assailant. Hoofbeats thudded on the forest floor behind him.

The man before him stepped down from his saddle, drawing a short sword. Weaver took up a defensive stance, blinking in an attempt to clear his head, but another horse barrelled into his left shoulder. A second cudgel blow, harder than the first, hit the back of his head and he toppled into darkness.

CHAPTER TWENTY-EIGHT

Alwenna stirred in her bed at Vorrahan, close to waking. There was something she'd forgotten, something important. Her horse trotted on briskly, unheeding as she commanded it to halt, to turn around. Hooves beat out a muffled rhythm over the carpet of pine needles on the forest floor. The gibbous moon rode high in the sky, strong enough to cast shadows between the trees. Then the shadows shifted and she spun away. Far below her Weaver fell from the saddle, rolled and reached for his dagger. Moonlight flashed on a blade. She tried to shout a warning but her words were drowned out by the crackle and hiss of flames. All around her buildings were burning: roof timbers were aflame, cracking with the intense heat, collapsing in bursts of embers which drove everyone back. Water turned to steam as bucketful after bucketful was hurled in an attempt to douse the inferno. The librarian staggered through the cloister, arms laden with precious manuscripts, smoke rising from the smouldering sleeve of his robe. She would have helped him, but behind her someone laughed, stopping her as she reached out. And there Vasic stood at the window of Highkell solar, exultant. In his hand was a sheet of parchment, and on that sheet a signature, firm and clear: Garrad.

This time her shout of protest was real. The sound still echoed in her ears as she sat up in the darkness of her bedchamber. Her limbs shook and her mouth was dry, foul with the tang she'd learned to associate with the sight. She stumbled over to the window, but there was no sign of fire, no sound as the precinct slumbered. She returned to her bed, wrapping the covers about her shoulders and waited for the pounding of her heart to ease. She sought to recall the vision, to divine what had happened to Weaver, to find some trace of him, some hint he'd survived the attack. There was nothing. Everything had been engulfed by flame, by Vasic's glee.

Nothing.

Sitting there in the dark, the only waking creature in the room, she had no doubt her vision was true. She was utterly alone, and Father Garrad had sold her to Vasic. She was defeated. The flight from Highkell had all been in vain. All it had done was bring about the deaths of those closest to her. Now Weaver's loyalty had been repaid with base treachery. What recourse had she, but to sit back and wait for Vasic to lead her back to Highkell in shackles? If not literally, she'd be shackled by wedlock soon enough, to secure his kingship over the territory Tresilian had ruled. She had no one to turn to, no place to hide. Tresilian's plan had failed.

She sank back on her pillows. Then it happened: that same fluttering sensation deep within her abdomen she had felt once before, so tiny she'd wondered if she'd imagined it. There it was again, a second time, stronger, determined, as the child within her kicked.

She couldn't give up. Not now.

CHAPTER TWENTY-NINE

Alwenna eased the door shut behind her and crept along the cloister, keeping to the shadows. No one stirred. She found the shore gate where the plan had shown it and, as she'd hoped, it was unmanned. The bolts were stiff, but yielded after a struggle. She eased the gate open but it gave out a raucous screech of rusty hinges. She slid through hastily and drew the gate shut, the grinding of the old hinges too loud in the silence of night. She thought she heard a faint scuffling from the precinct behind her. She listened intently, but all she could hear was deafening silence, a rushing sound that she realised was the blood running through her veins. Once again she felt that fluttering sensation deep within her womb. This time she was the one protecting an innocent life.

She hurried down to the place where the precinct boats were beached. Here was her first real difficulty: the tide was out, so she would need to drag the boat some distance to the water's edge. The smallest boat proved heavier than she'd anticipated. She managed to heave it over the short stretch of grass and onto the shingle where it grated against the stones, shattering the night's calm.

Alwenna froze, listening, but nothing else stirred. No

shouts of alarm sounded from the precinct. She summoned her strength and heaved at the boat again. It jammed against a cobble and she tugged harder. She couldn't fail now, not at the first obstacle. The boat gave way in a rush and she overbalanced, toppling backwards and landing with the boat jammed against her knee, pinning her leg to the ground. A look over her shoulder told her she'd only dragged the boat a fraction closer to the water. The muscles in her forearms were already taut with effort.

Then she heard the footsteps. Several people crunched steadily over the shingle towards where she was sprawled among the pebbles. She pressed in behind the bulk of the rowing boat, hoping against hope that she might not be spotted. A single set of footsteps stopped a few yards away, on the other side of the boat. Her pulse thundered in her ears. She held her breath lest it betray her whereabouts.

The footsteps crunched closer.

"Lady Alwenna. You appear to be in need of assistance."

Alwenna recognised Father Garrad's voice. She raised her head and sat up slowly. He gestured to the two priests who had waited some distance away and they hurried forward and lifted the boat from her leg.

Brother Drew bent to help her to her feet. "Are you hurt, my lady?"

"No, no, I'm fine, thank you." She straightened her knee cautiously.

Garrad cleared his throat. "That will do, Brother Drew."

The novice dropped her arm as if he'd been burned and stumbled back two hasty paces. "I meant no disrespect, father."

"No one ever does, Brother Drew, such is the insidious nature of sin. When we first set our steps along the path to ruin, we never mean any harm."

Drew bowed his head.

Alwenna looked from one to the other. "Father Garrad–"

Garrad pulled himself up to his full height. "A nobly born lady such as yourself may not be bound by the rules of our order, my lady, but see the effect your presence in our midst has on gullible novices. Damage is so easily done, yet so, so hard to remedy."

Alwenna gaped at the priest. "Father, you have received me here at my husband's behest, but if my presence creates difficulties for the community you have only to call the ferryman and I shall leave."

Garrad twisted his lips in something like a smile, but even by the forgiving moonlight it was a sorry effort. "Lady Alwenna, your understanding is greatly appreciated, but it will not be necessary for you to leave. If you are more circumspect about your movements and keep to your quarters there will be no further harm done."

"No harm to whom, father?" Alwenna's words seemed to hang in the air between them; everything about them stilled.

"Your perception does you credit. I seek only to protect the community here at Vorrahan. These are my people. What manner of leader would I be if I did not ensure their welfare?" He met her gaze levelly at first, then he turned his eyes away, to the precinct. "This has been my life's work."

"And thus easily you break your word to Tresilian? Your duplicity is breathtaking."

Behind her, Brother Drew stifled an exclamation.

She hurried on before Garrad could respond. "Father, you might restore some vestige of honour to yourself if you let me have use of a boat and oarsman now. I will ask nothing more of the brethren here at Vorrahan if you will grant me that."

"Alas, my lady, I gave my word you would remain here." His tone was unctuous.

"We have already seen your word counts for less than nothing."

"But you, my gentle lady, understand such matters and can embrace forgiveness. The one to whom I promised to deliver you is, I fear, less refined, and the consequences of breaking my word to him would be far more painful."

"If you won't help me then you'll have to stop me by force." Alwenna took hold of the boat, tugging it again towards the sea. Anger lent her strength. She dragged it a couple of yards before Garrad barked an order to the two younger priests.

"Stop her, you fools."

Drew hesitated. "But, father, if she wants to leave–"

"You've no idea what's at stake. Don't question my orders, stop her!"

The elder priest caught hold of Alwenna's arm and tried to prise her fingers loose from the boat. A moment later Drew took hold of her other arm in a gentler grip. "I'm sorry, my lady. The tide's running against you tonight." He stooped closer so no one overheard his next words. "It'll turn, you may count on it."

She made a token struggle, but the two priests pulled her away from the boat and marched her back to the precinct, Garrad following behind them.

"Father Garrad, it's you who doesn't know what's at stake. Reconsider, please. It's the only way to save Vorrahan."

"Save yourself the effort, I'm proof against your dark

wiles. Why do you think Tresilian sent you here in the first place?" He seemed to expect some answer.

"You were his trusted tutor."

This time his smile was much closer to a sneer. "No, you foolish girl. He sent you here because we can contain you safely, where your accursed powers cannot bring ruin to Highkell."

Her husband didn't believe in such backward nonsense. He'd told her so, every time Vasic had thrown that particular insult in her face. And she'd never had reason to doubt Tresilian's word. Until now.

Once back in her quarters the key was removed and the main door was locked from the outside. Alwenna threw herself down on the bed and closed her eyes, but she couldn't shut out the vision of Vorrahan burning: the smoke, the flames, the shouting. Garrad's last words circled in her head. Tresilian had insisted Weaver should accompany her and no one else: Weaver, who was renowned for being proof against dark magic. And renowned for defeating her kinsman in single combat. Was there more behind his choice than she'd first imagined? And what had happened to Weaver? She lay there in the dark, trying to draw on the sight, but she could find no trace of the King's Man.

Instead Gwydion waited in his cave, but he was somehow younger and more alert. "Don't let Garrad worry you with his closed mind. He has no idea, no vision. As for doubt, that's all that prevents men turning into monsters. Rest, my child." He turned away.

She tried to call him back but she could make no sound, couldn't even move her limbs as the cave pitched around her and she spun away into darkness.

CHAPTER THIRTY

Weaver woke in the dark. A voice somewhere had cried out. His face was pressed against cold stone, which was slick with sweat and urine. He eased himself upright, head spinning, pain throbbing, blackness pitching about him. Chains clanked, digging into his wrists. Reason began to reassert itself: the chains had to be fastened to something. He reached out a hand and sure enough there was a wall, the worn stone smooth and clammy beneath his fingertips. He shuffled over until his back rested against it. About him he could hear other prisoners breathing, mumbling.

Prisoners. He was a prisoner. In a rank, fetid dungeon. The place stank. His hair was plastered to the side of his head, matted. His scalp beneath it was tight, scabbing over and painful to the touch. He'd been lying in Goddess knew what kind of filth, while vermin scurried about. He let his head sink back against the stone. Reason was not his friend here. But now it had returned he couldn't banish it. How had he come here? The effort of thinking was too much. So much easier to yield to the dark that pressed about him. His eyes closed and he let sleep claim him.

Through the dark he could see trees. Many trees: a forest. Pine needles softened his horse's hoofbeats. Then his horse raised its head, ears pricked, and something crashed against Weaver's skull.

He woke with a start, his neck stiff. It was still dark, punctuated by the same scufflings as before, but this time he could remember. Alwenna, alone at Vorrahan.

He had failed.

The jangle of keys heralded a guard who unlocked the door to the chamber where Weaver was held. The sudden influx of light made him blink. He raised one hand to shade his eyes as best he could while hampered by the chains. The first guard waited at the door, holding his lantern high, while another guard crossed the room and stooped to unlock the manacles that shackled Weaver to the wall.

The guard's face was familiar, but it took Weaver a moment to place him: Curtis. He'd trained him as a raw recruit, years ago. Curtis had been skinnier then.

"His highness wants to speak to you." The guard met Weaver's eyes for a few seconds; it might have been compassion in his gaze.

Weaver stood slowly, trying to ease life back into cramped muscles that had been still too long. How long had he been in there now? How long spent unconscious before he arrived? Hours or days? He had no way of knowing. Curtis might be able to tell him, but not while his superior looked on. Still hobbled at the ankles, Weaver shuffled across the uneven floor, seeing too clearly the filth in which he'd been lying. He couldn't afford to be too particular right now, but he promised himself if he ever got out of there alive he'd burn his clothing. Climbing the steps proved difficult. Twice he stumbled on the uneven stone stairs. His head still pounded where his assailant's cudgel had landed, although the dizziness had faded. He was in no shape to make a run for freedom, even if the chance offered itself.

"In here." Curtis ushered him into an empty guardroom. For the briefest of moments he caught Weaver's eye, then glanced towards his superior officer and turned away. The door closed behind him and a key grated in the lock. It seemed they were taking no chances where Ranald Weaver, renowned King's Man, was concerned.

Weaver peered out of the guardroom window, eyes pained by the daylight. He already knew what he would see, but until that moment he'd been able to pretend he was prisoner at some lesser place than Highkell. The guardroom was above ground level, close enough to lower himself down and drop the remainder to the ground safely if he'd been in his usual condition. But even if he could have smashed the window unnoticed, it opened into the inner bailey. And that was crawling with as many soldiers as his clothing must have been crawling with lice. He'd only resort to that if he were desperate. He'd rather die a free man than as a prisoner in that stinking dungeon. But living as a free man would be preferable. And as he stood there with the daylight on his face he could indulge a moment's hope. They hadn't killed him yet, so they wanted something from him. Even a bargain of some kind might not be out of the question. His situation no longer looked as grim as before, at any rate.

The key rattled in the lock and he turned to face his captors.

Curtis stepped into the room, followed by his superior. They took up positions by the door, then Vasic himself entered, two men-at-arms following him and stationing themselves at either side. Apparently Vasic was as cautious as he was ambitious.

Vasic curled his lip in distaste and raised a scented square of fabric to his face. "This is the one?" He directed his question to the superior guard.

"Yes, sire."

Vasic swung his gaze to Weaver once more. "You are Ranald Weaver?"

"I am."

"Address his highness correctly, you oaf." The superior guard moved forward, raising a business-like cudgel.

"I am Ranald Weaver, your highness."

"And arrogant with it, I'll be bound." Vasic stepped closer, but took care to remain out of reach. "You were the most highly trusted of my late cousin's King's Men."

"You are well informed, your highness."

"Indeed I am. Yet I find it difficult to credit." Vasic studied Weaver, the handkerchief held beneath his nose.

"The dungeons here are not best equipped for washing, your highness." Whatever game Vasic was playing, he'd no doubt get to the point soon enough.

"That is not your habitual state?" Vasic studied Weaver over the 'kerchief. "I have no doubt the Lady Alwenna will be shocked to see you thus."

Had he captured her already? Weaver forced himself to remain composed.

"Come now, there's no need to make this difficult. You took the Lady Alwenna away from here, did you not?"

"I did, your highness." Vasic must have this information

from Father Garrad already, no need to provoke him unnecessarily. Weaver had had plenty of time to think and he had no doubt the ambush had been arranged by someone who knew the route he would take when he left Vorrahan.

"And where did you take her?" Vasic appeared uninterested.

"To sanctuary at the precinct on Vorrahan. In the care of Father Garrad, sire."

"And you have left her there?"

"Yes, sire."

"Upon whose orders were you acting?"

"Tresilian's orders, your highness." He hesitated; it might work. "I'm a soldier, not a nursemaid. I make my living with my blade."

"Indeed. Are you suggesting your blade is for hire?"

"If Tresilian is dead, I am no longer bound to his service."

Vasic laughed. "Would you have me believe you'd serve me, Weaver? Your reputation goes before you. Stanton would have brought you into my employ if you could have been bought. His death was your handiwork, I understand?"

"Stanton's dead? I had no idea, sire."

"False modesty becomes you even more ill than your current guise. But you may wish to know I myself put an end to Tresilian while you were busy with his wife."

So that was it. Weaver bit back his words of denial.

Vasic was smiling now. "Oh, yes, Weaver. Father Garrad shared all his concerns at how cosy you had become with your erstwhile sovereign's widow. Tresilian was ever the trusting fool. Let's have the truth of the matter."

"I obeyed his orders, nothing more. As I said, I'm no nursemaid, your highness."

"We'll see." Vasic returned to the door. "Take him back to the dungeon. I have more pressing matters to deal with before questioning him further."

CHAPTER THIRTY-ONE

Alwenna huddled in her bed, sitting up so she could stave off sleep as long as possible. She would have to give in soon, but sleep brought with it the visions: intense moments of others' lives intruding on her rest, fuelling her own fears. Whether they belonged in the past, present or future she couldn't tell. But if she didn't find a way to fend them off soon she'd end up as mad as old Gwydion. She was nodding off when she thought she'd heard some noise. She held her breath to listen but all remained quiet. An owl outside, perhaps. She settled back beneath her covers.

Then she heard it again. Metal grated on metal: the creak of the hinge on the outer door. Unmistakable. Who would be opening that at this time of night? Pointless to feign sleep. They would make enough noise breaking open the bolted door, and she was trapped in this room with no way out. She rolled over to the edge of the bed and grabbed the pewter candlestick. It was hefty enough to at least do some damage on her account. She lowered her feet to the floor, snatching up her clothing in case she had time to scramble into it.

Then came a soft knock at the door. Did would-be assailants pause to knock at doors?

"Lady Alwenna?" The voice was low. She couldn't quite

place it. She pulled her kirtle over her head, and dragged it into place as the unseen visitor knocked again, louder. "My lady?"

"Who is it?" She crept over to take up a stance behind the door, raising the candlestick in the air.

"It's Drew, my lady. May I enter the room?"

What on earth could he want? It could be some trick, but she would sooner go out to meet her fate bravely than cower in the dark until Vasic's men dragged her from the chamber. She reached out and slid the bolt open, drawing silently back from the door. "Very well. You may enter."

A glow appeared beneath the door as he lit a candle, then the latch raised and the door eased open. Drew stepped inside, halting when the light from his candle fell upon the empty bed. He carried no weapon that Alwenna could see, and his eating knife remained in the sheath belted to his waist. Bewildered, he scanned the room slowly. There was no feigning the alarm on his face as he discovered her holding the candlestick aloft.

He recoiled. "My lady, I mean you no harm."

Alwenna lowered the impromptu weapon, but kept hold of it. "What brings you here under cover of darkness, brother?"

"I have news, my lady. Father Garrad has taken care to keep me busy outside the precinct since that night on the beach: he fears I have been corrupted by your presence. But today – well, I overheard him speaking to Brother Irwyn." He paused the flow of words to draw breath.

"Brother Irwyn? Do I know him?"

"He has charge of the kitchens. But he acts for Father Garrad when he is called away on precinct business, so he holds his trust."

Alwenna nodded. "Go on."

"I was on the way to collect grain when I overheard them, out by the field-house. I ought to have revealed my presence, but I did not. Out of petty resentment, I confess, for the way I have been treated since I spoke up in your support. But that is neither here nor there. Father Garrad expects a detachment of soldiers to arrive shortly to take you back to Highkell. Vasic intends to be crowned king as soon as he has taken you as his wife, my lady."

"I see." Alwenna paced across the room. "This isn't entirely unexpected."

"I can take you away tonight, my lady, if that is what you wish."

She halted. "You would take such a risk?"

"My lady, I joined the brethren with a pure heart, but what I have seen of late sickens me." His words tumbled over one another in his eagerness to unburden himself. "The corruption here comes not from your presence among us, but the very head of our order. Father Garrad has been seduced by worldly concerns. He may be my superior, but I can no longer sit back while he meddles in affairs that should be none of our remit here at Vorrahan. To betray a guest of the order who was sent here by a generous patron – it is wrong. Father Garrad would have it that my head has been turned by your beauty and dark powers, of course."

He'd run out of words at last. "Indeed? It seems I have offended Father Garrad more than I ever thought possible. Either he is much changed since Tresilian was tutored here, or my late husband was much mistaken as to his character." She paused. "But tell me, brother, where do you stand with regard to my supposed beauty and dark powers?"

"My lady, I admire your beauty, and fear your power, but I believe you would never knowingly misuse either."

"Can you be sure, brother, that your faith is not misplaced?"

"My lady, that night in the brewhouse, Weaver spoke of your journey and... he extracted a promise from me that should any ill befall him I would be watchful for your care. And from what I overheard – if I understood correctly – he has already been captured." Drew's fingers clenched and unclenched around the candlestick he carried. "My lady, if you would leave Vorrahan it must be now, or we will likely run straight into Vasic's men before we are clear of the bay. There are horses in the mainland pasture."

"I would leave... but if you help me you risk everything, even your life."

"My life is worth nothing if I sit idly by while you are betrayed. It lies within my power to help you now. The tide runs in our favour but by daylight it will have turned."

"Brother, I ought not accept this sacrifice from you, but I am hard pressed. Are you sure? You may leave this room now and suffer no reproach."

"My lady, I leave Vorrahan tonight no matter what. I would offer you assistance and this is the only way I may. It is unlikely there will be another such chance."

"Then give me five minutes to make ready." Alwenna gathered such belongings as she thought might be useful, hastily throwing on the remainder of her clothing. She set a bolster in the bed to at least give the impression she slept there to a casual observer, then hurried from the room. Drew waited in the anteroom where Weaver had slept.

"Wear this habit over your clothes: it will help disguise you."

With the bulky habit over the layers of garments she already wore, Alwenna looked nothing like the slender lady Weaver had brought to Vorrahan. Drew handed her the knife and belt that Weaver had removed from one of Stanton's men the night they left Highkell. Alwenna fastened it, grateful for the familiar object despite such unpleasant associations.

"Which way do we go, brother?"

"Please, my lady, call me Drew. From this moment I am no longer a brother of this precinct."

"As you wish. Do we make for the shore gate?"

"No, that is guarded now. But there is another way through the stables and out through the hayloft door to the pasture. That is not watched, and I have a boat waiting nearby."

They moved quietly through the darkened precinct, alerting no guard to their presence, then, just as they were about to enter the stable, Alwenna felt a sudden apprehension. She laid a hand on Drew's arm, stopping him.

"Not that way," she whispered, trying to suppress the vision that clouded her senses, but she could no more stop it than stop water flowing downhill. The sky above her darkened until the pinpoints of stars were obscured by smoke, black and billowing. It welled from the stable roof while an inferno roared, devouring the timbers of the building. The yard was filled with monks passing water buckets along lines, throwing them into the flames which licked higher and higher with each offering of sweat. Father Garrad stood off to one side, watching the roof burn.

"They will pay. I'll see to that." His words were oddly

distorted by the crackling of the flames. Then the flames dimmed and she was looking down at a tame log fire in a hearth. A man's voice swore, at length, then tossed a piece of parchment into the flames. The edges turned brown, and the signature "Garrad' was visible before the sheet contorted, twisting up as the fire claimed it. The man straightened up, the curl of his lip instantly recognisable: Vasic. He was older than when Alwenna had last seen him, more mature.

"Count yourself lucky I wasn't there to have you locked inside, priest." Vasic strode away as the parchment crumbled to ash.

"My lady, please, we will be seen." Drew's hand at her elbow tugged her back to her surroundings.

She couldn't focus on anything. "Drew... guide me for a moment."

Drew hesitated then gingerly led her forward several paces. Then she heard the metal-on-metal grating of the stable latch as he lifted it and pushed the door part-way open. The sense of dread returned but the world slid back into focus – in time for her to see two pale figures in the straw, engrossed in a heaving, grunting tangle of limbs, illuminated by candlelight. Drew backed up abruptly, leaving the door ajar.

"I never thought... That's Brother Irwyn." He was visibly shaken by the sight of the two monks.

"Did he see you?"

"I... I don't think so." Drew gnawed on a thumbnail. "That's the only way into the hayloft."

"What now? Do we wait until they've gone?"

Drew shook his head reluctantly. "We could miss the tide."

"Then we must sneak past them. They might not notice."

He gave her a horrified look. "But..."

"What other option do we have?"

"The loft ladder's against the back wall. Maybe if we're quiet enough..."

Drew eased the door wider open, then slipped inside. She followed him, keeping her eyes on the ground where she walked while the monks continued their increasingly noisy tryst just a few yards away. Drew climbed the ladder with the ease of familiarity. Alwenna found she had to hitch her skirts out of the way to prevent her feet becoming entangled. She was halfway up the ladder when the monks fell silent. Not daring to look round, she tried to move more quickly, but lost her footing as she reached the topmost rung. The ladder creaked in protest as she slipped and bashed her shin on the offending rung. She clambered hastily over it and onto the loft, sending a loose clump of hay cascading down.

"Who's there?" The man's voice was harsh, but unmistakably that of Brother Irwyn. Drew's guess had been right. She joined Drew at the loft door where he wrestled with the iron loop that operated the latch. There were scuffling sounds from below. The latch lifted with an audible creak, but that was nothing to the groan of rusted hinges as the door swung open, or the clatter of the latch as Drew released it.

This time there was a single shout from below, followed by cursing and the creak of the ladder as someone set foot on it. Alwenna lowered herself from the door until she had to let go and simply drop the remaining distance. A pain shot through her ankle as she hit the ground, then rolled, regaining her feet as Drew landed beside her. They scrambled up and dashed across the field as a man shouted from the loft behind them.

Drew helped Alwenna scramble over the drystone wall, risking a look back. He cursed. "We're followed."

They ducked down behind the wall, hurrying as best they could until they reached a sheep pen. There Drew paused, before tucking in behind the corner of the wall. "They're not calling for help. We still have a chance." He picked up a cobble that must have fallen from the wall, hefted it in his hand, then pressed his back to the wall, waiting. Alwenna took up position next to him. The wall and the ground around it was rank with the smell of sheep. What would Weaver have done? Ensured neither monk could have left the stable in the first place, like as not.

It felt like a long time before clumsy footsteps drew near, though it could only have been a few seconds. Their pursuer was breathing heavily, as if unaccustomed to such exercise. Alwenna pressed tighter against the wall. Finding a loose stone beneath her fingertips, she took hold of it.

Stones clattered as their pursuer climbed over the wall and began making his way towards them. Drew tensed as the footsteps came closer, then paused. Then two more steps, firm and decided this time.

Drew sprang to his feet, cobble in hand, and there was a grunt of surprise as he hurled himself at their pursuer, followed by a hollow thud. All became confusion as the two tussled. Alwenna eased herself up to peer over the wall. Irwyn, with dark blood trickling down his forehead, had one hand about Drew's throat. Drew struck at him with the cobble a second time, but landed only a glancing blow off his shoulder and the stone fell from his hands.

Their escape was close to failure.

Alwenna dived for Irwyn, striking out with the stone she clutched. It connected with his skull with a sickening thud. Irwyn swayed for a moment, then toppled to the ground and Drew staggered clear.

Drew reached up to wipe his cut lip with the back of his hand, sucking in air with an effort. "Thank you, my lady."

Alwenna still gripped the rock in her hand. Was it her imagination, or could she see Irwyn's blood on it? She dropped it hastily.

A second monk was hurrying across the field, for all the world like an ungainly bird as his unbelted robes flapped loose about him.

"Brother Francis. He won't stop us." Drew caught hold of her hand and tugged her towards the shore and they were off, sprinting over the open ground, crunching over the shingle to where the boats waited.

Alwenna risked a look back as they dragged the boat to the water's edge. Francis was stooped over Irwyn, all thoughts of pursuit apparently forgotten.

A few minutes later they were rowing across the sound. Drew pulled steadily at the oars, helped by the tide, until they were out in open water and could see the precinct beyond the trees once more. Drew frowned, pausing with oars raised. Even before Alwenna twisted around she guessed what she would see. Smoke billowed from the roof of the stable and flames already licked at the stars.

"They had a candle with them in the stable." She could picture it clearly in her mind's eye: set on the floor among the straw. It must have been upturned in their haste at being discovered.

"Lucky for us, my lady." He was much calmer now.

"Even if they notice we're gone they'll have no leisure to do anything about it. And I doubt Francis will want to tell them." He pulled back on the oars again and they sped towards the mainland.

CHAPTER THIRTY-TWO

Garrad rubbed his eyes and set aside the letter he was composing. It had taken three days before the fire burned itself out. The library had been saved by the monks' efforts, but the stables had been completely destroyed. Rebuilding it was going to be costly: importing new timbers from the mainland, new slate, hiring labourers… The precinct was in desperate need of funds. His best hope had been finding the runaways on the mainland before they travelled too far, but the search parties had learned nothing. The pair of them had vanished without trace. He had anticipated generous treatment from Vasic for handing over the Lady Alwenna, but now he could look for nothing but displeasure. And Vasic's reputation for making his displeasure known had reached even this quiet corner of the Peninsula. Somehow he had to break the news to his new king. He couldn't put it off any longer. He picked up the part-written letter again, but this time was interrupted by a knock at the door.

Brother Irwyn entered the room. His hands and one arm were bandaged, while his forehead bore a livid scar. Rumour had it he'd carried out some heroic rescue during the fire, although no one seemed to know quite who or what had been rescued.

"You continue to make a good recovery, I see, brother. What brings you here?" Garrad set the letter down on his desk.

"Father, my conscience is heavy." The priest made show of wringing his hands together, every inch the penitent. The effect was marred somewhat by his bulky bandages.

"Indeed?" Garrad didn't have time – or inclination – for this.

"It concerns the night of the fire, holy father. It grieves me to tell you this, but... I've thought for a while Brother Drew was unreliable. He spent so much time chasing after the Lady Alwenna I feared he had lost his way. So I kept a close eye on him and – this is what I have hesitated to tell you – the night of the fire I saw them sneaking into the stable building, with a lighted candle."

"And you tell me this only now?"

Irwyn hung his head. "I cannot be sure this caused the fire, father. But I could not in all conscience withhold the information any longer." The man was a consummate actor, Garrad had to grant him that. "I called Brother Francis for assistance but they heard us approaching and fled over the fields. We gave chase, not realising the candle must have been overturned in their haste. The stable was ablaze when we returned."

"I see." Father Garrad steepled his fingers, regarding his second-in-command. Not for a moment did he believe this was the truth: the monk had waited until they were sure the fugitives had gone beyond recall. Nevertheless his tale might be turned to good use. "And you would attest to all this before the highest courts if necessary?"

"I would, father. Brother Francis will be able to confirm

everything I have told you. Brother Drew flouted the laws of our order, and broke his vows with that woman. I suspect witchery on her part, he was so smitten."

"Indeed, that is a possibility I had not considered. You were fortunate she did not turn her unholy powers on you, as she did on her dupe Ranald Weaver."

"The Goddess gave me strength to resist such worldly lures, your holiness."

Garrad was impressed. The man could lie as brazenly and adroitly as any he had ever known. "That is fortunate. Had you not intervened in such timely fashion the fire might have spread to the library. Our loss would have been incalculable."

Irwyn assumed an expression of great humility. "It was fortunate indeed, father. Divine providence guided my actions that night."

"Indeed." Garrad studied Irwyn. The monk met his gaze with every impression of innocence and righteousness. He would make an excellent witness. And Brother Francis, with his impeccable record at the precinct, would back every word. So very respectable in appearance, the pair of them. "Irwyn, thank you for sharing your suspicions. I shall send a full report to his highness King Vasic. He must be informed what manner of woman he seeks to take into his protection."

Garrad dismissed Irwyn and tore up the half-written letter, beginning again with a fresh sheet of parchment. He weighed each sentence carefully before committing it to the page. It took quite some time, but when he had dusted the sheet with sand to dry the ink and read through the whole, he felt satisfied with the end result. Every adverse event at Vorrahan could be laid clearly at the

Lady Alwenna's door. This should be more than sufficient to save his good name where Vasic was concerned. He sealed the sheet with wax, marking it with his signet ring. Tomorrow he would send one of the novices to carry it to the mainland. He poured himself a drink, savouring it as the liquor burned a fiery path down his throat.

Then he caught sight of movement from the corner of his eye. A figure stood by the window, wearing the familiar cowl of the novice monk required of all trainees at Vorrahan. It was Tresilian. He stared straight at Garrad.

"That was not well done, father. I see now I ought not have given my trust to you so completely." He paused, head tilted on one side as Garrad gaped at him in disbelief. "Alwenna is wiser than me, I think. And she knew Gwydion of old, long before you could begin to poison his mind. She will not be so easily manipulated. You will see." He raised the hood up over his head so it hid his face. "You will pay for every one of your crimes, father. You cannot hide the truth from the Goddess." He turned away and the candle flame guttered and went out, pitching Garrad into darkness. He sat at his desk, smoke from the snuffed candle curling into his nostrils, heart racing, scarcely daring to breathe as he listened for any hint of movement in the darkened chamber. Only when he was as certain as a man could be that he was alone did he rise from his seat and fumble his way to the door.

CHAPTER THIRTY-THREE

Drew's stomach knotted with anxiety as they approached the crossroads. If he intended to ask, this was the time. He glanced at the Lady Alwenna. She was sagging in her saddle, although a couple of hours' daylight remained.

"If I may suggest... my family live not far from here. I think they would gladly shelter us for the night. My lady?"

She glanced his way, frowning, clearly pre-occupied with her own thoughts. "I beg your pardon?"

"My family live nearby. We might shelter there for the night."

Her frown lifted for a moment. "That would be welcome. If you think we can trust them?"

"My ma'll be glad to see me, my lady. She never wanted me to leave. I... I would be grateful to see her once more before travelling east."

"Of course." She smiled and her face was transformed, but only for a few seconds. The Lady Alwenna carried too much sadness with her. If only Gwydion had told him more – told them both more. The old man should never have burdened her with the knowledge of ages. Then again, if he hadn't, that knowledge might be Drew's now. And everything Drew had seen told him that burden was a heavy one. To think he'd once envied her.

The mason's yard at the head of the valley was just as Drew remembered. They made their way along the foot of the rock escarpment, riding in the deep evening shadow. Workers looked up as they passed, with one or two nodding recognition. Before they reached the house at the head of the yard his brother Coll approached, smiling, bashing dust from his hands and his leather tunic.

"Drew? It is you. Well met! What brings you so far from Vorrahan?" Coll's eyes, filled with curiosity, slid to the Lady Alwenna. He straightened up, puffing out his chest, his smile widening. "Well, Drew?"

Some things hadn't changed. The knot of apprehension in Drew's stomach eased a fraction.

"My lady, may I present to you my younger brother, Coll? He is my father's apprentice." Drew waited for a nod before embarking on the story they had determined upon. "I'm escorting the Lady Selena to her family home. She is a widow, lately in refuge at the precinct after fever claimed her husband."

"The roads are perilous since the fall of Highkell. The usurper–" Coll bowed. "But he holds no sway here. Ma will be glad to see you."

Coll stepped back, lowering his head in deference, and Drew knew their father was approaching.

"Well now, I thought my eyes must be deceiving me. My own son, and travelling with a fine lady, no less."

Drew waited for the barb to follow the words, but there was none. He performed the introductions and explained their errand, the story slipping more easily from his lips with every repetition. The Lady Alwenna – or Selena, as he tried to think of her – smiled graciously upon his father, complimenting him on the work she saw being carried out in his yard and the fine sons he had raised. Within minutes she had him wrapped around her little finger. And the old man lapped it up as he led the way to the house at the top of the quarry yard.

Later that evening Drew was attending to the horses when the barn door opened, and the Lady Alwenna stepped inside, closing it softly behind her.

"I thought you might need some help out here."

Drew nodded. He understood perfectly well she sought a few minutes' peace. "My lady, how did you do it? You charmed him. So easily. Gwydion told me of such things, yet–"

"It's not difficult to show a man the thing he most desires to see." She shrugged and set about inspecting their tack as Drew finished grooming the horse.

"You need not do that."

"It's high time I learned to be useful, do you not think? You are not my servant, after all." She rubbed at the saddle with a scrap of cloth. "And I wished to speak with you, Drew." She rubbed a little harder, a slight frown on her face. "It seems to me your family might welcome you home. Your mother has been telling me how she regrets ever letting your father send you away. Your father, too, seems well disposed towards you now."

"I gave my word, my lady. First to Weaver and now to you. I will serve you as long as you have need of me."

"They would welcome you here, I'm sure of it." She spoke softly. "I think I can make sure of it."

"My lady, I cannot return to the life I once led here: it was a lie. I will never live the life they would have me lead."

She set the saddle down in some clean straw. "Drew, I can't promise you'll be safe if you go with me." She picked up one of the bridles and started cleaning dried-on grass from the bit, scraping at it with a thumbnail. "It'll be dangerous. There will be people who would use you to gain a hold over me."

Now was the time to tell her. All the things Brother Gwydion had told him. All the madness.

"My lady, when–"

The barn door swung open with a grinding of hinges and they both spun round, startled. Coll entered, smiling, and at the same time giving Drew a curious look. A surprised look.

"I was sent to tell you both that food's on the table." He offered his arm to the Lady Alwenna and led her back to the house.

Drew followed behind. It would have to wait.

CHAPTER THIRTY-FOUR

Drew was keen to move on early the next morning. Alwenna had no objection: his brother Coll asked a deal too many questions. An hour after dawn they had already climbed the hill out of the valley and joined the road leading between Westhaven and Highkell.

Alwenna hesitated, then turned her horse's head towards Highkell.

Drew hurried his horse alongside hers. "My lady? The road to Westhaven lies the other way."

"We're not going to Westhaven."

"But last night, at table you said—"

"I did. But I haven't the coin to take a ship from Westhaven." There had to be a diplomatic way to explain her mistrust of his brother's questions, but in the hour they'd been riding she'd failed to find it.

Drew frowned. "You lied?"

"I'd sooner think of it as setting a false trail. In case anyone from Vorrahan should think to question your family."

"I see." His sombre expression suggested he'd worked out the reasons for her decision. "Then you plan to ride straight into Highkell after all? Simply hand yourself over to Vasic?"

"Goddess, no. Weaver mentioned a packhorse path through the mountains to the north which the freemerchants use. It's impassable in winter, but by now it should be clear."

Drew smiled. "Ma grew up on the road. She told me tales of travelling that way when she was a girl." His smile faded as swiftly as it had appeared. "But I don't know how to find it."

Alwenna nudged her horse forward. "We'll work that out when we get closer. I'm hoping we'll meet some freemerchants along the way." She couldn't afford to dwell on the lack of detail to her plan. Anything was better than waiting at Vorrahan until Vasic arrived.

Drew rode alongside her. "Was the part about having family in The Marches true?"

"As far as I know. I left when I was eight so I won't recognise anyone. But I understand the people there remain fiercely loyal to my family so I might hope to raise support against Vasic."

"Would you invite further bloodshed?"

"My claim to the throne is nothing to me: I never sought it, nor welcomed it. The trappings of royalty..." She shrugged. "I was always warmly clothed and well fed. I know many have not had that good fortune. But as long as Vasic remains at Highkell, the people in The Marches will be denied such things. If I can improve things, have I the right to ignore any opportunity to do so, however fraught it may be for me personally?"

"I had not seen it in such terms, my lady."

"Nor did I, until the last year or two. I thought only of myself and my own convenience. My eyes were finally opened to the responsibilities of my rank."

A farmer's wagon approached and Drew rode ahead to make room for it, putting an end to their conversation.

They camped that night in the shelter of a belt of trees a short distance from the road. Alwenna would have preferred a more secluded spot, but this road was more open than the route she'd travelled with Weaver. She slept uneasily as half-formed images stalked her mind. Voices spoke but she couldn't hear the words for the crackling of flames. Figures moved through the smoke but their faces remained unseen. And from somewhere in the midst of it all she heard Weaver cry out. She woke with a start, to find a soldier standing above her, the point of his sword hovering above her throat.

The stranger's mouth twisted in a cold grin. "What have we here?" With the blade of his sword he pushed her travelling cloak aside. "Not too fat, not too thin. She'll do."

"Don't you touch her!" Drew struggled between two soldiers and earned a fist to the face for his pains.

The soldier glanced at him, then back to Alwenna. "It'll take more than you to stop me, lad. Take him away out of sight where I can't hear him whining. Keep him alive for now, he might be useful yet."

"You mustn't–" Drew's words were silenced with the crunch of a mailed fist against his nose, then another to his stomach. He doubled over, struggling to breathe, but his words were audible. "She's the Lady Alwenna. Harm her and you'll die."

The sneering soldier paused and studied Alwenna more closely. He frowned. "What's your name, bitch?"

"You heard the holy brother – he does not lie." Now her secret was out she might have more to gain by admitting the truth. I am the Lady Alwenna of Brigholm, relict of his highness King Tresilian, late of Highkell."

"The Lady Alwenna herself? Well now." The sword point still hovered over the lacing of her kirtle. "Vasic will reward me well for taking you to him. Well enough that I can forego a minute or two's pleasure. For now." He managed to make the words sound like a threat, nevertheless. But he sheathed his sword. "Don't stand there gawping, you fools, bring the horses."

CHAPTER THIRTY-FIVE

Vasic glowered out of the mullioned window at the mist that once again surrounded the keep at Highkell. What had possessed him to claim the accursed place? Highkell controlled trade through the passes between The Marches and the rest of the Peninsula. It was key to controlling all the business that came and went inland from the deep-sea ports of The Marches. Control of trade meant taxes and money and power. And he liked power. He liked power very much. But it wasn't as simple as that. It never had been.

The sky was growing darker even though it was scarcely after noon – another bloody downpour on the way, no doubt. He glared down at the gatehouse. A detachment of soldiers had returned, doubtless bearing more bad news and lame excuses. Then, in the midst of the group he spotted two prisoners: one wore a monk's cowl while the other was cloaked – a woman? Beneath the heavy hood he could not be sure, but the prisoner turned towards him and although he still could not see her face he was certain. Alwenna. She was never meant for Tresilian.

He hurried away from the window and had made it as far as the door to the antechamber before he stopped. He'd dismissed the rabble of hangers-on that he liked to call his court earlier that morning and they would be waiting there for him to relent. And he wanted no one to witness this meeting. He had to be in control of this situation. He was king, was he not?

He summoned a servant. "A detachment of soldiers has returned with prisoners. Bring the commander to report to me at once."

CHAPTER THIRTY-SIX

Alwenna approached the bridge over the gorge at Highkell with a dull sense of dread. The journey had tired her beyond belief. Their captors had maintained a constant suggestion of menace the whole way. Never a mile had passed without Alwenna dreading what might happen. Any attempts she and Drew had made to speak between themselves had been shouted down by the commander. Alwenna doubted she'd learned to hate anyone more than him, from his thick eyebrows and receding forehead to unshaven face. A natural predator, he was a powerfully built man, perhaps shorter than Weaver by an inch or two. But where Weaver resembled a mountain cat in its agile grace, the commander resembled a boar: swift to react, and single-minded.

The sky darkened and with it Alwenna's mood as they drew nearer her childhood home, and her childhood enemy. There could be little doubt what lay in store for her at Vasic's hands. She'd not been visited by the sight since her capture by the soldiers. This was the only thing she had to be thankful for in recent days as it left her so vulnerable – little better than blind – during the visions. For the first time in days Alwenna found herself thinking of the old man, Gwydion. There was a void in her mind where once there had been some connection with him. And for a moment she sensed something stirring, so distant she could hardly make it out, something shouting out in protest against... It had gone. She felt strangely heartened by the sense of another's pain. She might not be entirely alone after all. It was an unsettling sort of comfort.

The commander ordered Alwenna to dismount as guards strode out from the gatehouse to speak with him. Peveril, she finally learned his name was. She stored the information away. One day she would use it. Not through petty vengeance – although Goddess knew she would relish that – but because her sight told her it would be so.

A messenger dashed from the keep as Peveril exchanged words with the two guards who had stepped out to greet him.

"His highness requires the captain of the troop who has returned with prisoners to report to him at once. Alone."

"Secure my prisoners in the gatehouse." Peveril tucked his helmet under his arm and hurried away towards the main building.

Alwenna raised her head towards the tall mullioned window. She'd often watched the comings and goings in the courtyard from that vantage point. A man stood there now, watching. And she felt his tension – a mix of apprehension and arousal as he stared down at the hooded figure by the gatehouse. As the figure turned its head towards him, he caught his breath. This was her, he knew it. Finally after years of waiting, she would be his.

One of the soldiers caught Alwenna by the arm, none too gently. With a start she recalled herself to the present, unnerved by what had just happened and repelled by the sense of Vasic's thoughts towards her. The soldier hustled her into a small guardroom where Drew already waited. Both their hands remained bound. There was nowhere to sit but the stone ledge beneath the barred window, nothing provided for their ease but a chamber pot in the corner of the bare room. Alwenna sat on the ledge. On impulse she pressed her hands against the cool stone of her childhood home, as if it might offer her comfort. But it didn't.

Instead, she learned Ranald Weaver had sat in that same place. Many days ago. She closed her eyes, pressing her hands flat against the stone as best she could with her wrists bound together. Weaver was there, somewhere; the ancient blood of the line that had fashioned these walls told her. He was weak, the sense of his presence so faint she feared he might be close to death, but he was there.

In the dungeon Weaver sat up, too weary to brush the filthy straw from his clothing. He shuffled over to lean his back against the wall. Something had changed. Energy and hope seemed to flow into his veins and breathing became easier, as if a fever had finally broken.

Footsteps on the stairs announced the arrival of the guard with their meagre rations of food and water. Keys rattled in the lock and Curtis entered the room, carrying a ewer of water and a basket. He refilled the basin set on the raised stone platform in the centre of the cell before handing round dried bread. Unlike the other jailers he always did this, noting the condition of the prisoners as he went. He often passed on snippets of news from the outside world, usually inconsequential stuff, but mulling over the import of it helped Weaver keep his mind working. Today, however, the news was different.

"Scouts have returned from the west with prisoners. If their braggart captain is to be believed the Lady Alwenna has been brought back to Highkell. Travelling with a monk, so they say." He caught Weaver's eye then. "We face interesting times, lads." He shuffled out with the empty ewer.

Weaver picked at his portion of bread. With a monk? Only one? If she'd been sold to Vasic she'd surely have been sent under a full guard. He'd told her to stay on Vorrahan, but if Garrad had set out to betray them both... He had too many questions, and no answers.

In the guardroom higher up the tower, Alwenna curled up on the narrow window ledge, sliding into a deep sleep. Drew moved over to her and took hold of her bound wrists to check her pulse. He'd read of this, the deeper power that came with the sight. His own meagre ability couldn't hope to accomplish the working she'd just completed. Gwydion had told him how it would be, of course, but he couldn't help marvelling at her strength. There had been a time when he'd resented her, turning up and taking the legacy from Gwydion that would otherwise have been his. But when he'd witnessed the raw energy that had flowed between them he'd realised he should have feared that power, not coveted it. Events had overtaken them so quickly he'd had no opportunity to explain to Alwenna what Gwydion had taught him, yet somehow, he had to. As if he could hope to explain the ramblings of an old man he hadn't understood himself.

CHAPTER THIRTY-SEVEN

Vasic waited impatiently in his throne room, returning more than once to the window to look down into the courtyard, as if he'd see the woman there again. He couldn't believe it was anyone other than Alwenna – she'd always had that effect on him.

A cautious hand knocked at the door.

"Enter." Vasic turned away from the window. Hames entered the room, pausing to make a low bow. Behind him followed a soldier – sergeant or some such rank – bowing and scraping in the inelegant manner of one unused to making obeisance before a monarch.

"Enough grovelling, man, make your report." Vasic was in no mood for observing the social niceties.

"Your highness, on the road between Westhaven and Highkell our patrol apprehended a monk and a lady travelling on horseback. The monk gives his name as Drew, formerly of Vorrahan, while the lady claims to be the Lady Alwenna, relict of Tresilian." He paused for breath. "She answers the description given to us closely enough to bring her before you, your highness." The man bowed once more, making a more creditable effort this time. A fast learner. Perhaps too fast.

"A monk, you say?"

"Yes, your highness. A young novice."

Vasic had no trust for the monks at Vorrahan. They may have cheated him after all, trying to gain some kind of advantage. "Where did they say they were bound?"

"We found them travelling east, your highness, after hearing word of suspicious travellers bound for Westhaven from Vorrahan. I did not question them further once I heard the lady's claim. I felt sure you would wish to oversee any interrogation." He bowed again.

Oh, yes, he was a quick learner – or a smooth-tongued liar. "Have the prisoners brought before me here. Now."

A man-at-arms stationed at the door scurried away to do his king's bidding, his footsteps padding across the smooth stone hall beyond the doors.

Hames stepped forward. "Sire, I have here urgent despatches from Vorrahan."

"They can wait. I have more pressing matters to attend to."

"As you wish, sire. However, it may be worthwhile perusing them quickly – there may be information pertaining to your prisoners."

"You presume a deal too much, Hames." Vasic ran a hand across his brow. "Show me these despatches."

Hames handed him the single scroll of parchment.

Vasic cracked open the seal and frowned as he studied the sheet. "Curse the man, his writing's terrible. Who has written this? Garrad. And well he might." He read on a few lines and his frown cleared, his lips curling in something like a smile. "How providential. Hames, this is excellent news."

Hames bowed. "Your highness."

"She has played right into my hands. Father Garrad seems a little put out, but since he was so careless as to lose his prisoner before my soldiers could collect her... He has managed to make himself useful in this matter, nonetheless." Vasic lowered the paper. "You there, soldier, you said your prisoners were travelling on horseback? Describe the animals."

"Yes, your highness. They were quality, one grey–"

"And one bay." Vasic smiled. "You have done well, soldier. You may leave my presence. Hames, see he is rewarded with coin for today's work."

The soldier backed from the room and Hames followed in his wake, bowing with the grace of one raised on palace intrigue and risen to high rank through his aptitude.

Vasic sat back on the throne. "Our moment of reckoning approaches, Alwenna. You have over-reached yourself this time." His fingers flexed on the polished wood of the throne arms and he drew in a deep breath, closing his eyes. This promised to be exquisite.

CHAPTER THIRTY-EIGHT

Alwenna followed the guard up the winding stairs she knew so well. They paused outside the upper guardroom before entering the antechamber to the throne room. Drew scuffled up the stairs behind her, the old leather boots he'd donned when he left the precinct much the worse for wear. A fine sight they must have presented, both deprived of sleep and the means to wash for several days. Despite her bound hands she attempted to pull her hair into some kind of order as they waited to be admitted to the king's presence. Tresilian had never stood on ceremony like this, but he'd always been secure in his kingship, and in himself. Vasic had never enjoyed such a luxury.

The door opened and the guard motioned with his head. "In you go, now."

Alwenna studied him for a moment with a raised eyebrow, just long enough for the man to look discomfited. "You are new here, I think?"

The man shuffled under her scrutiny. "Aye, milady."

Alwenna looked him up and down once more. "Well, I never." Her voice contained just the right amount of disdain. Court ways: she hadn't forgotten them during her absence. Nor had she missed them. She drew herself up to her full height, then walked with a measured pace into the room. Head held high, she was more stately than she'd ever sought to be during Tresilian's tenure as king.

Vasic sat on the throne where her husband's place had once been. Alwenna recognised Hames standing off to one side. The petty administrator must have wasted no time making himself useful to his new employer. Vasic tensed, straightening in his seat as she crossed the floor. His fingers gripped the arms of the throne more than necessary. It seemed her first impression had been all she could hope for.

She stopped three paces away from the throne, inclined her head for a moment, then stood tall and straight as before. Drew padded up to take his place beside her and knelt there, his head bowed.

Vasic's eyes remained fixed on her.

She sensed the handful of advisors in the room hoped to see her make obeisance before Vasic. Doubtless a deal of money was about to change hands on the outcome of this meeting. Courtiers were ever fond of gambling, regardless of who sat on the throne. Alwenna waited as the tension in the room built.

Vasic's brow furrowed.

She let her lips curl in a hint of a smile, visible to no one in the room but Vasic. A hint of a smile, spiced with a tinge of derision. "Well, cousin. I see you style yourself king of the whole Peninsula these days?"

Vasic's eyes narrowed. "Curb your insolence, madam, and kneel before your king."

His words echoed round the chambers. Alwenna was aware of a movement from Hames, at the very edge of her vision.

"You may sit on the throne today, cousin, but you are no king here. You are nothing but a usurper. That throne is mine: by right, by law, and by popular support."

A murmur ran around the room.

Vasic's lips curled in a sneer. "You were ever headstrong, Alwenna. I was led to believe your husband taught you the semblance of manners, but it seems reports were exaggerated."

"Manners, cousin? You dare talk of manners?" Alwenna heard a nervous intake of breath from Drew as she marshalled her anger, combining it by instinct with some eldritch strength she'd scarcely known she possessed until this moment. "You summon me before you with my hands bound like a common thief, without offering water to wash or refreshment of any kind." She raised her voice so it rang about the chamber. "Like a common thief. I am not the one who presumes to sit on a stolen throne. I am not the one who tortured the rightful king on the rack to learn the whereabouts of his wife. I am not the coward who killed his own kinsman by slipping a knife between his ribs while he was bound there. I am not the one who consigned his body to an unmarked grave with hundreds of his loyal citizens. I am none of those things, but I am the one who will call you to account for every one of your misdeeds."

She couldn't hold the room in silence any longer, and for a moment feared she would lose consciousness as she heard men-at-arms rushing to restrain her from either side. But as soon as they touched her they fell back in fear and she felt her strength return.

Vasic watched her in fascination, as one might study a swaying snake that blocked the only exit from a room.

Alwenna smiled. "I am sure, cousin, you did not summon me to discuss that. What is your purpose in calling me here?"

Vasic's eyes never left her. "Hames, clear the room. I want no one left in here but yourself and two men-at-arms. You may wait by the far door."

"Your highness." Hames bowed lower than ever and the room emptied. Drew got up from his knees but Alwenna set her hand upon his shoulder. "Stay, Drew. You will be safer here with me, I think."

Drew gave her a wide-eyed glance, but he nodded. She could tell he thought she was playing an unnecessarily dangerous game.

Vasic glared at the youth. "I ordered the room to be cleared."

"Cousin, just as you have no wish to be alone in the room with me, I have no wish to be alone with you and your men. And I know you are not without clemency."

"Then let him stand at the far end of the room."

Alwenna nodded at Drew and he obeyed, setting himself apart from Vasic's men who were stationed before the door.

"Well, cousin, here we are, just the two of us. It is quite like old times. Will you unbind my hands now so we may talk like civilised human beings?"

"It may suit my purposes better to keep you tied, Alwenna." He let his eyes run over her body from head to toe, lingering over her curves with a return of his insolent bravado.

"I had hoped the passage of time might have wrought an improvement in your attitude. It would seem I was overly optimistic. It is of little import." She shrugged one shoulder. "Tell me why you have brought me here."

Vasic's brows snapped together. "You are my prisoner. I ask the questions."

"As you wish, cousin." She stood before him, tall, proud, unconcerned. She would show him no weakness.

Vasic glanced beyond her to the silent onlookers at the far end of the room. "Hames, bring me the letter from Vorrahan." Hames hurried up the hall and passed him a sheet of parchment. Vasic re-read the letter while Hames, now somewhat breathless, hastened back to his place.

"You may be interested to learn news of your escapades has already reached us here at Highkell." Vasic glanced at Alwenna; she took care not to react. "I fear Father Garrad lays some serious charges at your door." He frowned. "This does not surprise you?"

"Father Garrad promised me sanctuary, then betrayed me. I doubt I could be surprised by any lies he might concoct now."

"Indeed? He reports that while at Vorrahan you lived under the same roof as a common soldier, without servant or chaperone to preserve decency."

"I was obliged to live in the lodgings Father Garrad provided. He claimed it was safer, being within the precinct walls."

"I have only your word for that." Vasic shrugged. "He further informs me that not content with the attentions of a common soldier, you turned the head of a young novice, name of Brother Drew, and seduced him from his vows of abstinence." He let his eyes flick across the room to where the youth stood.

"Brother Drew was as sickened by Father Garrad's treachery as I was myself."

"Father Garrad is a loyal subject – you ought not speak against him in that way. Further, you stole two horses, one grey and one bay, both in care of the precinct at Vorrahan. And further still, you caused a fire to be started to cover your escape, destroying precinct property and endangering lives."

"We did no such thing. We came upon two brothers in the stable intent on breaking their vows. They had brought a candle with them and set it down in the straw."

"The community at Vorrahan has long been famed for its piety. Your influence there was baleful."

"And the charges Garrad levels against me are laughable." She forced her voice to remain perfectly even, perfectly calm. "Come to the point, cousin. I weary of your conversation as fast as ever I did in my youth."

"I see you are determined to make light of these matters. Your arrogance has brought you low, Lady Alwenna." He leaned forward, gripping the arms of the throne until his knuckles whitened. This, then, was to be the crux of the matter. "I am prepared to be lenient. I am prepared to overlook your past mistakes and grant you a pardon for these crimes. I am prepared to allow you to take the place you wrongfully claim is yours by right. All this I am prepared to grant, on the single condition that you become my wife."

There it was, out in the open at last. "A generous offer indeed, cousin, but one I cannot accept – not while honest men who served my late husband remain immured in the dungeons here. My conscience will not permit me to take my place here in luxury while they suffer."

"Madam!" Vasic rose to his feet. "You are in no position to bargain with me."

"As you wish, cousin. But your impassioned entreaties leave me unmoved." She doubted he would even notice her sarcasm. "I cannot accept the terms you offer."

"Damn it, you witch, you'll do as you're told."

"No. As long as the people who served me and my late husband suffer the consequences of their loyalty, I shall not accept your terms."

Vasic sank back onto his throne, speaking through gritted teeth in a low voice that only she could hear. "You forget your place here, madam. I am prepared to tolerate your presence, despite your arrogance. I am prepared to overlook your whoring. I am prepared to deal graciously with you. You are in no position to bargain with me – this letter details complaints of such severity I could have you executed for the heresies you committed at Vorrahan."

"Such are the decisions a man must take if he would be king. I wish you and your conscience joy of them, cousin." She smiled then, certain of what she must do. "Have your men lead me to the deepest dungeon. Let the people speak my name only in whispers lest they conspire against you. Spill my blood and see how it earns you their fear. You will never earn their respect, nor their loyalty. Harm me and you will inspire nothing but contempt in the people you would call your own. Take the throne on those terms and see what accursed blessings rain down upon you."

"Enough!" Vasic jumped to his feet. "Hames, secure the Lady Alwenna in her former quarters. Put a double guard at the door and ensure she has no means of escape. Whatever vile lies she may utter against the crown, let it be seen that I am merciful. I do not seek to silence her permanently, even though that lies entirely within my power as king of this realm. I understand the grief of a widow for her husband. I can see it has driven her wits from her to speak so; let us hope time brings a return to reason for the poor, afflicted creature. As for her lapdog of a monk, toss him in the dungeon. I'll deal with him later."

Alwenna twisted round in time to see two men-at-arms enclose Drew in their grip and drag him from the room. She turned her attention back to Vasic as more soldiers advanced up the room.

"As you wish, cousin. Let the people see which one of us is a stranger to reason. Continue as you are and history will be left in no doubt."

CHAPTER THIRTY-NINE

Weaver was still awake when Curtis opened the door to the dungeon and sent Drew into the chamber. Curtis nudged the former novice as he released his bonds and nodded his head towards Weaver. "You'll know yon fella, from the tales I've heard."

Drew blinked, disorientated in the dim light.

Curtis lowered his voice to a murmur. "He'll see you right, lad." He laid a reassuring hand on Drew's shoulder, causing the youth to flinch. As the door closed behind Curtis a deeper darkness enfolded the prisoners until their eyes adjusted.

Drew picked his way across the chamber, stumbling as he caught his foot on something – or someone. He was breathing hard by the time he joined Weaver and hunkered down against the wall at his side. "Goddess, this place gives me the chills. How fare you, Weaver?"

"I've been worse, brother. What of you? I'm sorry you have to join us in our filth."

"Brother no more. I've forsaken those vows. The precinct is tainted by corruption and I want none of it." He paused, easing his wrists where the bonds had cut into his flesh on the journey there. "She knew you'd been

188

captured. The night after you left."

No need to ask who "she" was. "You travelled with her from Vorrahan?"

"Aye. We took a boat from the beach."

"There are some you should know here." Weaver indicated the wiry man sitting on his right. "This is Lyall, who served with me in The Marches, long before I joined the King's Men."

"I warned him no good would come of befriending a king, but he was too wooden-headed to listen." Lyall's voice carried the accent of the Outer Isles. "You'll have noticed that, I daresay."

Drew smiled. "Aye. That, and the hollow legs to keep his balance."

Weaver snorted. "And now you're done maligning me, young Drew, you should also know Blaine. He did some handy work with his battle axe at Vorland Pass. He has more tales to tell about that than I have."

Blaine was tall and raw-boned; if he'd been better fed of late he'd be a huge man. He grinned, his teeth disconcertingly bright in the dim room. "If there's free drink to be had, I have the tales to tell."

"An honour." The lad sounded overwhelmed.

"What news from outside, Drew? We've heard nothing but rumours." Weaver wasn't sure yet whether to trust the lad or treat him as a potential traitor.

"Father Garrad betrayed you both." The youth's voice shook on the last word – anger or fear? It was hard to be sure. "I overheard him speaking to Brother Irwyn – I was keeping an ear open like you said – saying Vasic's men were on the way. We didn't reckon on meeting them on the road. It was as if they knew where we'd be." He gazed into the middle distance, sounding defeated. "And now it was all for nothing."

Weaver leaned forward, so his voice might not be overheard by the room at large. "Not so. By escaping you've discredited Garrad."

"We were called before Vasic. He questioned the Lady Alwenna about our escape, but he already knew everything. He had a letter from Father Garrad." Drew fell silent for a moment. "Garrad claimed we set fire to the stables, but it wasn't us. Two of the brethren had taken a candle into the stables with them. But that's by the by. He accused Alwenna of stealing horses – that was my doing. One was yours – it's here at Highkell now, in Vasic's stables."

"It can't be helped now, lad."

"That's not the worst of it. Garrad has accused the lady of base conduct – with you, and with me. He claims she caused me to forsake my vows. And he made much of the fact you shared the same roof at the precinct."

Weaver cursed inwardly. "And no doubt it'll suit Vasic to accept Father Garrad's version of events?"

"Aye, he seemed well pleased with what was written in that letter. Lies, all of it. Except for the horses," he added, scrupulously honest.

Weaver rested his head back against the wall. There was nothing he could do about any of it. "If I ever win free of this place I'll find Garrad and make him pay for every word of it."

Blaine laughed, deep and low. "You've changed your tune, Weaver. As I recall you were sick of kicking your heels at court while the king bedded his spoilt new wife."

Weaver shrugged, glad for the poor light at that moment.

"I misjudged her. She's not the spoilt child I once thought."

"Really? High praise from you." Blaine hesitated. "And the witchery?"

"She has it, sure enough, though I don't know the half of it."

"Old Gwydion told me…" Drew hesitated.

"Well?" Weaver prompted.

"He told me he'd seen none with such power as she has. He meant to spend time teaching her… but he became too ill. He'd chosen me to receive his legacy, if the Lady Alwenna had not reached Vorrahan in time. After that day in the cavern I've been thankful it wasn't me."

"You knew what he was about to do?" Weaver failed to make the question sound casual.

"Not that day, no. I swear it." Drew shifted nervously. "He spoke so often of the need to prepare for it."

"And you can still set store by that crazy old man's ramblings?"

"I see now Father Garrad did much to discredit Gwydion during his time at Vorrahan – he was subtle, with his cheery manner. And it must have been easy, for Gwydion was always uneasy in company. He knew so much of everyone's thoughts, you see…"

Did that mean Alwenna could do the same? Weaver didn't ask that question. If she'd been able to read his thoughts all this time, he was better not knowing.

CHAPTER FORTY

Alwenna soaked in the tub of warm water in her chamber. This was the one luxury of Highkell she'd truly missed. Set before a roaring fire and filled almost to the brim, it was a far cry from the shallow tub provided at Vorrahan by servants always pressed for time. The water eased her aches and pains, soothing wrists rubbed raw by the dirty leather straps she'd been bound with, dissolving away the grime from the journey until nothing remained but her anger against Vasic. That anger still burned, but slowly now, contained despite her frustration at having travelled full circle at such great cost.

She'd learned much at Vorrahan – things far beyond Vasic's comprehension. Unfortunately, her own understanding of them as yet might not greatly outstrip her cousin's. But she sensed this confrontation with Vasic had been bound to come. Perhaps it was better now, while Tresilian's child still remained hidden within her womb. Safe, where none would think to seek – not yet, while she did not show. The sickness was passing, just as Wynne had predicted. Poor Wynne. Gone, as was Tresilian. Vasic had to be brought to account. She shivered. The water in the tub had cooled as she was lost in thought.

Alwenna stood up and stepped out of the tub. Still shivering, she dried herself quickly and threw on the shift a silent servant girl had left ready. Alwenna huddled beneath the bedcovers until the girl had cleared away the bathtub. As soon as the door closed behind the servant, Alwenna hurried across the chamber to lock the door, only to discover she had no key. She opened the door and called after the girl.

"Where is the key to this door? There should be one."

The girl looked round, startled, then shook her head. "I don't know, my lady. I haven't seen one. Will that be all, my lady?"

"Yes, that's all." The girl wasn't one of the previous staff at Highkell. She seemed to be hard-working, but went about her duties with little joy. Vasic would have surrounded himself with people who were beholden to him, so Alwenna was disinclined to trust any of the servants. As she closed the door once more, she realised that line of thought raised interesting questions about the steward, Hames, who'd been a minor clerk during Tresilian's reign. Had he been Vasic's man all that time?

Before Alwenna climbed back into her bed she tied the door latch down with a belt, and slid a chair against it for good measure. She went over to snuff the candle that stood on the wooden kist next to the door, and noticed the wall-hanging above it: a small hunting scene she'd worked herself. How many hours had she spent bent over that? Tresilian's father had still been alive then and had pronounced it an accomplished piece. She ran a hand over the stitching, her fingertips tracing the irregularities where she'd unpicked a detail so often that the canvas had stretched, or finished a figure clumsily. How long since she'd completed it? Two years, or three? It might as well have been a lifetime ago.

She returned to the warmth of her covers, hoping she was too tired to be disturbed by the clamouring voices that had been Gwydion's gift, but here in her old chamber she could no more stop the past crowding about her than she could give up breathing.

CHAPTER FORTY-ONE

Alwenna didn't hear Vasic enter the room, so absorbed was she in the scene she was stitching. The design was taken from a painting in the great hall: a colourful array of beasts frolicked among the trees around the edge of the scene, while in the centre would be a group of hunters, hawks on their wrists and wolfhounds trotting at their heels. Vanishing into the forest were several deer, while clouds moved across a darkening sky. She'd originally planned a daylight scene, but as she worked she'd altered things so the hunters were riding home at nightfall, tired by their endeavours.

She was seated by the window with her back to the door to catch the best of the daylight, which was in short supply. Mist cloaked the forests and hills about Highkell and rain fell from an unremittingly grey sky. Soon she would have to stop working on the fine detail, as the light was fading.

Alwenna lifted her head as she heard a hushed exhalation, then hands were clamped over her eyes, pulling her head back as a voice whispered in her ear.

"Guess who?"

"Ow, that hurts. Let go." She tugged at the hands and

by chance rather than by design her needle stabbed into the joker's flesh.

One hand was snatched away and its owner swore. She twisted round, to find Vasic standing there.

"It was only a joke, there was no need for that." He glared at her.

She shrugged. "It wasn't funny."

"I heard you turned Tresilian down again."

"What business is it of yours if I did?"

"Dear cousin, I have a lively interest in your matrimonial plans. And we're long overdue a heart-to-heart about such things. You and I could make a fair fist of the job, you know."

"That would be funnier if it wasn't so ridiculous." She returned to her needlework. The needle was stained with Vasic's blood.

"Don't turn your back on me when I'm talking to you."

"If you don't like it then don't sneak up behind me when you want to talk to me."

"Tresilian's too soft with you by far." He wound his hand in her hair, then tugged her head back, tracing her throat with the fingertips of his free hand. "Since you don't want him, maybe you'll find me more to your taste."

"Have you gone mad? No." She jabbed at him with her elbow.

"By the Goddess, it's time you learned some manners, Alwenna." He tugged her head further back and with his other hand he began worrying at the lacing of her kirtle, a workaday gown she was wearing so she could dress without assistance. "First I'll show you why ladies of your station should wear back-lacing garments."

"No, get off–"

Vasic covered her mouth with his own, smothering her shouts. His breath was sharp with wine. Alwenna twisted away from him and her chair toppled, crashing them both on the floor with a splintering of wood. She tried to scramble away from Vasic but he threw his weight on top of her, dragging at her skirts.

She screamed out then. "No, stop!"

Footsteps hastened across the antechamber outside her small workroom and the door burst open.

Wynne's voice thundered across the room, echoing from the vaulted ceiling. "Stop that at once!" Vasic was dragged bodily off her, the hand entangled in her hair yanking at her scalp, making her yelp. Alwenna clambered away backwards as Wynne dumped Vasic on the ground at her feet. "You will leave now, young man. Your father will hear of this."

Fists clenched, Vasic sprang to his feet and advanced towards Wynne. "This is none of your business, you old hag. Get out of here now, and I won't mention your insubordination."

Wynne snorted. Other footsteps came running along the great hall and a moment later Tresilian appeared in the doorway.

"What's happened here?" His eyes moved from Alwenna standing at bay against the far wall, Wynne with the broken chair at her feet, and Vasic lowering his fists.

Tresilian advanced on Vasic. "You still haven't learned to take no for an answer, have you?"

Vasic squared up to him. "She's made it clear enough she doesn't want you. It's time you let someone else have the field."

Tresilian glanced at Alwenna. "Has he hurt you?"

"No, not really." She managed to keep her voice steady. "I'm fine."

"Not really?" Tresilian turned to Vasic. "What does she mean by that?"

Vasic shrugged. "Likely means she was enjoying it."

Tresilian snapped and swung a wild punch at Vasic, connecting with his jaw so hard his teeth clacked together. Vasic retaliated and in a moment they'd wrestled one another to the floor in a tangle of flailing fists.

Wynne skirted round the room to Alwenna. "Come with me, child. We'll leave them to it."

"But Wynne, shouldn't we stop them?" Alwenna stepped aside as the two combatants rolled in her direction.

"No, not this time. This is long overdue." She wrapped one arm about Alwenna's shoulders, ushering her away from the scene. Two men-at-arms hovered in the doorway, uncertainly.

Wynne spoke to the elder one. "See no lasting damage is done – step in if it looks likely."

"Aye, I can manage that." The bearded man-at-arms winked at her.

Wynne patted the man on the shoulder. "Just see it doesn't go too far."

The last Alwenna saw of the scene as Wynne led her away was Tresilian on top of Vasic, pounding his bloodied face.

"It's all my fault again, isn't it? If I'd just accepted Tresilian none of this would have happened."

"Don't think like that, my lamb. Those two have been after an excuse to go for each other's throats for years. If it hadn't been you it would have been over some servant girl, or an argument about handling hawks, or a hundred other things each more silly than the last."

"If I agreed, do you think this hostility between them would be at an end?"

"Frankly, no. Vasic's small minded, Tresilian's an idealist; they'd clash no matter what. Your uncle insists on throwing them together. He thinks they'll work through it that way. There was a time I thought he was right but now I'm not so sure. The grudge runs too deep." She opened the door to Alwenna's chamber. "But never mind their foolishness, did he hurt you in any way? You said not, but was that the truth?"

Alwenna fingered her lip. "It was the truth. I think he may have cut my lip, but it's nothing."

Wynne examined her mouth. "So I see. I know it irks you to hear this, but you should keep a servant at hand, always."

"Yes, Wynne. I admit you are right." She sat down by the fire, chilled by the realisation this wasn't the end of her problems, but only the very beginning.

Alwenna sought out Tresilian later that evening, at the high table. He sported a cut lip, while one eye was swollen shut. Vasic was nowhere in sight.

"Alwenna, I didn't think you'd join us this evening. Sit next to me." He moved along the bench to make room for her. She sat gracefully where he'd indicated and he leaned over to speak so no one would overhear. "You are none the worse for this afternoon's incident, I hope?"

"None the worse, cousin. I seem to have fared better than you."

Tresilian's grin was rather more lopsided than usual. "This is nothing. You should see Vasic." He took another mouthful of wine. Alwenna guessed he'd had several already.

She drew back a little. "Do you think you ought to make light of it like that?"

"Make light of it? I don't." He pushed back a tress of hair that had fallen over her shoulder. "I was never so angry before. Vasic's been asking for a beating for a long time, and I'm pleased to have been the one to deliver it. I hope he remembers it whenever he dares so much as look at you."

"Ho, Tresilian!" Stanton called to him from further down the table. There was another one who thought too highly of his own charms, although the ladies at court didn't seem to mind. "A toast to your health."

Tresilian grinned and raised his goblet. Alwenna felt a frisson of unease: Vasic would remember the scene in that chamber, she was certain of it. Every time he looked at her he'd remember it, and resent Tresilian – heir to the throne – all the more for it.

Alwenna shivered. She picked up her goblet, hoping the wine would warm her. As she raised it to her lips she glanced down the table past Tresilian to where a man-at-arms sat, watching her with a grim expression on his face. The wine stung the cut on her lip and she lowered the goblet, splashing wine onto the table and over her hand in her haste. She dabbed at it with a 'kerchief, and looked along the table once more. The soldier's eyes turned hastily from her to the tankard he nursed in his hands.

"What are you up to, Alwenna? Spilling good wine? For shame." Tresilian topped up her goblet, grinning.

"Who's the man-at-arms sitting beyond Stanton and his friends?"

Tresilian looked along the table, puzzled. "Oh, you mean Weaver? He's a fine fellow, come to us from The

Marches. He's as handy in a brawl as you could ever hope
to find. A widower, lost his wife a couple of years ago."

"That's sad." No wonder he looked so dour.

"I should introduce you." Tresilian turned, but the
soldier had already left the table and was making his way
to the door. "I'm sparring with him tomorrow morning –
you should come and watch."

"I might." She'd seen enough violence for one day.

"He gets tongue-tied when he's in company." He leaned
to murmur in her ear. "Especially with beautiful ladies
such as yourself."

She felt an odd thrill at Tresilian's words and for the
first time wondered if her reasons for resisting marriage to
him were all imagined. Embarrassed by her own thoughts
and feelings, she turned away and found Weaver watching
them. He'd paused on his way out of the room, hand on
the door. He inclined his head politely and turned as flames
sprang up around him, devouring the wooden door and
flaring up to hide him from sight in a matter of seconds.
The roar of the fire blotted out all other sounds. The heat
grew so fierce she was forced back and she had to turn and
flee, leaving everything she knew behind her.

Alwenna woke, drenched in sweat, her heart pounding,
her mouth parched. She was out of bed and halfway across
the chamber to the door before she realised she'd been
dreaming. There were no flames here, only fading embers
safe in the hearth. And there had been no flames then, on
that long-ago day.

CHAPTER FORTY-TWO

Vasic summoned Alwenna to his throne room at noon. As at their previous meeting his retainers were banished to the far end of the room, while her maidservant also waited there. As before, Vasic's eyes never left her as she walked the length of the room. With her hair dressed in formal style and wearing a richly embroidered gown, today she was dressed for her part, every inch a queen.

"Good day to you, cousin Vasic." She ignored the etiquette that required she remain silent until the king had spoken. She would miss no opportunity to remind him she rejected his claim to Tresilian's throne.

Vasic's eyes narrowed, but he ignored the slight. "Lady Alwenna. I trust you slept well?"

She hadn't, not after waking from the vision. "Tolerably, I thank you."

Vasic raised a sceptical eyebrow. "You have had time to reflect on my offer. I hope you have seen the wisdom of accepting. My generosity is not boundless."

"I recall your generosity of old, cousin. It was never offered without the hope of gain for yourself."

"Madam, do not try my patience. I am king of this realm now. I do you a great honour offering marriage –

you are, after all, used goods."

"The condition of the goods is immaterial, is it not, cousin? As king you might take those goods and use them in any way you wish. It is my lineage you need to secure your throne – and that is every bit as important for you as it was for Tresilian. Perhaps more so, since your claim is in opposition to my own as his widow."

Vasic smiled, that tight smile she knew of old. "As you rightly say I could take from you whatever I needed, but I am not so brutish a creature. You have chosen to disregard me and treat me as something lesser, but let me prove to you now that I am capable of refinement and delicacy in matters that warrant it."

He was working up to some new outrage, Alwenna could tell.

"You spoke yesterday, madam, of your concern for loyal servants of your husband who are my prisoners here. Consent to the match and when it is publicly announced all but two prisoners will be granted amnesty and released."

"All but two, cousin?" She was careful to control her reaction to his words.

"All but two. There are some seventy prisoners in my dungeons. I shall release sixty-eight of them, as my wedding gift to you. Think of it, Alwenna: sixty-eight souls, redeemed through your actions." Vasic was far too pleased with himself.

She forced herself to remain calm. "And what of the two, cousin?"

"One will be released after our marriage is consummated; the other must face trial for treason. You may choose which."

She drew a steadying breath. "That is a strange kind of justice, cousin."

Vasic's smile widened. "My dear, you would be wise not to pit your wits against me. I have the upper hand this time."

"And which two do you wish to single out for such treatment?" As if she didn't know the answer already.

"My dear cousin, need you ask?" His lips curled with glee. "Father Garrad attaches the blame firmly to you for bewitching these poor fellows, yet these commoners have presumed to look too high above their own station. Their crimes are too base, too self-serving – I cannot let them go unpunished. But even now I am prepared to be generous. One must be made an example of – there is no smoke without fire and there has been altogether too much smoke resulting from your time at Vorrahan, has there not?" He paused to enjoy his little joke. Alwenna's stony silence seemed to amuse him even more. "Once I have taken you as wife, one of these men will be granted a pardon, while the other must face charges. And you may choose which, my sweet: the novice monk known as Brother Drew, or the deserter Ranald Weaver."

"Your generosity is almost boundless, cousin. How am I even to know these loyal servants still live? If there are seventy prisoners you must let me see them and count them for myself."

"Alwenna." His voice dropped an octave, dangerous, caressing. "Would you question my integrity? Is my word not enough?"

"If I must weigh so many lives against my own happiness, I would look upon their faces first."

"I see no necessity. They are an ugly, unwashed bunch. They would offend all your senses, as well as being riddled with vermin and pestilence."

"Then let them wash and send healers among them, cousin. You cannot purchase my fidelity with the freedom of dead men."

"My sweet, you use such ugly terms. I am simply offering you a way to help your people escape the consequences of their actions."

"Let me see them, let me count them. If they are my people, I cannot make such a decision until I have walked among them."

"You may look and you may count, but I shall not permit you to walk among them."

"You will if you want my agreement." Alwenna shrugged. "When can you arrange it?"

Vasic studied her face. "Very well. An hour after noon."

"Then with your permission I shall withdraw until that time." She didn't trust Vasic to keep his word, but if she could buy the freedom of so many, how could she resist further? As for Weaver and Drew, how could she make such a choice?

"You have my most gracious permission, madam cousin."

Alwenna stalked from the room, skirts rustling in her wake.

CHAPTER FORTY-THREE

Alwenna descended the stairs to the dungeons behind Vasic. Two men-at-arms preceded them, carrying torches. A guard unlocked the dungeon door and pulled it open. A fetid odour of damp earth, unwashed bodies and worse lifted from the chamber.

Vasic raised a scented handkerchief to his nose. "You are determined, madam, are you not?"

Alwenna steeled herself and nodded.

"Very well." Vasic reached imperiously for her hand. After a moment's hesitation she set her fingers over his. He signalled the torch-bearers to enter the room before them, then led Alwenna after them. They moved between the prisoners, who stirred uneasily, squinting in the unaccustomed torchlight. At first she feared she would retch from the vile air that filled her nose and mouth, but her senses adapted and she was able to ignore it. As she walked through the suffering and the filth she was grateful her boots would be easy enough to scrub clean. She doubted whether her memory would be so fortunate. Some faces were familiar: men-at-arms who had served her husband and his father before him. Decent men, many of them with wives and families to support. She could secure their freedom, simply by agreeing to lie with the man who led her about the room now, watching her face for any emotion she might reveal. Her conscience would only allow her to do one thing. She attempted to count the number of prisoners in the room. Vasic's figure seemed to be accurate.

"You spoke of two others?" Her voice rang out, oddly strained in the eerie silence of the dungeon.

Vasic's lips curled in a predatory smile. He nodded to the guard who led the way to the far corner. The torchlight fell upon a familiar face, recognisable despite the cuts and bruises: Weaver. The pain of recognition was so intense she dared not let her gaze linger, but in that moment Weaver met her eyes. With a movement so slight she could not be certain he had moved at all, he shook his head. If he had opened his mouth and uttered the words aloud his meaning could not have been clearer: Don't do it. Somehow he must have learned of Vasic's ultimatum. Beside him Drew huddled, his gangling limbs tucked against his chest as he stared at the floor, one eye swollen shut.

Alwenna turned away, fighting to contain her anger. She would not give Vasic the reaction he sought.

"Have you looked your fill, my lady? I would not wish to curtail your pleasure." Vasic had changed little from the boy who used to pull the wings off butterflies.

"It is no pleasure to see honest men punished for their loyalty." One day soon she would wipe that self-satisfied smile from his face. "I shall not forget what I have seen here."

"I would not have it any other way, my lady." Vasic pressed a proprietorial hand over the small of her back.

Behind her she heard the clink of chains from the corner. She dared not look back.

Controlling the urge to twist free, she allowed Vasic to guide her to the door. More than anything she regretted being unable to pause and look back to that dark corner.

Vasic followed Alwenna up the stairs and put a halt to her precipitate flight as they entered the great hall. "I have done as you asked, my lady. Give me your answer now."

Alwenna pictured herself flailing her fists against him, scratching, biting, anything to wipe that smug smile off his face. And as he waited for her answer she saw a hint of doubt creep over his expression. He may have manipulated her into a corner, but she still had power over him, however limited. She might yet turn that to her advantage.

"You will free all the prisoners who are held for loyalty to Tresilian? All sixty-eight of them, and any others held on those grounds alone?"

"With the exception of the two who stand accused of intimacy with you."

"Those charges are false. Free them, too, and you will have my agreement."

Vasic shook his head. "Those were not my original terms. Accept those or nothing at all. Further, if you cannot agree to my generous offer today, then tomorrow one prisoner will be removed from the dungeon and executed. And the same will happen every day until you do consent."

He met Alwenna's gaze, unabashed. It occurred to her for the first time that he was, quite simply, without any kind of conscience. People meant nothing to him. Their lives were as insignificant as stray insects on the floor: there only to be crushed underfoot if he willed it. She hadn't been able to save Wynne, but she could save those sixty-eight lives.

She suppressed a shudder. "You have my agreement to your terms, cousin – make the announcement."

She left him there in the great hall and hurried up the newel stairs to her chambers. Once there she ordered hot water and washed from head to toe. But she couldn't be certain whether she was washing away the filth of the dungeon, or the taint of Vasic's hand upon her.

CHAPTER FORTY-FOUR

From the eastern window of her chamber Alwenna watched as the prisoners straggled across the courtyard in twos and threes. They made their way out beneath the gatehouse where families or other loved ones waited. She counted every one, and sure enough there were sixty-eight. Vasic had kept his word. She ought to have felt some kind of elation at this moment, but instead she felt empty. Worse than the knowledge she'd sold her own body to secure these people's freedom was the dread that Vasic would somehow go back on his word. All she could do right now was hope they put a great distance between themselves and Highkell before Vasic changed his mind.

Her head ached. She turned away from the light of the window and crossed the room, pausing in front of the hunting scene she'd crafted before her marriage to Tresilian. The dark sky and the alignment of the stars had come from her imagination, or so she'd once thought. She was drawn to set her hand on that dark sky, her mouth bitter with the taste that heralded the sight. She had nothing to gain by trying to fight it now; yield to it and she might sleep easier. She spread her fingers over the fabric and opened her mind.

The darkness was deeper and more complete than she'd ever known before. It closed in about her, held her pinned in a death grip. She couldn't breathe. The pain in her lungs was unbearable. She cried out but her throat made no sound. She screamed but there was no one to hear. This had to be what it was to be mad.

Then there was a sound: a scrape, a thud, muffled and far away. A slithering and scuffling, and then a sudden intrusion of fresh air cutting through the reek of damp stone and loose mortar, cutting through her madness. And light, burning her eyes, stinging them to tears. And a voice. A voice she knew. The words… she had no idea what they had been. That voice was all that mattered. Then there was more light tearing into her and she had to press her eyes closed against the dazzle of it. Tears escaped between her eyelids as the alien sounds resolved into something meaningful: the scrape and clunk as fallen stone was cleared away. And the voice again. A hand on her shoulder. Weaver.

"You came back." Her voice. It was hoarse and strange to her ears, but the madness fled. "You came back for me."

A hand brushed her face.

The maid's voice intruded. "My lady? Are you hurt, my lady?" The girl shook Alwenna's shoulder, nervously, as if she expected to be told off. Alwenna was crumpled on the floor beneath the wall hanging. She pushed herself up to a sitting position.

"I… I must have fainted."

"Let me bring you some wine, my lady."

Alwenna was about to stop the girl, tell her it wasn't necessary. But she was shaking from the horror of what she had experienced. What did it mean? She didn't recognise the scene. Had her mind played with the memory of Gwydion's cave? She'd fallen to the floor then – there had been the slick stone, the damp smell. Gwydion had spoken of seeing into the realms of the future and told her not to fear the darkness. As for Weaver, he was a prisoner in Vasic's dungeon and going nowhere.

Perhaps she'd simply fainted after all.

CHAPTER FORTY-FIVE

The clunk of the dungeon door opening woke Weaver. Two guards unlocked his and Drew's leg shackles, hauling the youth to his feet when he was slow to respond to the order to stand. Curtis was on duty at the door. He gave them a sympathetic glance as they passed, but nothing more. Weaver knew what to expect even before they were led along the dark corridor to the vaulted torture chamber.

When Weaver recovered consciousness he was tied to the rack, arms dragged above his head with damp ropes biting into wrists and ankles. One eye was swollen shut from the beating he'd been given. Above him was the vaulted ceiling, serrated with teeth of lime leaching from the damp stone. He couldn't turn his head far enough to see who else was in the room, but he recognised Vasic's voice.

"Are you simple, boy? Admit the truth of Garrad's accusations and all this will stop. You know you want to."

Drew's reply was little more than a whimper. "It's untrue. I... she... did nothing wrong."

Footsteps crossed the chamber, then returned. A faint sound disturbed the silence, and with it a singeing smell, then an unearthly screech.

"Are you sure? Let's try that again, shall we?" Vasic's voice was sweet reason itself.

"Let the lad be." Weaver's ribs spasmed with pain as he spoke up. "He never so much as looked at her. It was me."

"Don't listen to him," Drew gasped. "He's only trying to protect me."

"Each determined to protect the other? So noble. The Lady Alwenna will indeed be touched when I tell her." Leisurely footsteps crossed the chamber, then Vasic leaned over Weaver, smiling. "Who am I to believe? It matters little to me, as long as your presence here guarantees her compliance." His grinning face loomed closer to Weaver. "But her taste for low company surprises me. Which of you does she prefer, I wonder? The hardened warrior, or the eager young boy? She preferred the eager boy when she was younger – she married that one. And look where that got her."

Vasic moved out of Weaver's line of sight. For a moment he dared hope Vasic was tiring of his game. "You must tell me, Weaver: which of you does she favour?" Searing heat tore into Weaver's side and the stink of his own singeing flesh rose up around him. He couldn't contain the grunt of pain as the branding iron was released.

"My, my, hardened soldier indeed. Let's see how loud the young boy squeals this time." Vasic's footsteps moved away.

"No, let him be." Weaver's ribs spasmed with every inward breath. "I... I have her trust."

"Indeed. And how did you earn that, soldier?"

Weaver flinched, but no fresh pain was visited on him. "Tresilian ordered me to take her to Vorrahan. She turned to me for comfort once." It was no great stretch of the truth. She'd needed comfort but all he'd been able to think of was losing himself inside her. That was why he'd run away with his tail between his legs and got stinking drunk in the brewhouse. Drew shouldn't have to pay the price for Weaver's guilt.

"As I suspected." There was a clatter as the iron was thrown to the floor. "Do you have his words?"

An unknown voice replied. "Yes, your highness." A quill scraped on parchment.

"Can you write, soldier?"

"Yes."

"Then you may sign your confession. Untie him."

The ropes bit even harder into his limbs as guards fought to release the knots which had tightened as the rope began to dry. Weaver pushed himself upright. The movement set fresh spasms through his ribs and he couldn't take hold of the quill until they'd eased. The words on the parchment danced before his eyes, but they were the words he'd spoken. He wrote his name in an unsteady hand. Goddess forgive him.

CHAPTER FORTY-SIX

Alwenna was pacing restlessly about her bedchamber when, after a peremptory knock from outside, the door swung open before the servant girl could answer it. Vasic stood there, a smile of satisfaction curling his lips. Not a winning smile, but cold and calculating. He gestured to the servant girl. "You, wait outside."

The girl hurried from the room without a backward glance, her head lowered.

Vasic pushed the door shut then paused, surveying Alwenna. "I have news for you, my dear. I think it will be welcome news for you, since you will be spared a difficult decision after our marriage."

He could only mean Weaver and Drew. Alwenna was too late to rein in her reaction.

"I thought that might capture your attention. Your affection for the two commoners would be touching in other circumstances." His voice was unctuous.

"Speak plainly, cousin. What is this news?"

"You are so blunt, my dear. As a lady of refinement you might study for a less abrupt manner. Especially when addressing your future husband."

Damn Vasic. She was in no mood to play his games.

"You are in such a playful mood today, cousin, I can only assume your news pleases you greatly."

"Indeed it does. You remain as astute as ever." He smiled, and crossed the room to the table by the window. "You may see if you wish." He set down a sheet of parchment on the table top. "This is the soldier's signed confession, so you need not choose which prisoner to face charges, after all."

"But... we didn't..." She leaned over to see more clearly. Vasic kept one hand on the sheet of parchment. With his other hand he toyed with a tress of her hair that had fallen forward as she read the brief confession. He brushed the strand back over her shoulder and slid his fingertips onto the nape of her neck. She flinched away from his touch, unable to tear her eyes from the document he held. Weaver's signature was unevenly written, but legible. Each ill-formed letter spoke of his pain. She didn't need the sudden rush of sight as she pressed a fingertip to the ink to know what he'd endured.

"He will face charges of treason. His confession means he will be found guilty, of course, but not before the due process of the law is observed. You will find I am scrupulously careful about such matters."

Alwenna tried to remain impassive as she stepped away from Vasic's reach. "And the young novice?"

"He will be released, as per our agreement."

"Now you have a confession he should be released straight away." Alwenna tried to keep her voice level.

"No, my dear." Vasic spoke as if to a slow child. "He will be released after our wedding night. Those were the terms of our agreement. I was most particular to make them clear to you."

"But if he is not guilty you cannot hold him any longer."

He smiled. "My dear, it has never been a question of their guilt, but of your compliance." He raised a hand to caress her face and she pulled her head away.

His smile turned to a scowl. "That is an unflattering habit you have developed of late, my sweet. If I were a lesser man I might be offended by your lack of consideration for my finer feelings."

"Finer feelings? You have such things? I find that hard to believe when you seem entirely taken up with your own gratification." She regretted the words as soon as they had left her mouth.

Vasic's scowl deepened. "Cousin, I thought you had grown past this tiresome stage. Must I remind you of the respect due to me as your king and future husband?" He rolled up the parchment and stowed it away inside his doublet.

Alwenna bit back her instinctive retort. She needed to think through the implications of Weaver's confession for this charade. A professional soldier expected certain risks in the course of his career; a novice monk, well, that was different. Drew had chosen a very different path. If he'd not turned from it to help her he would not now be in this predicament and she owed it to him to mitigate the damage he suffered as a consequence. The confession had taken the choice out of her hands, although it was probably the choice she'd have made. Except now Weaver faced execution.

Vasic was studying her, his head tilted slightly to one side. "My sweetness, you haven't yet thanked me for bringing you this news." Unctuous as olive oil, but not as wholesome.

"That was remiss of me. It must have slipped my mind."

"Then thank me now. You may kiss the royal hand." He extended his hand to her, the hand bearing his signet ring.

She wanted to defy him; he dared her to do just that. She took his hand in hers and curtseyed low, pressing her lips to his fingers for the briefest of moments. As she straightened up again Vasic caught hold of her hand and drew her towards him.

She resisted. For a moment they faced one another.

Vasic shook his head. "Cousin, you will do what I require of you with good grace, or suffer the consequences along with your erstwhile playthings. Is my meaning clear?"

"Never more so, cousin." But when he leaned closer she couldn't help twisting away. Vasic caught hold of the front of her dress and shoved her back against the edge of the bed. She toppled backwards and he half-fell, half-clambered on top of her, pressing his mouth over hers, probing with his tongue, bruising her lips against her own teeth. She clawed at his face and he pulled back, cursing. Beside the bed stood a heavy candlestick and she made a desperate lunge for it, grabbed it and smashed it against the side of his head.

He slumped over onto the bed and she shoved his dead weight away so she could scramble clear, then she gathered up her skirts and ran, dropping the candlestick as she tugged the door open. She was halfway down the flight of newel stairs before Vasic bellowed for his guards. The soldiers on duty in the great hall gaped as she passed, before they realised the import of their master's shouts and gave chase. Alwenna's luck ran out when she reached the foot of the tower, as two burly guards stepped forward to block her path. She realised her mistake in abandoning her weapon as she dodged one, but the other tackled her to the ground, and she was bound and returned to the great hall. Vasic sat in state there, clutching a cloth to a bleeding gash above one ear while a healer fussed over him.

Vasic glared at Alwenna. "You have gone too far this time." He turned his eyes to the guard. "Lock her up, it's time she learned some respect."

The guard hesitated. "In her rooms, sire?"

"No, you fool. Put her in the cell off the guardroom. Let her have a taste of what her life will be like if she disobeys me again."

CHAPTER FORTY-SEVEN

The dungeon door clattered open, startling Weaver into wakefulness.

Curtis hurried over to unlock first Weaver's shackles, then Drew's. "We've no time to waste. Vasic's in a rage – you need to get out now."

Weaver scrambled to his feet and stretched to work some life into his limbs, sending a fresh spasm of pain through his ribs. "What's happened?"

"You'll be needing this." Curtis handed him a sword and belt that Weaver recognised as his own. Drew took a moment longer to get to his feet as he searched through the straw for something. But he rose lithely enough, fumbling with his voluminous sleeves, and accepted the dagger and belt that Curtis handed him.

Weaver buckled on his belt, wincing as pain shot through his ribs. "Tell us, Curtis. What are we getting into?"

"The Lady Alwenna tried to escape – she's been locked in the guardroom cell."

"She – how? Is she hurt?" Weaver tried to gather his scrambled wits.

"I don't know. We've no time to waste."

Curtis hurried away and was halfway up the broad staircase before Weaver and Drew caught up. Curtis signalled to them to wait as he sauntered up to the two guards stationed at the head of the stairs.

"All's quiet down there. I've got the dice with me, if you think your luck's better than yesterday."

The taller of the two guards glowered at him but the shorter man laughed. Weaver recognised neither; they must have come to Highkell in Vasic's army. Curtis fumbled in his scrip, ostensibly searching for his dice and moved round so the shorter of the two guards turned his back to the stairs.

Weaver was almost within arm's reach of the shorter guard when the taller one sensed movement and spun round, drawing his sword. The shorter man followed suit, sidestepping into Curtis who backed away towards the guardroom door. The tall guard tried to drive the prisoners back to the top of the stairs, but Weaver stood his ground. The pain in his ribs hampered him, but this would be his only chance to win free and he fought like a cornered rat, taking risks until he got inside the taller man's guard and smashed him in the face with the pommel of his sword. The tall man staggered. Weaver thrust his sword up beneath the guard's breastplate and he fell backwards. As Weaver withdrew his blade the shorter man lunged towards him, dagger in hand.

A blade flashed across from the stairwell, lodging in the guard's throat. With a dreadful gurgling he crashed against Weaver, and rolled to the ground, clawing at the knife and pulling it free, only to release a spurt of blood that sprayed across the flagstones, the wall, and his fallen companion. After a moment he lay still. Drew stepped forward to retrieve the blade, wiping it clean on the dead man's hose.

Weaver bent double, fighting the pain from his ribs. "You kept that skill quiet, lad."

Drew flashed a pained grin. "You didn't ask."

Curtis stripped the liveried tabards from the fallen guards, passing them to the others. "There'll be two more in the main guardroom."

They paused only to search the bodies, removing scrips full of coin, then turned their attention to the two guards outside the guardroom. These two were easily distracted by Curtis' gossip. Weaver garrotted one, while Drew slit the other's throat. Curtis grabbed the keys from the senior guard's belt and sorted through them, trying to find one to fit the locked cell.

"It's not here." Curtis tried the largest key, but it rattled uselessly in the lock. He cursed.

"Who's that?" Alwenna's voice was hoarse but unmistakable. A moment later her face appeared at the inspection grille. There was a fresh cut on her lip.

Weaver reached for her fingertips through the bars. Her hands were cold to the touch. "You are hurt…"

"Weaver! What's happening? Has he freed you?"

"We decided not to wait." He glanced at Curtis, who still rummaged through the keys. "Have you found that key yet?"

"I'm trying," Curtis grumbled. "I don't think it's here."

Alwenna's face fell. "The key to this door? Hames has it. He took it with him after he locked me in."

"Hames? Where is he now?"

Alwenna shook her head. "I don't know – with Vasic? He's his steward."

Curtis desperately tried the other keys. "It's no use. I

can't open it with these."

"Then we'll break it down." Weaver knew he was fooling himself – the door was new and solid. "Lever it off its hinges, there must be some way."

"It's set into the stonework, it won't open without the key. There's no time, Weaver." Curtis was sympathetic. "At any minute someone might come for the Lady Alwenna. Or you. We have to go."

"I won't leave her here."

Alwenna watched Weaver with a bittersweet expression on her face. "He's right, you must go. Get away. Then Vasic can't use you against me."

Drew was watching the courtyard from the doorway. "There's a merchant's wagon about to leave, with pack mules and outriders. We could slip in among them and walk straight out through the gate."

"I can't leave you here. Not with him."

"You must. While you still can." She released his fingertips and stepped back from the door. "Go. It'll be easier to handle Vasic, knowing you're beyond his reach."

Drew came over to add his urgings to the others. "Weaver, this is the best chance we'll have."

Weaver stepped away from the door, irresolute. The three of them couldn't storm Vasic's private chambers to find the key. He knew it. They were right. But to come so close to freeing her… "I'll come back for you. Just as soon as I can."

Drew was fumbling inside his sleeve. "My lady, you might have a use for this." He passed a small leather sheath between the narrow bars of the grille.

The throwing knife, Weaver realised. For the quiet son of a stonemason Drew was full of surprises.

Alwenna reached for it and took it from him, puzzled, her lips forming an "Oh" as she identified it.

"Hide it in your clothing. Once they know you have it they'll likely take it off you, but it might help you in a tight spot."

"Thank you." She tucked the blade inside her sleeve. "Now please, go, before you are discovered."

Weaver had to force himself to turn away. He had to put all thoughts of her out of his head and concentrate on the task at hand, or he'd put all three of them in danger.

Curtis had taken Drew's place at the door. "The merchant's setting off now. Are you ready, Weaver?"

"Aye." Weaver nodded. He followed Curtis and Drew out, aware that behind him Alwenna watched from the cell. He never once looked back.

CHAPTER FORTY-EIGHT

Weaver halted his horse at the summit of Vorland Pass, waiting for the others by the cairn that marked the boundary between Highground and The Marches. A few hundred yards below him a spring emerged from the ground between a jumble of boulders. It didn't look like much, but it was the source of the broad river that wound across the plain below them to join the sea at Ellisquay. On a clear day the city and its harbour could just be seen from here. But this was not such a day. The distance was lost in haze and cloud obscured all but the foothills of the Scarrow Mountains that rose across the plain. And between his vantage point and the plain was a steep descent over rough ground. Just looking at the so-called road ahead made the pain in his ribs worse. Right now the thought of drowning that pain in a barrel of ale was the only thing keeping him in the saddle.

Weaver couldn't shake off the uneasy sense everything would change beyond recall now he'd crossed that watershed. He told himself the further he travelled from the Lady Alwenna the better it would be for both of them. She would be married to Vasic and there'd be a new peace in the Peninsular Kingdoms, perhaps more lasting than the peace secured by her marriage to Tresilian. And she'd be as far beyond his reach as she'd ever been. He'd been a fool to imagine it could ever have been otherwise. He knew his place. And he knew better than to indulge in foolish daydreams about a woman. How many times would he have to be burned to remember it?

Drew brought his horse up alongside Weaver. "Can I ask you... Is this where it happened? The battle?"

What romantic ideas did the lad have about war? "Near enough. Why do you ask?"

"I heard about it from my father – and later from Brother Gwydion. On the second day you took on the eastern champion, Stian, single-handed?"

Champion. Goddess, the lad didn't think he was a hero, surely? "I volunteered to fight him."

"Everyone said he was twice your size, and had dark powers. And they called you the Peacemaker afterwards."

"You don't want to believe everything people tell you, lad. Especially not the likes of Gwydion. He was a crazy old man."

"He was right about many things, Weaver: about you, and about the Lady Alwenna. He knew she was coming to Vorrahan. He said she'd be the greatest seer the world has known since the time of Alidreth, but surrounded by non-believers."

Weaver snorted, sending a fresh spasm of pain through his side. "It doesn't take a seer to know their order has fallen out of favour."

"He – what he did that day to the Lady Alwenna – it was wrong. But he had no time left."

Now there was an understatement. "Better for all if the old man had died ten minutes sooner."

For a moment Weaver thought Drew was going to turn his horse away, but instead the lad had another go.

"Why pretend you don't care? When you fought Stian that day – you had some higher purpose, surely."

"No. I wasn't after peace. I didn't care about the outcome of the battle, or how many lives were in the balance. My only purpose was to wipe Stian from the face of the earth. And to cause him as much pain as possible in the process." Weaver paused. "As it was, he met his end far too quickly."

"They say–" The lad hesitated again. "They say you're a berserker. And you swore that day to wipe out every member of his family."

"You're the talkative one today. Do they also say how much I drank that day? It took me two days to sober up. There's no heroism in battle, lad."

"I– That wasn't what I meant. They said you fought like a man possessed."

"I fought like a man who didn't care if he lived or died. Stian very much wanted to live – on the day that gave me the advantage."

"They told me it was because–" Drew hesitated then rushed the final words. "Because of your wife. Stian slighted her."

"Who said that?"

"Gwydion."

There would have been gossip at the time. How else could the old man have known of it? "People talk." But could word really have spread as far as Vorrahan?

"He could divine the truth, whatever you say. And he began to teach me how. He would have taught the Lady Alwenna, too, if he'd been granted time. The Goddess claimed him too soon. But, Weaver, when you swore vengeance against Stian's family, on the blood of your enemy… Isn't the Lady Alwenna one of his kin?"

Curse the lad for his impudence. "Do you dare suggest I'd raise a hand against her?"

"No. But…" The lad grimaced. "Words of vengeance have a power all their own. Your enemies might one day use them against you."

"What's done is done. Leave the past where it belongs."

If the lad had a clever retort for that, Weaver was spared hearing it as Curtis rode up alongside them, his horse blowing heavily.

"Just my luck to get the broken-winded nag."

Weaver glanced at the horse. It was fit enough. "It's the horse who's out of luck. You've been eating too well in the usurper's kitchens."

Curtis flushed with anger. "You'd be in a sorry state now if I hadn't been."

What was that all about? "Don't think I'm not glad of it." Weaver had known him for years. They'd joke about Curtis' tendency to gain weight, and Weaver's failure with women, and they'd cover one another's backs in battle. That was how it worked. "We should swap horses anyway. Drew's half the weight of either of us."

Curtis laughed. "Aye, that's right enough." His moment of ill-humour had passed. Maybe he was regretting leaving behind softer living.

Weaver shrugged. If his memory served him correctly there was an inn at the foot of the pass. Goddess willing it was still there. He needed to get riotously, irredeemably drunk. And on the morrow if the worst of his problems was a hangover he'd count himself fortunate.

CHAPTER FORTY-NINE

Alwenna slumped on the floor in the least noxious corner of the cell. Someone must have been using the room as a urinal since her last sojourn there. Outside she heard various footsteps coming and going. Each time she tensed, expecting to hear the hue and cry raised against the escaped prisoners, but each time the footsteps moved away again. Weaver and the others must have been clear of the main gates by now. They had to be.

Finally someone entered the anteroom leading to the dungeons. There was an exclamation as, presumably, the new arrival spotted the fallen guards. A male voice swore, at length. Alwenna was diverted briefly trying to work out if the act he described was even physically possible. The prisoners had been gone at least an hour, probably more. And now, every profanity the man added to his litany meant Weaver and the others were several more paces clear of Highkell and any possible pursuit.

The relief left her almost euphoric. Almost.

The man peered through her cell door, belatedly ensuring she'd not fled with the others, then hurried away. She wondered idly if he would report the news himself, or perhaps find some unfortunate messenger to do the job for him.

Some time passed before other guards arrived, and while there was much discussion of the bodies strewn about the place they did nothing. They must have been waiting for their superior to inspect the scene. Sure enough, a few minutes later Hames arrived.

Alwenna waited quietly in her corner, knees tucked up, arms wrapped about them. It would not be long.

Sure enough, Hames barked orders at the other guards and they set about removing the bodies. Then the key grated in the lock and a moment later the door swung open. Having ascertained she offered no threat, he stepped inside and pushed the door shut behind him. He didn't advance any further into the room, but stood there looking down at her.

"Well, well. The high and mighty Lady Alwenna. Fallen from grace and all her friends gone off without her."

She made no reply.

"Cat got your tongue?" He took a step closer. "You'd do well not to ignore me. I am a man of influence now."

"Oh?" She glanced at him with indifference. As long as he kept his distance she'd have nothing to worry about.

"Have you nothing to say to that?"

"No, I don't think I have."

"Don't try to get clever with me."

"I'm trying to be polite. But I'll be honest – you make it difficult." She straightened up where she sat, gathering her legs beneath her so she might move quickly if she needed to. She folded her arms over her stomach. Drew's throwing knife was there inside her sleeve, the looped handle reassuringly solid beneath her fingertips.

Hames stepped closer, still remaining beyond arm's length. "What would you say if I told you Vasic's ordered me to teach you some manners?"

"These are strange times, certainly. But as strange as that?"

The steward glared from beneath pale lashes. Although greying, he still had the fair colouring typical of a southerner. He might well have been working on Vasic's account for years. She shrugged; it mattered little now. Every word wasted here saw Weaver and Drew a step further beyond Vasic's reach. That thought filled her with a strange elation.

"I'd say you're making it up. Vasic will have ordered you to do no such thing. Because you're a fool." She smiled, giving it just enough mockery, but hoping it wasn't too much. If he kicked her it would hurt.

Hames kept his distance. "Take care you don't regret this day's work, my lady." He didn't spit on the ground at her feet but he might as well have. "I'm an influential man now."

"I didn't believe you the first time you said that, why would I now? It seems to me you were in charge while two of Vasic's prisoners escaped."

He didn't rise to the bait; instead his fleshy lips curled in a smile. "And they left you behind. That can't be pleasant, not after everything you've done for them." He was enjoying this too much. But, if he liked to boast about how important he was – well, he would be privy to secrets she might find useful.

Alwenna shook her head. "All I ever did for them was get them imprisoned. I'm sure they're glad to be rid of me." That might be the truth, after all: hadn't Weaver been restless to be gone from her side ever since they had set off on their journey? As for Drew, he must surely have regretted the impulse to help her escape Vorrahan. No, they were well rid of her. Weaver had wanted to break down the cell door, sure enough, but that didn't mean anything. He'd sworn to protect her, hadn't he? And a man like Weaver lived by his word – without that he'd be lost.

"That's not what I heard, my lady. I heard you did a whole lot more for them. I heard…" He paused, grinning. "There are witnesses who have sworn to what they saw at Vorrahan on oath. They say you seduced the King's Man from his duty and turned the novice from his vows." Still he kept his distance. But he wanted this to be true, she could sense it.

"I wonder you dare enter this cell lest I corrupt you."

"I'm not scared of you, nor of any woman." The lascivious curl to his lips remained. "They say even two men couldn't satisfy you – but you'll find I'm a better man than either of those two."

The man's conceit really was astounding. He appeared to believe every word of it. "I doubt Vasic would be overly pleased. And he has a way of making his displeasure plain." The handle of Drew's knife remained within easy reach of her fingertips, but she wouldn't need it. Not this time.

"My lady, I already told you I have influence. I can smooth your way here at Highkell."

"How selfless."

"Treat with me and you will find me generosity itself."

"If Vasic were to hear what you have suggested, your situation here would become at best extremely uncomfortable."

"Would you threaten me? Let me remind you that you are the prisoner here. And everyone knows what you are. Do you imagine for one minute that Vasic would take your word over mine?"

Had the man's certainty slipped a fraction there? "I have known him a long time – longer than you, I suspect. He will take whoever's word suits his purpose. And as long as his purpose is to rule the Peninsular Kingdoms, he will have more need of me than of you." She rose cautiously to a standing position.

Hames backed away a half step. "Think on what I have said, my lady. The day may come when Vasic is no longer lord of Highkell."

"Would you take his place? Then you are bolder than I thought – I must take care not to misjudge you in future."

The preening fool straightened up at those words, sucking in his beer belly. He nodded graciously. "And I see you are as wise as your reputation would have it, my lady. We will have our day of reckoning, you and I." He stepped back to the door and opened it, keeping his eyes on her. Not so confident he would turn his back on her. Perhaps he was not such a fool after all.

She made no answer. The key grated in the lock of her door, then his footsteps retreated across the guardroom, and the outer door closed with a thud.

"Oh yes, Hames, we will have our day of reckoning." She couldn't believe a word the man said. Vasic had never been shy of doing his own bullying – he enjoyed it too much.

She returned to her corner and sat down again, resting her back against the wall and closing her eyes. The tiny life inside her stirred. Whatever she did next, it was not just her wellbeing depending on her choice: she had to make the right decision for Tresilian's child.

For a moment she'd forgotten: it was no longer just her needs to consider.

CHAPTER FIFTY

The first thing Weaver noticed as they entered the outskirts of Halesworth was the smell of scorched timbers. Looking about, he located the source. Beyond the houses ahead of them a plume of smoke curled upwards – not the smoke of a raging fire, but the sulky smoulder of doused flames making a last attempt to break from cooling ashes. The streets were quiet and the few people around hurried about their business. Some averted their eyes when they caught sight of the strangers, others stared with outright suspicion.

Curtis pushed his horse alongside Weaver's. "Friendly lot, ain't they?"

"Aye. Do we push on through?"

"We need to stop for provisions. We'll have to be careful." Curtis had never been one to go hungry if it could be avoided. "And Blaine was going to leave word if they found anyone hiring."

An old woman shuffling along in front of the houses stopped and glared at them. "We don't want your kind here – bugger off, before we set the dogs on you. You hear me, you filth?" She gestured wildly with her fist. "Don't pretend you can't hear me, you misbegotten sons of

236

whores. You're nowt but filth and wasters."

Weaver kicked his horse forward into a slow trot. Once they'd rounded the corner, the woman's cursing faded. Alongside him Drew clenched his reins with white knuckles.

"Times are bad. Pay her no heed, lad."

"She hated us. Really hated us."

"She's mad as a coot. That's how some old folk get when they've seen too much life."

"Gwydion didn't, and he saw countless other lives as well as his own."

"Maybe. But he never went hungry unless he chose to fast, and he never lost children or grandchildren to war. Grief like that can tear a person apart without leaving so much as a mark on the outside."

"It's left a mark on her for sure." Drew looked over at Weaver. "And... No, never mind." He studied the street ahead of them.

"If there's something on your mind, lad, spit it out."

"It was nothing."

Weaver suppressed a flash of annoyance. The boy was too damned deep sometimes.

CHAPTER FIFTY-ONE

Alwenna's guards came and went in silence for the most part. They were bearable enough, but Hames was a different matter. He would let himself into her cell daily – she kept track of the time passing by his visits. And he would talk to her. Or, rather, talk at her. Most of the time he didn't seek a response.

"He says he'll have you thrown from the curtain tower, his highness does." Hames grew bolder each day, yet despite his constant air of menace he hadn't so far attempted to touch her. She suspected he never would, for all his boasts. She was, in effect, his perfect woman: a captive audience.

"Does he, indeed?" The man was more annoying than a mosquito, but also, sadly, more problematic to crush.

"Onto the rocks at the edge of the gorge. A shame to smash open such a pretty skull. He plans to leave you there as a reminder to his subjects of what happens to those who disobey him."

"That sounds a pleasingly swift end, all considered. Why ever does he delay?" Hames was going to be no use to her. Any notion she'd had that he might help her cause had long since fled.

"It can only be a nostalgic fondness for your childhood together, do you not think, my lady?"

"I cannot imagine. Obviously you, enjoying his confidence as you do, must be privy to his innermost thoughts."

He actually smiled, the preening fool. He was oblivious to her sarcasm. He got all his satisfaction from taunting a prisoner who had no redress against him. Enough. How many days had it been now? Five, or six? She couldn't ignore his annoying buzzing any longer – she wanted done with him.

"There was a time I thought you ready to take his place – you admitted as much yourself. Has your appetite for danger weakened since then?"

"I never said any such thing. Do you hope to turn his highness against me with such lies?"

"How could I do that, imprisoned here? You have Vasic's ear, not I. I find myself at your mercy…" Would he rise to the bait? "If you were to think kindly enough of me to plead clemency from his highness, I would count myself fortunate. I have had much time to think of late."

Hames ran his eyes over her where she sat in her corner. She had his attention now.

"You would find me… not ungrateful." A tiny voice told her this was unwise, but she ignored it. She'd spent too long sitting in the dark with only that voice for company.

"I am a busy man – I have not time to exchange riddles with you. Speak plainly."

The smug bastard knew what she hinted at, but he wanted to hear her debase herself before him. Their reckoning inched closer. As did he.

"Would you not care for a token of my gratitude?"

She folded her hands in her lap in a submissive gesture. Mesmerised, Hames leaned forward. She smiled and he closed the distance between them, as if he could not help himself. She willed him to lean closer still, to reach out. He stooped down, extending his left hand to touch her.

It was the work of a moment to slip Drew's blade from her sleeve and plunge it into his neck. Hames' eyes widened with shock as she dragged the blade across his throat with all her strength. Warm blood gushed over her hands and with a terrible rattling breath he collapsed on top of her, limbs flailing. She shoved him away and his head hit the flagstone floor with a hollow thud of finality and his desperate movements stilled, leaving empty eyes staring upwards. A dark stain spread over the crotch of his woollen hose as his bladder voided.

"As if any woman in her right mind would have looked at you." Alwenna climbed to her knees and cleaned the blade on Hames' shirt, methodically transferring every smudge of his blood to the fabric.

She'd killed a man. Deliberately goaded him and, in cold blood, she'd sent a soul from this world. She drew in a deep breath and closed her eyes, quelling a sudden urge to laugh aloud. She ought to be revolted by what she had just done; instead she found herself exulting in it. What was it Weaver had said – something about death being the ultimate truth? She shivered. Goddess, now she understood him. She'd gone against every tenet by which she'd been raised, and broken the law of the land by taking a life without trial. And her only regret was it had been over too quickly.

She stood, and spat on the corpse. "You useless pile of meat."

The fool hadn't even locked the cell door behind himself. She stooped and loosened his belt, tugging the bunch of keys from it. She might not have much time. The guards would be used to him spending several minutes in her cell as his daily routine, but how long before one of them felt obliged to check? Perhaps, of course, they'd been warned not to interfere. In any event the anteroom was empty. She heaved Hames' carcass into the corner behind the door then stepped out of the cell and locked it. Peering back through the grille she could see only his boot protruding from the corner. She tossed the key down the garderobe off the antechamber. It amused her to think of them running around trying to find another key before they could release the dead man. A tiny voice told her she shouldn't find it as amusing as she did at that moment, but she shrugged it off as she stowed the short blade safely inside her sleeve. Now to find Vasic.

CHAPTER FIFTY-TWO

An odour reminiscent of boiled cabbage permeated the air in the taproom of the *Ferret*. The inn had gone sadly downhill since Weaver had last passed through Halesworth. Back then, anyone who was worth knowing drank at the *Ferret*. A man could find out who was hiring, who was a bad payer, who would honour a contract – that was how Weaver had stumbled into Tresilian's service in the first place. The shabby furniture didn't appear to have changed since those days, but the faces were unfamiliar. And most of those appeared world-weary and suspicious. At least the ale was cheap. That probably accounted for the number of people still frequenting the place.

As Drew and Curtis settled at a table near the door a tall figure detached from a knot of drinkers at the back of the room. Weaver's hand moved to his sword hilt before he recognised Blaine. The tall man ambled over to join them, grinning.

"We'd almost given you up. Finally outstayed your welcome at Highkell?" He slapped Weaver's shoulder in greeting as he sat down with them.

"Welcome got a bit too warm." Weaver sat on the bench opposite Blaine so he could see what was happening in the taproom. He straightened up to ease the biting pain over his ribs.

Blaine grimaced. "Like that, was it? The usurper'll have to find himself a new plaything."

"He has plenty of others to go at." They'd left him one in the cell off the guardroom. They could have tried harder to free her. Weaver picked up his tankard. The beer was lifeless, the sudsy head dissipating as fast as it had formed.

Curtis swore and pulled a face. "This beer tastes like piss."

"I wouldn't know," Blaine replied. "It does the job."

Curtis glared at Blaine. "You'd know if you'd sat through an eight-month siege. Call yourself a soldier?"

Blaine grinned. "Just now the only thing I call myself is out of work."

Weaver took a mouthful of his ale. Curtis was right, it tasted like nothing he wanted to drink. But it was cheap and wet, and now he'd paid for it he'd damned well drink it.

Curtis was glaring at Blaine, who was unbothered. Drew sat looking from one to the other, apparently uncertain what to make of Curtis' sudden flare of temper.

A draught swilled across their table as the taproom door opened.

Blaine glanced at the newcomer and his grin widened. "Lyall. Look who just got in."

Lyall frowned, until he caught sight of Weaver. He joined them at the table. "Well, I'll be damned. Curtis, you managed it? I'd buy you a drink if I had any money."

"Needn't bother here," Curtis grumbled. "Tastes bad enough to make a man give up."

"No luck finding work, then?" Weaver slid the ale jug over to Lyall, who shook his head.

"No one's hiring. Tresilian's army was billeted here until Highkell fell, and they moved on without settling their debts. Or so they say. Everyone here's out of food and out of charity."

"But they were sent to Brigholm." Weaver took an absent-minded mouthful of ale. "Did they never get that far?"

Lyall spread his hands wide. "That's what they're saying. This was always an army town, but they don't want us around now."

Blaine leaned over, speaking in a low voice. "I've heard there's some lordling hiring further east – they could have gone there."

Lyall made a dismissive gesture. "Doesn't matter where they've gone if they're not paying. Did nowt to help the rest of us who got stuck at Highkell."

Curtis interrupted. "The way I heard it they were never called back. Not by Tresilian."

"That's mad." Lyall drummed his fingers on the table. "He had two clear days before Vasic's army reached the gates – plenty of time to send word. You told me yourself, Weaver."

"True. But they'd have arrived too late to stop Vasic. Could still have caused some damage." Weaver shrugged. "Messages go astray. The usurper had scouting parties doing his dirty work in the west, he might have had more in the east."

Lyall scowled. "They left us high and dry. And as if that wasn't bad enough, they're not paying their dues. I'm not trailing east after them on the off-chance they'll honour what's already owed us."

Weaver recognised the weariness in Lyall's face.

"Sounds like you mean it."

"Aye. Reckon I do." Lyall drummed his fingers on the table again. "I'm getting too old for soldiering. And I've been too long from home."

Home? What was that? Weaver swallowed another mouthful of the dire ale. It didn't taste any better than the first had.

"See what I've had to put up with?" Blaine still grinned. "Tried to tell him it's deserting, but he won't have it."

"If Tresilian still held the throne it would be." Curtis set his empty tankard down on the table, wiping his mouth with the back of his hand.

"But he doesn't, does he?" Lyall shook his head. "His widow would have done right by us, but she's no better off than we are. She's bought us our freedom, and I'm not wasting it. I'm going home."

"We're not all as old as you." Curtis stood up, picked up the empty jug and headed for the bar to get a refill.

There was a dull ache behind Weaver's eyes. Home represented too many things he didn't want to think about. He downed the remaining contents of his tankard in one. It tasted bad, but it might still take the edge off if he swallowed enough of it.

"What about you, Weaver? You're a northerner, bred and born." Lyall watched him. "You still have a fancy to go back to farming? I have that patch of land to work."

"Not thought about it for a long time."

"Think about it now. The packhorse route through the mountains will be clear. No need to go near Highkell."

Weaver had never had any interest in working the family farm alongside his father. They'd both been a disappointment to one another as Weaver grew up. Their last contact had been several years ago when, in the first flush of delight, Weaver had sent news of his wedding. His father's reply had been a litany of self-pity: since his son hadn't chosen a northern girl he'd likely never see his own grandchildren – assuming Weaver survived his soldiering career long enough to make any. Weaver hadn't even bothered to tell him of his wife's death. He had no idea now if the man was still alive, or had joined his mother at last in the village graveyard.

Weaver set his tankard down, twisting it about. "I always swore I wouldn't go back without a scrip full of coin. And I've unfinished business here."

"What, with a barrel of bad eastern ale?" Lyall shook his head. "I've had my fill. I'm setting off in the morning."

"I'm a better soldier than a farmer. If there's a lord rallying opposition to the usurper I'll serve him."

Lyall shook his head again. "I'm telling you, it's a lost cause."

"Maybe. Maybe not." Weaver shrugged. He wasn't concerned about weighing the odds, not this time. This time it was personal.

CHAPTER FIFTY-THREE

Alwenna threw open the guardroom door. A startled guard spun round, a guilty expression on his face. The fingers of his left hand were still closed about a serving maid's arm. He relaxed for an instant as he saw it wasn't Hames about to tear a strip off him, then his eyes widened as he realised he was gaping at his erstwhile prisoner. His confusion was delicious.

"Close your mouth lad, or you'll catch flies." Alwenna smiled. "The pair of you should show deference to your betters."

The maidservant curtseyed to the ground, bowing her head. The guard gaped at Alwenna a moment longer before reaching for his sword. His hand moved slower and slower until it halted halfway to the scabbard. His eyes widened as he folded at the waist and bowed in a passable imitation of a courtier.

"You show commendable sense." The air was rank with his fear and she drew it into her nostrils as if it were the sweetest of rose scents. It was delicious, intoxicating. But they were a distraction. She had no business toying with some poor guard and his girl, not while her cousin went unchecked. She left them behind as she climbed the stairs leading up to the great hall.

The two soldiers at the entrance stepped forward, blocking her path to the door. She willed it otherwise and they seemed to melt back as she drew nearer, lowering their heads. One man reached forward and pushed open the door, bowing as she swept past him. This was her due, was it not?

Vasic was in the great hall, seated at the top table on the raised dais at the eastern end, presiding over a meal with some dignitaries or other. Vasic appeared to be unwell: his face had an unhealthy pallor while his eyes had a strangely sunken look to them. And his cheeks were gaunter than the day he'd cornered her in her bedchamber. Had he taken some infection from his injury? No, she could see the scar protruding from his hairline, red still but healing. More was the pity.

Vasic raised his head as he became aware of her approach. People ranged along the tables at either side twisted round to follow her progress, but none tried to interfere. She felt lightheaded, wanted to laugh out loud, to mock Vasic for a fool. Was that a shout behind her? No matter. Her business was with Vasic.

Her cousin's eyes widened, then he half rose from his seat, resting his hands on the table before him as if he needed the support. Alwenna saw his mouth moving, but his words failed to reach her. A pain rose up in her forehead, building and building until it resonated through her skull and blocked out everything around her. A haze danced before her eyes, obscuring everything around her until she had no idea where her foot would land when she placed it in front of her. She raised her hands in front of her eyes but couldn't see them, couldn't even feel them until she dug her nails into the flesh of her own face. Darkness enclosed her, blotting out every sound. She dropped into oblivion.

CHAPTER FIFTY-FOUR

The city of Brigholm sprawled across the floodplain. It had long since spread beyond the confines of the ancient walls, but the walls there had never been built for defence. They'd been built to ensure tolls were collected from travellers crossing the twin bridges to buy or sell at the market on the island in the middle of the river. Weaver had never planned to return to the place. Any fond memories he held of his years there had been wiped out by his wife's death. And now, the further east they travelled, the more he was haunted by thoughts of her. Sure, he'd avenged her and their unborn child's death, and the shame Stian had brought upon her. But his feelings for one of Stian's kinfolk had to be disloyal to her memory, however distant that kinship.

Weaver had half expected to see an army bearing Tresilian's standards camped on the plain, even though they'd passed no sign of them on the road. Somehow an entire army had disappeared like smoke on a breeze. Instead all they found were merchant encampments, and farmers who'd travelled some distance to sell their produce. Many of them seemed to be doing a lively – if illegal – trade without paying to cross to the island. All well and good until the city watch ventured out. The four travellers paid their modest dues and crossed the first bridge, setting up camp at the southern end of the island as was normal practice for the less wealthy.

The beer in Brigholm was at least better than in Halesworth. Just as well, since it was also a deal more expensive. Since entering the *Three Tuns* a few hours earlier they'd worked their way through a fair bit of the money taken from the fallen guards, but Weaver was no closer to taking the edge off anything but his tolerance for his companions' jokes. Maybe it was time to leave.

A bedraggled group of women had been eyeing them from a table in the corner. The youngest chose that moment to stroll over to their table and try her luck, smiling and pouting. One look at Weaver's expression was enough to make her turn her attention elsewhere. Her smile broadened when she got a good look at Drew: younger – and cleaner – flesh than she'd normally find at the *Three Tuns*. She pressed up beside the youth, all smiles and invitation, but he flushed deep scarlet and stammered something inaudible in reply.

Curtis cheered up. "What's your rate, love?"

The girl smiled and pouted some more as she told him an extortionate figure.

Curtis grinned. "Too rich for my blood."

She wiggled her curves again. Even Weaver couldn't deny she was pretty. "Well, sir, it's still early. I could give you a discount for a quick one."

"And you're lovely enough to tempt the very saints. But they likely have more money than me." Curtis made much of his disappointment. Weaver had seen the strategy work in the past, but even young as she was, this one wouldn't be fooled into handing it out for next to nothing.

Blaine watched with amusement. "How about the young lad here – let him dip his wick for free, first time round? He's good-looking enough, surely?"

The girl fluttered her eyelashes coyly at Drew. "We could come to some arrangement, I'm sure."

"No, no." There was more than a hint of panic about Drew now. "I wouldn't dream of offending you – I can't afford your full price."

Blaine laughed. "What say we all chip in for young Drew here?" He tossed a couple of coins on the table, and Curtis followed suit. The girl scooped up the coins and smiled enticingly at Drew.

The expression on Drew's face was one of abject horror. "No, really, it wouldn't be right."

She pouted and slid a hand beneath the table. "Come on. I'll be in trouble if I don't get custom soon."

Drew jumped to his feet, spilling his drink, and bolted for the door. Curtis and Blaine guffawed with laughter, and the girl withdrew, her face almost as scarlet beneath the powder as Drew's. She returned to her seat in the corner, favouring the three of them with murderous glares as she muttered to her two companions.

Weaver had finished his ale. Drew still hadn't returned, but there was little point staying in the tavern. If they were lucky their clothes might not yet be infested by whatever wildlife lurked in the straw covering the beaten-earth floor.

The barman wandered over to their table and picked up Drew's abandoned tankard. "Are you done with those? If I were you," he paused and sniffed for emphasis, "I'd be making my way for wherever it is you call home." He nodded his head towards the girl who was now deep in conversation with two middle-aged men. Every so often they glanced towards the table where Weaver and his companions sat.

"I've paid to enjoy my ale in peace," muttered Curtis. "The girl got money for nothing, what more does she want?"

"I don't want any trouble in here." The barman folded his arms, empty tankards dangling from one hand, waiting for their empties.

Weaver stood up. "We'll take our custom elsewhere." There was no point lingering in hopes of finding work: the place was dead.

"I'll drink this in my own sweet time," Curtis grumbled. "I paid good money for it and there's been a war on, if you haven't forgotten. Money's scarce." But he downed his drink and stood as Weaver had done. Blaine followed their lead wearily, but he didn't bother to argue.

Weaver led the way to the inn door, alert for trouble. The two men with the girl continued to fire hostile looks at them, but they didn't seem inclined to take it further – perhaps as a result of seeing just how well the three carried themselves now they weren't hunched over a table.

It was too easy. Weaver set a hand on his sword pommel as he reached for the door handle, nodding to the others. They filed out behind him in silence, pulling the door shut in their wake.

Weaver stepped out into the darkness and immediately to his right, the others peeled away to the left, alert for sounds of ambush. There were several figures leaning against the fence across the road, waiting. At least they hadn't been carrying crossbows. Weaver and Curtis strode off down the street, waiting to see who the men followed.

There was a moment's hesitation as they conferred, then they seemed to think better of it and crossed the road, returning to the inn. The door opened, lighting up the street for a moment, then darkness fell once more and the street lapsed back into silence.

Back at their camp Drew slouched by the fire. He prodded at the embers with a stick, twisting it until it began to smoulder.

Weaver sat down nearby. "Women, eh?"

Drew glared at him. "She should have taken the hint."

Weaver studied the lad. There was an intensity about his anger as he prodded the stick into the fire, out of all proportion to the difficulty he'd had at the inn. The teasing? It had been gentle enough. Had he had such a strict upbringing he couldn't face a woman, or even the thought of being with one?

The youth had been natural enough with the Lady Alwenna– And there she was again. Every time he thought he'd managed to put her from his mind she sneaked back in. Every damned time.

Weaver finally broke the silence. "She wasn't to my taste either."

Drew raised his head, about to ask something, then seemed to realise the answer. "Oh, I see. You mean you already have someone."

"Not so's you'd notice."

Some of the shadow lifted from Drew. "Don't worry, I'll tell no one. But you can't pull the wool over my eyes. Could see it when you arrived at Vorrahan."

There was no point denying it. "She's better off where she is."

"With Vasic? You don't believe that, do you?"

"I don't want to believe it. But she's highborn – spent all her life surrounded by servants. Living in a castle, plenty of food to eat, fine clothes to wear, courtiers to entertain her." He had to cling to that idea. She'd come to terms with her marriage to Vasic, probably long before Weaver would. "Can you see her living like this?"

Drew leaned closer to the fire. "I can." The words were a challenge. "I told you about when we left Vorrahan. She tried to steal a boat. All by herself. Sneaked out at night and dragged a rowing boat halfway down to the water before Garrad caught up with her."

If Weaver hadn't left her there... He should have kept himself in check, not run away at the first chance.

The shadow crossed Drew's face once more as if he'd read Weaver's thoughts. "That's when I knew I had to help her. I'd already decided to leave myself." He looked around before continuing, as if to make sure he wasn't being overheard. "That Brother Irwyn, in the kitchen – I don't know if you saw him?"

"I did." Weaver hadn't been told how Drew and Alwenna had escaped from Vorrahan, not in any detail. The youth had been circumspect about what he said in the dungeon, surrounded by potential spies. Now he seemed to need to tell the tale. Weaver had no objection to listening – not when it involved the Lady Alwenna – but Drew had fallen silent.

"Brother Irwyn?" Weaver prompted.

Once more Drew stirred the embers with the charred stick. "He was... not a kindly man. Nor pious. He tried– I had to get away."

Weaver nodded. He saw where the youth's story was leading.

Drew continued speaking. "I told you of two monks in the stable the night we left? That was Irwyn and Brother Francis, breaking their vows of abstinence. They must have knocked their candle over after we disturbed them. By the time we were crossing the sound the whole barn was on fire."

"And Garrad seized his chance to blame you both for setting it."

Drew nodded, his expression troubled. "I... was only glad to escape at last. And of course I was glad to help the Lady Alwenna escape. If I hadn't, Irwyn would have choked me for sure. She brained him with a rock – did I tell you that?"

"She what?" He must have misheard.

"She clobbered Irwyn on the head. With a rock. I didn't hit him hard enough the first time, and she saved me. No one else came after us because they were all busy dealing with the fire in the barn. If we hadn't crossed paths with a group of Vasic's soldiers..."

"You were travelling east by that time?"

"Yes. We stopped one night with my family. The Lady Alwenna charmed them all."

"I can imagine." Weaver knew how that worked.

"I'd do anything for her." Drew summoned a deep breath. "But not for the same reasons as you. They didn't know who she was, of course, but my father was much taken with the idea of me riding with a highborn lady. She let him think I'd been brave and chivalrous, and was off to become a proper squire. And so subtly, without uttering a word of a lie." He prodded at the fire again and the stick snapped. He threw it into the embers. "I doubt I'll ever see them again, but for once my father wasn't disappointed in me. He used to say the only place I was fit for was the precinct, because he couldn't beat me into becoming a real man."

And now Weaver understood Drew's reaction to the girl. The youth watched him warily, as if he expected a blow to be launched against him.

Weaver realised he was expected to say something. As if he was bothered where the lad chose to put it. "I see how it is, lad." To think he'd been jealous of any attention the youth had received from the Lady Alwenna. He'd bolted when he'd had his chance – or what he thought might have been his chance. Because of a promise made to a dead man. And now he was unlikely to see or speak to her again. And knowing he'd kept his word would do little enough to warm him at night.

CHAPTER FIFTY-FIVE

The surface beneath Alwenna yielded as she shifted her weight: a luxurious feather mattress – so comfortable. Yet every bone, every muscle ached. She sat up, stretching taut limbs. How had she come there? She'd been stripped to her shift by someone. And she was in her own bed at Highkell, enclosed by the familiar hangings. She racked her brain to remember what had happened, piecing together the fragments – courtiers shrinking back as she approached, the soldier and maid outside the guardroom, peering back through the grille to see Hames' boot poking out from the corner where he sprawled on the floor – and her nightmare resolved into full recollection. She'd collapsed at Vasic's feet before she could raise so much as a finger against him. How unutterably foolish. And how soon before she had to pay the price for her folly? She very much doubted being restored unharmed to her own chambers was any part of it.

Faint sounds warned her somebody was moving about the bedchamber. She flipped the curtain back, determined not to be caught unawares, only to see the startled face of a maid who was carrying a bundle of logs to the fireside.

"My lady." She bobbed her head, then set down the logs

with a clatter on the hearth. "Would you have water to bathe?"

The girl's full eyelashes, high cheekbones and fair hair were familiar. She'd seen those features recently. Ah, yes. Flirting with the guard.

The girl watched her cautiously. But not with fear – something more like speculation. Was she another of Vasic's spies? Or simply the closest to hand when Alwenna collapsed? Time would tell.

"Yes, thank you, I would have water to bathe."

"Very well, my lady." The girl turned and hurried for the door. As she reached for the latch, Alwenna spoke up.

"Do you have a name, girl?"

"Erin, my lady." The girl bobbed a hasty curtsey and reached for the door handle.

"I saw you outside the guardroom with that soldier." Last night – or had she slept longer? She mustn't reveal how little she knew. "Is he your sweetheart?"

"No, my lady." She spoke with quiet force, and the sharp jut of her chin as she raised her head in defiance suggested the words were spoken in truth.

"Very well. If he bothers you again, tell me. I would not have his sort near the private chambers." In truth Alwenna cared little what sort of vermin roamed loose about Vasic's keep, but she sought to know more about anyone who had access to her chamber – and to her person.

The girl gave her a careful look, her expression closed. "Yes, my lady." And then she slipped out of the door without more ado. The girl would tell her nothing: she would deal with any unwelcome advances in her own way, Alwenna was sure of that. And she didn't trust the mad woman lately returned from the cells. Not at all. Who could blame her?

CHAPTER FIFTY-SIX

Weaver had had enough of the inn. And Brigholm. They'd been chasing their own tails all day, trying to find a stranger they'd been told might still be hiring.

Curtis set down a full jug of ale, slopping some over onto the table as he clambered over the bench to sit down again. "Cheer up, Weaver, it might never happen."

Weaver took the jug from him and refilled his tankard. "Mind what you're doing. We've little enough to spend on ale without you spilling half of it."

Curtis laughed. "It's all going into your hollow legs. Try inhaling it instead of drinking it."

Weaver had forgotten how bloody infuriating the man could be. But he'd seen them right in Vasic's dungeon, he couldn't deny it. "And you never could hold your ale. Bugger off back to camp and leave the drinking to those who can."

"Mind your language, you'll shock the young 'un – he won't have heard the like."

Weaver was about to reply in more forthright terms when he realised Drew wasn't at the table. "Where is he, anyway?"

"Went out back a while ago. Probably spewing up your

precious beer. Hasn't the stomach for it." Curtis refilled his own tankard and was about to slide the jug over to Blaine but stopped when he saw the man had slumped over on the table.

"He hasn't drunk that much." The lad could nurse a tankard of ale longer than any Weaver had ever known.

"Trust you to keep an eye on him – always were a miser with the beer."

Weaver ignored him. The taproom wasn't so crowded now. After spending half the evening looking daggers at them, the whore from the night before had gone – probably found herself some custom. So, too, had the men who'd been whispering with her. Maybe they'd earned themselves a discount for their trouble. But a few of the other regulars who'd been lurking by the bar, muttering about the offcomers, had vanished, too.

Weaver set down his tankard, the contents untouched. "Something's not right," he muttered to Curtis. "Keep your eyes peeled. And wake Blaine."

Curtis snapped out of his merry mood at that. "Aye." He nudged Blaine, who mumbled in protest.

"I'm awake. What you wanna do that for?"

Weaver made his way out back, alert for any hint of trouble. The latrine backed onto the small beck, which ran shallow and noisy over its stony bed at this point. There was no sign of Drew there. Weaver paused to empty his bladder. If he could empty his mind half as easily he'd be a happy man. As he adjusted his clothing he became aware of some alien sound carried on the night air. He listened, cursing the lively flow of the stream behind the outhouse. Then he heard it again, clearly this time: shouting. Not the merry shouting of rambling drunks, but the angry shouting of a mob. He stepped back inside the bar room. The barkeeper's expression gave nothing away, but his manner was too studied. The man avoided Weaver's gaze, busying himself cleaning tankards. The disappearance of the whore and her menfolk along with Drew was too big a coincidence to ignore.

Curtis looked up, but the joke he had been about to voice died on his lips. "Trouble?"

"Aye, trouble." Weaver made for the door. Curtis nudged Blaine to his feet and he blearily stumbled after them, with a regretful look at the unfinished ale.

"Where are they?" Curtis asked as they dog-trotted down a dark street.

"Marketplace, from the sounds of it. You hear the crowd?"

"Aye."

Weaver should have heeded the bad atmosphere at the inn last night. He should have heeded his doubts. But no, he was hell-bent on drowning his sorrows. And even that he'd done badly, for his head was clearing rapidly.

"You think they've got the youth?" Curtis jogged alongside him.

"Seems likely."

"He might be under a hedge somewhere, sleeping it off."

"Could be."

Shambling behind them, Blaine coughed and spat. "Boy's prettier than the whore."

"I doubt they're offering him paid work." Weaver's head was crystal clear now.

Weaver halted at the end of the side street. A crowd of perhaps two dozen had gathered in the marketplace.

There was no sign of a night watchman – in Weaver's day this mob would have been broken up already. It was a merry gathering, out for some entertainment. A few of the rabble still carried tankards. The focus of their attention was slumped on the steps before the market pillar, unresisting. A couple of men stood over him, having clearly administered a beating. One of them stepped forward and delivered a rib-crunching kick to the figure, earning a pained grunt for his trouble.

"Step aside, or you'll answer to me!" Weaver barked in his best drillmaster's voice.

Both men turned, startled, and members of the crowd nearest drew back.

Someone among them jeered. "Think yer 'ard enough, offcomer? I've a handful of coin says yer not."

That was all the inducement Weaver needed. He'd walked away from needless fights many a time, but right here, right now, he'd welcome the release.

The crowd's laughter died as drew his sword from the scabbard and rolled his shoulders to loosen them. The two men nearest the figure on the ground drew back warily. The fallen man panted as he dragged himself up onto his knees. Weaver nodded to Curtis and Blaine, who went over to him and drew him to the base of the market pillar where at least his back was protected.

Weaver drew in his breath, filling his lungs. Goddess, he needed this. "Which of you inbred scum is going to be first?" A couple of the nearest men stepped away from him. Someone at the back of the crowd laughed. But not all were so hesitant. A big man emerged from the midst of the crowd, wielding a longsword. The onlookers fell back in haste.

"Big Mel will show him," someone shouted. Emboldened by this, the two who'd been beating up the youth also advanced, drawing business-like daggers with long blades. Weaver was aware Curtis and Blaine had stepped up to flank him. Old habits were taken up as easily as if it had been yesterday, despite several years having passed since these three last fought together.

Weaver grinned at the big man, a feral snarl with little humour. "What's the matter? Having second thoughts, you bastard? Or is it your night to go home and fuck your mother?"

With a bellow, the man charged at Weaver. There was no science behind his attack – he simply counted on his bulk to plough down his opponents.

Weaver sidestepped, deflecting the longsword and swinging round to slice open the man's leggings with his sword point, exposing a pair of flaccid buttocks. The man spun around and charged again, blundering about like an enraged bullock as his leggings slipped down around his knees. Weaver opened the man's throat before he could cause any damage, and he crashed to the floor. An uneasy murmur went through the crowd. The two ringleaders exchanged doubtful looks. Weaver made a covert hand signal to Curtis before springing forward at the taller man, on the left. A single arc of his sword severed the man's knife-hand at the wrist. The blade clattered to the ground as blood arced through the air. Before the injured man could stumble away, Weaver plunged his sword into the man's side. With a grunt the man's legs gave way and Weaver yanked his blade free, ready for more. Over to his right, Curtis grappled with the other assailant before punching his dagger straight into the man's heart through the gap around the armhole of his leather jerkin. To his left, Blaine kept a watchful eye on the crowd in case anyone still fancied their chances. There were one or two mutters of discontent.

Weaver pinpointed the speakers, but before he could do anything about it several metal-shod horses clattered into the marketplace. The riders spurred towards the crowd, who scattered in all directions.

Weaver, Curtis and Blaine stood their ground before the stone pillar. The soldiers were armed with spears. It didn't bode well, but Weaver was still in reckless mood.

"You there by the steps. Set down your weapons." The commander's voice was muffled by a full-face helmet.

"By whose order?" Weaver stooped and wiped his blade clean on the dead man's tunic as the others maintained defensive stances.

"By order of the commander of the city watch. And now I'll thank you to set down those blades, before more blood's spilled." The voice sounded familiar.

Weaver ran a mental stocktake of the members of the city watch he'd known back in the old days, but drew a blank. "I'm spilling no blood now. While your men are pointing those spears my way I'm disinclined to put up my sword."

The commander nudged his horse forward. "What's been going on here?"

"These men set on one of our party. Brigholm offers a strange sort of welcome to travellers these days."

"Aye." Curtis joined in. "It was a friendly town once over. Now a man can't have a quiet drink without being plagued by whores and their pimps."

The commander sat back in his saddle, studying Weaver.

After a moment he reached up a gloved hand and raised the visor of his helmet. "I know you: Ranald Weaver. Haven't seen you since… it must be Ardvarran. I fought alongside you in the bill line. Jaseph Rekhart, you must remember."

Of course. The once-skinny youth had filled out to match his height now, as best Weaver could tell by the poor light. "City watch? You've come up in the world, Rekhart. I should have known you from the damned tin can you're wearing." Weaver sheathed his sword.

Rekhart gestured to his men. "Stand down." He dismounted, striding over to shake Weaver's hand. "Well, Weaver. I'll be damned. Your arrogant ways haven't got you killed yet." He made a cursory inspection of the dead men on the ground. "Mel and his mates picked on the wrong one this time. Clear these vermin away," he ordered his men, then returned his attention to Weaver. "Last I heard, you were cosseting the royal whelp. Are you in town long? We have to catch up."

"That about sums it up. There's not much more to tell." Weaver introduced his travelling companions. "This here's Curtis, you'll likely remember him, and Blaine. And this here…" He gestured at the lean figure who sat hunched beneath his hooded robe on the market steps, one hand pressed to his stomach. The figure straightened up and pushed back his hood to reveal not Drew's cropped hair, but freemerchant braids and a stranger's lean face with an aquiline nose.

CHAPTER FIFTY-SEVEN

Alwenna pushed her tapestry frame aside and stood up, pacing over to the window. She had no appetite for the work. Rain drizzled down the glass, distorting her view of the outside world. Mist obscured the treetops on the ridge across the gorge. It had been raining for ever. The outer wall of her chamber was slick with condensation, beads of moisture oozing down the stone to darken the floorboards where they met the wall. They would rot away if these conditions continued. She poked at the end of one of the floorboards and it yielded beneath her fingernail. How long before she too rotted, trapped here in this room? She wasn't suffering in any physical way, but waiting to learn what Vasic's next move would be and hearing nothing, day after day, was wearing beyond belief.

Maybe he'd tired of his obsession with her at long last – perhaps even found someone more willing and more suited to be his queen. Long ago there'd been talk of the daughter of a well-to-do family in the Outer Isles...

A knock at the door heralded the arrival of the maidservant, bearing a tray with Alwenna's main meal for the day.

"My lady." The girl curtseyed. "Shall I set this on the table as usual?"

"Yes. Thank you, Erin." Alwenna wouldn't risk eating until the maid had gone. The sickness could still catch her unawares when she first tasted food after a few hours' fast. If Weaver had recognised her condition there was every likelihood a country girl would, too. Eventually the child would begin to show, but she would hide the truth as long as she was able.

The girl bobbed a sombre curtsey and moved over to the fire, stirring the embers into life and adding more logs. The girl attended to her duties in a methodical way, yet without any sense she was present in the moment at all. Alwenna turned her back to the window. She was hardly the liveliest of company herself, these days.

"Your accent isn't Highkell. Did you have to travel far to find work here?"

"No, ma'am. My da used to farm down south of the bridge."

That was the longest speech Alwenna had heard from her. For some reason she felt determined to persist today. Anything would be better than brooding over things she couldn't change. "Used to farm? Did Vasic's army destroy your crops?" She recalled the devastated farmstead she and Weaver had passed and realised how insensitive the question was.

"No, ma'am. My da was a tenant of Lord Stanton. When he died his uncle reclaimed the land for himself."

So much for trying to get to know the girl better. Her family had been evicted on account of the man Weaver had killed the night they'd fled the citadel. That was one secret she'd better not confide in the girl, for sure. "That's terrible. Could he do that legally?"

"My da said not, and he brought us all here to petition

the king. But the king says until peace has been established he can't hear our case in a proper court. He's taken the land and says he's holding it in trust until it's..." She cast about for the right word. "Resolved."

"Then I hope he resolves the matter to your satisfaction."

"He gave me an' Da work. Da's in the stables. Some of the horses used to be ours, but the taxman took them."

"Your father must have bred good horses."

"Oh, yes'm. Our horses were fastest over the half mile at the last three spring fairs." The girl lit up. "Our young stock got top prices at the autumn sales. Every year since, oh, forever."

"And you worked with them? It must be difficult for you working indoors here."

"Aye, m'lady. It's warm an' there's plenty to eat, an' I don't smell of horses or have to clean mud off my clothes all the time, but..." The girl seemed to decide she'd said too much and fell silent.

"You said Lord Stanton's uncle inherited his estate?" The courtier hadn't been married. One reason for his popularity with the ladies... and hadn't she herself once been just as taken in as the rest of them?

"Aye, m'lady. Lord Marwick. From down country."

Alwenna remembered him from court, an old man without wife or children. "Lord Stanton was to be his heir."

"Aye, m'lady. It didn't work out that way."

Indeed. "There are things that might be done to restore the land to your family. How long had your father held the farm?"

"Since his great grandfather's time. He came with Norris' vanguard from the east."

"Then you have a strong claim. I know those at court

who might help. Let me think, and I will give you the names of people most likely to support you. Things have changed at court since Vasic's arrival, and I cannot take up your claim myself, but there is much I might do."

"You would do that, m'lady?" The girl appeared doubtful, even suspicious. She was trying to find the catch. "Why, my lady?"

"Why?" It was a fair question. Why try to help a surly young servant, who had no conversation, no power and nothing to trade for the favour? "It's what I was raised to do, as queen. I was taught to have concern for the people, and to do what I might to mitigate any ills they suffered. If I may help in some small way to undo the damage caused by my cousin's obsession, then I shall."

"I see, m'lady." The girl looked at her as if she thought her entirely mad. "I... I must take your laundry to the green now, m'lady." She gathered up a bundle of linen and hurried to the door. "I swore I would never be beholden to anyone again after I came here." With a determined expression she turned and left the room.

"So that was, 'Thank you, my lady, but I don't need you to meddle in my affairs.' And now I'm talking to myself." There was nothing Alwenna could do here but sew pretty things and await Vasic's... what? Pleasure? Judgement?

She'd killed a man. In self-defence, she might argue, and she was sure if Vasic had known what Hames planned he'd have disposed of him ruthlessly. And far more slowly. She might have been wiser to confide her suspicions in Vasic. Instead, by dealing with Hames herself, she'd delivered herself straight into Vasic's hands: he now had a genuine charge of murder to lay at her door, as well as the false charges from Garrad. If Vasic was waiting for a suitable moment to make an example of her with a summary execution, he'd surely act soon.

The fact he'd returned her to her own rooms, and the fact he'd never questioned her – or had her questioned by others – about Hames' death had to signify something, but what? Did he know the truth? Or was he waiting for some message from her? That, now the possibility occurred to her, seemed most likely. Vasic had never wavered in his obsession over the years. Was he finally playing a waiting game – intending her to go to him as supplicant, to seek his forgiveness for her crime?

That made sense. If he'd continued to persecute her, to give her a reason for anger, she'd have resisted him every inch of the way. But if she went to Vasic to seek forgiveness, after brooding over her crime, the death caused by her own hand... Once she took that step towards submission, he'd as good as won. If she were shown only kindness and understanding, she had nothing to fight against. Wasn't that, in the end, how her opposition to the match with Tresilian had been worn down? And if the road ahead meant peace and prosperity for "her" people, could she, in conscience, resist and cause more grief for them?

Maybe he dared not kill her for fear of repercussions, while he feared her too much now to make her his wife and risk having her plunge a convenient knife into his body one night as he slept. Maybe he would leave her here for ever in silence. Waiting for some sign of clemency from him, or even some sign of anger. And if that sign never came, he could not have hit upon a more sure way to break her.

CHAPTER FIFTY-EIGHT

The freemerchant pushed himself to his feet, one hand clutched to his stomach. "My name is Marten. May the Hunter be my witness, I owe you gentlemen my sincerest thanks. But I fear you may have mistaken me for someone else."

Weaver took only a few seconds to decide the freemerchant had a great deal too much to say for himself.

"A thousand pardons, gentlemen. I, too, was drinking at the *Three Tuns* this evening – a victim of my own curiosity, I must confess. When I went out to the privy I was set upon by those worthy citizens." He gestured towards the corpses. "My curiosity has been assuaged, for I have learned the place deserves its reputation as a haunt of thieves and worse. One of them has my purse: green leather with a pewter clasp. When that is restored to me I can express my gratitude in some more meaningful fashion than this surfeit of words."

Weaver shrugged, paying the man's prattle no heed. Where the hell had Drew gone?

Rekhart set his men to search the bodies and drew Weaver off to one side, leaving the others to listen to the freemerchant who was still holding forth. "So, Weaver, what brings you east after all this time?"

"Same as ever, looking for work."

"Heard about Highkell. Bad business, that. But you got clear?" Rekhart made the question seem innocent enough.

"It's a long story. There were traitors at court."

Rekhart nodded. "That's what we heard. Bought by southern money, they say."

Weaver shrugged. "That's likely the way of it. You can count on wealthy men to rally to the largest purse."

"Spoken like a poor man."

"I wouldn't be needing work otherwise." Weaver hesitated. "Anything doing here? In the watch, maybe?"

"These are hard times for honest folk. I'd give you work at the drop of a hat, but there's a price on your head throughout Highground. If anyone started asking questions…"

"Aye. I thought as much."

"You'll need to be careful. They've got long memories round here, and they're still loyal to the old family." The younger man shuffled the helmet in his hands. "And to the Lady Alwenna. They say you–"

"There's not a word of truth in it."

Rekhart raised a hand in a conciliatory gesture. "I never thought there was. But once a rumour gets out… You know how it is. Your name will mean trouble round here."

"What are you saying? You're going to clap me in irons and send me back to the usurper?"

"No. We're still on the same side, you and I. But I must have been mistaken when I thought I recognised you – the light isn't that good in the square. While you're in town I can turn a blind eye for a few days. I wish I could do more."

Weaver nodded. "A word of advice, Rekhart."

The younger man stiffened.

"You want to see a healer about your eyes before they get any worse."

The younger man laughed. "The longer I've been in this job, the worse they get."

Weaver, Blaine and Curtis made their way back to camp. They fully expected to find Drew waiting there, but there was still no sign of him.

Blaine was unconcerned. "That lass must have given him a discount after all."

It was shortly before dawn when Weaver was woken by the sound of someone approaching their campsite through the trees. He reached for his dagger cautiously, easing it from the sheath. He could have sworn Rekhart would be as good as his word, but he wasn't taking anything for granted. He could hear only one set of footsteps, a little unsteady. Whoever it was stumbled over a tree root and muttered a curse. Drew's voice.

Weaver slid the knife back into its sheath. "You took your time, lad. Did you get lost?"

"No, not lost." He dropped down onto his blanket, yawning. "Sorry, I didn't mean to wake anyone." He pulled the blanket over himself.

"Good night, was it?"

Drew grinned. "Yes. It was." He rolled over and was snoring within a minute.

CHAPTER FIFTY-NINE

The servant knocked at Vasic's door. Vasic set down the hand mirror, stood up and crossed over to the window so he was standing with his back to the light. He'd never imagined his mother's vanity would stand him in such good stead.

"Enter."

The door pushed open and a timid servant stepped just inside. "The Lady Alwenna's maid is here, sire."

"Admit her, then leave us."

As ever, the maid entered the room with her head bowed. She moved silently, as if she wished to leave no trace of her presence in the keep. Vasic would not have chosen her as his agent, but in times such as these even royalty had to work with the tools fate handed to them. The girl halted several paces away from where he stood, hands clasped before her, eyes lowered.

"Well, what have you to report?"

"Nothing new, sire. The Lady Alwenna continues to work on a tapestry. She bathes daily. She... she would have me believe she can help me reclaim my father's farm."

Why did the girl hesitate then – was she holding something back? "Have you seen her using any strange amulets, talismans? Anything out of the ordinary?

Anything that could be a sign of witchcraft?"

"No, I have not, sire." The girl kept her eyes to the ground.

"And does she remain calm and even-tempered?"

"Yes, sire. Except…" The girl hesitated again.

This could be it. "Except what?"

"She is restless at night, sire. She talks in her sleep."

"What does she say?"

"I cannot make out the words, sire."

"You must try to do so. I want to know everything she says. Leave me now."

The servant girl hurried from the room as if she meant to be gone before he could change his mind. As if. Once had been enough with that one.

He returned to the table and lifted the mirror once more. It told him no lies. With dismaying honesty it reflected the dark hollows beneath his bloodshot eyes, the gaunt lines over his face, and the lankness of his hair which had developed an alarming tendency to fall away with the comb. The healer had found nothing wrong, and suggested blood-letting. Or that the water at Highkell did not agree with him.

Vasic set the mirror down sharply and picked up the letter from the high seer at Lynesreach.

"It is unfortunate the Lady Alwenna's guardians did not heed our advice when they established her as a child at Highkell. Had she been raised with us here – as we earnestly advised – Highkell might have continued to prosper. As it is, she is no longer of an age to be admitted to our order and we regret that we are unable to offer her sanctuary at this time, despite the generous provisions you are prepared to make."

No one could nurse a grudge like an old fool. And the seers clung to the remnants of their self-importance like ticks to a dog's muzzle. Doubtless if they waited long enough every single one of their jaded predictions would eventually come true, one way or the other. Meanwhile Vasic was acutely concerned about which came to pass in his own lifetime. A lifetime which at present he feared might be somewhat attenuated, if not abruptly curtailed. If he couldn't rid himself of the Lady Alwenna honourably, there were other ways. But they were last resorts. He'd had his fill of kinslaying. It was one thing in the aftermath of battle – a ruler was expected to make his mark in no uncertain terms. That was a lesson Tresilian might have done well to learn for himself, but his cousin had always lacked resolution – look how he'd havered over his marriage to Alwenna. And much good it had done him. And now Vasic found himself vacillating over her. He had no wish to rid himself of her at all. Quite the reverse. He should be bold and seize the moment.

If Alwenna were somehow behind the illness that plagued him, surely restoring her to her rightful position as queen would solve that particular problem. It had begun about the time he'd thrown her in the cells, after all

She knew how these things worked. She'd never been keen to take Tresilian as husband but she'd capitulated in the end. Wed her with honour and all due deference, bed her, get her breeding. What more could she ask? With her honour restored, her witchery against him would surely cease. In fact, now he'd reached his decision he felt much improved already. A wedding would be just the thing, unite the people – his aunt had always insisted there was nothing like a good wedding to make trade prosper. And he would ensure the only knives within his happy bride's reach were blunt ones. She'd come round to the idea. Let Garrad perform the ceremony – everyone would see the match had the blessing of the precinct.

Vasic took up his pen. If this plan failed she would have to go, but really, the more he thought about it, the more fitting it seemed. Of course she wouldn't yield to him without the blessing of wedlock – that was no more than her due as royalty. Yes, now he was on the right path.

CHAPTER SIXTY

Weaver was to meet the freemerchant in a small kopamid house in the ancient heart of the city. Many eyes followed his progress down the cobbled backstreet. He had no reason to suspect it was a trap, but it wasn't unusual for a stranger to these parts to become lost in the maze of narrow alleys and never be seen again – never missed, never recognised. Such was Brigholm. The rich lived up on the hill while the poor teemed among these alleys, working when they could, supplying the mine companies with what they needed but earning little in return. Small wonder the city was a source of discontent in difficult times. Vasic's armies hadn't ventured this far, but food supplies from the south had been disrupted and bread was costly for poor folk. And bread made peace like no other foodstuff. Full bellies were content ones.

Content or not, no one interfered with Weaver's progress through the labyrinthine streets. Heads turned when he entered the kopamid shop, but the freemerchant was already there, awaiting his arrival. A youth hovered in the doorway behind Weaver, having followed him most of the way. Perhaps an escort to vouch for his good character if the locals had taken exception to his presence.

Or a guide to intervene if he took a wrong turning. Either way, the freemerchant's eyes flicked towards the youth for a moment and there was the slightest of nods to acknowledge his errand had been discharged. If Weaver had nursed any preconceptions the nomadic freemerchant might be uneasy in the cramped confines of the city he had to revise them, for Marten appeared very much at home here.

"Greetings, Weaver. You found the place without difficulty?" He performed the traditional gesture of greeting, but it was perfunctory at best – he might as easily have been gesturing towards a seat in welcome. A freemerchant who could slip between the worlds of traveller and city dweller with consummate ease. A renegade, or a sign of changing times? Marten may be outward-looking but he had not gone so far as to break with centuries of freemerchant tradition and shake hands – such direct contact led to exchange of disease, the landless people maintained.

Weaver echoed the man's gesture. "Greetings, Marten." Weaver took his seat in the booth opposite the freemerchant.

Marten set about pouring spiced kopamid into the ornate globe-shaped vessels favoured in the region. Ritual required it be poured in the presence of the guests, and that the host should drink first. Not that Marchers had a tradition of poisoning their guests, but like many rituals this one had its origins in practical matters. Marten set down the pot and took up his cup.

"You are familiar with our eastern ways, then, Ranald Weaver?"

"I served here for several years." And would have made the place his family home, had they not been destroyed

by one of the foremost nobles in the region. Doubtless the
freemerchant knew all about that – he was not as artless
as he wished to appear.

"Then let us drink. To brisk trade." He held the vessel
beneath his nose for a moment, inhaling the aroma, then
swallowed a generous mouthful of the spiced kopamid
and set his cup down.

Weaver took up his own. "To brisk trade." Trade was
everything to the freemerchants. They were allowed no
other income. He inhaled the aromatic spices, blended
in the same way his wife had made it in the tiny room
they rented below the barracks. The wave of nostalgia the
smell inspired was so powerful it caught him off guard. He
gulped a mouthful of the hot liquid. Hot enough to bring
him back to the here and now. He replaced his cup on the
table.

"Your messenger said you might be able to put me onto
some work?"

"Indeed I might." Marten smiled, undoubtedly intended
to charm, but secretive as a snake under a blanket of
leaves. "Since our first meeting I've made a few enquiries
about you, Weaver. Our new king would pay well to see
you returned to his hospitality at Highkell."

A secretive and prudent snake. One to be given a wide
berth. But Weaver was hungry, with no prospect of work
in sight. He took another sip of the spiced kopamid. He
should never have come back, not this far east. He should
have gone north, back where he began, price on his
head or no. Back where there were no broken dreams to
torment him. "And did you learn much else from your
enquiries?" It wasn't too late, he could hang up his sword
and learn how to plough again.

"I learned much to confirm what you told me. And more about your deeds in battle than I doubt you would ever own. Farmer's son risen to King's Man, no less."

Weaver shrugged. "Common gossip may be common, doesn't mean it's true."

"Ah, yes, rumour is a fickle mistress. But for our landless people rumours are a commodity – what other stock can a man carry in such quantity that will never burden his mule, yet cannot be seen by would-be thieves?"

"Will your rumours put food in my belly?"

"In time they will. I heard you were loyal and true to the dead king. Am I right in thinking you would seek to displace the usurper who's taken his throne?"

"My loyalty's my business. I'll not discuss it with one who so easily fell foul of a bunch of drunkards. Secrets can be taken by anyone with a will to extract them. And then they'll hang a man faster than any rumour. It's true I was loyal to the old king. He's dead now and I'm King's Man no more."

Marten nodded. "There's a fine discussion to be had about the nature of truth and the nature of rumour – many a truth may prove to be, after all, a rumour substantiated. And armies have mobilised for belief in things no more substantial than rumours. But I see you are in no mood for philosophical debate. Your old cause may not be as dead as you think, if you've stomach to continue the fight."

"You think I'll fight for an ideal now? I'm ready to turn my hand to the plough. You've been listening to the wrong rumours."

"Is that so, Ranald Weaver? My sources have been reliable in the past. You were unstoppable at Vorland Pass, they tell me. And they told me you lived for battle."

"That was years ago. People change."

"This cannot be denied. My own kinsman tells me he saw you riding away from Highkell as Vasic's army approached from the lowlands. With a fine lady, no less. Now there's a fascinating tale. So much room for conjecture."

"What are you suggesting?" Weaver downed the last of the kopamid. He wanted a proper drink, one that would numb his senses and chase away the ghosts. If he didn't need more coin to buy it, he wouldn't be listening to this prattling fool now.

The freemerchant met Weaver's hostile gaze without embarrassment. "I suggest nothing, but people do talk. Your king is killed in the siege, yet you escape unharmed and his lady is committed to his cousin's control? This has not escaped notice."

"Then you accuse me of turning coat? I've killed men for suggesting less."

"Of course not, but people do talk. Along with the convenient matter of your escape from Highkell, the commander of the city watch here is your friend. There are some who believe you have already thrown in your lot with the new king." The freemerchant smiled.

"So they would have it I'm here to bring down any last traces of rebellion? Foolish beyond belief." Weaver pushed his cup into the middle of the table. "We've nothing more to discuss."

"If you would prove them wrong, there's opportunity here for you." For the first time Marten's expression suggested the conversation was not going his way.

"Opportunity to get myself hanged by talking treason? If the east were going to rise they should have done it when Highkell first fell, instead of bleating about taxes. I'll take my chance with peacetime."

Marten spread his hands wide in a theatrical gesture. "I've heard this peace will be short-lived."

"More rumours? Continue like this and you'll be even shorter-lived."

"Not rumours, Weaver. Reliable information. This opportunity will be to your advantage."

Farming had never looked so good. "I see no opportunity here. Unless you mean me to watch while you talk the new king to death." Weaver stood up.

"Would you leave the lady where she is?" It seemed the freemerchant would stoop to any means to recruit him.

"Don't drag her into this."

"She belongs with her own people, and they stand ready to welcome her into their hearts."

"Then you'll have no need of me. We're done here."

The freemerchant bowed. "Very well. If you change your mind, Weaver, ask for me here. They'll know how to get word to me."

Weaver turned on his heel, striding from the kopamid shop. He needed a drink – several drinks – to dull the ache in his head, and to drown the nagging doubt that accused him of once again failing the lady he'd sworn to protect.

CHAPTER SIXTY-ONE

When Vasic finally spoke to Alwenna he did it with a remarkable lack of fanfare. The door to her chamber opened and in he stepped. A guard waited until the maid hurried from the room, then the guard followed her out, closing the door.

Alwenna looked up from where she sat at her tapestry frame. Her cousin's face was even gaunter than when she'd last seen him. Had he been unwell? That would account for his absence. "Cousin. I thought you had done with me entirely."

Vasic crossed over to the window embrasure where Alwenna sat, stopping a couple of yards away, well beyond arm's reach. "And if I had, could you wonder at it?"

"Of course not." She set another stitch in the canvas, stabbing the needle through the taut fabric with a "pock" sound.

"And would it please you to know I have indeed considered setting you aside entirely?"

"I think it would be a wise choice on your part. But I have no wish to see out my days as your prisoner."

"'Prisoner' is a harsh word, dear cousin. I wish to keep you safe from harm."

"Indeed? Your loyal servant Hames suggested otherwise."

Vasic's fingers clenched then unclenched, a nervous gesture Alwenna remembered from childhood. "He proved to be unworthy of my trust. My judgement was perhaps wanting."

"Wanting in many ways, cousin." Alwenna stabbed the needle through the canvas again. A strange hunger filled her once more. She recognised an echo of the reckless fire that burned in her veins the day she'd killed Hames. But only an echo. She crushed it. Right now she would hear what Vasic had to say. She needed to know what he was thinking or, better yet, what he was planning.

He watched her now with something that might have been apprehension. A strange wariness had taken place of the acquisitive way he'd been wont to look at her.

Stab, into the fabric, pull the thread through. Why did he not speak? Stab, draw another stitch through. Stab. This silence was impossible. "I know how you killed Tresilian."

Vasic made a gesture of annoyance. "You disappoint me, Alwenna. You've lived here long enough to know you cannot believe idle gossip." He paced away from the window, arms folded.

"Idle gossip? I know the very words you whispered to him."

"That is nonsense." He raised one restless hand to cover his mouth.

"You tortured him. I know you did. He asked you to finish it and you bent down to whisper in his ear."

Vasic's eyes widened as he stared at her.

"You asked if it would be a kindness. And he said you hadn't the mettle."

Vasic's hand moved, then settled again over his mouth.

"Do you still care to tell me it's idle gossip, cousin? Can you deny you told him he'd always underestimated you as you pressed your knife against his ribs? Dare you deny it? You stabbed your own cousin – not just kingslayer, but kinslayer. Doubly damned by your own hand."

A tremor shook the fingers he still held over his mouth. He clenched then unclenched them. "How could you possibly…"

That echo grew louder. Alwenna's needlework was forgotten.

Vasic paced across the room to the table and turned to face her again. "I don't know who you've been speaking to, but it doesn't matter now. All that is in the past. It is with the future we must concern ourselves."

"I have little confidence it would be a long future, cousin. Or should I call you kinslayer now?" The scowl on his face told her she'd overstepped the mark. She should have curbed her tongue. The echo of that raw, wild hunger faded, leaving her strangely bereft, drained of the will to do anything at all.

Vasic took a couple of steps towards her. He'd come into the room all conciliatory, but now he was back to the familiar bluster. "Let me tell you how it will be, Alwenna. You and I will be married, in proper order. I'll have no one claim it was done in haste. The announcement will be made this very day and the wedding will take place on the next holy day. I have made my decision and it is for you to accept it."

She'd been foolish to hope he'd had second thoughts. "Vasic, I know you've long sought this marriage, but do you really believe you are getting a good bargain in me?"

His eyes narrowed, as if he suspected some new trick on her part. "We will unite south, east and west for good.

This will be a new age of prosperity for the Peninsular Kingdoms."

"There is another way." Once the idea took hold she could not shake it off. "You could still do all those things if I were to abdicate my authority to you. I could go into exile. I could leave the Peninsula and there would be no cause for unrest then. I could go to the Outer Isles – further, even."

"Come now – do you think me such a fool? You would be rallying supporters against me before you were out of sight of the citadel."

"I would not, I swear it. I would support your claim to the throne unequivocally." She had to make him understand. "I have no appetite for the business of royalty. Keep me here and I'll be a constant reminder of Tresilian. And people will seek to use me to influence you. Let me leave and the kingdom will truly be yours. It makes sense, Vasic."

"You would choose poverty over staying here at my side in your rightful place?"

Was he considering it? A little flattery couldn't hurt. "You would be too generous to leave me in poverty, cousin."

"No." He shook his head. "You will remain here, as my queen. I am decided. And all will be as it should be. You will have no cause to reproach me."

He turned and left the room.

Alwenna stabbed her needle into the canvas. She'd dared hope for a moment. She'd never be able to trust Vasic. She never had, even before he'd killed Tresilian. And how long before she went the same way? She wouldn't wait to find out. Vasic would get little joy of this marriage.

CHAPTER SIXTY-TWO

Weaver hunched before the campfire and pressed his hands to his temples, nursing another sore head. This would be his last hangover. Not because he'd sworn off drink, but because he had nothing left to buy drink with. Not even an old friend on the city watch had been able to use his influence to secure work for him. Times were hard in Brigholm. Times were hard everywhere.

Curtis was busying himself adding more wood to the campfire, every so often glancing towards Weaver.

Weaver recognised his expression of old: a man with something to say, but aware this wasn't the right moment. There never would be a right moment. "Well, spit it out, man."

Curtis turned his eyes away briefly. It was clear he didn't want the conflict. But Blaine had gone in search of something to put in the cooking pot and Drew was away in town, working, supposedly. There wouldn't be a better opportunity.

"You've got something to say, say it before the others get back."

Curtis shuffled his feet and dropped the bundle of wood by the fire. "We go a long way back. A long way. And it's not for me to question your choices, but... We need to decide what to do next. There's nothing to keep us here – there's no work going. Not the sort we're fit for, leastways."

"And you think I should drink myself into oblivion somewhere more congenial?"

"Eh? No, I never–"

"I get it. You think it, but you were never about to say it." Weaver picked up a small pebble from the ground, turning it between his fingers. He should never have come back to Brigholm at all. It brought the past too sharply into relief. His wife's and child's deaths, Stian, and, because of him, the Lady Alwenna. All of it was pressing in on him, demanding his attention when all he wanted was to forget the whole sorry lot.

Curtis cleared his throat. "What I was going to say is there's no point sticking around here. We've already taken that much firewood, we're like to outstay our welcome. I'm for pushing further east. The more distance we put between us and Highkell the better, I'd say. Now we've got prices on our heads and all."

Nobody made you break me out of prison, Weaver thought. And nobody even asked you to. "How much further east? The mining towns? There's not much else, but they won't be hiring fighters. And after that there are just mountains." He hadn't mentioned the freemerchant's promise of work. Now would be the time if he was going to. But he didn't trust Marten. In the past it hadn't stopped him taking money for a day's work, but... something didn't smell right. He realised Curtis was speaking.

"Y'know, the big port? What's it called – Ellisquay?" Curtis straightened up, with a hint of his old enthusiasm. "There's labouring work to be had on the dock, or ships

– and merchants hire protection for cargoes, overland as well as by sea. What better way to drop out of sight?"

Weaver considered. Curtis had a point. Attached to a trade caravan, cash-in-hand, staying nowhere too long – the idea had merit. They would disappear from Vasic's view, for certain. The image of the farm on the northern coast faded and died. The road he'd travelled had led him too far away from it after all. He couldn't hope to get much further from Highkell without getting on a boat. Trouble was he didn't really want to get away from Highkell. Not while Alwenna remained captive there. Common sense told him the longer he hung around there in Brigholm the less likely he ever was to move on. He should find himself an accessible woman and cure his fixation with the one he couldn't have.

He was distracted by the sound of someone whistling as they drew near to the campsite. Drew, sounding remarkably pleased with himself, came into sight between the trees. He carried a small bundle slung over one shoulder.

"Fancy some newly baked bread? And eggs? Fresh from the market this morning." He grinned. His hair flopped over his eyes, growing rapidly out of the severe novice's crop.

"From the market?" Curtis didn't need a second invitation, reaching up to unwrap the bundle.

"I came by some money," Drew said, still grinning. "Honestly," he added when he saw the doubtful look on Weaver's face.

"And there I was thinking you'd taken to robbing old ladies."

"I told you I'd found work. I've been running errands for a trader uptown. He says I can stay on."

The lad looked remarkably pleased with himself, still. Now he was up close Weaver could see heavy shadows beneath his eyes. Seemed he was working night shifts. He'd found himself rather more than a job, if Weaver knew anything about anything.

"Steady work?" Weaver asked.

Curtis had already set about cooking the eggs in the one pitted pan they'd gleaned in town.

"Oh, yes, steady. I've the chance of a room above the shop." Drew radiated happiness.

Weaver tilted his head sideways. "It's that way, is it? I'm glad for you." He hesitated. "We're talking about moving on. There's no work in sight for us here."

Drew's face fell slightly. "You've had no luck? That's a shame. I…" He rubbed one hand awkwardly on his leg, looking troubled. "I think I need to stay here. It's a good opportunity for me… If you don't mind?"

"Mind? It's your life, lad. Better we split up – we'll be less easily recognised if Vasic's men come searching for us."

"I hadn't thought of that. Do you think they will?" Drew looked anxious.

Weaver shook his head. "I doubt it. Not now. He'll have more urgent matters to bother him. We'd already served our purpose."

For a moment the youth looked downcast. "I don't want to seem ungrateful – I owe you so much, but I'm no fighter. And that's the work you're looking for, isn't it?"

"Aye. You'll be better off here. It's far enough from Highkell for you to rest easy, I'd say. And a big enough city for you not to stand out. But you don't owe me anything – you cleaned out one of Vasic's guards, remember?"

"That reminds me – something I heard in town

last night." Drew hesitated. "It's news you might find unwelcome, but… it's public knowledge, so you'll hear soon enough."

Weaver could guess what it was. He nodded. "Tell me, then."

"It's the Lady Alwenna. She's to marry Vasic on the next holy day. There are town criers proclaiming it throughout the Peninsula."

Weaver shrugged. "It was bound to happen."

"There was a lot of talk about an age of peace and prosperity for the people. I guessed you wouldn't like it, but… I thought you'd want to know. I hope I haven't done wrong?"

"No, lad." He'd done it out of consideration, after all. Not from malice. And yes, it was better to learn here, away from the public eye. Here, where none would press an advantage because of it. Weaver gave himself a mental shake. "How did the crowd react?"

"They didn't cheer." Drew considered. "Some muttered a bit, but I couldn't hear much of it. They seemed to think they'd be better treated once she was installed as true queen – that's his intention – queen rather than his consort. If Vasic dies without issue the crown will be hers."

"Is that so? Generous. I'll hazard he sleeps with guards by his bed from now on." Weaver grinned despite himself. "That was ever Tresilian's mistake: his advisors insisted she shouldn't be given equal status, even though her claim cemented his. He'd have had less trouble from The Marches if he had." Perhaps Vasic was not as foolish as he looked. He'd laced Tresilian's court with his own adherents readily enough, after all. And perhaps he'd treat the Lady Alwenna well enough. He could offer her all the comforts she was accustomed to. Maybe it would be a good thing for the kingdom. Maybe.

Of one thing he could never convince himself: that the Lady Alwenna would welcome the match. Whatever she claimed about duty there'd been times when she'd smiled for Tresilian and he'd felt he was intruding. She'd never smile on Weaver that way. Not now. The match could bring the people the political stability they sought and he ought to welcome it on those grounds. But he never would. His faint hope that he might somehow wrest her untouched from Highkell withered and died.

Blaine returned at that moment with a brace of rabbits which they hung ready for supper. And they set about their unexpected breakfast of fried eggs, slightly smoked-tasting from the green firewood they'd had to use. Weaver's hands shook as he juggled the food into his mouth – another situation that wouldn't improve any time soon.

They were lazing about the fire enjoying the luxury of full bellies when Drew sat up, startled.

"That's horses! Could it be Vasic's men after all?"

Weaver listened. "It's just one horse, and too slow. Make yourself scarce, lad. You've not been seen with us for a few days now, better keep it that way."

Drew grabbed his meagre bundle of clothes and ducked away beneath a low branch, pausing. "If you need to find me, the shop's on Soulard's Gate. The door's green–"

"That's plenty, lad. The less I know, the less anyone can find out from me. Goddess be with you."

Curtis muttered a farewell as he got to his feet. Blaine grunted something non-committal.

Drew nodded tightly and ducked away beneath the branch, vanishing into the cover of the trees. Weaver stood up, stretching knotted muscles as he buckled on his sword belt. He fumbled the strap into the buckle with unsteady hands. What he wouldn't give for a drink right now.

Curtis watched him. "Are we expecting trouble?"

"Could be he led someone straight to us," Blaine grunted.

"No, he's sound." Weaver rolled his shoulders. "Trouble wouldn't move that slowly."

The three of them spread across the small clearing, between whoever approached and their horses, which were tethered at the other side of the camp. All three held their hands over the pommels of their swords.

A large bay horse pushed into sight between the trees. Weaver recognised the tall figure astride it straight away. Curtis and Blaine glanced towards Weaver in question. He shook his head and moved his hand from the sword pommel.

The freemerchant halted his horse several paces away in the centre of the clearing and smiled. "My greetings, gentlemen. May the Hunter watch over your fires."

"And so may you be blessed, traveller."

Marten inclined his head in greeting and Weaver did likewise. Damn the man, what was he up to? The smile playing about his mouth was too smug by far.

"I bring you news, King's Man. May I dismount by your fire?"

"I'm King's Man no more, as I've already told you." But he quelled his instinctive reaction to tell him to ride on and take his damned news elsewhere. Rarely had he taken such a dislike to a man. He'd had many dealings with the freemerchants over the years. His own wife's freemerchant relations had all danced at their wedding, for Goddess's sake. But he kept his feelings in check. "You may dismount if you're still of a mind to."

The freemerchant smiled, and swung down from the saddle, fastening his reins back behind the stirrup leathers. He approached the fire, spreading his empty hands wide. "I come to you unarmed. You may trust me, Weaver, although I doubt you will."

"Then finally we agree on something. What makes you think I want to hear more of your news?"

Curtis set about boiling water.

The freemerchant crouched down by the fire, warming his hands. "Mornings can be cold this close to the mountains."

"Aye, they can. But I'd sooner you answered my question."

The freemerchant glanced pointedly towards Curtis and Blaine.

"You can talk freely in front of them."

"Very well." The freemerchant appeared unconcerned by Weaver's hostility, maintaining his easy smile. "They may find this news of interest, too. Put in simplest terms, Weaver, the king you swore allegiance to is not dead." He paused for effect, looking round his small audience. "Tresilian lives."

CHAPTER SIXTY-THREE

The freemerchant showed every appearance of believing his outrageous claim.

Weaver shook his head. "I've heard some tall tales in my time, but that must be the tallest."

"Sometimes the truth is the hardest thing to accept." The freemerchant studied him. "You are disinclined to believe me?"

"Vasic himself bragged to me of stabbing him."

"And Vasic, is, of course, renowned for his honesty and forthrightness." He spread his hands over the fire.

The kettle tilted where Curtis had set it in the embers. He reached over and adjusted it. "I carried his body out. He was dead."

"Ah, yes. And you pocketed a handy sum for putting his body in a freemerchant's wagon, despite the orders to throw him in the pit with the rest." The man smiled.

Curtis coughed and spat into the flames. "Could be."

"The same freemerchant who waited for you by the gates when you freed Weaver? And who told you where you would find cheap horses?" Marten clasped his fingers together, watching the three comrades with a benign expression.

Curtis nodded slowly. "Aye, the same."

Weaver shifted irritably. "This proves little, freemerchant. Only that you have reliable sources of information. And are meddling in affairs that are not your own."

Marten shrugged. "Perhaps. As I've said before, rumours are our stock in trade. And we pass on only what is accurate – our livelihood depends upon it. Tresilian lives. And he will be in need of loyal men in his army. Loyal men such as you three. Let me take you to him and then you will see for yourselves."

Weaver rubbed the back of his neck. "And how are we to know you wouldn't lead us into a trap?"

"If you will not trust me, trust what you know of your king. Hasn't he always treated the freemerchants with respect? He had a great deal of time for us, did he not?"

"The same could be said of any of his subjects."

"Your caution does you credit, Weaver. He would not have gullible fools in his new army, but I have nothing to lose by revealing my hand now. Tresilian would have me convince you to rejoin his cause. After all, you never left his service, did you?" The freemerchant studied Weaver's face.

It was said they, too, had the sight. Weaver turned his attention to the fire. Swearing allegiance to his former master's widow had been a continuation of his duty to his king. Nothing had changed. Nothing outward, anyway. He met the freemerchant's gaze again.

"Many saw him dead. I won't follow you on a fool's errand without proof."

The freemerchant sighed. "Of course. You may have tried to lose yourself in the ale barrel, but you haven't pissed away your common sense with the rest of it."

Weaver jumped to his feet. "Away and play your cat-and-mouse games elsewhere. You're under guest rights here at our fire, but next time we meet don't expect me to show you courtesy."

The freemerchant got leisurely to his feet, uncoiling long limbs with practised ease. "This is no game. This is about life, and death, and the places between. You and I serve the same king, Weaver, and we always have. The night you took the Lady Alwenna from Highkell, I was there. Who do you think Tresilian sent to cover your backs? Why do you think the men following you didn't run you down at the watergate? They went the same way Stanton did. And it was my blade that sent them on their way."

Weaver prowled around the fire, glaring at the freemerchant. Could he have learned this from anyone else? Or was it nothing more than a series of lucky guesses about events that night? "What blade would that be? Your people boast of never carrying them."

The freemerchant smiled again, mirthless this time. "Indeed. But I would be an imprudent man not to carry some means of defending myself, would I not?" With a theatrical gesture he shrugged, and spread his hands wide. This time his hands were not empty, but in each a throwing blade lay across the palm, held loosely in place by his thumbs. His attitude remained unthreatening.

"A nice trick." Weaver shrugged. "You are more the courtier than I guessed."

"But I have yet to convince you?" The freemerchant tucked the blades away inside his sleeves.

Weaver nodded. "Your sources may be every bit as accurate as you brag, but you have yet to convince me."

"Very well. The night Tresilian ordered you to take the

Lady Alwenna away? I was listening from the garderobe the whole time. You had thrown your cloak over the settle. When she entered the room her eyes fell upon it first, in disgust. She protested she had to take the servant Wynne with her on the journey. She and Tresilian whispered, so you could not hear. But I could. She asked if he'd told you everything, and he replied–"

"Enough!" All eyes were upon Weaver now.

"Tresilian handed her a bundle of homespun clothing. Drab, brown stuff, more suited to a merchant's wife than a monarch. But she wore it when–"

"I said enough."

"I too had the king's trust." The freemerchant smiled again. "My admiration of the lady was open, so he sent her with you, the man who hadn't looked at another woman since his wife died."

"What are you suggesting?" Weaver growled.

The freemerchant spread his hands wide again. "I suggest nothing. I seek only to convince you we serve the same king. He would have you rejoin him now. All of you."

Weaver exchanged looks with Curtis and Blaine. Each nodded, almost imperceptibly. Whether Tresilian lived or no, they all needed to eat.

"We'll put your rumours to the test, freemerchant. But only if the terms are good enough." And if the braggart was not telling the truth, Weaver promised himself, he would cut out his lying tongue using the freemerchant's own deceitful blades.

CHAPTER SIXTY-FOUR

From the window of her tower room Alwenna could see the washing green she and Weaver had crossed in the darkness, so many days ago. It seemed like an eternity since the blood-drenched night in the alley, when she hadn't known for sure whose side the taciturn Weaver was going to take. Today there were washerwomen at work, even though they had no hope of drying their laundry outside in this weather.

She could just make out the dark mouth of the culvert she and Weaver had escaped through. The water was running higher than it had been that night. She felt as though it had been raining forever, rather than a matter of weeks. It reminded her of the weeks following her arrival at Highkell. The rain had been unceasing then. Rainclouds had settled about the citadel, masking the summits either side of the gorge, and the rain had fallen and fallen. And she'd believed Highkell the most desolate place on earth. Now she knew the same sense of despair. Cheerless fog threaded between the trees and ridges of the hillside opposite and the water poured from the culvert over the waterfall in a steady rush that seemed to reverberate through the fabric of the building. She could hear it where she stood on the upper floor of the tower, sense it beating against the stonework of the curtain wall. She rested her hands for a moment on the stone sill: so much water, such power. If it had been like this the night she and Weaver had left it would surely have swept them off their feet and over the edge of the gorge.

And maybe, just maybe, that would have been better for all concerned. And she wouldn't be facing this farce of a wedding.

Goddess knew she'd done her best the first time round with Tresilian. What was it Weaver had said? They hadn't managed the business so ill. No, they hadn't. That didn't mean she wanted to go through it all again with Vasic. But there were still other people depending on her. The common folk. People whose lives had been torn apart because of what had been, in the end, little more than a childhood squabble. And she'd been the source of discontent. She could make amends. And so she would, although it gave her no joy.

She stared out through the rain. If she leaned to her right she could see the main gate where a merchant's caravan trudged in, pack ponies laden with barrels. Wine or ale for the common folk at the wedding feast, no doubt. Vasic would never drink anything hauled in so recently.

There was a knock at the door, and Vasic's new steward stepped over the threshold. He was tall, skinny and nervous, where Hames had been broad and bullish. "My lady, his highness is ready for you to join him." He bowed hastily.

She'd forgotten it was time to enact the daily farce of dining with her future husband. "Very well. We must not keep his highness waiting."

Vasic still looked gaunt and pale, but since declaring their wedding date he'd recovered some of his old bravado. He looked her over now with proprietorial approbation, a glass of red wine in his hand. He refused to use the old goblets, claiming they tainted the flavour.

Alwenna picked at her food, conscious of the need to keep her strength up and thankful that her sickness had passed. Vasic hadn't guessed her secret yet, but she didn't see how she could keep up the pretence much longer. She was aware of her own waistline thickening, and it would be visible to the perceptive observer soon enough, however much care she took to choose concealing garments. Not for the first time she regretted her decision to urge Weaver and the others to leave without her. Could several strong men not have broken down the door after all? Even without the keys? She pushed the thought away. Regrets served no purpose.

"You look melancholy, my dear."

I am not your dear, she thought. "I have spent so much time cooped up indoors of late. I miss riding out beyond the citadel walls."

Vasic snorted. "Is that so? You must grow accustomed to it, my lady. It is not safe for you to venture abroad at this time. There are bands of brigands roaming the countryside. Tresilian was lax when it came to matters of law and order."

"Indeed? When last I travelled abroad the only brigands I saw were doing your bidding, cousin."

Vasic swallowed the last of his wine and dabbed his lips with a clean handkerchief. "Do you think me so easily fooled, my dear? I know you are far from reconciled to this marriage." For a moment an expression of sadness crossed his face. "I will do my duty by you, nevertheless. You will be married with all honour, and accorded all the respect due to one of your exalted status. None will be able to criticise my treatment of you." He stood up, watching her closely for a reaction. "In fact everyone will be able to see how you have been accorded every courtesy. If after that you cannot accept our marriage, well…"

There was a knock at the door.

Vasic glanced round in annoyance. "What is it?" he snapped.

The door opened a fraction and a serving boy peered round the edge, bowing after a fashion. "Your highness, I'm to tell you your guest has arrived from the west."

"Very well. Have him escorted to the throne room. I shall speak to him there." The boy vanished, pulling the door shut. Vasic pushed himself slowly to his feet, clad in finery surpassing Alwenna's plain everyday gown. "I hope we will enjoy a long and fruitful association, dear cousin. But I would say it is very much down to your behaviour – accept the honour I accord you with good grace and do your duty." He smiled. "I am not so lost in admiration for you that I cannot see how you store up resentment. Abandon any idea of turning against me, dear cousin." He paused at the door. "Many's the fresh-faced bride who's been lost in childbed, after all."

Goddess, had he guessed her secret, or was this nothing more than his old habit of pulling wings off trapped butterflies? "Threats, cousin? You choose a strange way to win me over."

"Dear girl, we both know that day is long past. Do not misunderstand me: I would grieve deeply if I were to lose you now. But I must bear in mind the best interests of the state. Such is the lot of a king." He opened the door himself and stepped out through it, his lips curling in that self-satisfied smile she'd hated since childhood. It was a measure of Vasic's capacity to bear a grudge that none of the old childhood scores had been forgotten. And that, in itself, was proof he couldn't have guessed her secret yet. Learning she carried Tresilian's child would eclipse all of those.

Childhood memories chased her through her sleep that night, intermingled with visions. Some she recognised: the collapse of the road beneath her parents' carriage as they arrived at Highkell; the smell of wet earth as it thudded against the carriage, entombing her; the long-ago discussion beneath the cherry trees when Tresilian told her they were expected to marry; Vasic cornering her in the garderobe; her precipitate flight down the stairs; how good the air tasted as she paused to draw breath, rain misting her face and flattening her hair to her head. But the rest made no sense: the smell of dust and masonry settling about her, clogging her mouth, making her cough and her eyes stream; darkness, unremitting and chill; a voice in the darkness, soft, caressing; the sense she no longer knew who she was, but only that something mattered, something that lay beyond recall; the murmur of water against a lakeshore, driven by a light breeze that raised goosebumps; a blind need, desire, the rush of cold air against heated flesh; voices calling in the darkness; hands lifting her from her tomb into light too bright, too dazzling to bear; murmured reassurances, hands moving over cold flesh; lungs struggling to draw in air, burning with pain yet so cold, such need for warmth; more heat, desperate need, soft hands answering that need; a moist cloth pressed over mouth and nose, shutting off the air, shutting off everything–

Alwenna woke, gasping for breath. The dream had been too vivid, too real. She sat up, her whole body shaking and her heart pounding with panic as she drew in great gasps of air, relieved to find it filled her lungs. Her mouth was foul with the taste of the sight, just as it had been the night she witnessed Weaver's ambush.

Was he in trouble again?

But it hadn't been Weaver, she was certain. How she could be so sure, she didn't know, but it had been someone else. Someone she felt she should know, yet somehow alien to her. She shivered at the memory of the cloth pressing over her – well, someone's – face. There had been a strange smell, sharp yet cloying. Her mind was filled with the sense of it still, but she couldn't place it at all.

Within her that tiny life shifted and stirred, pressing momentarily against her bladder, the sensation reassuringly grounded in the here and now. It was still dark outside, but she could no more go back to sleep than take wing and fly. She propped her pillow against the head of the bed and tucked her knees up to curl against it. Someone had been part of her nightmare. Someone was undergoing some kind of ordeal. Not Weaver. Someone else. Had she witnessed their last moments as they were smothered in their sleep? She shuddered. There had to be some way to stop the sight.

CHAPTER SIXTY-FIVE

Erin fastened the clasp of the necklace in place. "You look very fine, my lady." Wrought in the shape of a garland of leaves, Vasic's gift to Alwenna struck chill against her skin.

"I'll do, I suppose. You will make a finer lady-in-waiting than any of the rest, Erin."

The girl bobbed a curtsey, not entirely at ease in an elegant gown. "Thank you, my lady." She was less than delighted by her newly enhanced status but at least she hadn't refused the honour.

"Vasic was always fond of keeping up appearances." Alwenna stared at her reflection in the mirror. The fitted gown could not disguise the slight thickening about her waist. But it was only slight; apparent to her, but hopefully not even to those who had met her daily since her marriage to Tresilian. By her good fortune – sad though it was – there were few of those present at court now, and none of them well acquainted with her.

The maid watched her in silence, her expression conveying nothing. Had she guessed the truth yet? Watchful as she was, it seemed more than likely. Whether the girl had or not, Alwenna could do nothing about it now. She had a growing conviction their fates were entwined more closely than either would once have believed possible. And probably more closely than either of them would have chosen. But choice was a fickle friend, more often than not illusory. If Alwenna's fortunes turned then the girl would find herself once more in the scullery, fending off the advances of every guard who happened by in a dark stairwell. That might be enough to ensure the girl remained close with any secrets she'd learned about her mistress, rather than risk losing her position.

Alwenna took one more look in the mirror. If she twisted her head it made her reflection shift and distort and she found herself looking at a stranger, yet a stranger who was somehow familiar. Her hair was bound up in traditional style, just as it had been for her wedding to Tresilian. She was now less than two years older. The events of that day seemed far off yet at the same time they jostled about her, demanding her attention.

Goddess, not now. She recognised the dizziness that presaged the sight. Everyone was waiting for her in the throne room. She clasped her hands together to counter their unsteadiness and tried to will herself to remain calm. It seemed to help.

She could see the reflection of the maid behind her, watching her, dispassionate. At least the girl didn't actively hate her. Not yet. Where had that thought come from?

Alwenna twitched at the folds of her dress, ensuring the skirts fell in smooth lines to the floor. Green silk, for fertility, with inset panels of purple to denote her royal status. It was a shame about the shadows beneath her eyes, but she wouldn't disgrace her family. Not this day.

Again the thought surprised her. She pushed it away. Now was not the time for morbid reflection. Her ladies-in-waiting were in the antechamber, ready to escort her into the king's presence. They'd all been hand-picked by Vasic, from households loyal to the southern king. If she heard the word usurper whispered that day they would be directed at her, not her soon-to-be husband.

Her head felt clearer. Had she managed to subdue the sight for once?

"Are you ready, my lady?" The maid's voice seemed to come from some place far away.

Alwenna turned and took a step towards the door but never reached it as the room pitched about her. The voices woke. Thousands at once, all clamouring to be heard, a monstrous babble from which she could discern no meaning, no sense. They increased in volume until they blanked out everything, even the daylight. She didn't know she'd fallen until she awoke with her face pressed against the cold floor – except she was not herself, she was him. She was Weaver, shackled in the dark and kept alive only by the burning shame of his failure. And through the dark in another time and place someone moaned, a whisper answered, two lovers locked in desperate communion. And she was gazing into grey eyes, pupils dilated, locked on hers. Then the eyes widened as they recognised her and a woman screamed out loud.

CHAPTER SIXTY-SIX

A hand pulled at her arm. "My lady, you must stand. Everyone is waiting. My lady, please." The hand tugged more insistently and Alwenna pushed herself up to a sitting position, the bloody taste of the sight filling her mouth. No, not just the sight, she'd cut her lip against her teeth. Her fingertips came away red with blood and she spat a mouthful out onto the floor before she could contain her disgust.

"In a moment... Bring me some wine. Strong and sweet."

The girl's footsteps hurried across the chamber to the side table. Alwenna kept her gaze fixed on the woodgrain of the floor in front of her until the last of the dizziness faded and she could focus clearly once more. She could see the myriad of tiny flecks criss-crossing the grain of the oak, her eyes able to discern tiny variations which her fingertips couldn't detect. She shivered. The sight had passed and with it the ghastly lightheadedness that had dogged her footsteps all morning.

Erin handed her a goblet of wine and she gulped it down, shuddering as it coursed down her throat and crept into her stomach, blazing a trail of fire that staved off the chill the sight had left.

"Can you stand now, my lady?"

Alwenna forced herself to concentrate on the present. She had to do this. "Yes."

With the girl's assistance she stood and they shook out the folds of her skirts once more, cleaning off dust from the floor. The girl worked in silence, taking care to remove every trace of Alwenna's collapse. Doubtless she'd be punished if her lady was not presented in accordance with Vasic's wishes. She even took time to tidy Alwenna's hair, though it was still perfectly presentable.

"That will do, Erin. Open the door, please, before my nerves get the better of me again." She doubted the girl believed a word of that particular lie, but Alwenna felt more confident now. The lingering after-taste of the sight had gone and her mind was sharper, clearer. The voices had been banished for now and she could face the coming ordeal with more assurance. Thank the Goddess it had happened before she'd left her chamber. She'd been a fool to imagine she could deny the sight. She didn't know how she'd manage with a new husband to hide it from. With luck he wouldn't require her to spend much time in his company. She intended to ensure she wasn't a sufficiently stimulating companion. She couldn't suppress a smile at that thought.

"My lady, are you all right?" The girl watched her apprehensively.

"Never better, Erin. Open the door."

In the anteroom below, Erin announced her to the ladies-in-waiting. Alwenna walked forward with certainty as they backed away and curtseyed before her. She might as well have staggered out like a drunkard for all they could see with their eyes pinned to the floor. Foolish sheep, they were. Vasic seemed to enjoy their vapid bleating. That one there at the end, the blonde one. Alwenna had seen her in a vision, gasping as Vasic had her up against the wall. He'd appeared to enjoy that uncommonly.

She drifted regally past them, not waiting for them to fall into line behind her as she paced with determination towards the great chamber. She noted the scuffling as they hurried to take their places. This, too, amused her. The wine had been strong. Perhaps she ought to have had another goblet before leaving her chamber. No matter. There would be plenty more at the wedding feast.

The great chamber was packed. Vasic had ensured all his supporters were there to witness their union. And if this crowd was any indication his supporters were plentiful indeed. Or his detractors were prepared to play along for the sake of an easy life. Which was it? Perhaps, in truth, most of the people assembled there didn't really care who ruled as long as there was some kind of stability. It saddened her to think Tresilian's untimely passing might have been of so little consequence to them. He'd arguably been a better man than Vasic. Kinder, certainly. But perhaps it wasn't in a king's best interests to be kind? That was one issue she could expect to debate with Vasic, far sooner than she would have chosen.

She made her stately progress towards the dais where Vasic awaited her. Beyond him a priest in ceremonial robes knelt, head bowed in prayer as he blessed the wedding cup. She glanced over the ranks of subservient dignitaries and reflected that perhaps ruthlessness was the most desirable attribute in a king.

Minstrels played on the gallery over the door by which she'd entered the room. The music they played was sombre, better suited to a funeral than a wedding. Suitable gravitas for a state occasion, but to her it spoke of departures, not new beginnings. Not that it mattered. None of it would matter soon. The stone-cold certainty brought a chill of recognition: this was a truth she could not alter, ought not attempt to. This would be an ending.

Immutable.

For whom, she could not yet see.

She trod towards it with her head held high.

CHAPTER SIXTY-SEVEN

Weaver signed the freemerchant's contract, inscribing his name beneath where Curtis and Blaine had already made their marks. The last thing he'd put his name to had been the forced confession damning the Lady Alwenna. At least this time it was only himself he betrayed.

The freemerchant stowed the parchment away inside his surcoat, smiling in his supercilious fashion. He had a way of looking sideways at the non-freemerchants that irked Weaver. They couldn't claim to be one with the other people of the Peninsula, yet hold themselves aloof the way they did. Then again, who was he to criticise? He'd chosen his own path since leaving the family farm. If Marten knew he'd once had a wife with freemerchant blood he hadn't mentioned it. Perhaps he was one of those who believed freemerchant blood shouldn't mingle with that of the landbound.

The road they took now led them east out of Brigholm, towards the mountains. They climbed steadily all day, vegetation around them thinning as trees grew sparse. The freemerchant had told them they would be three days on the road. He'd recruited others besides Weaver and his companions: dead-eyed sell-swords who'd obey orders as long as the pay kept coming. And who'd steal whatever they deemed their due the instant the money ran out. The only cause they believed in was holding their own bodies and dubious souls together. The freemerchant was playing a risky game with some of his acquisitions.

One of them – Scoular by name, a solidly built man who fancied himself as something of a leader – watched as Weaver sat in their overnight camp, sharpening his dagger on a borrowed whetstone. The blade didn't need work, but Weaver's hands needed occupation – anything to take his mind off events unfolding at Highkell. The feast would likely have started by now. They'd be drinking to the bride's health. Given the opportunity he'd have drunk himself senseless hours ago. Instead, he sat there with the whetstone, removing non-existent flaws from a perfectly honed blade.

Scoular stood up and wandered over to where Weaver sat. "Carry on like that and you'll have no blade left."

Weaver ignored him and continued honing the blade.

Scoular cleared his throat. "I said–"

"I heard you." Weaver gave the blade one last pass over the whetstone and inspected the edge.

Scoular spat on the ground at Weaver's feet. "I hate to see good steel wasted."

"So do I." Weaver slid the blade into its sheath. "That's why I won't be gutting you with it. Not this time."

Scoular snorted with derision. "I heard you were hard."

Weaver pretended to think over Scoular's words. "Should I know you?" He rose to his feet, the movement carefully controlled. He was half a head taller than Scoular, but the other man had the advantage when it came to weight. He had the kind of bulk that would run to fat easily, but it looked like solid muscle right now.

Scoular raised his chin. "Most folks have in The Marches."

Weaver nodded. "Is that so? The womenfolk tell the children tales about you to keep them in their beds at night?"

"Don't try to get clever with me." Scoular circled round Weaver, flexing his arms. "You've lost your bottle – it's plain as–"

A bellowing voice broke in. "What's going on here?" Marten strode across to where the two men faced one another. He was openly carrying a sword on this journey. Were they about to find out if he could wield it?

Scoular eyed the ground in sullen silence.

Weaver shrugged. "We're just swapping tales of the old days. You know how it is."

"I know." Marten glared at them. "If there's any fighting you're both out of the company. I don't pay you to damage each other. Is that clear?"

"Aye, sir," Scoular mumbled before slouching off to rejoin his companions.

"And you, Weaver – is it clear?"

"It's clear."

Marten studied his face for a moment. "Don't make trouble for me, Weaver. There's more riding on this than you would ever believe."

"I won't make trouble, but I can't speak for Scoular. If he starts something I'll have no choice but to finish it."

"Then you'll both be out of the company. Is that understood?"

Weaver nodded. "Understood." Either the freemerchant

had realised he had a bad bargain in the sell-swords, or something more fundamental wasn't going to plan. Whichever it might be, time would tell.

CHAPTER SIXTY-EIGHT

Alwenna halted before the dais while the ladies-in-waiting gathered her skirts so she might ascend the short flight of steps with all due ceremony. The air vibrated with tension, as if a thunderstorm approached. Could no one else in the room sense it?

Vasic studied her with his lips curled in a smile of welcome. It was the smile of the victor, about to claim his prize. Poor fool. Let him enjoy this moment – it would not last long. Again, that certainty. Stone cold, it burned within her, setting nerve ends afire and gripping her in a strange rapture a thousand times stronger than that she'd known after Hames' death. She smiled.

A burst of rain lashed against the window beneath which the priest still knelt, his back to the room. A man of slender build, he rose easily to his feet. A shiver of recognition ran down her spine. She knew him before he even turned, his hands raised in benediction. Instinct recognised her enemy before he even spoke. And he spoke with Garrad's voice, Garrad's duplicity.

"You will join hands and kneel, that we may beseech the blessing of the Goddess upon this marriage." His eyes slid over her, cold, without any hint of welcome. Strange, since she'd not been good enough for Tresilian, that he should look with approval upon her marriage to Vasic, his chosen lord. A puzzle, but of little consequence. Not now. She was certain.

Vasic took hold of her hand and gave a subtle tug in a downward direction. She resisted, but did not remove her hand from his grasp. She was aware he'd turned his face to her, but she kept her gaze fixed on Garrad.

The priest avoided meeting her eye. "You will kneel, that we may beseech the blessing of the Goddess upon this marriage."

"I will kneel before the Goddess, but not while this abomination presumes to mediate on her behalf." Her voice rang out loud, startling in its clarity. All the years of elocution training she'd endured were finally worthwhile.

A shocked murmur ran around the room behind them.

"Cousin, this is not the time to cause trouble," Vasic hissed.

"Then remove the traitor Garrad from my presence."

Another murmur rose, louder than the first.

Vasic's grip tightened on her hand. "Garrad is the most exalted priest of the brethren at Vorrahan, and he is my loyal servant."

"He has been loyal servant to many kings, often to more than one king at once." She had no doubt most of the assembled onlookers had heard her words. But her next words were for Vasic alone. "You would be wise to heed my warning."

Vasic dropped her hand as if she'd burned him.

"Dismiss him, Vasic, if you would have me trust you."

He wouldn't. It was certain.

Immutable.

All she had to do was wait.

The rain hurled itself against the window harder than ever and the sky darkened. Alwenna suppressed a shiver. It would be soon.

"I warned you, your highness. She is cursed, I tell you." Garrad pointed an accusing hand at Alwenna, his voice reverberating about the great chamber. "She is the abomination in this room."

Alwenna smiled back at him. "The Goddess will speak soon enough, Garrad. And I call everyone here to witness her decision." Alwenna raised her own hands in mimicry of his benediction.

For three heartbeats there was silence. Then, minutely at first, the floor began to resonate.

Garrad gaped at Alwenna in disbelief that changed swiftly to anger.

The vibration grew stronger until the floor shook palpably. Behind them onlookers raised their voices in alarm. At the back of the chamber the doors were pulled open, the groaning hinges drowned out by the buzz of panic as people fled.

"Curse you, you hell-spawn bitch!" Garrad's voice carried over the commotion, and he pulled a ceremonial dagger from his belt. The jewels glinted, as if waking from a deep sleep. Alwenna had seen that knife before: held in Vasic's hand, in a dungeon, spilling her husband's blood.

"No!" Vasic caught hold of Alwenna's hand, trying to pull her away.

"Stand clear, cousin. Let him try his worst." Alwenna shook off his grip and spread her hands wide, palms uppermost, smiling. "Come, holiest of fathers, do your work."

Face suffused with rage, Garrad took a step towards her and the floor pitched more wildly. A stone fell from the outer wall, crashing through the timber dais barely two yards from where they stood.

Garrad spun to face it, struggling to keep his balance, then turned back to Alwenna.

"End it now, Garrad," she goaded. "Let all those gathered here witness it."

Garrad's expression of hatred crumbled, giving way first to doubt and then to rank fear. He stared at Alwenna as if mesmerised. Gripping the dagger in both hands, he raised it above his head. Beneath his fingers the jewels in the ornate hilt glinted and his gaze was drawn to them, an expression of wonderment overtaking the fear. An expression of ecstasy. "My Goddess, I am your faithful servant. I do only your bidding."

He plunged the dagger deep into his own throat, blood spurting over Alwenna and Vasic where they stood.

Vasic staggered back in horror.

Alwenna felt a bubble of laughter rising within her chest and she saw no reason to contain it. She laughed out loud as Garrad crumpled to the ground. The knife clattered to the floor and lay there, the blood-spattered jewels still glowing with vibrant colour.

"Cousin, the Goddess has spoken." Alwenna smiled at Vasic, but he backed further away from her.

The floor continued to shake and more masonry fell from the top of the outer wall above the window. "Truly, Vasic, you are wiser than I once thought. But this time you have nothing to fear." The floor pitched sideways and they all staggered. The dagger rolled over and over until it came to rest against the wall. Screams from the back of the room intensified as the remaining onlookers fought to escape.

And their fear was delicious. Alwenna could taste their panic as she breathed it in, more intoxicating than any wine.

She was dimly aware that Vasic had turned and bolted for the door; dimly aware, too, of a determined tug on her arm.

"Highness, you cannot stay here." The servant girl; the silent, watchful servant girl.

"I'm safe enough, Erin. The Goddess has not finished with me yet. Not this day."

The girl gaped at her in horror and tugged harder. "My lady, the wall." She pointed to where the ornamental dagger lay. Alwenna was just in time to see the glint of the precious gems as the dagger rolled away, falling out of sight through a yawning gap that split the wall from floor to ceiling. As they watched, the gap grew ever wider and the floor tilted steeper, threatening to pitch them over the edge after the dagger. Then Erin lost her footing and slid towards the abyss. Without thinking, Alwenna snatched a handful of her robe and heaved her upwards, away from the sheer drop. She caught hold of the edge of the tilting dais and somehow they scrambled together towards the door at the opposite side of the window alcove. Alwenna had no thought in her mind at all but she saw the twisted snakes that formed the door handle and grabbed them. Together they clung there. Screams grew louder from the far end of the room, and with a great rushing and rumbling a whole chunk of the outer wall fell away, the floor sliding after it, sending up a great cloud of dust that stung their eyes and filled their mouths and eyes with grit.

The deafening roar of falling masonry died away and

the dust cloud began to settle, revealing they were clinging to a doorway near the edge of what remained of the floor. Then once again the ground beneath them pitched and the walls reverberated. With an ominous cracking sound another section of floor sheared away, dropping down the precipice. Then with a great shudder the whole wall began to peel off in its wake, dragging the two women down with the doorway in which they clung as dust boiled up to engulf them.

CHAPTER SIXTY-NINE

Weaver was out of shape. The time he'd spent in the Highkell dungeon had taken its toll on him, as had the time he'd spent contemplating the bottom of an ale tankard since. A morning back in the saddle after their first long day on the road was doing nothing to help the nagging pain in his ribs, despite the fact they were travelling at an easy pace. He thought briefly of that farm on the northern coast, but there was no turning back. He'd signed the freemerchant's contract and now it was down to him to earn his keep. The road wound ahead of them over the plain, climbing almost imperceptibly towards the distant mountains. Scrubby vegetation dotted the rock-strewn landscape. It was said this had once been a vast sea that froze so hard every living thing was turned to stone. It was an uneasy place, too silent by far. Occasional creatures scurried away out of sight, startled by their approach. The same nondescript colour as the sandy ground, the creatures dived into burrows dug in the shade of the rocks.

The freemerchant slowed his horse to ride alongside Weaver. "If you're fast enough and hungry enough you can catch them, but dried beef's better for travelling here. Well salted."

"Better than fresh meat?"

"They're too much work for precious little meat. The birds that prey on them are a better bet. But even they're scrawny." The freemerchant scanned the sky. "They're not often to be found in the middle of the day, though. I prefer to keep my head down and get across as fast as possible, without overtiring the horses." The freemerchant hadn't been silent for more than two minutes at a time since they'd set off.

"You travel these plains often?" Weaver still didn't trust him, but he wanted Marten to think he'd won.

"Too often, lately. There's better game to be had in the foothills and plentiful water. It all runs deep underground here. It's no great wonder this place is known as the Blighted Sea."

Weaver grunted noncommittally. This was one of the rare occasions when he agreed with Marten, but he saw no reason to admit it out loud.

"Have you travelled this far east before, Weaver?"

"Not by this route. Skirted the plains a few times."

"I hadn't taken you to be superstitious."

"I'm not. Just fond of fresh meat."

"Yes, I'd heard that was the case." The freemerchant smiled lazily.

There were one or two close friends who might have got away with that joke. The freemerchant was not one of them. "A man with your experience knows not to set store by idle rumour."

"Indeed." The freemerchant grinned and kicked his horse forward, riding ahead to the front of the file of horses.

Weaver watched his retreating back. He'd find out what

Marten was really after, one way or the other. Blighted
Sea, indeed. The name suited the sere landscape well.
But the unwelcoming vista didn't bother him. What did
make him uneasy was the sense that nothing good would
come of this journey east. He couldn't shake the growing
conviction that he ought to be travelling in another
direction entirely.

The conviction was so strong that he twisted round in
his saddle – sending a searing pain through his ribs as he
did so – to look back over the ground they'd covered. And
he glimpsed movement, far off in the distance. Something
was raising a cloud of dust. He halted his horse and turned
it round, the better to study the movement.

A single rider, moving at speed, following the same line
they'd taken over the arid landscape.

He called for Marten's attention. "We have company."

Marten rode back to his side, studying the distant figure
with a frown. "So it seems."

"Riding straight for us. Are you expecting stragglers?"

"No." Marten's frown deepened. "They're riding fast."
He appeared more concerned by the rider than Weaver
might have expected. "Any urgent news for me is likely to
come from the east, not the west." He glanced at Weaver.
"We've time to push on to the top of this hill – that's a
good place to wait and see what this rider's about."

They didn't have long to wait. By the time their horses
had had their regular rest-stop the rider was climbing the
hill in their wake. Minutes later he came clattering up to
them, a skinny youth mounted on an expensive horse.
Weaver recognised Drew with surprise. He signalled to the
others where they lay in wait, arrows nocked. The horse's
flanks were heaving, but it was lean and fit, and clearly

used to such arduous journeys.

"Hold hard, young Drew." The rider halted abruptly, scanning the rocky ground. The horse sidled, still keen to keep moving.

Weaver stood, sheathing his sword as he approached Drew. "What's this? You taken to thieving horses?" It was a quality animal, bred for racing unless he was much mistaken.

Drew grinned fleetingly. "No, it's only borrowed."

"From your new employer?" A wealthy man, if the horse was anything to go by. What had the lad said he did? A trader? Or had that just been another evasive answer?

"That's right." The youth nodded as he slid down from the saddle, looking more uncomfortable than the horse that had done most of the work. He led the horse towards Weaver. "I had to come find you."

As he drew closer Weaver could see his face was drawn and he looked as if he'd passed a sleepless night.

"I couldn't think of anyone else who'd help – and I was pretty sure you'd want to know. Even if…" He fell silent as he caught sight of the freemerchant.

Marten sauntered out of cover, hand on the pommel of the sword he now carried openly, quietly asserting his role as leader of the mismatched band. No, he was no ordinary freemerchant. Weaver would be glad of a chance to ask a few questions of other freemerchants about his new employer – he imagined they'd have some colourful views.

"Have we met?" Marten's voice was quiet, but assertive.

"No, no I don't think so…" Drew hesitated.

"Saw you with Jervin, didn't I? A few nights ago, at the *White Ox*?"

Drew nodded. "You may well have. I– I have news for Weaver."

"Not a new recruit who missed us in Brigholm, then? Be quick, we've some distance to travel today."

Drew glanced nervously over to where the freemerchant waited as he hurried to Weaver's side. "I didn't know what to do. Jervin loaned me the horse. I had to tell you…"

It was bad news. It could be nothing else. "Then tell me and get it over with."

"It's the Lady Alwenna. She's in trouble. Terrible trouble. Last night…" Drew tailed off, a haunted expression crossing his face. He pressed his hands to his temples. "Goddess, I can hardly bear it…"

"What trouble? How could she–" They were to be married – when? Yesterday. The Lady Alwenna and her accursed cousin.

"That's the worst, Weaver, I can't tell. She's trapped. In darkness. I don't know what's happened. But – it's really bad. She's terrified, in pain. And she's calling for you."

Weaver studied the lad's harrowed expression. "How? How could you possibly know this?"

"She's… in my mind. I can hear her, trapped in the darkness." Drew's voice shook. "I… I told you once how Gwydion planned to make me his heir? I have some of her gift, only the tiniest amount. But I know she's in trouble. She needs your help, Weaver."

Was the lad telling the truth? Weaver studied him. He'd never been able to lie to save himself. Whatever was happening, Drew believed Alwenna was in danger.

"How long? When did it start?"

"Yesterday afternoon." Drew choked out the words. "I felt such a burst of rage… and then… at first I couldn't tell what it was, but by nightfall I knew. And I set out to find you."

"I can't just drop everything and leave – I've signed to this company. I can't help."

Goddess, he might as well have kicked a puppy.

Drew gaped at him in disbelief. "But she's calling for you."

"So you say. If she's in a dungeon at Highkell I won't be able to get her out." He'd sworn to protect her. Could he live with himself if he failed her again?

"But she's not in a dungeon." Drew's eyes slid from side to side as he considered. "No, if she were, she'd not be so – she's terrified. It's dark, and she can't move, I think, and – she needs your help." If this was a trap for Weaver it couldn't have been set more certainly.

Weaver turned to the freemerchant, who watched them with undisguised curiosity. Weaver suspected Marten would happily stick a knife in him simply to see his reaction – and probe his innards just to learn what manner of a creature he was. "The lad brings bad news from Highkell."

"We have a contract, you and I. I hope you have not forgotten already."

"I haven't. Hear me out first." Weaver led Marten further away from the group so they would not be overheard. "The news concerns your patron's lady wife. She's in danger. Would you have me ignore it, simply to bend my knee to my king a day or two sooner?"

The freemerchant tilted his head to one side, considering. "I think you mean to answer this summons, no matter what."

"I swore to Tresilian that I would protect her. And when

I believed him dead I swore the same to the lady herself. I can't ignore her plea for help."

"You would break your contract to answer it?" The freemerchant toyed with the cuff of his sleeve.

"If all is as you claim then I continue to serve my king as loyally as ever."

Marten considered. "Then of course you must do what you may. Which is what, precisely?"

Weaver glanced at Drew. "She's trapped, that's all we know."

"We?" The freemerchant turned his eyes to Drew, who blushed and shuffled his feet.

Weaver couldn't spend time arguing with the freemerchant. Not now. "The lad has the sight."

"Indeed?" Marten studied Drew more closely. "You have freemerchant blood?"

"Aye, I do. On my mother's side… and… my true father."

"Then we are well met, young brother." Marten made the gesture of greeting and, after a moment of hesitation, Drew responded in kind. "Outcasts together. We will speak more of this later, I hope, when we have more time." He smiled, before turning his attention back to Weaver. "This news changes things. I am already overdue at our destination but you will turn back to rescue the lady and bring her to safety. How many men do you require?"

A good question. What did they face? "Let me take Blaine and Curtis. We are used to working together."

The freemerchant nodded, his face giving away nothing. "Very well. When you return, follow this road east for a further six miles and you'll come to an inn at a crossroads. Ask for me there by name and they will give you directions. And think on, Weaver. If you attempt to cross me now I will see you regret it."

"I've never broken a contract yet."

The freemerchant studied him. "I don't doubt it. But have a care, nonetheless." He returned to his horse and took a bag of coin from his saddlebag and tossed it to Weaver. "You may need this to ensure the lady's wellbeing. I shall expect you to account for every coin when you rejoin us."

CHAPTER SEVENTY

The girl settled her porcelain-faced doll on the carriage seat. "How much further? It's nearly dark." She started swinging her legs back and forth.

"Not far." Her mother glanced at the man dozing beside her, his arms folded, legs stretched across the floor to the opposite seat. "Don't wake your father." She tucked the folds of her travelling cloak closer about herself.

Alwenna sighed, then spoke in a stage whisper. "Will there be–?" With a crunch the carriage pitched sideways. Outside the coachman shouted and horses' hooves scrambled as the vehicle lurched, flinging the girl against her mother. The floor tilted, creaking as the horses struggled outside against the weight. Then with a crack of snapping wood the body of the coach lurched sideways and it rolled over, flinging its occupants against wall then roof then wall, over and over. Soil and stones cascaded down the bank in its wake, clattering against the roof of the upturned vehicle. A great weight pressed down on Alwenna. Woollen fabric smothered her face and she clawed it free, fighting to breathe.

Alwenna woke to stillness. The crumbling, falling

nightmare had ended. The same old nightmare, yet still so vivid, so real. The imagined weight of her father's broken body pressed down on her legs. She could almost taste the loosened earth, the grit in her mouth, the dust caking her lips. Her eyes stung with grit when she opened them and tears streamed unbidden.

Dust? Grit?

She raised her hand to rub her eyelids, but something hampered the movement. She jerked her arm reflexively and freed it. Her action set something in motion with a tiny skirling hush that stilled after a moment or two. What? It sounded like pebbles. Or sand. The smell of mouldering plaster rose up around her. She blinked, looking for the chink between her bed curtains where moonlight or firelight always shone, but the night was too dark. Disorientated, she tried to push herself up into a sitting position, only to find one foot was pinned by tangled bedcovers. Impatiently she tugged it and pain ripped through her ankle. She yelped out loud and subsided. More cautiously she explored the darkness with her free hand. She was covered not by woollen blankets, but by a blanket of grit and small stones, crumbled plaster and mortar. This was not her old nightmare. Not now. It had propelled her into a new, waking one.

She could feel a jumble of stone to one side. When she reached up – at least she believed it was up – her fingertips found a slanting rib of smoother stone. Her fingers dislodged a fall of mortar which cascaded onto her face, stinging her eyes anew. She pushed her hand against the stone rib. It did not move at all. She probed around the uppermost side of it and her finger pricked on a sharp, cold edge and came away sticky with blood. Glass.

Window glass.

The twisting, shaking floor. The collapsing masonry, the terrible rumbling slide as the dust cloud engulfed them. She had scrambled to the doorway by the window and now she must have been pinned beneath it. The keep of Highkell had swallowed her whole.

Her limbs began to tremble and she tried more desperately to free her foot from the weight that crushed against it. It wouldn't move. She couldn't even feel any pain in it now. She thrashed wildly, trying to tug it out by throwing all her body weight against it. Something shifted, then bit deeper into her ankle and she screamed aloud, until the pain overwhelmed her and she slid into darkness.

The next time she woke she could hear voices. Many voices. Some sobbed, some shouted, some cried out for help, some whimpered. In the blackness she could not even tell if they were next to her, somewhere just beyond reach of her fingertips, or if they were only imagined. Too many voices. She couldn't make out the words. They collided with one another in her mind, ran up against the barricades surrounding her and trickled away in the darkness before she could make any sense of them. But she finally understood. At some point in time, every one of them was, had been or would be real. And she had no way of knowing which were echoes of things past, which were things yet to happen and which belonged here and now. She was a revenant pinned there between the layers of darkness, suspended between past and future yet denied the present in this nightmare made real. Her head ached and her eyes stung, whether she held them open or closed. The dust on her face was encrusted by her tears, dragging her skin tight across her cheekbones. She was going to die there, parched with thirst, weak and hungry. Inside her womb the baby kicked. They were both going to die there.

CHAPTER SEVENTY-ONE

First there was darkness. And within it, pain, clamouring in his chest. A deep dragging sensation threatened to tear him apart. Then, where he could have sworn there had been nothing, there was a tingling rush as air drew into his lungs. The uneven rise and fall of his chest settled into some kind of rhythm, and he heard the flow of air, the pulsing of blood through his veins. And it was familiar. Achingly familiar.

Sounds where there had been none.

And his chest rose and fell, rose and fell. So familiar... and yet...

The awareness crept up on him almost imperceptibly: he was alive. His pulse quickened, and the rush of blood through his veins threatened to deafen him. There was something, at the edge of his consciousness, something he ought to know...

Renewed pain seared through his chest, but it burned out almost immediately, settling to a dull, dragging ache. And there were other sensations now: coolness as an unseen hand mopped his forehead, warmth as hands moved over his ribcage, dispersing the pain, and the rise and fall, rise and fall, became less laboured, until he didn't need to think about it at all – it simply was.

And then he became aware of sounds around him: the swish of fabric as someone moved nearby; a faint grinding sound some way away – a pestle and mortar; further still, birdsong; the susurrus of leaves stirred by a light breeze. More and more sounds. His fingers twitched. And now he sensed there was light but his eyelids weighed too heavy to lift and he gave up the struggle to open them.

He couldn't say how many days passed in this way. Sometimes when he woke it was dark, and he caught the rank smell of tallow, recognised it and understood this was not what he was used to. Other times there was light beyond his closed eyelids. But every time, as soon as he stirred, even so much as a fingertip, something damp and cool was pressed to his lips and as he quenched his thirst he slid away from consciousness once more as a deeper weariness overcame him. Until the day came when he woke more fully and realised he was in the place where he had woken the day before, and the day before that, and all those times in between.

Footsteps approached and he recognised the sweet, cloying scent of the thirst-quenching stuff he had grown used to. He parted his lips, ready to take the scant moisture. Then the footsteps halted. Fabric swished close by and a hand pressed for a few moments upon his forehead.

A soft voice spoke. "You have returned to us, at last, my lord. May the Goddess be praised for her mercy. Let us give thanks." The voice was soft, husky. A woman's, he realised. Still something eluded him, something he thought he should know. With a supreme effort he opened his eyes but the light was overwhelming and he had to squeeze his lids shut again.

The woman murmured words he didn't recognise: soothing, rhythmic words. He let them carry him along, drifting on the current of pleasant sensations. He felt the lightest of motions over his chest, followed by a rush of less warm air, and realised such garments as he wore were being unfastened. The hands began to massage his upper body, kneading his chest and ribs. He relished the sensation, his chest rising and falling in time to the rhythmic motion. Then the hands moved lower still and his body responded, hardening as she worked her fingers over him. The hands left him for a moment and he heard fabric, lifting, settling.

"It is time for us to thank the Goddess." She straddled him. Warm flesh pressed against his own and he felt the heat in his loins grow. He opened his eyes again then, just long enough to see she was every bit as beautiful as he had imagined, with long, fair hair and firm, rounded breasts. He yearned to explore her with his own hands, yet when he tried to lift them they might as well have been made of granite.

"Save your strength," she murmured, leaning forward to kiss him. He closed his eyes again as she teased at his mouth with her tongue and her breasts brushed against his chest. Rise and fall, rise and fall, rise and– She lowered herself onto him and began to move, slowly at first but each sway of her hips more certain than the one before, until he released himself inside her.

"Your first act on waking is for the Goddess. May she bless your offering with new life." She spoke unevenly, her voice taking a moment to recover its earlier lyrical quality. "Now she will walk at your side always, and favour you above all men." She lifted herself off him then. A blink of his eyes showed him her firm, neat waist, vanishing beneath a shapeless robe.

He would have struggled to sit up at that point, to call her back to him, but the sweet-tasting sponge was applied to his lips again and he slid away into a deep sleep, vaguely aware he still had not recalled the thing that was so important.

CHAPTER SEVENTY-TWO

Weaver wasn't prepared for the scale of devastation that greeted them at Highkell. They'd halted their horses in the cover of trees on the ridge opposite the citadel. Or rather, what remained of it. It was as if a giant's fist had punched a hole through the cliff on which the citadel stood. The cliff beneath the breach was soused with water seeping from myriad cracks. Below stretched a scar of freshly exposed rock. Soil stripped from the slope had been swept down to the bottom of the gorge and come to rest in a jumble of uprooted trees and fallen masonry. Above the breach...

Weaver swore.

Above the breach the whole of the King's Tower had gone, taking with it one wall of the great throne room which now stood open to the elements. The curtain wall gaped either side, revealing a great gash in the ground cut away by the collapse of the tower. A section of soil still topped by turf curled out over the drop – all that remained of the washing green. The curtain wall to the town side of the citadel leaned drunkenly out from the cliff top. Further up the gorge, the main city gate opened out onto a sheer drop, the bridge carried away in another landslide, along with several hundred yards of the approach road on their side of the gorge. Highkell was effectively cut off from the south.

Despite Drew's insistence something was badly wrong, Weaver had never quite believed it. Now he struggled to comprehend the scale of destruction. "Where in the name of the Goddess do we begin?"

Curtis shook his head. "No one could survive in that."

"She's here. I know it." Drew studied the rubble below them, intent on something none of the rest of them could detect. "There." He pointed down the gorge, some distance below the point where the tower had stood. "We need to get down there." He sounded sure.

Weaver studied the citadel. Labourers moved among the wreckage above the breach, clearing fallen masonry and shoring up damaged walls with timbers, but there was no evidence of archers or other guard patrols. For the time being the only way down from Highkell would be by rope, or a circuitous route over the steep ground from the west gate. There seemed every chance they might search the rubble without interference.

"Weaver, how do we get down there?" Drew was insistent.

"We'll need to go further downstream, to where the bank hasn't washed away. There'll be sheep trods we can follow. We'll leave the horses up here, out of sight among the trees."

Drew nodded. "Then let's not waste time."

Once they'd reached the mounds of rubble, their task looked impossible. The debris shifted underfoot, however carefully they tried to pick their way through it. Drew, lighter than the others, took the lead. "She's here, I tell you." Drew clambered up the precarious pile of rubble, teetering over loose blocks of masonry, searching for something only he could sense. Then he doubled back and crouched down, setting one hand against a huge stone lintel which jutted from the rubble. "Here. This is it." He beckoned urgently to Weaver, and he and his comrades clambered up the fallen masonry to his side.

"She's here. She's alive, Weaver. I'm sure of it."

The lad believed it. Weaver daren't. But he began clearing the fallen stone aside, and they worked to uncover the lintel. It formed the top of an ornate window, and was still attached to one jamb. A few panes of leaded glass still hung from one mullion. The big window from the throne room? She might well have been there.

They worked in silence, alert for any sudden movement of the loose stone surrounding them. Weaver and Blaine between them heaved a large block aside, revealing a cavity formed by the fallen lintel and door jamb. And beyond the trickling dust, something moved. There was the faintest of sounds, little more than an exhalation. Drew still insisted it was Alwenna. It could be anyone in there. They worked faster, clearing more rubble away until an accumulation of loose mortar rushed inside the cavity and there was a yelp of protest.

At last Weaver believed.

The rubble around the spot was becoming increasingly unstable. They'd cleared enough to allow light into the cavity, revealing dust-covered fabric – a silk gown. They worked swiftly to clear the rubble from about her. At one point, Drew stepped back, frowning, and looked around before returning to their work. A fallen timber had come to rest across her legs and it took some time to clear away enough stone to lift it. She moved, twisting around in an effort to get to her feet. Drew reached inside the cavity and helped her scramble out.

Weaver caught a glimpse of the girl's fair hair, and his disappointment was crushing. It wasn't Alwenna.

The girl held one hand over her eyes as she squinted in the daylight. "Thank the Goddess..." Her voice was dry and cracked even on those few syllables. She held her left arm awkwardly against her side and trembled with exhaustion.

Blaine helped her away from her precarious perch among the loose rubble. "Easy now, lass. Lean on me."

"You're not from these parts." She squinted at them a second time through streaming eyes. "Those aren't Vasic's colours..."

Nearby, a quantity of masonry subsided with an ominous rumble and a couple of stones rolled loose and clattered away down the gorge.

"We're here to find the Lady Alwenna."

The girl caught her breath. "Then you'll need... She saved me, pulled me from the edge..." The girl drew a ragged breath.

Weaver's heart seemed to stop beating.

"She was right beside me, I know she was. I heard her, in the dark."

After a few more minutes' effort they uncovered more fabric. Green, this time. Ornate, such as an important bride might wear on her wedding day.

Drew, slightest among their party, peered through the gap they'd cleared. "Her feet are pinned. It's—" He twisted round, then pulled his head and shoulders back out of the hole. "Bring me a length of timber, two if you can find them. We need to be sure it doesn't cave in."

A block of stone tilted beneath Weaver's foot. He froze. Every shift of weight was now fraught. Drew peered inside the cavity once more, speaking calmly to the trapped woman. "Not long now. We'll shore up this rubble to be sure it's safe before we free your legs." He withdrew again and pointed to the section of rubble against the window jamb. "Keep clearing away there, Weaver. That window's wedged solid at the back, it's going nowhere. I need room to get inside with the timber props."

Weaver attacked the fallen stonework with renewed vigour. One of the others returned with a length of timber that had once formed a window lintel.

Drew hefted it. "Perfect. Another of these, two if you can find them. That should do it, Weaver – be ready to pass the prop to me when I'm inside." Drew lowered himself feet first through the gap Weaver had created. He paused partway in, twisting round and feeling his way with his feet, pausing again as small stones cascaded inside, then ducked out of sight.

The moments stretched as Weaver waited. Drew appeared at the hole. "She's doing well. Her leg hurts, but that's a good sign. Hand me the prop." Weaver passed it to him, supporting the end until Drew had moved out of sight and took it in after him. Weaver faced another anxious wait punctuated only by clunks and thuds as, presumably, Drew wedged the prop in position. Drew's head popped out of the hole once more after what seemed an impossible wait. "Begin to clear this section here. When it comes to this stone you'll need me to support it from this side." He set his hand on a large block of stone at shoulder height.

The men worked swiftly, without wasting energy in conversation. Inside the rubble Alwenna remained quiet. Weaver redoubled his efforts. If they were too late... They couldn't be too late. Drew would have said something, surely.

A moment later and the huge block Drew had pointed out began to shift. "Wait!" he yelled, straining to hold the block in place. "Take the stone from beneath it so we can roll it away."

The three of them scrabbled frantically and a moment later Drew heaved the block out over the top and they dragged it down in a controlled slide. A few small stones to one side of it toppled into the cavity.

"Give me more daylight to free her legs." Drew stooped, scrabbling in the debris they'd just uncovered, and picked up an ornate dagger. He tucked it away in his belt and continued clearing stone.

Finally Weaver could see inside the cavity where Alwenna lay trapped. And it was Alwenna. She lay with her eyes closed, trembling. Her breathing might have been unsteady, but she was breathing.

Drew worked by her legs. "We're nearly there, my lady. We'll have you out of here in a matter of minutes. Keep still now, it won't take long."

There was no visible response from Alwenna. Were they too late after all?

Weaver clambered over the remaining rubble, leaving the other two to clear more space, and stooped at Drew's side. A large cornerstone pinned Alwenna's leg to the rubble beneath.

"Take that end, Weaver. We need to lift this clean away

without causing any more damage. On the count of three."

He counted.

They lifted.

Alwenna uttered a stifled cry as they lifted the block clear of her leg.

From somewhere on the tumbled hillside there came a shout of warning.

The servant girl screamed. "Get down!"

A volley of arrows rained down nearby, clattering among the stones several yards short of where they worked.

There was a muffled curse from Curtis as he dived for cover. "The whoreson bastards are firing on us."

Weaver wrestled the block into a safe place where it couldn't cause further damage. "We're all known here. You turned coat, after all."

Curtis crouched among the rubble. "They've bloody good eyesight if they can recognise me from there, that's all I'll say."

Drew was already dragging Alwenna out from beneath the lintel that had prevented her from being crushed.

Another volley of arrows followed the first. From the rubble below them, Blaine cursed. "Half a dozen archers on the curtain wall. They'll have our range next time. We need to move."

As if they'd heard, the next volley of arrows skittered against the stones around them. None of them were hit, but it left no doubt they were being targeted.

Drew helped Weaver lift Alwenna from beneath the stone lintel and out into full daylight. The servant girl was already on her feet, scrambling down towards the road with Curtis. Alwenna couldn't carry any weight on her injured foot so Drew and Weaver supported her between them. A further volley followed them, falling short, and they scrambled faster, but the exertion of recent days was finally catching up with Drew. He staggered and almost fell, stepping back so Blaine could take his place when the next volley clattered around them. Drew gasped and stumbled against Alwenna.

"Drew, no!" The first words she'd spoken were a near-inarticulate scream of anger. She tried to pull him to his feet, but Blaine slung the youth over his shoulder as if he were no weight at all and dashed for the cover of the trees. Weaver set off behind them but Alwenna twisted round, pulling free from his grip as if she would return to Highkell.

"My lady, this way." Weaver caught hold of Alwenna's shoulder to turn her back to safety but she resisted, her muscles rigid beneath his fingertips.

She raised her face towards the curtain wall where the archers were nocking their arrows, almost ready to fire again. The wall shuddered and soil tumbled away from the base before it gradually peeled out from the citadel. The wall slid down into the gorge, voices crying out in terror as flailing figures dropped from the crumbling masonry. Weaver tugged at her shoulder again, but still she resisted. Then the tension in her muscles eased and she turned, a hard expression on her face such as he'd never seen before. She focused on Weaver, yet didn't seem to recognise him at all.

And in that moment Weaver hardly recognised her. "My lady? We must go."

Alwenna pressed her fingertips to her forehead. "Yes, of course." She took a step forward and stumbled as her damaged ankle failed. Weaver pulled her arm about his shoulders, supporting her weight as they followed after the others who were already scrambling up the bank in the shelter of the trees.

CHAPTER SEVENTY-THREE

The others were already mounted up by the time Weaver and Alwenna reached them. He boosted her into his saddle and vaulted on behind. They had no time to linger, with every likelihood of pursuit from Highkell. He led them on a circuitous route through the forest, and they rode hard for several miles once they'd reached the road east. The servant girl was mounted behind Drew, doggedly supporting him as he gradually slumped lower and lower in the saddle. She seemed tough as old boots, but she called a halt as they approached a shallow ford.

"I can't keep him in the saddle any longer. Not with only one good arm."

Blaine dismounted and half-lifted Drew down, half-supported him as he fell. The girl stayed seated, flexing the arm she'd been holding Drew in place with. She looked every bit as haggard as the Lady Alwenna. There was blood soaked into the front of her dress. She stared at it blankly, as if it took her a moment to work out how it had got there, then looked at Drew who hung limply in Blaine's grip.

"Take him in among the trees, out of sight. It's time we dealt with that wound." Weaver rode his horse into the cover of the trees, finding a suitable clearing where he dismounted. If Drew's wound wasn't tended to now there was every chance they'd lose him on the road. There was, to be fair, every chance they'd lose him anyway, judging by his pallor.

"My lady? We'll rest here awhile."

Alwenna looked at him dully. "Rest? Have we time?" Her voice was hoarse.

"Drew's injured. We need to tend to it before we ride further."

Her eyes widened. "Of course." She'd been silent the whole journey. Now she looked about her, apparently at a loss as to what to do next.

"Let me help you dismount, my lady."

"Thank you." She winced as she swung her right leg over the back of the saddle.

Weaver supported her weight as she slid down. It wasn't elegant, by any means, and she couldn't put weight on her injured ankle, but she seemed a little more aware of her surroundings. He turned his attention to Drew's injury. They'd summarily snapped the arrow shaft so they could ride without causing him further injury, leaving enough protruding so they might remove it later. The wound had almost stopped bleeding, which was good news after seeing the amount of blood on the servant girl's gown.

Weaver studied the injury, gauging the tip of the arrow had travelled most of the way through Drew's shoulder. A careful examination with his fingertips as Blaine and Curtis held the lad still confirmed this. Removing the arrowhead by the way it had entered would cause more damage than it had on the way in. They found a stick for Drew to bite on and pinned him between them as Weaver made ready to thrust the arrow the rest of the way through. Drew sagged between them, drifting in and out of consciousness. Alwenna watched, wide-eyed, forgetting to tear the shirt she'd been given into strips. The servant girl moved to the edge of the clump of trees, ensuring there was no one close by. She nodded to Weaver, who took a careful hold of the arrow, gauged the angle, then thrust it forward. Drew screeched, but the barb burst through the front of his shoulder. Another moment and Weaver had removed it. The servant girl set about washing the wound.

Curtis was all for stitching it, but the girl was stern. "No, stitching a deep wound can trap dirt inside – as long as he doesn't bleed too much, let it stay open."

"You sound mighty sure of that, lass," Blaine observed.

"My da kept racehorses. A bit of salt in the water would be best. Makes it heal faster."

Drew sat up, muttering under his breath as the servant girl set about bandaging his shoulder. Twice she had to remind the Lady Alwenna to hand her the strips of fabric. It was as if Alwenna's attention was fixed in some other place. It made Weaver uneasy. Whatever ailed her would take more than salt water to heal.

CHAPTER SEVENTY-FOUR

He was lying half-asleep among the tangled sheets when he recognised the fair-haired priestess' footsteps. His body hardened in anticipation. He sat up, reaching for her with a smile of welcome, but she shook her head, lowering her eyes modestly.

"My lord, you must not overtax your strength. Nine days you lay alone as one dead; nine days we will lie together before I must retreat into seclusion and pray the Goddess blesses our union." Her voice was even, with no hint of the husky tone he had learned to expect from her.

"Nine days?" How much time had passed already? He had no idea. It had never occurred to him to keep count. "But you need not leave me yet. What is your name?"

"We who serve the Goddess have no name until she blesses us. We are but empty vessels until that day, awaiting our time to serve her as only a woman made in her form can." The priestess had bound up her hair and was wearing the shapeless robe.

He swung his legs round to set his feet down on the floor. The stone flags were cool, sending a shiver running through him. "If you have no name, how am I to address you?"

She smiled. "As you do now, my lord." A gaggle of servants arrived, bringing with them a bathtub which they set down close to the bed, and steaming pitchers of water. "Today you will rise and bathe. It is time to rebuild your strength so we may – if the Goddess blesses our union – rejoin the world together."

The servants came and went with more pitchers of water until the tub was two-thirds full. The nameless priestess loosened her long hair and moved around the tub chanting an incantation in a language he did not recognise, sprinkling herbs and flower petals over the water and, finally, dashing a handful of salt into it. With elegance she knelt and stirred the water, three times one way, then three times the other way, then three times more as she had begun. All this he watched from where he sat on the edge of the bed.

She took him by the hand, encouraging him to stand. After a brief hesitation he did so, startled to discover how weak his limbs were. It had not always been this way, he knew, yet how he knew he could not be sure. And how it had once been he could not remember. The priestess led him by the hand to the tub and unlaced the neck of the voluminous chemise he had been sleeping in. She gathered up the garment from the hem and pulled it off over his head. The air against his naked flesh was cold and clammy with vapour from the tub. He shivered and his teeth began to chatter.

"The water will warm you, my lord. And the herbs will heal you."

She supported him as he cautiously raised one foot and stepped over the rim of the bathtub, wobbling precariously as he struggled to balance with one foot off the ground.

He lowered himself into the water, setting a hand on either side of the bath to support himself. This was something familiar, something he recognised. He lowered himself until the water had risen to his waist and his buttocks came to rest on the base of the tub. His arms trembled from the unaccustomed effort. He let them sink into the warm water, resting his head back and closing his eyes. In his mind's eye he could see another room, larger than this chamber, with a floor made from stone of redder hues. The walls, of the same red stone, were hung with lavish tapestries, the workmanship of the best quality, the detail fine. He knew it to be true. He opened his eyes. The priestess watched him, her hands clasped together, head bowed.

"Do I have a name?"

"Yes, my lord, but I do not know it. You will remember when the Goddess wills it. When you are healed."

CHAPTER SEVENTY-FIVE

That stranger was there in her mind again, waking in the darkness to a sensual touch. Alwenna pulled away from the contact, sitting bolt upright in a different darkness, her pulse thundering. She was in the forest. Around her, her companions slept. Someone on the far side of the fire snored gently. She shivered. Was she simply hearing someone else's dreams? Was she hearing Weaver's thoughts? No, she'd swear this stranger was not him. And yet… Could it be Vasic? He was familiar in some elusive way. Stanton's ghost haunting her? She shivered again and got to her feet, pulling her blanket round her shoulders. Maybe she ought to be grateful he'd driven away the memories of being trapped in the dark, but, whoever he was, she didn't need to know what he was getting up to right now.

The trees crowded in around Alwenna, shutting out such moonlight as there was. Too restless to sleep now, she decided to walk to the water's edge. She took up her walking stick and, leaning heavily on it, hobbled away from the fire. Doing her best not to wake anyone – especially Curtis who was ostensibly on watch – she picked her way round the edge of their campsite.

From the lake shore she could see the sky, the stars

bright, moving in their unending cycle. The Hunter, tall and proud, kept watch over their fire. A bright star hung just above the tree-line on the far shore, reflected on the surface of the lake. She knelt at the water's edge and set her palms in the water, watching the ripples spread outwards, distorting the reflection. Already she could breathe more easily and she felt her tension slipping away.

A twig snapped behind her and she turned to see Weaver approaching, his shirt ghostly in the moonlight. He hadn't paused to don his surcoat.

"My lady, is it wise to go so far from the fire?"

"I couldn't sleep." She turned back to the water, shivering again as its chill struck through her veins, bringing with it a delicious sense of being alive. A light breeze stirred the surface of the lake, obscuring the stars' reflections altogether and taking with it her moment of serenity.

She heard the crunch of footsteps as Weaver walked over beside her. "More bad dreams?"

"Yes." Could she tell him why these particular visions were so unsettling? She shouldn't, of course. He still clung to the euphemistic use of dreams, after all. She could tell him of her terror of being trapped again. Or should she not tell him that, either? "I wish I didn't need to sleep. I can't stop them then."

His mouth twisted in that expression she recognised so well, more revealing than any words.

"You still don't believe me, do you?"

"I know you're troubled, my lady. But we should go back to the others, before you catch a chill."

"You go if you want. I'm staying here." She sat down on the edge of her blanket and settled the rest more firmly around her shoulders. "I'm not cold."

After a moment's hesitation Weaver hunkered down beside her.

"What, can't you sleep either?"

"Not knowing you're down here by yourself, doing Goddess knows what."

"I'm not going to do anything stupid."

"I didn't suggest you were."

Alwenna shrugged. "I just feel better by the water. In among the trees – oh, I don't know, I find the forest oppressive."

"I've noticed that. The more sky you have, the more alive you are."

"That's it exactly." She turned to him in surprise. "Do you feel the same way?"

He sat with his forearms resting on his knees, his gaze fixed on the open water before them. "Can't say I do. But I noticed, up on the ridgeway."

That was Weaver all over, noticing everything and saying as little as possible. "Do you ever allow yourself to feel anything, Weaver?"

"No, my lady." He turned to face her then. "I've learned it rarely ends well."

"I don't believe you."

Weaver shrugged. "That's your choice." He picked up a flat pebble from the shore and sent it skimming out over the water. It bounced nine times before sinking beneath the surface. "I was worried about you yesterday. I think you're feeling better now."

This was the moment she could tell him everything, and he'd listen. The voices, the stranger, all of it. He'd listen. She shrugged in turn. "I don't do well in the dark."

Footsteps crunched over the lake shore towards them. Deliberately noisy footsteps, unless Alwenna missed her guess. Weaver jumped to his feet, reaching for a sword he wasn't carrying.

It was Erin. "My lady? Drew's asking for you."

Alwenna's initial suspicion the girl had been spying on them faded as she saw her serious expression. "What? Is he worse?"

"He has a fever, my lady."

Weaver helped Alwenna stand, lending his arm for support as she hobbled back to their campsite. The servant girl had already run on ahead. The silence stretched between them.

Drew was fretful when they returned to the camp. "My lady, when I saw you gone... I realised Jervin will have had no word from me in days – he'll be worried."

"Jervin? I don't know him, I think."

"He might be angry with me – he didn't want me to leave. You will explain it was necessary, won't you?" He caught hold of her sleeve, his grip strong. "You will tell him how it is, won't you? He doubted me when I said how important it was. But... Gwydion chose us. I should have told him sooner."

"Of course, I'll explain everything. But you'll see him yourself soon enough." She tried to smile reassuringly, but was assailed by a terrible sense of dread.

"I... I fear it may be too late for me."

"Nonsense. You feel bad now, but you'll soon heal."

Drew gave her a wistful smile and sank back on the folded surcoat that pillowed his head, closing his eyes. She hadn't convinced him, she could sense the sombre direction of his thoughts.

Erin wrung out a cloth in cold water and pressed it over his brow. "I beg your pardon for interrupting, m'lady. He woke almost as soon as you left the fireside."

"There's no need to apologise. You did the right thing."

The girl glanced up as Weaver approached, then busied herself mopping Drew's brow.

"An infusion of these leaves will help bring a fever down." He handed her a small fabric pouch. "Steep them in boiling water for five minutes. Enough for him to drink and to bathe the wound."

"Of course, sir." The girl jumped to her feet and hurried away to stir up the fire and boil water.

"Tell her there's no need to call me sir, could you?"

"You could tell her yourself," Alwenna murmured, taking Erin's place beside Drew. His eyelids flickered as he responded to some dream or vision. A dark one, by the way his features contorted.

"I thought she might take it the wrong way if I said it."

"How?" Alwenna looked up at Weaver, frowning. "Oh, I see what you mean." She wrung out the cloth again and replaced it on Drew's forehead. "I don't think she's sweet on you. She just hasn't worked out where you fit in all this."

"That makes two of us," Weaver muttered.

"What do you–' She didn't need the answer to that question. "That reminds me. Who's Jervin?"

"A trader in Brigholm. Likely he's given Drew work."

"Work? Drew seemed to think he'd be concerned about him. Isn't it rather more than that?"

"Well, the lad hasn't spelled it out, but I'd say you're right."

"I'm glad, if that's the case. I only hope he makes a good

recovery. He needs a healer."

"We should reach Brigholm tomorrow afternoon."

"It's serious, isn't it?"

"It's too soon to tell." Weaver's expression was sombre by the firelight.

Alwenna wished she could have stayed down by the lake shore. As the fire faded the trees pressed in around her, closer than before.

CHAPTER SEVENTY-SIX

They were perhaps half a day's ride from Brigholm and had halted in woodland to water and rest the horses. Drew's condition had not improved. The arrow wound was inflamed and the fever left him weak and sometimes rambling. As she helped Erin cleanse and re-dress his wound, Alwenna noticed the jewelled hilt of the knife stuck in his belt. She knew it straight away, even though the stones were dull and lifeless now. Those stones had glinted in Garrad's hands as he plunged the blade into his own throat. A thousand voices seemed to clamour at once and the scene played out again in her mind: the floor pitching, choking dust rising all around. She snatched up her stick and hobbled away to the riverbank, seating herself on a fallen tree trunk. The chatter of water usually helped to lull the unwanted voices, but it couldn't drown the tormented memories. Not this time.

She'd not been there long before Weaver joined her. "Something is troubling you... my lady?"

Alwenna noticed the pause, absently. "It's fair to say many things are troubling me, Weaver."

"It might help to speak of it." He seemed to have guessed she'd deflected his question. He sat down by her side, as he once had before, at the Holy Well at Vorrahan. Scant weeks ago, yet it seemed like an age. How far they'd travelled since then, only to return full circle.

Weaver plucked a length of grass and began picking the individual grains from the seed head. He was restless. Alwenna studied his profile. Several days' growth of beard covered his face, but didn't disguise the hollowness of his cheeks, a legacy of his sojourn in the dungeon at Highkell. She was distracted briefly by the thought that even the dungeon must have collapsed in the landslide.

The landslide. Her landslide. Had she willed it? She thought back to the moment the floor tilted. Before that. Garrad's scorn. His hatred of her simply for being born who she was. And in the end, perhaps, she'd earned it.

"Do you believe I did it?" She blurted the question before she changed her mind.

Weaver turned towards her, frowning. "Did what?"

"The landslide. Do you believe I caused it?"

"Ah, that." He turned his attention back to the seed head in his hands, and stripped the remaining grains with a single swipe of his thumbnail. He twisted the dry stem about his finger before glancing sideways at her. "Would you like me to say it's impossible, and nothing but superstitious folly?"

Of course she would. She needed that reassurance – something stable in a world that had changed beyond recognition. Weaver believed none of that, after all. If he couldn't touch it with his own hand, see it with his own eyes, he wouldn't believe it.

But he hesitated. Too long.

"I see." He, too, believed she was some kind of monster. She gathered her feet beneath her, ready to stand.

Weaver reached out and set his hand on her forearm. "Wait."

"What?" She pushed herself to her feet, leaning heavily on the stick.

"Don't you want to hear my answer?"

"No. I can see I shouldn't have asked." She began to hobble back to rejoin the others. Weaver threw the grass stem to the ground and walked alongside her.

"I was about to say there have been plenty of landslides at Highkell in the past. The road has been washed out several times over the years – it's common knowledge."

"And the last time was when I arrived there as a child."

"Nothing more than coincidence. The real wonder is the road didn't wash out again until now."

Too little, too late. "They did a lot of work to strengthen it."

"That might have diverted the water under the tower instead. Water's powerful stuff."

He made it sound almost plausible. If his response had been immediate she might have been convinced. She stood still. She had nothing to lose by asking. "Drew's carrying a dagger, an ornate thing... do you know where he got it?"

"Ornate? He favours plain and lethal, balanced for throwing."

"There's one in his belt. With gemstones set in the hilt."

"I don't–" Weaver frowned. "Wait – he picked one up from the rubble. Near where we found you. Why?"

"No reason."

"There's always a reason."

"It looks like–" The voices began again, and she felt as if the ground was pitching beneath her, and her nostrils filled with the smell of blood mingled with dust... She clenched the fingers of her left hand until her nails dug deep into her palm. The voices faded. "The one Garrad had. The blade he turned against himself."

"Garrad was another madman who finally overreached himself."

She would have loved to clutch at the straw he offered. But in her heart of hearts she knew it was not the case. "According to you the world is filled with madmen. He would have attacked me with that dagger if I hadn't invoked the Goddess." She didn't tell him how the jewels had shone with a strange light. Or how the wall fell away after the dagger rolled against it from Garrad's dead hand. How the floor... She stopped her thoughts pursuing that line any further as the voices began to murmur again.

"If Garrad was close by it's no great surprise Drew found it as we moved the rubble."

His words made perfect sense, as always, but it was Drew who'd been struck by the archer's arrow when they were almost out of range. "If it's the same one, I think it's an ill-omened thing."

"What, do you believe Garrad is a great loss to the world? You could as well believe it to be lucky – what if that arrow had been destined to kill Drew outright? It's a dagger, no more, no less. It'll be valuable. By all means stow it away in a bag, to be sure he doesn't injure himself in his fever."

He was right, of course. And yet... "So many strange things have happened. Do you still insist there's a simple explanation for all of them?"

Weaver hesitated again. "It was Drew who told us you were trapped. And he led us straight to the spot where you were buried."

This was not the reassurance she sought. "And?"

Weaver folded his arms. "I have no way to explain that."

"If you allow that, then you must allow the dagger could be ill-omened. You can't have it both ways."

"A blade is just a blade. Good or evil lies in the mind of the one who wields it."

"What if I told you I saw the gemstones in the hilt gleam when there was no sunlight to brighten them? What then? If the world is filled with madmen, Weaver, what does that make me?"

Weaver's mouth narrowed to a tight line. "I don't know, my lady." He turned and walked away.

CHAPTER SEVENTY-SEVEN

A servant opened the door in answer to Weaver's peremptory summons. A tall, thin man, his eyes widened as he took in the dishevelled group waiting outside the door. But he confirmed this was indeed Jervin the trader's house, and he would inform his master of their presence.

"Be quick about it then. Inform your master that Drew is one of our party, and badly injured. I doubt he would want him left waiting on the doorstep a moment longer than necessary."

The servant ran suspicious eyes over the group again before closing the door. Drew, still slumped in the saddle, was hooded and wrapped in a warm cloak to protect him from the worst ills of his fever. Weaver would have lifted him down while they waited, but the servant's manner left him doubting they'd be made welcome by Drew's putative employer.

The sound of hasty footsteps came from within and the door was flung open by the servant, now flushed with embarrassment.

"My master bids you all welcome and please to come in. If some of you would be so kind as to lead your horses round to the stables, the head groom will make all the necessary arrangements." He stepped back, gesturing them inside. Weaver and Blaine lifted Drew bodily from the saddle and carried him between them up the front steps. Alwenna hobbled behind, leaning heavily on her stick, but carrying a saddlebag slung over her shoulder. The servant cast a doubtful eye over her bedraggled gown, but he bowed and offered to take the bag from her.

She paused to look the servant up and down, raising one eyebrow. "That will not be necessary, thank you."

Curtis and Erin led the horses round to the stable yard at the back of the house. The servant closed the front door behind the rest of them and they had a moment to take stock of their surroundings before a door burst open at the back of the hallway and a stranger hurried forward.

"My name is Jervin. I welcome you to my home."

He was tall, of lean build, fair-haired. His eyes moved over them swiftly, coming to rest on Drew, supported as he was between Weaver and Blaine. "I knew this would end badly. What have you done?"

Drew summoned a weak smile. "I... foolishly stopped an arrow. But it's just a bit of fever. Now I'm home..."

Jervin clapped his hands and half a dozen servants appeared. In an instant he had sent one hurrying to bring the healer, while two more took charge of Drew and carried him through to the room from which Jervin had emerged. He instructed the oldest servant, a man Weaver guessed to be perhaps in his mid-fifties, to arrange hot water for them all.

"You will be my guests tonight, I trust? I can only offer you space in my hall, but the day is well advanced and I am sure you are travel-weary. We will dine at sunset."

Weaver glanced at Alwenna before speaking. She

looked exhausted, but nodded agreement. As well for her that they rest here. "Thank you. We are happy to accept your hospitality. Might I request the healer attends the ladies once he has treated Drew? The road has not been kind to them." He bowed then. "My name is Weaver."

Jervin bowed in return. "You are welcome, Weaver. And this, I think, must be the Lady Alwenna?" Weaver was not sure he liked the way Jervin eyed Alwenna. Then again, Drew had galloped off whole to save her and returned broken, so perhaps his attitude was understandable.

She smiled politely – her court smile – and said what was proper. "I cannot thank you enough for sparing Drew to help us. Without him we would have been in a sorry state."

Jervin bowed politely. Curtis and Erin emerged from another door at the back of the house and Weaver performed the necessary introductions before Jervin, clearly anxious to speak to Drew, left them. A servant led them through a door in one side of the antechamber to the great hall. A fire was already kindled in the grate and more servants were busy filling tubs with hot water in two small rooms off to one side. Whatever trade Jervin was involved in, it had to be a highly profitable one.

CHAPTER SEVENTY-EIGHT

Jervin was civil to his guests as they ate at his table, but it was clear it was a matter of doing his duty as host rather than any wish to get to know Drew's friends. After they'd finished eating Alwenna asked if she might visit Drew, to see how he was faring.

"We will have little opportunity tomorrow – Weaver tells me we must ride on early in the morning."

"You must? You are, of course, welcome to rest for longer – you have been through a terrible ordeal." Jervin met Alwenna's gaze as he uttered concern, yet she suspected he was relieved to hear her announcement.

Weaver spoke up before she could reply. "With regret, we must leave as soon after first light as may be. We have a long road before us."

Had they indeed? She would ask him about that. But she said nothing in front of Jervin. She was as keen to be gone from under his roof as he was to see them leave.

"Permit me to take you to him now, my lady." Jervin rose graciously from his seat. When Alwenna stood, Weaver did likewise. Doubtless he'd added their host to the ever-growing list of those he didn't trust. He'd been right about Garrad, so she made no objection to him accompanying them.

Drew was dozing on a daybed but stirred when they entered the room at the back of the house.

"You have visitors, Drew." Jervin's tone was surprisingly soft. "They must leave in the morning, and wished to reassure themselves you were recovering."

Drew was propped up on pillows, a clean dressing over his wounded shoulder. He smiled as he recognised Alwenna and Weaver. Already he looked much improved. Jervin reminded them the healer had stressed the importance of rest, then he withdrew, claiming urgent paperwork to do for his business.

"I couldn't leave without thanking you for coming to my rescue. If I can ever help you in return, you must call on me." As Alwenna spoke she realised she had no idea where or how she might be found in future.

"You must leave so soon?" There was disappointment in Drew's voice.

Alwenna glanced at Weaver. "We have an early start and a long ride ahead of us tomorrow."

"Of course." Drew nodded.

"We wouldn't leave you if we weren't convinced you were in good hands." Alwenna offered.

"The very best hands." Drew sat up, wincing as his wound tugged. "Jervin's an excellent fellow. If he seems a little distant, it's only because he was worried about me."

They chatted for a few minutes, until Drew began yawning, then they took their leave. They were almost at the door when Drew stopped them.

"Wait – I almost forgot. There's something I must give you."

Alwenna and Weaver exchanged puzzled looks.

"I found it in the ruins." He gestured to the court

cupboard at the side of his room. "It's in the top, left-hand side. It's important. You should have it, my lady."

Weaver crossed over and opened the door. He lifted out a cloth-wrapped bundle.

"Yes, that's it. I think… it's not intended for my hand."

Weaver closed the door and returned to the bedside, partially unwrapping the bundle to reveal the hilt of the ornate dagger.

"I found it when we were clearing fallen stone – I turned aside to lift a particular stone. I had to. And this was underneath."

Weaver raised an eyebrow. "Why think it's not for you? You found it."

"I can't keep it. The visions I had in my fever – the Lady Alwenna will need it." Drew's fingers plucked at his bedcover, straightening and smoothing it. "I know it's not for me."

Weaver glanced at Alwenna.

"I don't want it." She recalled the flash of the gemstones as Garrad plunged the blade into his throat. "It's ill-starred."

"You must take it, my lady. It'll not serve me. But one day it will serve you." Drew's voice was oddly modulated.

Weaver examined the dagger. "Visions, you say?"

Alwenna had expected him to voice scorn at the very suggestion the knife had some predestined properties. Now it was out in the open she couldn't draw her eyes away from it. There were dark stains in the runes engraved on the blade, presumably remnants of Garrad's blood. But the gemstones remained lifeless as Weaver turned it over in his hands.

Drew shook his head. "It was all confusion. Shouting, and fire. The Lady Alwenna took up the blade – I saw it in her hand. I know it is hers. She needed it. To defend…

her... child?" Drew looked from one to the other.

Child? She'd never told him. Unless Weaver had? From the look Weaver sent her way he was asking himself much the same question of her.

Weaver returned to studying the blade. "It's a fine piece of craftsmanship. You could sell it for a pretty sum."

Drew shook his head. "I told you. It's not mine to keep or to sell."

"Then we'll take it with us." Weaver flipped the cloth over the blade and wrapped it up. "Don't breathe a word of this to anyone else, Drew."

Drew sank back on his pillows. "I won't, I swear."

"Weaver, is it wise?" Had he listened to nothing of what she'd told him by the river?

"The Goddess will watch over you, my lady." Drew smiled. "I'm sure of it."

Weaver handed the bundle to Alwenna.

She couldn't refuse it, not in front of Drew, not when he so clearly believed she needed it. She took hold of it as gingerly as if it might shatter in her hands. Nothing happened and she felt suddenly foolish. A blade was just a blade.

"Thank you, Drew. I remain in your debt."

They took their leave then. The anteroom was empty and Alwenna paused there. "Did you tell him? About... this?" She set her hand upon her lower abdomen.

"No. I never would." Weaver hesitated. "You didn't?"

Alwenna shook her head. "No. Drew's sight is perhaps stronger than Gwydion believed." Were they right to leave Drew behind here? But what alternative did they have? He wished to stay. "Jervin is not at all keen to have us here, is he?"

"I've known warmer welcomes."

"But we're safe enough here, surely?"

"I've no wish to be beholden to his hospitality a moment longer than necessary."

"Beggars can't be choosers. Isn't that what they say?"

"He should show you more respect, my lady."

The candle in the wall sconce had gone out, and the only light in the antechamber came from fading embers in the small hearth. The darkness pressed about Alwenna. And waiting for her in the darkness were the voices. There was just enough light to see Weaver move over to the door. Any second now he'd open it and step through it to rejoin the others.

"Weaver, wait. You said we need to leave early tomorrow. Was that just for Jervin's benefit? Only... You haven't discussed it with me." She didn't mean the words to sound like an accusation, but his back stiffened and he stepped away from the door. At the back of her mind the whispers began. Somewhere the unknown lovers were stirring. She heard the sigh of a robe sliding to the floor.

"I wanted to see how he reacted." He hesitated, one hand moving to the back of his neck.

"Why?" Her heightened sense could almost taste his unease in the dim room. What was causing it? The lovers were already engrossed in the contact of fingertips on warm flesh... She pushed them to the very back of her mind. "You could have asked me what was in our host's mind: I knew he didn't want us here. Gwydion's gift is not entirely without use."

"I never thought of..." He paced across the room. "You can do that? Tell what people are thinking?"

It was so tempting to tell him yes. The lovers were

kissing, she knew, in that darkened room she was trying to close her mind to. "No, not in so many words." She was losing the thread of their conversation. "I can tell when people are lying. Sometimes. Not always."

Weaver cleared his throat. "I'd have stopped Gwydion that day. If I'd known what he was going to do."

"You made that clear at the time." She looked across at Weaver. His embarrassment was plain even by the dim firelight. "Tresilian himself told me to go to him. I've never understood why."

Weaver shifted awkwardly. "That reminds me. There's something I haven't had time to tell you." He folded his arms.

Somewhere in the darkness flesh goosebumped, exposed to the night air as more clothing fell away. Alwenna shivered. "What about? Tomorrow?"

Weaver pressed his hand to his chin. "Yes. Tomorrow."

This was going to take some time. "Well? Tomorrow's almost upon us." The other voices had stilled. Right now she and Weaver were alone with the two lovers.

"It is, my lady." He looked down at her with an unreadable expression on his face. Maybe the only emotion he could express was anger. "We will ride east, to meet with a freemerchant named Marten. He claims..." Weaver hesitated. "Well, there's a faction there who would restore you to your birthright."

"Indeed?" She took a step closer to him. "And when will you ask whether I wish to fall in with such plans?"

Weaver stared at her. "Why wouldn't you? You are queen of The Marches."

"And I've been tugged back and forth between rival factions all my life." Her skin burned with the lovers' hunger. All she wanted was to lose herself as they were. "Have you any idea how it is to be raised for duty? To be told every day what you must do for other people, because it is your duty. Twice now I've been obedient and given up my own hopes for duty and this time I'm done with it."

"But, my lady–" He rubbed the back of his neck.

"I have a name. Just for once, why don't you use it?" She turned her back on him as she tried to regain some semblance of control. Damn those lovers. Their willing flesh. Their hunger.

"But, my–"

She spun round to glare at him. "Didn't you hear me?" The bundle in her hand slipped from her fingers and fell to the floor, the fabric flopping open to reveal the knife. Muttering in annoyance, she stooped down to pick it up.

The gemstones in the hilt glowed faintly in the dim room.

Alwenna froze, her hand inches away from the knife. "Do you see that?"

Weaver moved round until he blocked the light from the fire. The stones still shimmered. "I see it." His voice was impassive.

"Tell me it's some trick of the light."

"Move away from it, my lady."

He'd told her what to do once too often. She stretched her fingers towards it and the colours in the gemstones intensified. Such a beautiful thing...

Weaver flicked the knife out of reach with his foot. It spun away across the floor with a clatter, the gemstones fading as it came to rest.

Alwenna straightened up, sending a burst of pain through her ankle. "How dare you?"

Weaver picked up the cloth from the floor, and scooped up the knife with it, wrapping the cloth around it.

All the fight fell away from Alwenna. She pushed open the door to the great hall and hobbled over to the corner where Erin had laid out her blankets, ignoring the startled looks from the others. She curled up beneath the blankets, hating the smell of horse that lingered about them, hating her so-called freedom, hating everything.

CHAPTER SEVENTY-NINE

The stable yard was still deep in early morning shadow when Curtis returned with the horses he'd acquired for Erin and Alwenna.

Erin jumped down from the rail where she'd been sitting. "I hope you didn't pay too much for these." She circled the horses, eyeing them critically.

"There wasn't much choice at such short notice. Likely the army cleaned out the best of their stock a few weeks back."

Weaver had been lounging against the stable wall in frowning silence as they waited, but he roused at this news. "Tresilian's army? Any word on where they went?"

"None." Curtis shook his head. "If they knew where they were bound they kept tight-lipped about it. But there's word from Highkell. Vasic was injured in the collapse, but he survived."

"More's the pity." Erin looked up from inspecting the new horses' feet. "You paid too much for these animals."

"They're both sound." Curtis pretended to be affronted by her close inspection. "I had them trotted up to be sure."

"Next time you have to buy a horse, send me to do it."

Curtis grinned, looking pleased with himself. "Fine way

to thank a man for going to all that trouble."

"It's a good job we're both light, that's all I'll say." Erin removed the saddle and ran her fingertips over the underside, before checking the horse's back.

"As soon as you're done counting that horse's legs, we can go." Weaver fastened his saddlebags into place.

"It'll take me five minutes to check the tack. Or would you rather lose hours down the road when there's a problem?" Erin set the saddle back in place and tightened the girth. "This one will have the easiest paces for my lady." Erin handed the reins to Weaver, before subjecting the other horse to a similar inspection.

Weaver led the horse over to where Alwenna waited. "If you're ready, my lady?" His expression was closed.

"So we go in search of this freemerchant?"

"Have you a better suggestion?"

She scowled at him. "You know the answer to that."

"Well, then." He gestured towards the waiting horse.

She readied herself to mount and he legged her up. Right now she needed his help, but they would have a day of reckoning. Soon, she promised herself. She took up the reins. "The dagger. Do you still have it?"

"Yes." Weaver looked up, his expression revealing nothing of his thoughts. "Do you want to carry it? It's yours."

"No."

"Very well." Weaver turned away to his horse. "Aren't you done yet?" he asked Erin, who was still fussing over her tack.

"I'm done." She vaulted into the saddle. Grinning, she turned her horse to face the gate. "Never let it be said I'm the one holding us back, windbagging."

CHAPTER EIGHTY

The healer stowed the last of his equipment in his bag. "Your back continues to mend well, your highness, and I can find no sign of serious illness. I can bleed you again if you wish, but I doubt it will improve matters."

"No, I'm tired enough as it is." Vasic gestured the man away irritably.

"As you wish, your highness." The man bowed low, the bald centre of his head sun-tanned in contrast to the grey hair surrounding it. "Ensure you eat red meat at every meal. That will help counter the tiredness." He took up his bag, bowed once more, and backed out of Vasic's private chamber. What the healer lacked in insight he at least made up for in deference.

Vasic pushed himself up from his chair. Even that small effort was a struggle. His limbs were leaden, and the pain in his side deepened as he moved – the pain the healer swore was nothing more than trapped wind. And then there was the dream. Every night now, for how long?

That was the worst of it. Every night, over and over, he was forced to relive Tresilian's death in his sleep. If it had been the collapse of the tower, the warmth of Garrad's blood as it spurted against his face, or the horror on

Alwenna's face as she and the servant girl were swallowed by the rubble... That he could have understood. Events like that could – should – haunt a man, unless he were less than human. But Tresilian's death?

That had never haunted him. It had been a simple matter of expedience – the only common-sense action for a usurper to take. Of course, only she had dared call him that. Alwenna. His second cousin. The driving force behind everything he'd done for as long as he could remember.

He took up his ornate walking cane – he would never use the thing in front of witnesses – and made his way over to the window. Once it had looked along the curtain wall to the main tower. Now it perched above the massive cleft torn through the curtain wall. At the bottom ran a desultory trickle of water from the spring for which Highkell had been named.

Below, masons and labourers were erecting a wooden framework from which to begin repairing the broken wall. The engineers had pronounced the remaining structure sound. According to them the old watergate had been too narrow to allow floodwater to escape and the heavy rain had proved the final straw. Their explanation was sweet reason.

Everyone knew the power of water. The engineers proposed to build a larger watergate, supplemented by others at intervals through the curtain wall so the water would never be so disastrously dammed back. The expense would be ruinous, but he would save money by not rebuilding the fallen tower. And they could salvage stone from the wreckage, once they'd repaired the road through the gorge. That had to be his first priority: without the tolls from passing trade, Highkell was nothing. If the road remained washed out for too long the merchants would find other ways to move their goods around the Peninsula. And all his machinations would have been for naught.

He leaned on the window sill, watching the workers move over the broken curtain wall. And for the first time he doubted he would live to see the wall restored to its former strength. Did grief affect a man that way? He could abandon Highkell. Leave it now, return to his fortress in the south. Yet his need to control Highkell had driven him so long he couldn't imagine life without it. Just as he couldn't imagine life without the Lady Alwenna. But they'd pulled no one alive from the rubble. And after the second collapse of the curtain wall had taken a whole contingent of archers with it, they'd abandoned any hopes of reaching anyone buried on the lower slopes.

He turned away from the sunlight, which only seemed to taunt him, and shuffled back to his chair, leaning heavily on his cane. The healer insisted his illness was spiritual, not physical. But the healer hadn't been there to sense the raw power unleashed when Alwenna invoked the Goddess. Only after that had the floor begun to shake.

It was nonsensical, of course. And it was Garrad whom Alwenna had cursed. She'd told Vasic he had nothing to fear, yet his strength had fallen away day by day ever since. Should he return to the south? Better, perhaps, than staying here among the ruins of all his hopes. He could leave a steward to oversee the repairs. But he doubted he had the energy to undertake the journey, certainly not by horseback, having wrenched his back, scrambling clear as the floor collapsed. And his carriages were trapped in the stable yard at Highkell until the road was reopened. The indecision was worse than anything else. He lowered

himself into his chair, distributing his weight carefully on
the cushions. There had to be some cause for this accursed
weakness. And if the healer insisted it wasn't physical he
would investigate other possibilities.

He summoned a servant. "The high seer from Lynesreach
is waiting in the guest lodgings. Bring him to me now."

CHAPTER EIGHTY-ONE

Alwenna's eyes stung from the grit and dust that billowed over the Blighted Sea. Her face burned, scoured by the thin wind despite wrapping a scarf about her head as the freemerchants did. She ached from a long day spent in the saddle. Her damaged ankle throbbed even though she'd slipped it out of the stirrup early on in the journey so she could keep the joint moving. Even Erin, riding at her side, was slumped in her saddle, head bowed as she tried to keep her face out of the wind.

Ahead of them Weaver twisted round to say something. His words were snatched away by the wind. In the direction he pointed Alwenna could see through the dust a shape too big and too regular to be yet another boulder. To the windward side of it was a clump of trees. Proper, tall trees with trunks, not the scrubby bushes that were scattered over the plain. The inn. It had to be.

The inn was a long, low-eaved building, built around three sides of a courtyard. The fourth side was enclosed by a ramshackle set of stables. At some point in the past the walls had been rendered with clay and painted with lime-wash, but it was now so weather-beaten the overall impression was one of sun-bleached terracotta. Shabby or not, the relief the courtyard offered from the scouring wind was sublime. Alwenna slid down from her saddle, careless of her injured ankle until she landed half her weight on it, and yelped.

"My lady, you should have waited." Erin handed her the walking stick.

"I didn't think." She tested her weight on her ankle again, gingerly. "But I'm sure it's getting better. I couldn't have done that yesterday."

Nearby, Weaver stood where he'd just dismounted from his own horse, watching Alwenna. When she caught his eye he turned away, unwinding the scarf from his head, and stopping to shake the dust out of it once he was clear of the horses at the edge of the yard.

"You likely won't be able to put any weight on it at all tomorrow." Erin began disentangling her long hair and dusty scarf. They made their way over to where Weaver waited, and Alwenna tugged her own scarf loose.

The inn had two main rooms – the tap room where a bar held barrels of ale, and a room lined with tables for serving food. This was currently empty, although the tables were well-worn. Alwenna assumed the recent spate of windy weather had deterred most travellers from venturing over the Blighted Sea. Certainly, the landlord hurried over to serve them eagerly enough.

Weaver ordered a plain stew and requested it be well salted. "I'm to meet the freemerchant, Marten. He told me you'd be able to give me directions to find him."

"Well now." The landlord straightened up, rubbing his ear thoughtfully. "There are plenty people would like to find Marten, but there's nothing to say he wants to be found by all of them. You're a stranger to me, and I've never seen you here with him, so you'll have to give me your name first."

"My name's Weaver." He drummed his fingertips on the smooth-scrubbed table. He didn't appear at all easy about this business with the freemerchant. Unless the strange incident with Drew's dagger had left him in such a foul mood. Perhaps with some good ale inside him, he might be a little sweeter – and more forthcoming besides. Alwenna couldn't shake the conviction he was being less than frank with her.

"That's a common enough name in these parts."

"Ranald Weaver." Weaver's fingertips stilled. "Marten himself told me to ask for directions here. I doubt he'll be pleased to learn you're playing games with his people."

His people? What did he mean by that? Alwenna turned her full attention to the exchange.

The landlord frowned. "I never play games, not where business is concerned. And not where my important customers are concerned, neither."

Weaver stared back at him and they froze thus for a moment before the landlord nodded, glancing at Alwenna as he spoke. "He's left a message for you – I'll bring it."

"Very well. I must trust Marten's in no great hurry to see us."

The landlord vanished through a door behind the bar. He reappeared almost immediately, bearing a sealed letter which he handed to Weaver without ceremony. "He's paid up front for a room for the lady, and one for yourself. The rest can take space in the attics."

Weaver nodded again, waiting for the landlord to leave before cracking open the wax seal. Alwenna, seated opposite, couldn't see the text. Weaver read it then folded the paper, stowing it away without comment. He looked up to find her watching him.

"We're to join the freemerchant at the summer palace – your old family home, my lady. He pulls longer strings than I once imagined."

"My family home? I haven't seen the place in over twelve years." She'd had a sunny room with views over a tumbling mountain stream. There had been a huge dining table, polished to such a sheen she could see her own reflection in it. Her father had sat at one end, her mother at the other. Only rarely had she joined them. And then she had disgraced herself, pulling faces at her reflection while her father spoke. Had that been at the summer palace, or the city residence in Brigholm? None of it seemed terribly familiar now. She certainly had no recollection of crossing the Blighted Sea before.

Weaver was watching her as if he expected some kind of reaction.

"I remember very little about it." Right now she was more concerned about that letter. It had been addressed to him, of course, she'd seen that much as he read the single sheet. So really it was none of her business, yet... She was sure Weaver was hiding something from her.

The rooms the landlord allocated to them were along the landing at the far end of the building from the stairs, above the dining room.

Erin checked the bedding suspiciously once the landlord had left them. "Well, I've seen worse."

They'd not been there long before servants arrived with hot water and a tub which they filled before the fire, setting up a discreet folding screen.

Alwenna eased herself into the water with relief, glad

of the first real opportunity to ease her aches and pains.
The bruising was coming out on her ankle now, and it
was a grotesque purple, but the swelling was reducing.
She lay back, sinking as low as she could in the water.
The tub wasn't as luxurious as the one she'd been used to
at Highkell, but it was adequate. And the water was the
perfect temperature. She closed her eyes.

And she was there at Highkell again, pacing back and
forth across one of the lesser guest chambers. Her arm
was in a sling and it pained her if she moved too quickly.
Everything had gone wrong. She didn't know how she
knew, she just did. She explored her feelings with a strange
air of detachment: so much frustration, so much pent-up
anger, and behind it all a deep-rooted fear. And it was all
Alwenna's fault. She coughed, and had to stop pacing back
and forth as pain seared through her ribs. She pressed a
hand to the spot where it hurt. And then she was in a
dungeon, Vasic leaning close, smiling, wine-laced breath
warming her face. "Would it be a kindness to you?"

"You haven't the mettle." Every word took a supreme
effort, every inch of her body ached. For a moment the
scene dissolved and the dull pain eased. Was this death?
Had she been wrong to fear it all this time? Then Vasic's
face swam back into focus. His words were distorted,
indistinct. But somehow they amused her. "Such irony."
She began to laugh, but a pain tore into her ribs. A pain so
stark she cried out and then it stole the air from her lungs
so she couldn't even–

"My lady? What happened?" Erin bent over her,
alarmed. "Are you hurt?"

Alwenna gaped at Erin. Dazzling spots swam before her
eyes and her chest was tight with the need to draw in air.

Somehow she opened her mouth and sucked in a harsh lungful, and another, and her sight began to clear. She sat up abruptly, shaking as her body clamoured for her to fight, to flee, to save herself.

"My lady, what is it?"

It was all Alwenna could do to breathe. She folded forward, wrapping her arms about her knees, and gradually the pressure on her lungs eased.

There was a clatter at the door and Weaver crashed into the room. "What's going on? Is–"

He halted, staring at Alwenna. Bare-chested, one half of his face was clean-shaven, the other lathered, a spot of blood mingling with the lather on his jawline where the blade had slipped.

And she couldn't help but laugh, shakily at first. Wide-eyed, Erin snatched up a towel and held it in front of Alwenna to spare her blushes.

Weaver's face coloured with embarrassment. "I thought you were being murdered."

Alwenna tried to get her breathing back under control, gulping for air between bursts of laughter. "No," was all she managed.

"Then by the Goddess's name what happened?"

Tears were streaming down her cheeks and she splashed her face with water. That helped her regain control. "I dozed off. It was a nightmare, that's all."

"That's all?" His mouth twisted with distaste, the way it did every time she mentioned the sight. It was enough to sober her up.

"That's all. Truly." She could almost breathe normally again, and the sensation of pain in her ribs was nothing but a bad memory. She shivered. "It was an unpleasant one, but I do apologise, for I've made you cut yourself."

He raised a hand to his jaw. "It's nothing. You're unhurt?"

"I'm unhurt." In that shadowy place she didn't know, a woman was murmuring soothing words to a man who'd woken from a nightmare. Her nightmare. Yet how could that be? She shook her head to clear it of the whispers.

Frowning, Weaver studied her face, clearly unconvinced. "Are you sure, my lady?"

"Why ever would I say I was unhurt if I wasn't? If you don't mind, I would very much like to get out of this bath, but there's a terrible draught from that doorway." She gathered her knees, ready to stand.

"I beg your pardon, my lady." Weaver turned away and she caught a glimpse of a raw wound on his ribs before he shut the door abruptly behind himself.

"The towel, Erin, if you please." Alwenna stood and the girl hastily offered up the towel, attempting to assume the mask-like composure she'd worn throughout her time at Highkell.

CHAPTER EIGHTY-TWO

The high seer from Lynesreach precinct was a portly man whose substantial belly and air of self-consequence invariably preceded him into the room. His flesh brimmed up around the ostentatious signet ring he wore on the middle finger of his left hand, suggesting he hadn't always been that way. Vasic had no real wish to speak to the man, but he was clutching at straws. And the High Seer Yurgen of Lynesreach was a very substantial straw indeed. If Vasic should make it through this mysterious illness, he intended to inspect the precinct at Lynesreach. If the rest of the brethren had grown even half as hefty as Yurgen, he would raise their taxes.

Yurgen was surprisingly supple for his build and he bowed in creditable style, his nose almost scraping the floor. The haughty note from his letter to Vasic before the wedding was absent today – instead his manner was all appeasement. The days he'd spent kicking his heels in the guest lodgings since the wedding might have sweetened him somewhat.

"Highness, I am your most loyal servant, humble and eager to do your bidding." He straightened up, folding his hands in pious manner, keeping his eyes lowered in a gratifying display of humility.

Could Vasic even rely on the man to tell him the truth, should he know it? The seer had all the appearance of one who was determined to please, whatever the cost. Vasic stroked his chin. His beard was growing apace. He loathed the feel of it, but it served to hide the worst ravages of his mysterious illness.

As ever Vasic was tempted to say nothing. The sight would tell the seer what he wanted from him, would it not? Yurgen waited in silence, an ingratiating smile plastered on his face while he kept his eyes deferentially lowered. Really, the man was an intolerable sycophant once he was within range of immediate consequences for his actions.

Vasic sighed. "You must be frank with me, high seer. I know you are well able to cast aside concerns of precedence and status where matters of the sight are concerned – I have your reply concerning the Lady Alwenna as proof of that."

The man paled visibly and lowered his head further. "Your highness, the sight is impartial. It grieved me greatly to write such–"

Vasic raised one hand in the air and the man fell silent. With his face directed at the floor his peripheral vision had to be remarkable indeed. Vasic lowered his hand again, resting it on the arm of his chair before the tremors could be seen.

"I make no recrimination for that letter. It is over and done." He drew in a breath, looking for the words to phrase his query in as roundabout a way as possible. "Today I would have you tell me what visions the sight has brought you since then."

"Your highness, the sight is a fickle thing, it ebbs and

flows like the tide. It is ever secretive and the glimpses it grants us are often obscure."

"Yes, yes. I know that. Just tell me what you have seen."

The man licked his lips nervously. "Highness, I hardly know where to begin…"

He was indeed pale. Paler than Vasic could ever recall seeing him before. Something about his manner reminded Vasic of… himself. His own haunted sleep and feverish night-fears. "Tell me, Yurgen, do you have visions that recur, night after night?"

Yurgen's eyes widened and for a moment, in his surprise, he looked straight at Vasic. "Highness, I do." He seemed at a loss as to what to say next.

"Then perhaps you might begin with those, before we both die of old age."

Yurgen shuffled his feet. "You must understand, highness, that the sight is often imprecise, and can defy rational explanation." He hesitated, looking up at Vasic with apprehension.

"Yes, yes, of course." Was the old fraud about to reveal something he needed to hear for once? Vasic snapped his fingers. The guards at the door stood to attention. "Leave us. You will remain outside and ensure we are not disturbed until I give you further orders." He waited until the door had closed behind them before turning his attention back to the high seer.

"Very well, Yurgen. Tell me what the sight has revealed to you."

Yurgen bowed again, nose almost to the ground once more. He shook as he straightened up, clasping and reclasping his hands in the time-honoured pose of the overly pious. "This week, night after night, your highness,

I have seen… death. And with it darkness, such a darkness as I have never seen before. It corrupts all it touches. It is tainted, it runs against all natural order, an abomination." He shivered. "This much I can sense, but where the darkness is situated I cannot tell, or what form it takes. Its origin is… hidden from me. Unknowable."

Once Vasic would have scorned the man's words, sneered at his lack of solid information. Once. But the high seer's palpable fear convinced him. The man had always been holier-than-thou and arrogant with it. But now his composure had quite deserted him as he spoke of this mysterious darkness. Vasic fingered his beard. Darkness. The seer's words resonated with his own sense of foreboding.

"What else, Yurgen, besides this darkness?"

"Your highness, the darkness runs through everything, it reaches out across the kingdom. It… I think… it would engulf you if it had its way."

This was not the complacent litany he was used to hearing from seers. This was something raw, elemental. The man's fear was so heavy he could almost taste it on the air. This time, the seer believed. For once he would hear the truth, insofar as the man understood it. "If it had its way? It has a will, then?"

"Nothing is certain, your highness. I… I cannot examine it, every instinct forces me to turn away."

"And do you believe this is some elemental thing the Lady Alwenna's curse has conjured into being?" This was the question that most concerned Vasic. He expected the old man to crow over him, and upbraid him for not heeding his oft-repeated warnings by keeping Alwenna at Highkell.

The seer shifted uncomfortably. "No, your highness. It is an ancient thing, as old as death itself. And it reaches out for her, too. It hungers…"

"She fell to her death. None could have survived." He spoke the words almost without realising.

"Highness, it still hungers for her. For all who are of Gabrennir's royal line."

A cloud moved across the sun at that moment and Vasic shivered despite himself. A darkness that hungered for royal blood? Even beyond death? The whole thing was preposterous, yet… it had a ring of truth he could not easily dismiss, without knowing why it was so. "Pour us both drinks, Yurgen." He indicated a decanter of wine on the side table. "I must know everything you can tell me."

CHAPTER EIGHTY-THREE

It was only when Alwenna walked into the dining room and saw Weaver, freshly shaven and cleaned of the grime of several days' travel, sitting there with the others that it finally hit her: she'd survived. Whatever had happened to Vasic, he wasn't sending soldiers after her or they'd have overtaken them long before now. And those archers had fired on them, so they had to know someone had been retrieved from the rubble. Then again, all the archers had fallen with the final section of curtain wall that collapsed. The Goddess had been watching over her, it seemed. Her next religious observance would be very different from the ritual she had always performed out of duty. She still had no reason to believe the Goddess had truly spoken, and it was probably just coincidence. But... belief... As a child her prayers hadn't been answered. It was fair to say her non-belief had been shaken.

She realised Weaver was holding a chair ready for her to sit. "Thank you. There's no need to do that – I'm just another traveller on this road." She sat. In a plain kirtle she was once more anonymous, but not if Weaver insisted on treating her as a grand lady.

Weaver raised his eyebrows, but he didn't argue. "We've

been hearing more about Vasic. Rumour has it he's not just ill, but gravely ill."

Was that to be laid at her door too? "What would they know in an out-of-the-way place like this?"

"The freemerchants say rumours travel fastest along good roads. Roads meet here from all four corners of The Marches – it's hardly out of the way."

"Well, if the freemerchants say it is so…" That reminded her of the letter from the freemerchant, Marten. What was it that other freemerchant had said on the road to Vorrahan? He'd claimed her as sister. There they were, scurrying about the kingdom, passing on their nuggets of news. It was a strange kind of freedom to be always on the move like that.

The food arrived while she was lost in thought. She felt strangely lightheaded. She'd been keeping the voices at bay since her vision in the bath, but she could sense them now, growing more determined, nibbling at the edges of her resolve. Perhaps food would help.

Conversation ebbed and flowed around her, yet she felt unable to contribute to it. She picked at the stew, aware she needed to eat but she had little appetite. When she pushed her unfinished portion aside she still felt oddly detached from her surroundings. She was missing something of import – something crucial. When the menfolk started delving into the ale she decided to withdraw to her room. Weaver looked up questioningly as she stood. He glanced to where Erin was engrossed in conversation with Curtis. Alwenna shook her head. She could manage perfectly well without assistance. Erin and Curtis might make an odd couple, the one skinny as the other was solid, but let them seize a rare moment of happiness.

Alwenna had reached her room door before she knew what she was about to do. She paused, hand on the latch, checking back along the dim corridor. The corridor was empty. There were no locks on the room doors here – they could be bolted from the inside, and each room contained a strong chest that was secured to the floor, where valuables might be locked away. She turned and walked the few paces back to Weaver's room. Even though there was no one nearby to hear, she thumbed the latch cautiously so it would make no noise and slipped inside. The room was identical to hers, with shabby furnishings and a chipped and battered bed frame that had clearly seen better days. The fire in the grate still gave out warmth, banked up with ashes to keep it smouldering slowly.

A faint odour of horse wafted from the corner where his travelling clothes had been draped over a chair. That was the surcoat he'd been wearing when they arrived. She hunted through the pockets, outside and in. There were more than she'd expected – she could see how it had been possible for him to conjure up so many small necessities on their journey. She found his flint and some dry tinder stowed deep in one of the inside pockets. Elsewhere she found string, spare leather laces, crumbs in the pocket where he must have kept the oatcakes, but no sign of the letter, beyond a fragment of the wax seal that must have broken off when he pocketed it earlier that evening. Had he kept the letter with him when he'd changed clothes? Or even destroyed it so it wouldn't fall into the wrong hands? Wrong hands like hers, perhaps. He'd told her often enough he trusted no one.

In which case it was high time she earned his distrust. She hunted through the rest of his clothing but found nothing beyond a deal of horse hair. The lovers had begun their nightly tryst, discarding their clothing as she searched through Weaver's. She pushed their voices away as she tackled the noisome saddlebags. They only contained a tangle of spare clothing and other odds and ends. Buried underneath them, her fingertips met a cloth-wrapped bundle. A shiver of recognition told her straight away it was the dagger Drew had given her; she didn't need to unwrap it. She snatched her hand away and dropped the saddlebags hastily in the corner before turning to the merchant chest. It was the only place left. He might have locked the letter away in there. She dropped to her knees beside it. The key was right there, in the lock.

She twisted the key and lifted the lid, then peered inside. Empty. If he still had the letter, he carried it with him. She lowered the lid shut, sinking back on her heels. The lovers' hunger flooded her mind, as if they'd been waiting for her guard to drop. Who were they? There must be some reason they lurked there at the edge of her awareness, night after night. But maybe that was her mistake – trying to apply reason to anything that had happened since she left Highkell. They might not even be real, just some shameful fantasy conjured up by her own madness. She would end her days as crazy as old Gwydion. Or even crazier.

Behind Alwenna the door latch clicked and someone stepped into the room. She froze, the tiny hairs on the back of her neck standing on end as she realised she was being observed. Too late to snuff out the candle on the mantelpiece. Too late to hide.

There was a hushing sound as the door swung shut and a soft clunk as it closed.

"My lady."

It was Weaver. The tension slid from her shoulders and she could breathe again. She twisted round to see him standing in the doorway, looking down at her where she sat on the floor next to the chest. It had to be crystal clear what she'd been about.

"My lady." He repeated the words with the deliberation of a man who'd drunk well that evening, but not so much he slurred. "This is unexpected."

"Yes, it is." Too late to dissemble. Far, far too late. Better to brazen it out. "I never imagined you'd be back so soon. Not with so much drink at the table."

"No. Sometimes I surprise myself." He stepped around the end of the bed so he could see her fully. "But not as much as you surprise me, my lady." He took up the poker and stirred the fire into life, added a log, then turned back to where she sat on the floor, watching him.

"It appears for all the world as if you've been searching my room. Might I have the temerity to ask why?"

"That's a fair question." Still she sat. She had no idea how best to deal with the situation. At the back of her mind the two lovers communed eagerly. Her skin prickled with awareness of their passion.

"Are you likely to answer it?" Weaver took a step closer, watching her as if he expected her to sprout wings and fly away.

"I daresay." She began to get to her feet but a stab of pain shot through her ankle when she tried to put weight on it. "Perhaps you could help me up?"

Weaver's face was in shadow as he leaned forward and held out one hand. She clasped it and he tugged, none too gently, but she was able to stand and gingerly set weight on her injured ankle. She straightened up but he clasped her hand still. And for the first time she could gauge his mood. A thrill of heat tugged deep within her abdomen. There was no thought of duty here. Not tonight.

Somewhere the lovers were losing themselves in one another.

"Thank you." She ought to release his hand now, but instead she leaned closer. Why shouldn't she? Why shouldn't they? She was rewarded by an audible intake of his breath and his fingers tightened about hers.

"You were about to tell me why you were searching my room, my lady." Was his voice hoarser than usual? "I imagine you were looking for the dagger?"

"The dagger? No." It was tempting to seize on that as an excuse, but then she'd be no further forward. And she had little to lose now. "It was the letter. I wanted to read it."

He frowned. "You– What? What letter?"

"From the freemerchant."

"But why? It was nothing."

Mention the sight now and he would freeze, turn away. "It was the way you looked at me after you read it. Then you folded it and stowed it away. And I thought there was something in it you didn't want me to see."

"So, naturally, you asked me about it." Still he held her hand in his.

"I didn't think of that." She couldn't help leaning closer. "Can I see the letter?"

"I burned it. I would show you it if I hadn't – there was nothing you couldn't have seen."

"Then why such secrecy?"

"If it ever fell into the wrong hands... Even our two names in association could be enough to condemn us."

"Laudable, I'm sure." The lovers had fallen silent, spent

for the time being. Alwenna envied them their certainty.

"You don't agree?"

"You've already signed a confession. What difference would that letter have made?"

"It can't be used to make things worse. I'm a cautious man." Slowly, as if he acted against his better judgement, Weaver slipped his free hand round Alwenna's waist. "I've always been a cautious man."

"Are you? I'm not convinced." It was the most natural thing in the world for her to move closer, so close their breath mingled. She set one hand on his chest and stood on tiptoe to murmur in his ear. "A cautious man would bolt that door before we go much further."

Weaver laughed and pulled her up close. "I'll bolt the door if you promise you won't run away."

"With this ankle?" She tugged at the drawstring fastening of his shirt. "I won't run away. Not tonight."

CHAPTER EIGHTY-FOUR

Alwenna was eight years old, hurrying down the tower stairs.

Tresilian followed several steps behind her. "You can't. We'll get into trouble."

She gestured to him to be quiet. "Only if they catch us, stupid."

They crept up to the door to the king's chamber and pressed against the wall to listen. Voices rose and fell in the room beyond, but Alwenna couldn't make out the words. She reached for the handle. Like the others in the old keep at Highkell it was fashioned in the form of three snakes twisted round in a loop, each one devouring the tail of the snake in front. She hated them. Rather than touch the vile things, she took hold of the latch and hefted it up from the metal catch so she could pull the door open. Just a fraction. The grown-ups were sat at the table, the remains of a meal before them. There were no guards or servants in the room.

Alwenna recognised her grandmother's voice.

"... empty platitudes. The question is, what should we do with the child?"

Alwenna eased the door a fraction further open so she

could see Tresilian's father.

"That's easily answered. We can't relinquish control of the eastern estates to her father's family."

The old woman nodded. "There at least we agree. Would you raise her here?"

"Of course. As her closest relative the duty is mine."

The old woman tilted her head to one side as she studied her nephew. "I thought you might not wish to risk it."

"What – the seers' superstitious nonsense? That child is a danger to no one."

"Once I would have agreed with you, but lately…" She bent forward, seized by a coughing fit. "Already there are rumours it was no accident that killed them both."

"It's not the first time heavy rain has loosened that stretch of road." He shrugged. "I have no time for such folly."

"Folly or not, you'd do well to heed the mood of your people."

"They're happy as long as their bellies are full. And I can ensure that by uniting The Marches and Highground under one crown."

"They'd be unwieldy to administer and impossible to rule. How would you hope to keep order and still secure the southern border?"

"You grow old, Aunt Vanna. It's a challenge for someone younger, more ambitious."

"Someone such as yourself?" She snorted. "Over-ambitious, I'd say. Even without warnings from the seers."

"The seers! As ever you set them above worldly concerns, but they feel cold and hunger in winter like the rest of us. Think how it would enhance their standing – and fill their coffers – to have a descendant of the Venerable Alidreth within their precinct. Alwenna will stay here – she and Tresilian are of an age, after all."

"So is Vasic. Raise her to be loyal and send her to form an alliance with the south. Don't forget that girl from the Outer Islands – she would do well for Tresilian. Take care you don't–" Vanna was seized by another bout of coughing.

Alwenna heard footsteps descending the stairs behind them and spun around–

Alwenna woke in the darkness, disorientated, expecting to find herself at the foot of the newel stairs at Highkell. Instead there was warmth. An arm wrapped about her...

Weaver.

She burrowed against him. His arm tightened about her, fingertips pressing against her ribs.

"You're a restless sleeper."

"I'm not asleep."

"But you were just now."

"I dreamed I'd just arrived at Highkell. Wynne caught us eavesdropping when the grown-ups were talking about what to do with me."

"Did you get into trouble?"

"No. She never told anyone." Everything had been so simple then. "I'd forgotten all about it, but it was like I was right back there." She slid a hand up over Weaver's chest, her fingertips exploring the scar tissue from an old injury. His life was mapped on the outside, for all to see, yet he never spoke of it. Hers was mapped on the inside, in her mind, and hardly made enough sense for her to speak of it. "They were talking about the seers – how they said I was dangerous. Tresilian and Vasic used to tease me about it, even though everyone said it was nonsense."

Beneath her hand, Weaver tensed. Always the same reaction when she mentioned anything to do with the sight.

"I suppose they were right," she ventured.

Weaver drew in a breath, as if to speak, but he remained silent.

"What – do you think I'm dangerous too?" She pushed herself up on one elbow to study him by the dim firelight.

"No."

There was something he wasn't saying. "But?"

He raised a hand and pushed back a stray strand of hair from her face. "A man like me keeping company with the likes of you… that's dangerous. You're a queen. You grew up with future kings."

"Kings or not, they started out as little boys. They're no different." She trailed her fingertips down his sternum, felt his muscles tighten as her hand reached his belly. "And no better."

"Kings don't like commoners messing with their women."

"So? There aren't any kings here." She slid her hand further down. "This is no time to talk caution."

"Maybe not, but… Alwenna, we both know it can't end well." His body responded to her touch, putting the lie to his words.

"It won't end tonight, though, will it?"

Weaver drew in a deep breath. "If we had any sense it would."

"Oh, listen to you. When did you get so old?" She wriggled up against him.

"I'm just trying to say–"

She silenced him with a kiss. "Nothing I want to hear tonight."

"Understood." Weaver rolled onto his back, pulling her with him. "And now I'll have you know I'm not old, just short of sleep."

"There'll be plenty more time for sleeping." She bent forward and their tongues entwined once more as they found far more pressing things to do than talk.

CHAPTER EIGHTY-FIVE

Several heavy-eyed people gathered about the breakfast table the next morning. Curtis and Erin sat next to one another, sharing secretive smiles, leaning close every now and then. Weaver had stationed himself across the table from Alwenna, but when she looked up from her food and caught his eye, he too smiled. Perhaps smile was too generous a word for the infinitesimal change of his expression. At least they were a little less obvious than the other two love-birds. They'd both agreed they should be discreet when they'd parted company outside Alwenna's door sometime shortly before dawn – but there was something of the old, silent Weaver about him now. Blaine was nursing a heavy hangover, and impatient for them to be on the road. They didn't linger over breakfast, gathering their belongings and loading up the horses without wasting any time.

Weaver waited to give Alwenna a leg up into her saddle. "My lady, are you ready?" His hand touched her shoulder for the most fleeting of moments as she turned to face the saddle, then he legged her up in business-like manner. As she arranged her skirts she smiled at him, but he lowered his eyes when she would have held contact with him for longer.

Weaver turned away to mount his own horse. As they rode out of the inn yard he took up position in front, telling Curtis and Blaine to follow up in the rear, behind the two women.

They were an hour along the road, crossing gently rising ground, when three horses appeared in the distance ahead of them, descending the hill in single file.

Weaver halted and called Curtis forward to join him.

"What is it? Trouble?" Alwenna moved her horse alongside his.

He glanced her way. "No, my lady. Not of the kind you mean."

There was little to see from this distance, beyond the fact the riders rode tall bay horses.

"What – are there different kinds of trouble?"

"We don't know yet what we'll find at the summer palace, my lady. I know what the freemerchant told me–"

That letter again. There had been more to it after all. "Then tell me. This sounds like something I should know."

Weaver took a breath, his eyes flicking over to where Curtis waited. "This isn't the time or place." He dismounted from his horse, delving into his saddlebag to retrieve a cloth-wrapped bundle.

Alwenna recognised it instantly. "The dagger? Why now?"

"In case you need it. I–" Weaver shrugged. "It's no good to you in my bags, is it?" He stowed the knife in her saddlebag.

"You said you don't expect any trouble."

"No, I'm just–"

"Being cautious?"

He didn't smile. "Yes, my lady."

"But, Weaver, you didn't want me to carry this."

"Drew said you would need it. And there might not be another chance – this freemerchant is watchful."

"And is he one of them?" She indicated the riders in the distance.

"He may be."

Weaver vaulted back into his saddle and he and Curtis moved on again.

Alwenna followed, a knot of anxiety tightening her stomach. Deep inside her womb the baby shifted uneasily. It, too, sensed all was far from well. Somehow, the path she was travelling had taken another turn. Darkness lay ahead, and all she could do was continue riding towards it.

As the unknown riders drew near, two of them halted. They waited casually in the road on loose reins, their horses stretching their necks. The third, a tall and lean man who sat on his horse with easy grace, rode forward to meet them. As he drew closer Alwenna could see he wore his hair in freemerchant braids.

"Greetings, fellow travellers. May your roads be clear and the water pure." He raised his right hand to his left shoulder and bowed his head. He ran his eyes over the group, pausing briefly on Alwenna then halting at Weaver, who responded with the same gesture, albeit a more perfunctory version.

"And so may your road be blessed."

"Weaver, my brother in arms." The freemerchant smiled. "The Hunter has indeed watched over you. This, I take it, is the Lady Alwenna."

Weaver performed the necessary introduction, punctiliously polite. Alwenna responded as she had been taught, with courtly dignity.

The freemerchant, Marten, inclined his head again. "We will be honoured by your presence among us, my lady. I am delighted to be able to escort you for the rest of the journey. If we ride on now we can expect to reach our destination before the worst of the afternoon heat is upon us. You will be able to rest in the shade of your family home."

Again that stirring of apprehension. Alwenna nodded politely. "That will be most welcome."

Marten smiled, then turned his horse about to lead the group, signalling Weaver to ride at his side. Weaver had not so much as a glance to spare for Alwenna as he took his place alongside the freemerchant. She was left in no doubt Weaver actively distrusted Marten. This must have been what he'd been trying to warn her of the night before, though she couldn't fathom why he'd found it so difficult to speak up. It was clear she, too, had to be cautious unless she wanted their secret redistributed to the kingdom at large for the freemerchant's gain.

CHAPTER EIGHTY-SIX

They reached the summer palace by mid-afternoon. It was as unlike Highkell as Alwenna could have imagined. The site was surrounded by a high wall with a robust gatehouse and watch towers along the length of it, but it was not designed to withstand serious attack. As Alwenna rode in beneath the gatehouse there were no glimmerings of recognition. The sight stirred, lazy as rolling mist, although for once she was able to see the real world through it and she knew this place featured in Gwydion's store of knowledge. But that was not what she needed to know. The sight subsided. That had happened more of late – was she finally learning to control the visions?

Beyond the gatehouse lay a second, lesser gate. This led into a cloistered courtyard, colonnades running along either side to a three-storey building across the head of the yard. A flight of stone steps led up to an ornately carved entrance door with tall columns either side supporting a portico. Now this was familiar. The carving on the door was an elegant tracery of grape vines, stems entwined in symmetrical profusion. As a child she'd set out to count all the grapes, many times, but had always been hampered by her lack of height.

A steward hurried down the steps, clapping his hands to call forth servants from doors either side of the steps at basement level to take the horses.

Weaver dismounted quickly and came to Alwenna's side, ostensibly to help her dismount. He leaned close, speaking in a low voice that would not be overheard. "Have caution around this man, he plays some deep game of his own. You must know I am sworn to his service. I would have told you sooner, but... He claims to have–"

A servant arrived to take her horse and Weaver handed her the walking stick and stepped back with a deferential bow, his eyes directed to the ground. Alwenna had a thousand questions she might have asked, but she was obliged to remain silent.

Marten approached, the steward following a couple of paces behind, and bowed to Alwenna, smiling. "My lady, let me offer you my arm."

She had no choice but to acquiesce. For a few precious hours following her rescue she had been nobody, with nothing to worry about other than being. Now she was being pitched back into the world of court. But Weaver needn't have troubled to warn her: she knew how to play this game. She'd been bred for it and raised according to its rules. Marten walked with her past planters filled with scented lavender and helped her climb the steps. The air about them shimmered, but she couldn't tell whether it was the sight warning her of danger ahead or simply an effect of the afternoon heat. She was obliged to lean on Marten's arm more heavily than she would have chosen. But that might be to the good: let him believe her to be weaker than she was. Let him believe her a hapless, witless thing. Everything would be easier that way.

Up close the ornate doors were coated in dust which blackened the tops of the grapes she'd tried so hard to count in the past. The dust was ingrained, the accumulation of years of harsh sun and drifting sand, refusing to be dislodged by the pressure of her fingertip. The doors she remembered had glistened, giving off the scent of beeswax. Inside, the summer palace was shady and cool. It had the air of a place waking from long slumber, still struggling to catch up with a changing world. And woken too fast. Everywhere were telltale traces of hasty preparation: grime in corners that had escaped the mop, pitted dust in the deep relief of carved wood, spots of mould on ceilings. This was the home of Alwenna's early childhood, and yet it wasn't. The changes were there to be seen, overlying her recognition of once-familiar things. They were subtle. And dark.

Once inside, the party was divided, the men being led to a room at the front of the atrium, while Alwenna and Erin were escorted by a servant to a room at the back. Tepid water was provided in bowls for them to wash off the worst dust of their journey.

Erin prowled round the small room, peering out of the window. "This is not what's due to a lady like yourself, if you'll pardon me saying so."

"Perhaps our host doesn't believe I'm any such thing." Alwenna crossed to the glazed window. It overlooked a stable yard. Weeds grew between the cobbles, while the roof of the single-storey stables was gappy and uneven. Broken roof tiles lay on the ground where they had fallen. Could their host be one of her uncles? Stian was dead long ago, of course, at Weaver's hand. It seemed unlikely he would be in their employ now. So who?

"The summer palace has been shut up for many years. This may be the best our host can offer."

"Perhaps, my lady." The girl's expression was sombre, as it had been at Highkell.

"This would be a good time to ask, Erin: what is your wish in all this? We brought you with us from Highkell, but you are free to choose – you need not remain here if you do not wish to."

"I must serve you, my lady." The girl's voice was matter-of-fact. "I would have fallen to my death at Highkell, had you not saved me. It is the will of the Goddess." There was no joy in the girl's expression. She would do her duty as she perceived it. Alwenna knew how that worked.

"I will be grateful of your service, but if you wish to leave I will release you – at any time, you have only to speak up."

The girl curtseyed. "Thank you, my lady. But the Goddess still has work for us." She hesitated. "Drew told me. On the way to Brigholm, while I was nursing him. He said a great many things while he was ill."

"Might that not simply have been his fever?"

The girl frowned. "I don't think so, my lady. He talked the way you often do in your sleep. He was Goddess-touched."

The girl appeared to believe implicitly in every word she'd spoken.

"I didn't realise you were such a devout follower."

"I'm not, my lady. Leastwise I wasn't before your wedding."

"You don't think it was just the rain washing out the foundations?"

"It wasn't rain made that priest do what he did." Erin

hesitated. "If the Goddess has some purpose for me I'll not flout her will. Not after what I saw that day."

Alwenna was spared the need to answer by a knock at the door. A maidservant stepped into the room, bobbing a hesitant curtsey. "You're both to come with me, if it please my lady."

And if it didn't please her, what then? Alwenna took one last look out of the window at the run-down stable yard. That was no answer to send this girl away with. "Very well."

It was time to learn what she faced.

CHAPTER EIGHTY-SEVEN

Weaver and the others were already waiting in the antechamber with the freemerchant when Alwenna and Erin joined them. This room, at least, tallied with her memories. The smell of beeswax filled the air. The walls were panelled with hardwood which had been buffed to a high sheen. Beyond lay the great chamber which had been used for special occasions. Those had involved a great deal of dull talking on the part of the grown-ups. Since her presence hadn't enhanced such events, she'd spent little time there.

Marten bowed. Of all their party he was clad most like a courtier, but she recognised the distinctive loose-fitting freemerchant tunic, re-fashioned in more elaborate style. "My lady, now our party is complete it is time I presented you to our host."

Alwenna felt at a distinct disadvantage in her travel-stained gown of common weave, but she smiled and nodded and said what was proper.

Marten returned her smile. "Your arrival has been most eagerly awaited, I can assure you."

"You are too kind." She couldn't see how that was possible, for she'd still been at Highkell when Weaver had set out with the freemerchant. Weaver had told her how they'd turned back when Drew brought the news. She could see him standing stiffly beyond the freemerchant, jaw clenched. She'd seen him in many moods – ranging from boredom through annoyance to outright anger – but this was the first time she'd seen him look apprehensive.

Marten held out his arm. "Permit me to support you."

"I cannot impose on your kindness, sir. I must lean more heavily on my stick than you would find comfortable or seemly."

The freemerchant closed his heavy-lidded eyes momentarily. "As you wish, my lady. I shall walk at your side."

As they passed Weaver he avoided meeting her eyes, but he took his place behind them.

The great double doors, as ornately carved as those at the main entrance, swung open before them. On the dais at the head of the room stood a man. The light of the afternoon sun streamed through the great window behind him, so his features were in shadow.

Marten moved sedately forward, matching his pace to Alwenna's. She was aware that the others followed behind, but she made no attempt to hasten her steps. This entrance was ungainly enough without hobbling any faster. Her stick made hollow clacking sounds on the stone floor as they progressed between the long tables that ran down either side of the room. Alwenna concentrated on placing her stick securely on the ground with each step, keeping her eyes lowered so she wasn't dazzled by the sunlight.

They'd travelled almost the length of the room when a cloud passed over the sun. Alwenna raised her eyes to the figure on the dais and came to an abrupt halt.

There before the window, hands clasped behind his back as he watched her approach, stood Tresilian, her dead husband.

CHAPTER EIGHTY-EIGHT

This was not possible. Alwenna had seen Tresilian's death with her own eyes... But no, she hadn't. She'd dreamed of it. That wasn't the same thing. Not at all. And there he stood before her, tall as ever, if a little leaner.

Tresilian's face was gaunt, and his cheeks hollow, but when he smiled it was the familiar lopsided smile she'd known since childhood. It might have been her imagination that it lacked the usual warmth.

"My lady wife. You join us at last." His eyes moved to those standing behind her. "And Weaver, too. I hear you have been busy." The smile tightened.

Alwenna's stomach knotted. How could he possibly know? She stared at her husband. It was him, there could be no doubt. An awful silence stretched out until Weaver stepped forward to stand alongside her.

Weaver bowed low before his king. "Your highness. We heard that Vasic killed you."

Again that lopsided curl of Tresilian's lips. Alwenna suppressed a shiver.

Tresilian turned his eyes to her, as if he had heard her movement. "I am not so easily killed – as you can see." He spread his arms wide, smiling now, truly smiling. This

418

was the old Tresilian, delighted at catching them out with his joke.

Some of her tension dissipated. This was her husband standing before them. She ought never have set so much store by the visions. Yet the visions had perfectly shown her other things she knew to be true, such as the ambush on Weaver... And now she understood Weaver's reluctance to meet her gaze earlier. Had he already known Tresilian was alive? Nonetheless, he appeared as stunned as her to see Tresilian.

Finally she found her voice. "You have been alive all this time, yet never sent word?"

Tresilian raised an eyebrow. "My spies have kept me well informed. They could not have done so if I used them as errand boys. If they'd been running hither and thither at my beck and call our enemies would have removed them long ago."

"Everyone believed you dead." Alwenna could think of nothing else to say.

"Dear wife, I might almost think you were disappointed to find me alive and well." Still he smiled, hands clasped behind his back once more, entirely at his ease.

"It is something of a shock. Our old tutor's lessons somehow failed to prepare me for this." Tresilian knew how bitterly she'd complained of the never-ending etiquette lessons. As she waited for his reply she caught a glimpse of movement at the back of the dais. There was a door there that led – if she was not mistaken – to private quarters beyond. Tresilian didn't turn his head as he continued to study Alwenna, but gestured for the new arrival to sit on a bench set against the wall.

The figure stepped out from the shadow of the corner

and was revealed to be a slight young woman with long, fair hair, dressed in the robes of a priestess. She carried her hands clasped together in front of her, as if in prayer, her head bowed submissively as she moved over to the bench and sat down. She looked up and met Alwenna's gaze then. The girl had large eyes, with pale lashes. And even at that distance that was enough.

Those were the same eyes Alwenna had seen night after night as the unknown lovers sated their passion. And now they seemed to gaze into Alwenna's very soul, until she had to look away or risk yielding up every secret she had ever held – or so it felt at that moment. Alwenna drew in her breath and risked glancing towards the young priestess again. The girl now sat in meek pose, eyes fixed on some point on the floor, her lips curled in the hint of a secretive smile.

Alwenna looked up to find Tresilian still watching her.

"We have much to discuss, lady wife, and so we shall this evening. But first I am persuaded you would rest awhile, to recover from your journey."

"That would be welcome." It wasn't the journey throwing her into confusion – it was the damned shock of finding her dead husband not only alive and well, but apparently one of the mysterious lovers who had occupied her mind these past nights. And if the sight had shared that truth with her, over and over, how could it have misled her into thinking he was dead?

He appeared substantial enough as he smiled, and completely untroubled by any trace of guilt. "Then rest well. We will dine at sunset. You have been allotted suitable rooms in the west wing. My steward will ensure you are provided with the necessary servants. And, perhaps, a change of clothing."

Alwenna told herself she was foolish to imagine his comment was barbed. "Thank you, my lord husband." Alwenna followed the steward from the hall, signalling for Erin to go with them, while Tresilian turned his attention to the men who remained there. She couldn't catch much of what he said, but he seemed to be thanking one of them. The door closed behind them with a waft of beeswax polish, and the rest of his words were lost to them.

CHAPTER EIGHTY-NINE

Weaver kept his eyes fixed on Tresilian as the Lady Alwenna limped from the hall. It really was him, there could be no doubt. He could see the tiny scar just below his right eye from the battle when a pike had shattered, sending splinters flying everywhere.

"Well, gentlemen." Tresilian favoured them all with a sweeping glance. "It appears my thanks are in order. You have joined me here in exile and restored my lady wife to me. I could scarcely ask for greater proof of loyalty." His eyes lingered on Weaver. "There are questions I must ask in the fullness of time. But first – to business. I have need of more loyal King's Men and would appoint Curtis as such. You have served me well, and well again. You will wear my livery henceforth."

It was Curtis' turn to bow. "Highness, you grant me a great honour."

"I reward loyalty such as yours." Tresilian's eyes flicked to Weaver again. "Blaine, I would appoint you to the household guard. We are few in number here in The Marches, but that will change soon." Tresilian gestured to a servant who waited nearby. "Marten, you, too have proved your loyalty and I have here the first part of the reward we discussed."

The servant hurried forward, carrying a heavy bag of what looked and sounded like coin. This he passed to Marten, who bowed with grace.

"Your highness, I thank you on behalf of all my people."

Tresilian looked down at the men who knelt before him. "We will speak again presently, Marten. For now you three are dismissed. My new guards will report to the barracks." Tresilian paused. "You, Weaver, will stay where you are. I wish to speak with you further."

Here it was. Tresilian had already been told of Weaver's confession. Or he was about to demand an explanation as to how Alwenna had fallen into Vasic's hands after all. Whichever concerned him most, the outlook was bleak.

They waited in silence until the others had left the chamber. Tresilian signalled with his hand and the guards at the doors at either end of the room withdrew.

With a clunk the last door shut and the two of them were alone in the chamber together for the first time since Tresilian had instructed Weaver to take Alwenna from Highkell.

"So, Weaver, these rumours." Tresilian strolled over to the window, pausing to look outside before he turned to face Weaver again. "I confess, they disquiet me."

"Highness, Garrad sought to discredit the Lady Alwenna by spreading lies about her."

"Lies?"

"Poisonous lies, your highness. Not one word of his accusations was true." Not then, at any rate.

"The rumours have been spread by more than Father Garrad."

"After the journey we undertook, that is inevitable.

You know I have always had the utmost respect for your queen."

"Indeed. Respect, you call it?"

"Highness, she is as far beyond my reach as it is possible for a person to be." Weaver chose his words with care. "I could never ask her to stoop to my level, even were she not your wife."

Tresilian moved over to the throne-like seat on the dais and sat down, drumming his fingers on the arm. "I would like to believe what you say, Weaver. We have travelled many miles together and I have never before had cause to question your loyalty." Again he drummed his fingers. "Nevertheless, I understand you signed a confession to intimacy with the Lady Alwenna. My wife. The one you claim is so far above your reach. You can understand, I'm sure, why this concerns me."

"That confession was a falsehood, your highness. Extracted under torture by the usurper, Vasic."

"I would dearly like to believe you, Weaver, but... can you prove any of this?"

Weaver raised his head. He should tell him the whole truth. Tell him just how many times he took his wife on stained sheets in a common inn. Tell him how she moaned with pleasure. Tell him... "I bear the scars of Vasic's branding iron."

"So I have been told. Convenient for you." He looked at Weaver thoughtfully. "You capitulated to the usurper's demands, then? What reason could you possibly have for putting your name to a lie that would so damage my wife's reputation?"

"Highness, the usurper threatened the novice monk who helped the Lady Alwenna escape Vorrahan. I'd asked him to do what he could to help her in my absence. It would have been poor reward for the lad for doing as I asked him. I never imagined she'd face such betrayal, from Garrad of all people."

"A selfless act, then?" Tresilian gazed into Weaver's eyes as if he could read every thought that crossed his mind. "I wonder. This troubles me, Weaver. The rumours are so widespread I would be seen as a trusting fool if I let you resume your post as King's Man. Yet the Lady Alwenna enjoys such popularity in these parts I should be criticised for persecuting her if I were to make anything of these same rumours."

Weaver fixed his eyes on a knot in the plank in front of Tresilian's foot. "I understand, your highness."

"I wonder if you do. In the end what I require is not your understanding, but your obedience." Tresilian studied Weaver in silence, then appeared to reach a decision. He stood up and approached the edge of the dais before which Weaver stood. "In these difficult times I would be foolish to lose such a talented soldier as yourself. Do I still have your loyalty, Weaver?"

"You do, your highness."

"Then kneel before me."

Weaver obeyed, bowing his head. Tresilian watched him in silence.

"I understand you turned back – against Marten's orders – when you heard the Lady Alwenna was in difficulty. Was that the act of a loyal man?"

"The novice who brought the news has the sight, your highness. He told me she was in great danger."

"You believe in the sight now? That is a remarkable change of heart for you, Weaver."

"The Lady–" He had better not speak her name again. "Your wife described such scenes as I could no longer doubt it, your highness."

"I see. Yet it troubles me still that you flouted Marten's authority."

"I confess at that time I still believed him to be a pedlar of lies. I fully expected to find some pretender here claiming your name."

"So you say." Tresilian returned to his makeshift throne and sat down. The silence lengthened. The uneven stone flags were beginning to dig into Weaver's knees.

"You must swear fealty to me again, Weaver, before the assembled court tomorrow morning. You must be seen to be humble and obedient."

"As your highness wishes."

"Then so be it, Weaver. But words are easily uttered. Once the first lie is spoken, others hurry after it, lie upon lie. It is so easy, I know myself. Understand this: your oath of allegiance will be for others to see. I have another way for you to convince me of your loyalty. And until such time as you have convinced me, you will serve in my king's guard." Tresilian smiled a tight, strange smile. "You may leave me now."

No sooner had the words been spoken than the slender priestess rose to her feet and, in silence, crossed the dais to Tresilian's side.

Weaver got to his feet and bowed. Tresilian had already leaned over to speak to the girl. She turned her pallid eyes momentarily towards Weaver and his skin prickled with apprehension. He'd seen her give just such a look to the Lady Alwenna.

CHAPTER NINETY

Alwenna had bathed and dressed in the gown provided by Tresilian's servants. Upon Alwenna's insistence Erin had been similarly attired in her capacity as lady-in-waiting. The sun was still some distance above the horizon, and now all they could do was wait.

The girl sat in silence as Alwenna paced the floor. The voices were crowding in on her, clamouring to be heard, but too indistinct for her to make any sense of them. Of the lovers there was no trace, for which she was thankful.

A knock at the door stopped Alwenna halfway across the room. Erin jumped to her feet and went to unbolt the door.

A maidservant waited outside. "His highness requests the pleasure of your company before dining, my lady."

Did he indeed? Was he foregoing his usual assignation with the lithe priestess? So tempting to make him wait. Alwenna toyed with the idea, but dismissed it as childish. She needed to understand what had happened since she left Highkell, although she doubted Tresilian was prepared to tell her. He'd been taking lessons in diplomacy from Vasic if their first encounter was any indication. "Very well." That was all she could say. "Erin, you will accompany me."

"My lady, he said to bring just you." The servant looked apprehensive.

"Don't worry, I will tell him I insisted."

The servant dipped a curtsey. "Thank you, my lady." She appeared relieved, more than Alwenna would have expected of one of Tresilian's servants.

Tresilian waited for her in a smaller chamber off the great hall – the room from which the priestess had emerged earlier that day. Alwenna told Erin to wait outside and the girl took a seat on the bench set on the dais against the wall. It had been carefully positioned out of earshot. The single guard stationed at the far end of the room would no doubt suffice to prevent anyone sneaking closer to eavesdrop. Vasic would have had two men at each door. It was debatable whether that was a sign of Vasic's insecurity, or of Tresilian's lack of resources. Alwenna directed the maidservant to knock on the door, and she did so, opening it when Tresilian gave the command. The girl stepped over the threshold to announce Alwenna, then hastily withdrew.

Alwenna entered the room, leaning on her stick as little as she could manage. The pervasive scent of lavender was even stronger here. Every room was filled with the stuff – was it all that grew here, or simply a hasty measure to counter the fustiness of a building that had been unoccupied for so many years? She clenched her hand, digging her fingernails into her palm. She dared not let her mind wander. This meeting was important.

Tresilian waited by the fireplace where a small fire had been kindled, not so great that it would overheat the room in this warm spell, but enough to lend a little cheer to the proceedings. Two settles were arranged on either side of it, facing one another. At the other side of the room was another raised dais, with a table set in the deep window embrasure. Like the anteroom to the great hall this room was panelled, but any smell of beeswax polish was overwhelmed by the lavender. She counted six pots before she realised Tresilian was waiting until he had her full attention.

"Well, my lady wife. Here we are." Tresilian smiled. Alwenna was able to see his features clearly for the first time. He had aged visibly in the weeks they'd been apart. His face was deeply lined, and his eyes appeared sunken, ringed by deep shadows.

"My lord husband." She made such a curtsey as her ankle permitted, determined to set a fence of formality between them until she understood this new situation.

"Please, sit down. You must be weary after your journey."

"Thank you." She sat, taking her time about arranging her skirts decorously and propping the stick against the arm of the settle. Then she waited.

Tresilian looked down at her, his expression thoughtful. "So, Alwenna, where do we begin? I trust you are well, aside from that ankle injury?"

"Well enough, thank you."

Tresilian sat down opposite. "And our child?"

"Our child is well."

"That is good. I take it the sickness has passed, for you look well."

"It has." She felt as though she were discussing her life with a stranger.

"Excellent." His shoulders relaxed visibly. "And does anyone else know our secret?"

"Only Weaver. He recognised my symptoms as we travelled to Vorrahan."

"Is that so?" Tresilian rubbed his chin in the manner Vasic was wont to do. "I take it he took good care of you?" The question was casual enough. If he intended any double meaning it was not evident from his expression.

"He did. Until your Father Garrad betrayed us, in any event."

Tresilian smiled. "Yes, Father Garrad. I never took him for such a zealot." He didn't appear remotely surprised by her revelation. Or indignant.

"I gather your spies have already told you of this?"

"Why, yes, they have. You always were perceptive." He steepled his fingers, studying her as if she were some strange new creature. "Nevertheless, Alwenna, I find you have changed in these few weeks."

"Is that a surprise? You sent me away – cut me loose from everything and everyone I held dear. Sent me off into the wilderness with a common mercenary as protector. How do you imagine I thought of myself after that?" Once Wynne had gone, the only familiar thing in all that time had been Weaver. Weaver, whom she'd despised. Weaver, who dealt death with ruthless efficiency. Weaver, who, in the end had saved her from her own personal hell, had seen her at her very worst and brought her back to the land of the living. He'd shown her more loyalty than her husband.

"It was necessary."

"Necessary? Is that all the explanation I'm to get? You sent me into the clutches of an enemy. You trusted Garrad – you fool – and he sold me straight away to Vasic, without hesitation. The very moment Weaver left."

"My father warned me you'd always be a handful." He spoke with indifference.

"Is that any way to speak to me when I kept our secret safe all this time? You told me to seek out Gwydion and I did as you asked. That crazy old man who spent his days shut in the dark – whatever possessed you? And still I trusted you."

"That was your duty. All of it was necessary, to save Highkell, and to assure its future. Yet despite all my precautions you still managed to destroy it. Our childhood home. That saddens me."

"That's nonsense, I did no such thing. It rained for days. The water washed out the foundations."

"That discussion can keep." Tresilian brushed her words away as if they were nothing more than an annoying insect. "Garrad was right about you all along. And you killed him, too, did you not?"

"No. He took his own life." But the blade in the priest's hand had been meant for her until she spoke up. The doubt on his face had only appeared after that, then his agony as his life blood sprayed against the wall. The floor pitching beneath them. And her descent into– "He took his own life."

"A pity. I could have made better use of him."

"He betrayed us."

"Quite so. Your people can be... remarkably creative with the blood of an enemy."

"My people?" Her people had been at Highkell, Goddess knew what had happened to them. All but Weaver. And Drew. They were her people. Perhaps she ought to number her husband among them, if she could believe the evidence of her eyes. Yet...

"Yes, your people here in The Marches with their

heathenish ways." His lips curled in a tight smile.

"Heathenish? Need I remind you without our marriage, you are nothing to the people here? Think on that as you disdain us all, husband."

"You misunderstand me, Alwenna. It is not disdain I feel for your people and their mysteries. Far, far from it." Tresilian pressed a fingertip to his forehead, as if it pained him. "I have such things to tell—"

Oh, yes, he'd changed. His eyes saw something new where she stood. He seemed to see beyond the loyalty, beyond the fair looks that had always drawn him, beyond the anguish and the struggle to remain loyal. And beneath it all he saw her guilt. That she had, in the end, turned to Weaver. And somehow she suspected it no longer mattered to him: she'd become nothing more than a tool to be used to serve his purpose.

"I'm not the only one to have changed. You have, too." The thought filled her with an overwhelming sadness that stripped away all her anger as suddenly as the weather changing on a high ridge. "What happened, Tresilian? I... I saw you die."

He raised an eyebrow. "Indeed? You intrigue me." This time he wanted to hear what she had to say.

She twisted her fingers together. "I saw it happen. In the dungeon at Highkell. Vasic stabbed you – I saw it all. It was as if I was in there with you."

He raised his hands in the air, smiling. "Do I look as if anyone has stabbed me?"

"I saw it." She pressed her hand over her own ribs. "Right there."

"Well, well. Crazy old Gwydion was right after all." With a twisted smile he stood up, tugging his shirt out from the waist of his leggings. "There's no point denying it. You're bound to see it sooner or later." He hitched the fabric up so his abdomen was exposed. And there between his ribs was an ugly, puckered scar with an angry network of veins radiating from it as if his blood had been poisoned, far worse than Drew's shoulder.

Alwenna stared. How could he have survived such an injury?

"You can touch it if you want." Tresilian stepped closer and she pushed herself up from her seat before he could lean over her.

"Go on, touch it. You are my wife, after all."

She reached out an unsteady hand and set it over the wound, not sure what to expect. The flesh there was heated and there was some inflammation, but it was undeniably healing. And, yet every instinct told her it was wrong. Unnatural. She snatched her hand away and stepped back.

Tresilian laughed and let his shirt drop over the injury, leaving it hanging loose. "Satisfied now, my dear?"

It hardly seemed possible. "So Vasic's blade missed your heart? You didn't die?"

"Oh no." Tresilian grinned. "I died."

Impossible.

Alwenna took another step away from him but found herself backed up against the wall. The baby in her womb shifted fretfully.

"The bonds of kinship, my darling, run deep. Deeper than you or I ever imagined, innocents that we were." He leaned closer, then set one hand over her abdomen, where their baby lay. "Through all those years we never even guessed. And now, what wonders we have wrought between us."

"You must be mistaken." Alwenna fought the urge to edge towards the door. "These people must have lied to you. No one could–"

He frowned. "No, dear wife, you are mistaken." He raised his hand and gently traced the side of her face with his fingertips, bringing them to rest at the point on her throat where her blood pulsed. "It wasn't at all easy, of course." He smiled, not quite the lopsided smile she knew. "You will see in due course."

Alwenna pulled away, and he made no effort to stop her.

"It will be good to have you dining at my side once more."

Alwenna looked back as she opened the door. He still stood where she'd left him, watching her with that same smile. Oh, yes, he'd changed.

CHAPTER NINETY-ONE

Alwenna had already eaten what little food she felt need of. On her right side Tresilian was deep in conversation with the freemerchant, Marten. In the bustle of the hall her husband's manner seemed less sinister – so much so she began to wonder if she'd imagined it in her initial shock at finding him alive. She surveyed the room from her vantage point at the high table, unable to shake off the sense she was being watched.

Weaver was seated halfway down the long table on the left, eating in a desultory fashion while Curtis and Blaine beside him were drinking and laughing over some joke. Something jarred about the scene. For a moment she couldn't pin down what it was, then realised: Weaver was clad in the livery of the king's guard, while Curtis wore the emblazoned tabard of King's Man. That could only mean one thing. But did Tresilian know the truth – just as she knew about him and the priestess – or had he acted on the basis of Garrad's false accusation?

What was done was done. If she'd known her husband lived she'd never have turned to Weaver. Or so she liked to think. And then, Tresilian claimed to have died. Where did that leave marriage vows made in a former life? Her tutor's etiquette lessons had neglected to address such niceties. She drained her goblet of wine. It was poor stuff, and burned a raw path down her throat. At least it was strong enough to dull her mind and to soften the edges of this strange new court she'd blundered into.

The household at the summer palace was nothing like as large as at Highkell. There were familiar faces at the tables, even though she'd only been there a short time – Tresilian's portly steward for one, and the guard who'd been on duty outside the king's quarters that afternoon. And there, towards the top of the right-hand table, she found the person who was watching her.

The priestess sat with her hands clasped in her lap, grey eyes fixed on Alwenna. Alwenna knew those eyes. She'd seen those eyes, leached of any hint of colour, beneath Tresilian as he laboured and sweated in her dreams. And he presumed to judge his wife, after he'd cast her adrift in the first place? The girl met Alwenna's gaze with quiet determination. Let the girl have him. Let her warm his bed and tend to his insecurities. Then her own unborn child wriggled with her. Could she deprive it of its birthright because of her own capricious fancy for a common soldier? And even if she could, would Tresilian be prepared to let her? She shivered. What a wonder they had wrought, indeed. She took up a wine jug and refilled her goblet.

When Alwenna looked up again the priestess had gone. Her relief was short-lived, for a moment later Tresilian pushed back his chair, scraping it across the floorboards. With a word of apology to the freemerchant he withdrew from the table, striding out through the door that led to his private chambers.

Marten moved over to sit at Alwenna's left-hand side.

"My lady, have you had sufficient? You will find this dish less rich than the rest." He offered her some concoction made with what looked like chicken, at her best guess. Even the food in the land of her birth was unfamiliar.

"I have eaten well, thank you." She smiled just enough to take any sting out of her refusal, although she doubted he was much concerned either way. She knew a conversational gambit when she was offered one.

The freemerchant set the dish back down. "You must be overjoyed to be reunited with your husband, my lady."

Was he fishing for a reaction? Probably. "Of course. The more so because it was so unexpected." Alwenna swallowed another mouthful of the rough wine. Good luck to him gaining insight into her current state of mind. She'd be glad to know herself.

"Unexpected, my lady? I had no doubt Weaver would tell you."

"Weaver knew?" The words escaped before she could stop them.

"Why, yes, my lady. I must confess he did seem reluctant to take my word for it."

Alwenna glanced towards the lower table where Weaver sat. He'd been watching them, but lowered his eyes immediately. "Weaver is a famous sceptic. He once told me he believes nothing he's not seen for himself." At the back of her mind the voices began, the lovers immersing themselves in their communion. But this time behind it all was a note of doubt, of disharmony. Alwenna's head ached. The great hall had become too full, too noisy.

"Then I owe you my apologies, my lady. I ought to have anticipated that."

"It is of no consequence." She pushed herself to her

feet, taking up her walking stick. "Pray excuse me. I need some fresh air."

"Allow me to assist." Marten stood and offered his arm.

She wanted space to herself, not assistance, but it was easier to accept rather than make an issue of it before so many watchful eyes.

Marten led her to a door at the other side of the dais which opened onto a courtyard garden enclosed by high walls. The garden was not as pristine as she recalled, but the air was clear and she had room to breathe. The night air was far cooler in the foothills than it had been on the plain, but welcome after the stuffiness of the hall. Lavender plants still flourished here, although weeds grew in profusion between paving stones. The fountain that had once played in the centre of the garden was silent, the green water in the basin giving off a dank smell. Everything changed, of course. She couldn't expect it to be otherwise after all these years.

The moon, almost full in a clear sky, had not long cleared the horizon. It cast long shadows across the flagstones. She sat down on the broad rim of the fountain, recalling how her mother had sat there on hot summer days, trailing one hand in the water. Marten wandered about the garden, frost-blown flakes of stone crunching occasionally beneath his feet.

The air at this altitude was sharper, clearer, less laden with humanity's grievances. Somehow she seemed to be less at the whim of her sight here. Despite that, she couldn't push the two lovers entirely from her consciousness. It made more sense now that she should have been aware of them for so long, since one of them was Tresilian. She couldn't rouse any righteous anger against them. She'd believed him dead for weeks and faced up to the fact their marriage had been more a matter of duty than choice, at least for her. She'd once believed it had been otherwise for Tresilian, but his absorption in the priestess suggested she had been mistaken. She was more troubled by his impossible claims to have died. Her only certainty right now was Tresilian had changed, and not for the better.

"You are more comfortable now, your highness?" She'd almost forgotten Marten was there. It took a moment for her to realise the honorific still applied to her, despite recent events.

"Why, yes, thank you." Court small talk. She could remember how it went. "It is a beautiful, clear night."

"It is indeed – the Hunter watches over us all. An auspicious night for new beginnings."

Beginnings? She doubted this was any such thing. But she suspected Marten had accompanied her here for a specific purpose. And he would get to it in his own time, no doubt. "Tell me more about the Hunter. I understand he is your freemerchant god?"

"We worship the Goddess as well, my lady."

"Indeed? I did not know that." Alwenna had no need to feign surprise.

"I understand everything you learned of freemerchant lore would have been taught by the brethren from your local precinct?"

"That is true." She remembered fidgeting throughout the tedious lessons on warm summer days, counting the hours until she and Tresilian could go riding or exploring the royal estates. "Very dull lessons they made of the subject, too."

"And doubtless called us heathen, my lady?" There was no reproach in his words.

"I fear they did, sometimes." Tresilian himself had used the same word, that very day, and claimed it signified admiration in his mind. But... Not all was what it seemed with Tresilian. Not now. "What ought the brethren have taught us?"

"It is simple enough. The Hunter watches over our campfires and ensures our trade prospers, while the Goddess watches over mothers and children and ensures our health prospers. They are of equal importance: for what use is good trade if a man has no family to send forward into the world and no heirs to speak his name?"

"So family is important to freemerchants?" She recalled the string they had encountered on the way to Vorrahan, mother and children riding quietly behind the freemerchant Nicholl.

"Family is everything, my lady. And yet we have nothing to bequeath them but our names. That is all the law of the kingdom will permit us."

Here was the crux of the matter, then. "And you would have it otherwise?"

"I would have a great many things otherwise, my lady. I would have the brethren teach the truth about our ways. I would have our children enjoy the same rights as other children in the kingdom. And I would have the law changed that I might leave mine something more substantial than a name to be carried where the wind would take it. I would call a place home. A place where I may plant and grow. A place where my family might flourish. Not some hole scraped from a barren cliff."

Weaver had told her Marten was not like other freemerchants. He was certainly the only freemerchant she'd seen carrying a sword. "Would you surrender your freedom to travel for this?"

"You have spent much time on the road of late, my lady. Do you not feel the call of home all the more strongly because of it?"

Home. Where was that? Not here – she had no ties to this dry place. Not Brigholm, where she had been born. Was it Highkell, the place she had lived longest, the place she had destroyed? She shivered. "Mostly, Marten, I feel the call of a place that is... elsewhere. Is that not the call of the road?"

"It is the call of your blood, my sister. And the call of your ancestors' blood, back to Alidreth and beyond."

Nicholl had welcomed her as sister... Before she could ask Marten more, the door from the great hall opened, releasing the buzz of conversation across the courtyard, along with a burst of warm light.

Weaver. She knew it before he was closer than a dozen paces. The thrill in the pit of her stomach told her. Goddess, let her not make a fool of herself. Not before Marten: he saw too much.

"My lady. Marten." Weaver bowed, a cursory movement.

"Join us, Weaver. We have been stargazing, my new sister and I."

Weaver nodded. "It's a fine night. And unpleasantly warm indoors." He shuffled his feet, fidgeting with a loose button on his surcoat.

"Sadly, that is where I must return. I have papers to prepare for tomorrow." Marten bowed before Alwenna, then straightened up, nodding to Weaver. He'd taken a couple of steps towards the great hall before he turned back. "I would offer a friendly word of caution: we are watched here, wherever we go. You would do well not to add more fuel to the rumours." He turned away and strode to the door. Again there was a burst of light and conversation then the door closed, leaving Alwenna and Weaver alone in the courtyard.

Something must have prompted Weaver to join her outside, but he seemed reluctant to discuss it.

Alwenna broke the silence. "Does Marten know? About us?"

"He may have guessed. He's an astute man." Weaver drew a breath, then cleared his throat. "I ought not have followed you out here, my lady, but–"

"What – have you forgotten my name so quickly? I wonder you bother to speak to me at all."

"No!" Weaver took a few paces across the yard, so there was a respectable distance between them. "I... wanted to tell you I didn't believe Marten. If I'd known he told me the truth I'd never have..." He tailed off into wretched silence.

"The truth about what?" She wanted to make him say it.

"About the king."

"Oh. You mean my dead husband?"

Weaver winced. "I thought we'd find some pretender here..."

"It wasn't the most pleasant surprise." She picked at a clump of moss growing from a joint between two stone slabs forming the fountain rim. "You might have warned me."

"I did try, my lady."

"How many days and nights were we on the road from Highkell? You could have tried harder." She would never be certain what her choice would have been had she known Tresilian was rumoured to be alive. "I wish you had."

"As do I, my lady. We should go back indoors before we are missed."

Alwenna shrugged. "It doesn't matter. I'm sure Tresilian knows already. He doesn't care – he's too busy with his priestess to worry about what I've been up to."

"But... my lady, it was a mistake. It can't happen again."

"So you sought me out to tell me this is our ending? You presume a great deal, Weaver. Do you imagine I'd return willingly to your bed knowing you lied to get me there in the first place?"

Weaver's face was hidden in shadow. "No, my lady. I only sought to–"

The door clattered open and a strip of light darted across the courtyard. A moment later a gaggle of drunks spilled outside, laughing and joking. They were so preoccupied with their laughter they didn't seem to notice Alwenna and Weaver standing in the shadows.

"Let me return you to your seat, my lady." Weaver offered his arm.

"No. I need nothing from you. And I want nothing from you." She left him standing by the fountain and stalked away, ignoring the pain that ground through her ankle at every step.

The great hall was even noisier and warmer than when she'd stepped outside with Marten.

Erin hurried over to her side. "Is all well, my lady?"

"Well enough, but I think I shall withdraw for the night. I have a headache." There was no sign of Tresilian – not that she'd expected to see him there.

Curtis, however, stood up and came over to join them.

"My lady, I will escort you to your lodgings." He gestured to two guards who waited at the side of the room and they fell in step behind him.

"That is kind, but there is no need to trouble yourself." Was she not to be granted a moment's peace?

Curtis straightened up, puffing out his chest. "It is the king's orders, my lady." The tabard strained over his ample belly. Doubtless there hadn't been time to make livery to fit the new King's Man.

"Indeed? So thoughtful of him." Alwenna led the tiny procession back to her lodgings as slowly as possible, leaning heavily on her walking stick all the way. She took a petty delight in the knowledge her armed guard must have looked ridiculous trailing behind her like so many ducklings. It was only a very little delight, and short-lived. When Curtis withdrew, promising she need have no fear for her safety, he left the two guards outside her door. She had little doubt she'd become a prisoner in her own rooms.

CHAPTER NINETY-TWO

The great chamber was thronged with people. Alwenna tried not to fidget too obviously in her seat as she eased her back, stiffened from sitting too long in the unyielding chair on the dais next to Tresilian. Her husband seemed to have developed a taste for kingly spectacle since being overthrown by Vasic. Much of the daily business he'd once been happy to carry out behind closed doors now took place in public chambers. Today he was hearing petitions from his subjects. Many sought redress for the depredations of Vasic's troops along the borders; others sought remuneration for providing lodgings for the army that currently protected his new eastern court at the summer palace. Perhaps it made sense to be seen to be dealing with such matters. At Highkell he'd happily delegated such minor business to his steward. But if he hoped to inspire his people with his greatness, he might be doomed to disappointment. The whole business was deadly dull for onlookers. As she stifled a yawn Alwenna noticed movement at the doorway, then spotted the freemerchant pushing his way through the crowd. A head taller than most of the men there, he made a distinctive figure.

The steward called for order. "As noon approaches, if

there are any more petitioners, let them speak up now."

Marten's voice rose above the crowd. "Yes, here! I bring documents relating to matters discussed previously with his highness. I would beg his signature this day." Alwenna straightened in her seat, her discomfort forgotten. This was what he'd mentioned the night before, in the garden. His face was drawn and his eyes heavy; he appeared to have been working all night on the papers. From the corner of her eye she could see Weaver. Stationed on guard duty at one side of the dais, he stood to rigid attention as he had throughout the morning. On the bench against the wall at the opposite side of the dais the priestess sat, once again in that meek pose, her grey eyes focused on nothing at all. Alwenna was aware of the slight lifting of the girl's head as the freemerchant approached.

Marten bowed as if he'd spent all his days gracing royal courts. The steward took the documents he held out and carried them up to Tresilian, bowing as he presented them. Alwenna longed to push the fat fool off the dais. He reminded her too much of Hames. The thought set the same dull echo running through her mind. Was the sight warning her this man was another such? She couldn't afford to yield to the assumption the sight was doing her any kind of service. It hindered her more often than it helped, disturbing her senses and clouding her judgement when she needed to be sharp and alert. As now, for she'd missed Marten's words.

Tresilian made a show of perusing the documents, although he could only have given them the most cursory glance.

"You will find it all as we discussed, your highness," Marten prompted.

Tresilian handed the papers back to the steward. "I shall study these at length later." He frowned towards Marten. "I need not study them to find one glaring difficulty: Vasic remains on my throne at Highkell and controls the bulk of my treasury. Until the cuckoo is removed, I fear you have not upheld your side of the bargain."

Marten's eyes narrowed but he maintained his composure. The crowd behind must have seen nothing.

"Highness, granting these rights now will cost your administration nothing. We do not expect you to buy our land for us: we will do that ourselves. We seek only for you to repeal a damaging law – one which serves no purpose in these modern times."

Tresilian glanced sideways to the priestess before he replied. Almost imperceptibly, she shook her head. Alwenna would not have noticed had she not followed her husband's eyes to the girl at that precise moment.

Tresilian raised his voice as he addressed Marten. "Do not presume to tell me my business, freemerchant. The terms of our agreement were clear: you have not yet fulfilled your part. I am not prepared to discuss this further until you have done so."

The freemerchant straightened up, his jaw clenched. "As you wish, your highness." He turned and strode from the chamber, head held high and back stiff. He had no need this time to push through the crowd of onlookers for they parted to let him pass, a buzz of excited conversation rising in his wake.

"And the business of this court is completed for today." Tresilian rose and walked away to his private chambers, gesturing towards the priestess, who stood and followed after him, looking neither to the right nor to the left.

Years of training from the succession of tutors her uncle had provided enabled Alwenna to maintain a mask of indifference. The irony was not lost on her, but she might have found it more amusing had her husband attempted even a modicum of discretion. With the aid of her walking stick, Alwenna made her way to the steps leading down from the dais. There, as she began to descend them, Weaver stepped forward and supported her.

"Allow me, my lady." He released her arm as she reached the stone floor of the great hall.

"Thank you, Weaver." She smiled, but he averted his eyes. The murmur of conversation rose up as the room emptied.

Weaver spoke again, his voice toneless and correct. "If it please your highness, the king has requested I escort you safely back to your chambers."

"Indeed? His consideration for my wellbeing surprises me more each day."

A momentary stiffening of his shoulders was the only sign from Weaver to suggest her sarcasm hadn't been wasted this time. They walked in silence through the hall, with only a few servants remaining to witness their progress. She purposely did not speak until they reached the open – and empty – cloister.

"Tell me, Weaver, what do you make of our king?"

He mis-stepped. "I beg your pardon?"

"Do you find him much altered?"

Weaver hesitated. "He has been driven from his rightful place – he will not be the same as the man who believed himself secure there."

That almost made sense. "Do you think that sufficient to account for the change in his manner?"

"My lady, I cannot presume to answer that. He is my king and I am sworn to serve him."

"Without question? Have a care, Weaver. Something is seriously awry." They had almost reached the door to her rooms. "His little priestess – have you any thoughts about her?"

"He... tells me she is from a healing order."

"Is that what they call it now?"

Whatever reply Weaver might have made was lost as footsteps hurried up behind them, accompanied by the metallic clatter of plate armour. Weaver spun around, setting himself between Alwenna and whoever approached, his hand on the pommel of his sword. Alwenna recognised the livery of the King's Man, flanked by two men-at-arms carrying long pikes. Curtis. Affable, bumbling Curtis, whose most important business of the day had once been securing his next meal.

"We have orders to search your rooms, my lady." He wore his new dignity with an uneasy air.

Weaver took a half step forward. "Orders from whom?"

"From the king." Curtis squared his shoulders.

If Weaver challenged Curtis' authority, no good would come of it. Alwenna spoke up. "I have nothing to hide. What is it you seek? I may save you some trouble." In truth she had so few possessions it would take them next to no time to rifle through the lot.

Curtis stepped towards the door, keeping a wary eye on Weaver. "I am not at liberty to discuss my orders, my lady." Finding the door bolted from inside, he knocked loudly.

Weaver's shoulders tensed and Alwenna set her hand upon his arm to still him, hoping it was not visible from where Curtis stood. Marten's warning the evening before was already being borne out.

"Then please, be my guest."

From within Erin opened the door, eyes widening as she took in the scene.

"Erin, please admit these gentlemen. They wish to search my rooms."

Erin stood back, allowing Curtis and the two soldiers to enter. Weaver was about to follow them in, but Alwenna closed her fingers about his arm. "Did you know of this?"

He spoke over his shoulder, his face grim. "No. Nothing." He would have moved away then but she delayed him a moment longer.

"And Curtis? Why is he King's Man in your place?"

"A reward for services to the king's cause."

"For rescuing you?"

"For that." Weaver nodded. "And for who knows what else besides."

She released his arm. "So you were ordered to escort me back just now? And Curtis ordered to follow us in turn?"

"Quite so, my lady." Weaver stepped aside so she might enter her rooms, while he waited outside the open door.

Curtis was watching as the two soldiers flung clothes and bedding out of the heavy chest against the wall. Erin watched, too, hands on hips and lips pursed as carefully folded items were strewn over the bed. A bundle of cloth fell from beneath one armful and landed on the floor with a solid clunk.

"Hand me that." Curtis pointed to the bundle and one of the soldiers picked it up, the fabric unwinding in his hands. The ornate dagger fell from it with a clatter.

"Have a care," Curtis muttered. "That is a precious item." He bent and picked up the dagger with finger and thumb, examining it closely. The gemstones were dull in the cool light of the chamber.

Dull and lifeless. As if the thing waited for the right hand to claim it, the right voice to command it. Alwenna shivered. Weaver would say that was fanciful nonsense, but she couldn't shake off her sense of foreboding. No one spoke, all in the room gazing at the dagger. Curtis took the fabric from the soldier's hand and wrapped it up once more. Alwenna let out the breath she hadn't realised she'd been holding.

Curtis stowed the bundle inside his leather jerkin. "This rightfully belongs to his highness."

Again that sense of foreboding. "He need only have asked and I would gladly have brought it to him," Alwenna said. Unless Tresilian had very specific reasons to not want Alwenna to bring the dagger to him herself. How much did Tresilian know about Garrad's death? He didn't have the sight, surely. She would have known, wouldn't she? She had too many questions and no answers.

The only certain thing was that she would learn nothing from Curtis and his men. They'd found what they were looking for and now withdrew, Curtis bowing politely with something of his former good humour. She surmised he might have been uncomfortable about carrying out this commission. Weaver, after a brief nod in her direction, followed after them. He might have more luck learning something from his comrade in arms. Whether he would share what he learned with her was another question entirely.

Alwenna turned to survey the mess the soldiers had left in their wake. "Who knew so few possessions could create so much chaos?"

"I'm sorry, my lady. I'm so, so sorry." Erin stared at her in horror.

Alwenna looked at her in surprise. "It won't take long to put these things away." She picked up one of the silk gowns Tresilian had provided and began folding it.

"But… my lady… Don't you see? I told him." The girl was stricken.

"I don't see at all."

Erin pressed her hands over her mouth, then seemed to collect herself. "I just didn't think. He made out he was so pleased for me, becoming a proper lady-in-waiting. And… I believed him. I thought he meant it."

Alwenna turned and sat on the foot of the bed. "I don't follow – who are you talking about? Not Tresilian?"

"No, my lady, Curtis. He… We… Well, at the inn…"

"Ah, yes, at the inn." It had been quite the night for their happy band.

"He's a kind man, my lady, and he was good to me, and I thought… When he asked me all those things I thought he was interested in me… I see now…" The girl straightened up, squaring her shoulders. "I told him about the wedding, the dagger, the old priest, and the tower collapsing. All of it. And he must have told the king every word." Her shoulders slumped again. "It's all my fault."

"Not at all." Alwenna couldn't afford to have the girl retreat into silence again now. "If the king had troubled to ask me, I'd have told him exactly what happened at Highkell. As it is we've learned the dagger is more important to him than I would have guessed."

"It must be valuable, with all those gems. He could sell it to raise an army."

"Perhaps he will." But it seemed more likely he had

some more arcane use for the blade. And she had no doubt it was the blade that mattered here. That thought troubled her. Almost as much as the fact that the new Tresilian had resorted to subterfuge to obtain the dagger in the first place. The old Tresilian – the one she'd grown up alongside, the cousin she'd cared for, the man she'd eventually married – would simply have asked. He would have told her why he wanted the dagger. And he would have done so himself, not sent underlings to carry out the task for him.

As for the dagger being his rightful property – well, she'd never seen it in his possession, nor had she ever seen it in the armoury at Highkell. The first time she'd seen it had been in her vision, gripped in Vasic's hand before he stabbed Tresilian, the jewels glinting bright and harsh. It was part of the puzzle. Somehow her husband who had died but not died and the blade that had killed but not killed him were connected. Whatever that connection might be, it could only be an unwholesome one.

CHAPTER NINETY-THREE

Alwenna followed the servant along the cloistered walkway that led to the great hall and thence to the king's apartments. The sun had been at its highest point in the sky when the servant arrived and the early afternoon air was oppressive without hint of a breeze to relieve it. She would sooner have rested in her own rooms than answer the peremptory summons. The old Tresilian would have come in person to speak to her, she was sure of that. Her head ached, a dull pain that made it hard to concentrate. Even Erin seemed subdued by the heat as she trailed along in their wake.

Tresilian waited alone in the chamber off the great hall. He sat there now, his manner relaxed. Alwenna stepped inside, her walking stick making a hollow sound on the timber floor. She glanced around to be sure they were indeed alone as the door closed softly behind her. No advisors, no servants, no guards. And no pale priestess. The air reeked of lavender again.

"Dear wife. I am glad you could spare the time to join me."

The ache in her head deepened. The air in this room was stifling, heavier than outside, despite the shade afforded by deep window recesses. An uneasy feeling had settled in the pit of her stomach, accompanying the bad taste in her mouth that usually presaged the sight. But instead of voices clamouring to be heard, her head was filled with leaden nothingness. Her vision clouded and she faltered a few steps into the room, leaning heavily on her stick, her hand clammy about the handle. Every instinct cried out to go no further, but her body was too heavy to move at all, forward or back.

And then Tresilian was beside her, supporting her elbow. "The heat has overcome you. Just a few steps more and you may rest, Alwenna." He guided her to a chair and for a moment he was the familiar Tresilian, the old one. Her childhood friend, the cousin who was concerned for her welfare. "Sit here now, the breeze will cool you."

Tresilian eased her into the chair and, sure enough, there was a movement of air here, between the open windows. She shivered, setting her hands on the arms of the chair. It was made from dense wood, so old it was almost black, and was of unusual design, with concave arms fashioned so her forearms rested in them rather than on top of them.

Tresilian's expression was troubled as he bent over her. "That's better, your colour's returning." He straightened up, then took a couple of steps away. "That is all for the good, for I have a favour to ask of you. Since my... injury, my strength has been returning, but my cure is not yet complete. Marten is working to ensure that for me, but in the meantime..."

Marten. He'd been reprimanded because he hadn't removed Vasic from Highkell. How could that complete Tresilian's cure?

But Tresilian was still speaking. "I would ask a favour of

you, dear wife. I would not ask if it were not imperative, but there is only so much the order can do. You can help. Will you do one small thing for me?" Tresilian studied her face. He licked his lips, as if apprehensive, then set a hesitant hand upon her head, in a clumsy caress. "You will, won't you? You will help me?"

Instinct told her to say no, to run, to leave the summer palace, take a horse and ride until she could ride no further. But duty said stay and hear him out. A thousand childhood secrets shared said stay and help him out. And the child they'd created rested still and quiet in her womb, as if waiting to hear if she would ensure its father's health.

"A small thing, you say?"

"A very small thing – for you – but of great importance for me." His eyes held hers for a moment, then slid away again. His hand moved, stroking her hair.

Her apprehension doubled, and their unborn child kicked and twisted. "A very small thing? Will you grant me a favour in return?"

"Of course. Anything you ask." His thumb moved gently, an idle caress to the back of her head.

Marten's anger as he strode from the throne room rose unbidden to her mind. Tresilian's word couldn't be trusted, but she arguably had a deeper claim to his loyalty than the freemerchant. There was only one way to find out.

"If you wish me to help you, Tresilian, you must first tell me what this small thing is. And then, if I agree to it, you will set aside your priestess and she will leave the summer palace."

The gentle motion of his thumb stilled. She'd said the wrong thing.

"I cannot do that, truly I cannot." Then, to her

surprise he knelt in front of her, taking both her hands in his. "Alwenna, I wouldn't ask this of you if it were not necessary. You know me well enough to believe that."

Did she? "I did once."

"If you want our child to meet his father, grant me this boon." Now he gripped her hands fervently, too tight for her to simply pull them away. His fingertips dug into her palms, and his hands struck cold against hers.

She tried to pull her hands free but he hung on. "You still haven't told me what this boon is."

"You'll hardly feel a thing, I promise." His eyes were over-bright, feverish.

"No." She tried to tug her hands away again, but his grip tightened painfully. She struggled against him, her heartbeat racing, desperate to break free. She should have trusted her instinct all along. Behind her she felt a rush of air as a door opened, then closed again. Over the pounding of her headache she heard footsteps approach over the timber floor, steady and measured with military precision.

"All is ready, your highness." The priestess' voice. Alwenna had never heard her speak outside those heated visions. Now the girl knelt at her side, setting something down on the ground where Alwenna could not see it.

Beyond her stood Weaver, his face a closed mask.

Pinning her against the chair with the weight of his body, Tresilian pressed Alwenna's left arm down onto the chair arm. As calmly as if she were straightening bedding, the priestess wrapped a leather strap about Alwenna's forearm and tightened it until her arm was gripped against the dark wood. Alwenna fought Tresilian's hold on her remaining arm with all her weight, but he pinned her down while the girl fastened it like the first. A moment

later her feet had likewise been bound to the cross-rail of
the heavy chair.

"Be still, my lady. It will be over in next to no time." The
girl spoke with calm detachment, feeding another strap
around Alwenna's upper arm and pulling it tight until
Alwenna felt her veins throbbing against the pressure.
"She is ready now, your highness." The girl reached down
and lifted a small metal bowl in her hands. It flashed and
gleamed, and Alwenna could see runes carved around the
outside. Runes which looked familiar.

All Alwenna's attention had been on the priestess and
her pale grey eyes. Now Tresilian knelt before her with his
head bowed, as if in prayer.

She had not long to wonder where she had seen those
runes before. Tresilian stood, and in his hands he held the
ornate dagger. Runes glinted on the blade like quicksilver.
The gemstones were vivid and brilliant in the cool shade
of the room.

Alwenna stilled. She had nothing to gain by fighting.
And at the back of her mind was the spectre of what
had happened at Highkell. If she lost control now, what
cataclysmic events would ensue? She dared not find out.
She tried to calm the frantic beating of her pulse, which
seemed horribly amplified in the silence of the room.

"Thank you, my cousin. And my wife. Your gift to
me will be doubly blessed." Tresilian set the blade of
the dagger across his palm, then turned to Weaver, who
waited, stony-faced, as Tresilian held out the knife to him,
hilt-first.

"Weaver. You know what you must do."

Weaver took two steps forward, then lifted the knife
from the king's hands. Tresilian moved over to flank

Alwenna's right side while the priestess waited on her left.

Time seemed to stand still as Weaver turned to stand before Alwenna, then knelt slowly, oh so slowly.

"No. Please don't." The words came out as an agonised squeak. Weaver lifted brown eyes towards Alwenna, but they were empty of any compassion and he leaned closer, raising the dagger. Light danced off the blade as tremors shook his hand. He set the icy edge against the flesh in the crook of her elbow. She held her breath, bracing herself as he pressed the tip of the dagger into her skin above the blue vein. The colour of the gemstones enclosed between his fingers seemed to strengthen. Blood welled over the edge of the blade, spreading along the inscribed runes, a thin thread spilling down over her arm to drip into the bowl the priestess held beneath it.

"We need more, your highness." The priestess' words were as calm and matter of fact as before.

"Weaver, do as she says." Tresilian's voice was cold.

Weaver hesitated. Alwenna felt a tremor run through the blade, but then he dug the point deeper and ice bit into her arm until she lost all sensation in the limb. All she could do was watch as the bowl filled, drop by precious drop.

She must have passed out. When she became aware of her surroundings again Tresilian was unfastening the last of the leather straps. A bandage had been tied over the cut. Weaver stood to attention at the side of the dais, eyes focused on the wall opposite. The priestess was behind her, presumably at the altar-like table in the window, chanting some kind of incantation in a strangely muted voice.

"You are with us once more?" Tresilian's voice was almost caressing. He straightened up, having freed the last of the straps, and clapped his hands. The door at the far end of the room opened and the servant hurried forward, closely followed by Erin.

"Take your mistress back to her rooms. She must have red wine to drink. See she rests." Tresilian turned away, leaving Erin to help Alwenna to her feet and support her from the room. Weaver gave no sign of seeing her pass him by. Only the slight rise and fall of his chest as he breathed gave any indication he was not made of stone.

Alwenna glanced back once from the doorway. Silhouetted in the light from the window, the priestess and Tresilian were bent over the bowl, as if praying. Then Weaver stepped into her line of sight as he followed them out of the door. The door thudded shut and Weaver took up guard in front of it, as before avoiding eye contact with Alwenna at all. Garrad, Tresilian, Erin, Curtis, and now – worst of all – Weaver. Was there anyone left who had not yet betrayed her?

Alwenna could no longer contain her rage. She turned back towards him meaning to accuse him, to strike him, anything to reawaken some expression in that stony face, but dizziness overwhelmed her and she found herself staggering against Erin.

"Come, my lady, you must rest."

They had passed perhaps halfway along the cloister towards her chambers when Marten appeared striding towards them. "My lady, I would speak with you." His expression turned to one of concern as he drew nearer. "By the Goddess, what has happened? Are you ill?" He hurried to Alwenna and drew her arm about his shoulder, supporting her weight the rest of the way back to her lodgings.

The solitary guard stepped forward to block the door as they approached. "There's none permitted to enter other than the lady and her servant."

"The lady is unwell, you fool." Marten glared at the man.

"I've got my orders."

"Step aside, or I'll make sure to tell his highness how you made his queen's illness worse." The guard stepped back hastily.

Marten set Alwenna down on her bed. As he stepped back he caught sight of the bandage on her arm. "You are injured. Who did this?"

Alwenna laid her head back against the pillow, hoping the dizziness would pass. "It was... Weaver. Weaver did it." Voicing the words made the betrayal no less bitter. "On Tresilian's orders – he and the priestess took... took my blood." Her voice wobbled on the final words. Tremors shook her whole body. She opened her eyes to find Marten frowning down at her. "Marten, why did they want my blood?"

Marten pressed his fingertips to his chin. "Some ritual, I daresay."

He knew exactly why, but he wasn't prepared to tell her. Her head throbbed with pain, and dazzling sparks clouded her vision. She had to ask the right questions to get answers. But if she knew which were the right questions, she wouldn't need to ask them in the first place.

"It looked, as I left, as if Tresilian was going to drink it."

Even through her clouded vision she could see the dismay on his face. "You must have been mistaken." He straightened up, looking around the room. Again he frowned. "All this lavender – it is not good for one who has the sight." He turned to Erin. "Throw it all out. Immediately."

The lavender? She'd been choking on the stuff ever since they had arrived at the summer palace. "But, it's everywhere. In what way is it not good?"

"It suppresses the sight, and dulls the senses of those who are susceptible. And it would prevent one such as yourself from wielding their strength."

This time she had no doubt Marten was speaking what he believed to be the truth. Alwenna nodded at Erin, who had hesitated. "Do as he says, if you please."

The girl hurried to do her bidding while Marten made his way to the door. "Try to sleep, my lady. You will feel much restored afterwards."

He left, closing the door firmly behind himself. Alwenna scarcely noticed as she sank into a dizzy oblivion.

CHAPTER NINETY-FOUR

Alwenna's mouth was sour with the taste of the sight as she climbed the stairs, one winding step after the other. She'd climbed them countless times before, as a child, laughing with Tresilian. Once, furtively, after sneaking down to eavesdrop on the grown-ups deciding her future. Other times laughing in glee as the cousins played hide and seek.

And this time. It would be the last time she ever climbed these stairs. The very last time. She climbed slowly, struggling to catch her breath, the biting pain in her belly slowing her, making each upward step a struggle, her back protesting at the extra effort. One last time. And this would be the end of it. Full circle.

The twisted snakes forming the door handle were pitted with rust, but there was no need to touch them this time. The door hung open, skewed, with one corner resting on the stone floor, the top hinge cracked. No one had seen fit to repair it – why would they? And for all Tresilian's protestations, for all her uncle's scepticism, she had been the one to destroy Highkell. Three walls of the great chamber remained in place, but daylight cleft the western wall, where the stones had been torn away with the collapse of the curtain wall.

Her doing.

She crossed the room. The remaining floor tilted slightly now, but was still supported by the vaulted ceiling beneath. The effect was a mild sense of drunkenness. Perhaps this was how it would end: with her return the stones would finally give up their unequal fight against gravity and the floor would fall away beneath her weight. And this time her body would be buried for ever. If that was how it must be, let it be so. Let Highkell take its vengeance on her.

She closed her eyes, and could hear nothing but the pounding of her heart, the rise and fall of her chest as she caught each breath. And softer still than that she could hear the gentle settling of friable mortar between the loosened stones.

So be it.

She waited.

Nothing happened.

She moved over to the single remaining casement of the window, averting her eyes from the dizzying gap in the wall. Several of the tiny panes of glass had cracked. Last time she had seen this window, rain had been sluicing down it. Now it was dry, sunlight finding its way between the clouds. She gazed out, not seeing the landscape before her, but the scene she'd witnessed from the very top of the tower so many years ago, the huddle of people about the two open graves. It had been raining then. Just as it had rained at Highkell almost continually since. Highkell had taken her parents from her. She'd been cast adrift, rootless, and now she'd torn the foundations from Highkell. Perhaps the vengeance was hers and balance had already been achieved. Was that how it was all meant to play out?

Far below she heard the creak of metal hinges. The scuff of leather boots on stone flags. A murmur of voices. Male voices. They'd answered her summons after all. She turned away from the window and the view across the gorge so she could see the door from the stairs.

For the first time since she had fled Highkell with Weaver she knew calm. She knew what had to be done. She waited patiently, as they approached up the stairs.

Full circle.

The footsteps drew closer. A shadow fell across the wrecked doorway.

Alwenna woke. Her mouth was parched, her head throbbing as the vision receded, leaving her mind empty.

It took her a moment to realise for the first time since she'd arrived in The Marches that her mind was truly empty. The unwelcome voices were silent. In their place was rock-solid certainty.

Alwenna sat up, throwing back her covers. She pressed one hand over the barely discernible mound of her stomach where the baby slumbered. It wouldn't end here, that much was clear. And it wouldn't end yet. But, Goddess willing, it would end.

CHAPTER NINETY-FIVE

There were two guards outside Alwenna's door again when she left her chambers for the evening meal. They tucked in silently behind her and Erin as they made their way to the great hall.

Tresilian was already seated at the top table, and greeted her with magnanimous civility. "My lady wife. I trust you are well rested?"

"Well enough, husband." He really was becoming more like Vasic with every day that passed. It wasn't an improvement. Beneath the bandage her arm stung. She surveyed the hall as she sat down. Weaver was sitting well down one of the side tables, speaking to no one, all his attention on his food. There was nothing about him to suggest he'd enjoyed the day's work, rather the opposite. Alwenna found that discovery perversely satisfying. She would reckon with him at some point over this afternoon's deeds.

She picked at her food, relieved of the obligation of speaking further with Tresilian as he discussed something with the man seated on his right. The stranger's garments suggested some religious order. Sharp-faced, he was one to whom she determined to give a wide berth, particularly if he was anything to do with the little priestess. But now her attention had been called to the man, she began to notice others seated about the hall, wearing similar robes. Had they been there other nights? She couldn't be sure.

As the night before, Tresilian left the table early, this time in the company of the unknown priest. Alwenna watched as they left. Tresilian looked like the man she'd married. He walked like the man she'd married. But he no longer talked like him, nor acted like him.

The table lurched, as another diner arrived at her left-hand side. Marten leaned heavily on the table as he sat down beside her with none of his accustomed elegance. He brought with him a strong smell of wine.

"My lady." He performed the gesture of welcome without his usual panache. "It is good to see you… so well recovered."

"Thank you. Your advice was invaluable."

He spread his hands in a gesture of acknowledgment. "I am glad you found it so, my sister." He sprawled back in his chair, slurring his words ever so slightly. "There are things we must discuss, you and I. Things I have learned this day which might interest you."

Alwenna glanced over her shoulder. There was no one within earshot at the top table. Her two guards were slouching by the foot of the steps to the dais, eyes on a servant girl who was laughing and joking with an off-duty soldier as she poured his wine. But further down the hall Weaver had raised his head and was watching her now. For once he didn't look away as she made eye contact. Alwenna raised one haughty eyebrow and returned her attention to Marten. She was petty enough to smile warmly at the freemerchant.

"You intrigue me. But I am conscious of your advice earlier. Is it wise to speak here? I have two shadows now who follow me wherever I go." She glanced to where the two men-at-arms loitered.

Marten followed her gaze. "Humour me, my lady. A man as drunk as I could not possibly be discussing anything of import."

"As you wish." She slid a dish of chicken over the table to him, leaning closer as she did so. "Speak, my brother."

Marten slouched over the dish, apparently deliberating over which morsel to choose. "Your husband has made a mistake this day. He thinks he no longer needs me. I cannot hope to bring Vasic to him alive, and he uses this as an excuse to dispute the agreement we made years ago."

"Excuse? Not incentive to you to bring it about?"

"He thinks our cowled friends will give him what he needs by another means." He didn't slur now. "And, to be blunt, my sister, now he has you."

In her mind's eye Alwenna saw the dull gleam of the jewels in the handle of the dagger as the blade bit into her flesh. Marten took up a chicken leg from the dish. He was not half as drunk as he appeared.

Alwenna smiled her best court smile. "As you say, he has me for the time being. Whether he keeps me is another matter."

"Precisely so, sister." Marten swayed away from her, gesturing with the chicken leg for emphasis. "The bond of kinship is a powerful thing. You, Tresilian and Vasic share the same blood. You even share some of the same memories. And now, unless I'm much mistaken, the dagger has tasted your blood. Tresilian's father primed the blade long ago. It's no coincidence Vasic chose it to deliver the fatal blow to your husband. It's no coincidence you were able to turn it upon Garrad. And no coincidence your friend Drew found it in the ruins."

"Come now, Marten. That makes a fine tale, but Garrad turned the blade on himself."

"Did you not will it so, my lady?"

Alwenna shivered, despite herself. "You're drunk, Marten. These are tales to scare children into obedience, nothing more."

Marten selected another chicken leg from the dish. "My lady, you called upon the Goddess. You know it is the truth."

"Then why did the blade not turn upon Vasic when he stabbed Tresilian?"

"The answer is simple: your husband sought death at his cousin's hand."

"No. How could that be so? He'd have to be a madman."

Marten raised his eyebrows. "Indeed, my sister. Tresilian returned much changed from war in the east, did he not?"

He had. Alwenna could remember it clearly. Tresilian had left as an irresolute youth, and returned as a man, steeled by the death of his own father in battle. "He grew up. There is no great secret there."

"He embraced darkness." Marten held his chicken leg aloft, swaying slightly in his chair. "It found him there on the battlefield, and he embraced it."

"That's another fine tale, Marten, but how can you claim to know so much of it?"

"How, my sister?" He leaned closer. "Your husband made a deal with darkness and I – I am the man who brokered it."

A chill of recognition ran down Alwenna's spine at his

words. She straightened up. "That's preposterous. Tell me again when you are sober, and I might listen." Alwenna pushed her seat back and stood up, ignoring the pain that gnawed at her ankle.

He caught hold of her arm. "Sister, I'll tell you over and over until you listen. We must call a halt to this business, you and I. He grows stronger by the day. We must stop him now, while we still can."

This was no drunken maundering. Marten meant every word.

"What do you imagine I can do about any of this?"

"You can call upon the Goddess again."

"No. You overestimate me." Alwenna tugged her arm free and swept from the table, his words chasing after her, taking hold and hanging on. To call upon the Goddess was to take responsibility for what had happened at Highkell. For all the lives lost, indiscriminately, in the rubble. People had died alongside her, while she'd survived. All that kept her going now was her conviction it had been coincidence, the work of groundwater over many years. And the flashing of the gemstones had been a trick of the light. And Drew leading the rescuers straight to her, finding the dagger, handing it to her, that…

If she believed everything Marten said, then she also had to believe she was a monster.

CHAPTER NINETY-SIX

Weaver watched the two guards hasten after Alwenna as she limped from the room, her face tight with pain. He'd have no chance to speak to her while they followed her everywhere, especially since one of them was Scoular. Maybe that was for the best: she'd flay him with one disdainful glance. She'd been in such haste to leave she'd left her walking stick propped against the top table. Marten lounged there, wine cup in hand and a drunken smile on his face. Weaver could use a barrel or two of whatever the freemerchant had been drinking. For a moment he'd thought the man was speaking to Alwenna in earnest.

Marten noticed his scrutiny and grinned, raising one hand as if to catch Weaver's attention. He pushed himself to his feet, scooping up his wine cup, then twisted round to pick up the wine flagon gracing the now-empty top table. He made his way unsteadily down the steps and along the hall to where Weaver sat.

"Off duty? You'll join me in a toast to our fair queen, I've no doubt." The freemerchant sat down heavily, and grinned at Weaver. He slopped some wine into Weaver's cup and topped up his own – the bulk of its contents seemed to have found its way down the freemerchant's tunic front. Marten raised his cup. "To the Lady Alwenna's health. Long may she prosper."

Weaver raised his cup, keeping his eyes on Marten. What was the fellow about now? He'd no sooner trust him than a cornered rat. Was he about to take issue with Weaver for the day's events? The Lady Alwenna must have given him a full account over the dish they'd shared. Unwise, perhaps, for Tresilian to have left her alone at the table.

"Well, will you drink with me? The lady's health?"

"The lady's health." Weaver lifted the cup to his lips, inhaling carefully. It smelled of nothing but wine.

"Don't worry, it's not tainted. You're no use to any of us dead. And I doubt the king would have you brought back, however good your sword arm."

Weaver swallowed some of the wine – a better vintage than the rough stuff served at the lower tables. "I'm in no mood for your prating tonight, freemerchant."

Marten shrugged one shoulder. "I can understand that. It was an ill turn you served the lady this afternoon, was it not?"

Weaver glared at Marten, who met gaze for gaze, unblinking. His eyes were the same green as Alwenna's. Was it true all freemerchants had some measure of the sight?

"That cannot be easy to live with, Weaver."

Weaver downed the rest of the wine. "I swore loyalty to the king. You brought me the contract, remember? Or are you too far gone for that?"

Marten smiled. There was no trace of a slur as he spoke in a low voice. "I never forget a business agreement. And until now I've never broken one."

"Nor have I. I told you, I'm in no mood for your games."

"Then take another drink with me instead."

"I've had enough." Weaver pushed to his feet and left the freemerchant there. He strode to the main door, which stood wide open to ventilate the stuffy hall. In the cloistered yard the air was cooler. He was getting too old for this. He should have gone to Ellisquay and got work on the dock like Curtis suggested. All that time he'd thought Curtis had been helping him, and instead he'd been helping himself to the honour of King's Man. Weaver deserved the freemerchant's mockery. Here he was professing loyalty to the king who was busy right now with that colourless priestess, while his true wife was held under guard in her own palace. Worst of all, he was the one who'd brought her here.

As for Tresilian – had it all been some conjuring trick? Some elaborate gambit to flush out the traitors in his court? Or had he indeed died and been reborn? Stronger and wiser than before, he'd claimed. A wise man wouldn't keep his queen prisoner in her own palace for long – not here in The Marches. Once word got out, there'd be trouble. Whatever the truth behind Tresilian's condition, Alwenna carried his legitimate heir. Reason told Weaver she'd be safe until the child had been brought into the world. Except there was that business of the blood-letting. Instinct whispered she might not last that long.

Whether Tresilian had meant to test Weaver's loyalty or to punish them both, he couldn't have chosen better. Alwenna would never forgive Weaver for that piece of work – he'd seen the hurt in her eyes at his betrayal, even while his own gut roiled with distaste. He couldn't face doing that again.

He could go over the wall, desert his post. Turn his back on the whole sorry mess. But that would mean leaving the Lady Alwenna without a single friend at the summer palace. He suspected Marten had an inclination in that direction, but of late Marten, too, had fallen from royal favour. And that decision was as unlike Tresilian as anything Weaver could recall.

Weaver halted at the edge of the cloistered yard. Marten was far from pleased by the king's actions. Now was not the time to sulk like some adolescent. He should be mining the freemerchant for information before he sobered up and recovered his usual caution.

Weaver turned and strode back along the cloister.

CHAPTER NINETY-SEVEN

Alwenna slammed the door shut, waking the servant girl, who was dozing in a chair. "Erin, bring me water – as much as you can. A bathtub full would be best."

Erin blinked and rubbed her eyes. "But my lady, you bathed this morning."

"I don't need this for washing."

"It'll take time to heat it. The fires will be damped down for the night."

"Cold water will be better. Freshly drawn best of all." She couldn't say how she knew, but there again was the rock-solid certainty.

Erin stared at her. "Very well, my lady." She hurried to do as she had been bidden.

Alwenna stripped off her clothing and stepped into the water: fresh water, untainted by any trace of herbs or essences, untarnished by smoke or fire. The cold bit into her flesh, first one foot then the other. Her skin prickled and the chill snatched her breath as she lowered herself into it. She lay back and closed her eyes, waiting until the water stilled, waiting until only the rise and fall of her breathing disturbed it. Her mind cleared, darkness and confusion falling away, dissipating until all that remained was cold, calm certainty.

Tresilian lay alongside his priestess in a tangle of sheets. The girl sat upright in alarm, pulling up the sheet to cover her breasts. She stared into the night, eyes darting around as she tried to find Alwenna. "You mustn't do this," the girl mouthed. "You mustn't."

Alwenna moved on.

Weaver and Marten, heads together over a table, wine cups in hands, a half-empty flagon before them. Doubt, mistrust, recrimination. "All well and good to be wise after the event," Marten was saying. "She's in danger."

Weaver looked up with a start as her gaze passed over him, then set down his wine cup and pushed it away.

She moved on.

Curtis, snoring in a bunk. He stirred uneasily. This was not what she sought.

She moved on, faster now. Past horses in the stable. They shifted, stamping their hooves. A kitchen-boy crouched against the courtyard wall, crying, too immersed in his own misery to sense her scrutiny. Tresilian's steward, hunched over a parchment, working by the light of a single candle. He turned his head uneasily towards the door.

Not what she sought, none of them. She was wasting time.

On.

Towards a huddle of buildings to the east of the summer palace. Girls slept in dormitories, rows of spartan beds down either side of a long room, each one identical to the next. Then she came to a door and hesitated. The handle was fashioned in the shape of three snakes, each devouring the tail of the snake before it, identical to the handles at Highkell. She'd hated those snakes as a child and she hated them still. But she couldn't turn back now.

She pushed on.

Inside the chamber monks chanted, marking the passing of the night. Row upon row of candles burned on an altar. There was enough light to make out the drab colour of their habits – a brown homespun. Half a dozen monks sat apart, on raised pews. Their habits were grey. One raised his head as she approached. A livid scar ran down one side of his gaunt face, cutting through the socket where his left eye should have been. His remaining eye stared straight at her and she stopped with a jolt of recognition: Tresilian's father.

The shock jerked her back to bitter cold, a shout dying in her throat.

Erin snatched up a towel and hurried to her side. "My lady, you were gone so long I thought you wouldn't return." Gulping for air and shivering, Alwenna climbed out of the bath, wrapping the towel about her shoulders. She climbed onto the bed, heedless of her wet skin, and curled up there, pulling the blankets about herself in a bid to stop the tremors running through her body.

"My lady, what's wrong? What has shocked you so?" Erin stirred the embers in the hearth to life and added another log to the fire.

How to explain? The girl seemed accepting of the sight – at least she didn't try to pretend Alwenna had fallen asleep. "I saw Tresilian's father. He's here."

Erin looked blank.

"Erin, he's been dead these past three years. He fell in battle near Brigholm."

CHAPTER NINETY-EIGHT

Erin chopped at the last tress of Alwenna's hair with the newly sharpened eating knife. "It's done, my lady."

"Will I do?" Alwenna tugged doubtfully at what remained of her hair.

"Aye, my lady, you look nothing like a highborn lady now. Just mind you leave the talking to me." Erin gathered up the shorn hair and they tossed it on the fire, offering up a prayer to the Goddess to watch over them. As an afterthought, Alwenna repeated the freemerchant blessing invoking the Hunter, too. The hair contorted, twisted and sizzled away in the flames, leaving only a faint odour of singeing in the room to show it had ever existed.

Alwenna threw on a plain travelling cloak and covered what little remained of her hair by wrapping a scarf over her head.

The first light of the sun was showing in the sky, setting the undersides of the clouds on fire.

"It's time, my lady, if we're to do this." Erin eased open the bolt on the door.

Alwenna set one hand on the girl's arm; she was all skinny sinew beneath the homespun. "Are you sure?" The words were little more than a whisper.

Erin nodded, her expression determined. "Aye, my lady." She slipped out through the door. Alwenna pushed the door almost shut and set her foot behind it, peering out through the crack. Only one voice. Only one guard. Thank the Goddess. The other must have sneaked off with his lover again, as Erin had said he would.

"What, more bath water?" The man stepped forward, occluding Alwenna's view of the anteroom outside.

"Nah, just me this time. She's asleep." Erin's voice was bright and flirtatious. "I thought maybe you an' me, y'know…" The guard shifted and Alwenna could see Erin backing away, a mischievous grin on her face. "Not here! We might wake her. There's an empty garderobe round the corner." She turned away, glancing back over her shoulder, and the guard followed after her. As soon as they were out of sight Alwenna slipped from the doorway, empty bucket in hand, and began to make her way towards the well courtyard, moving slowly so she wouldn't put too much pressure on her injured ankle. She'd not gone far before hurried footsteps and the rustling of skirts announced Erin's approach.

Alwenna could smell blood, although it didn't show on the girl's clothing.

"Did it go as planned?"

"Aye, it did." The girl nodded tightly, rolling up her hooded cloak into a tight bundle. She'd been wearing it when she left the room.

"Are you all right?"

"Aye. That one got what he deserved." There was steel in her eyes, and a certain determination about the girl's movements that reminded Alwenna of her final encounter with Hames.

The guard at the entrance to the well courtyard let them pass without a second glance. There was more activity out here as stable boys were busy filling buckets to water the horses. The washing green lay beyond this yard, through a gate at the far side. Alwenna had a sudden premonition they wouldn't reach it.

She caught hold of Erin's arm. "There are too many people here."

"Nonsense. We are washer women going about our business. Just keep your head down. You carry this while I fill the bucket." Erin thrust the blood-soiled cloak into Alwenna's arms and took the bucket from her, then strode out to the well. Alwenna shuffled after her, doing her best to hide the weakness in her ankle. She kept her head low, wishing she could pull the hood of her cloak over her head, but they'd decided that would have looked out of place here within the palace walls.

Alwenna was halfway across the cobbled yard when a vision began pricking at her consciousness. She willed it away. She couldn't lose concentration now. But the sight was determined. Sparks danced before her eyes, veiling the courtyard. She fanned the flames, watching them climb higher and hotter. Then a gust dashed the sparks into her face and she was breathing wood smoke and ashes. The air wasn't filling her lungs, but searing them, making her cough and retch. Breathing was impossible. She was choking. She dropped to her hands and knees to crawl beneath the smoke and heat, lost her balance and her head smacked sharply against the cobbles.

"Keep back. The sight of your ugly mug won't help her none." Erin's voice penetrated the darkness. Alwenna blinked, and discovered it was daylight. Her forehead throbbed. She pushed herself up onto her hands and knees. Her right elbow stung where she'd grazed it.

"Is she ill?" Broad hands, presumably belonging to the owner of the deep voice that had just spoken, tugged her to her feet. Alwenna rubbed her hands down the front of her cloak and drew it shut to hide her clothing, keeping her head down.

"Let her be. She doesn't want your paws all over." Erin shoved Alwenna's would-be helpers back and bent beside her, gathering up the cloak that had fallen to the ground.

"'Ere," a deep voice asked. "Ain't that blood?"

"Well, what of it?" Erin snorted. "You think we'd be bothering to wash clean clothes?"

One or two of the onlookers laughed. Erin shoved the bundle into Alwenna's arms and steered her towards the well.

"That's a deal of blood." Deep Voice disliked being laughed at. "Fresh, too."

Goddess curse him for his damaged pride. Alwenna's head pounded so hard she couldn't think.

"Of course it is – how else do you think we're to wash it out? No chance once it's dried in. Did the midwife drop you on your head when you were born? My mistress is just back from a bad birthing. She's been up all night an' if we don't get this clean for her I'll catch it in the ear." Erin prodded the big man in the chest and he stepped back warily, an expression of distaste on his face. "Are you done poking your nose in? Some of us have work to do." She took hold of Alwenna's arm and guided her to where the bucket waited, full of water.

"Midwife, you say? Thank the Goddess." An educated voice broke in. A familiar voice with only a hint of the freemerchant lilt. "My wife is in need of her assistance. Take me to her at once, and I'll buy her a hundred new cloaks to replace that one."

Alwenna raised her eyes to find Marten studying her. Any hope he might not recognise her faded and died. He took a firm hold of her arm and led her away to another door leading to the guest lodgings. "Quickly now, bring that with you. There's no time to be lost."

Erin hesitated, apparently ready to argue – or even to run – but at a nod from Alwenna she hurried to join them.

CHAPTER NINETY-NINE

Marten kept tight hold of Alwenna's arm as he escorted her to his lodgings, giving her no chance to break away from him. Erin walked alongside, wary as a young horse. She still carried the bucket, the water in it sloshing with every step.

The guest lodgings were situated along the opposite side of the cloistered yard to where Alwenna had been housed, backing onto the well courtyard. The room contained a bed, a chest and a wooden bench.

"Ladies, pray be seated." Marten smiled. "I cannot offer you lavish hospitality here, but I can at least protect you from the eyes of the overly inquisitive."

Alwenna sat, ramrod-straight, on the bench and set the bundled cloak down on the floor at her feet. Next to her Erin followed suit.

"You suffered no great harm from your fall, I trust, sister?" He appeared genuinely concerned.

"No, I did not. But I thank you for your concern."

Marten smiled. "But for that your escape bid might have succeeded. Your servant's initiative is to be applauded." He nodded towards Erin, who watched him warily. "You are clearly dressed for travel. But, my lady, did you hope to cross the Blighted Sea without a guide?"

"We crossed it but two days ago. The way was clear enough." Erin's chin jutted in defiance.

Alwenna admired her presence of mind – their plan had been to skirt the arid land, but it was far better not to reveal anything of their intention. She had no wish to throw herself on Marten's mercy, not that she could be too particular now their plan had failed.

"It is the time of year when dust storms blow up without warning. Squalls so wild the sand shreds the flesh of the unwary traveller. So powerful they can redraw the landscape in a couple of hours. So enduring they can block out the sun for days at a time."

Erin pursed her lips and said nothing more.

"Discussing the weather is all well and good, Marten," Alwenna said. "But we should be on the road already, and now the whole palace is astir. Do you mean to help us or hinder us?"

"I mean to help you, of course. I named you sister, did I not?" He prodded at the bloodied cloak with his foot. "Whose is this?"

"The cloak, or the blood?" Alwenna hardly cared what he thought at that stage. It could only be a matter of time before the dead guard was found. Their bold escape plan had only taken them from bad to worse. And now Erin – hitherto free of any suspicion – was drawn in by her guilt.

"They do not belong to one and the same person? By the Goddess, you have been busy."

"The cloak was one of Tresilian's providing. The blood – on the cloak and my hands – belongs to one of his guards." Beside Alwenna the servant girl drew in a breath. Alwenna nudged her and she remained silent.

Marten examined the cloak doubtfully. "A great deal of blood. I can scarce credit you would do such a thing, sweet sister."

Alwenna smiled. "I may yet surprise you. Sometimes unpleasant deeds are necessary." Again Erin shifted beside her, but didn't speak up.

"Indeed they are. More often than one would like." Marten shrugged, then stirred the fire into life and dropped the cloak on it. As it began to smoulder he removed the stopper from a small bottle, releasing the scent of aromatic oil into the room. He dashed some onto the cloak and it burst into flame, sending up dark smoke that would be noticed by anyone outside who cared to stop and look up. "Tell me where to find the unfortunate fellow. I have the means to hide him in a more permanent way."

Alwenna looked at Erin. Dare they trust the freemerchant? Erin shrugged her shoulders. They had little option now. "In a garderobe. Just beyond the door to my chamber."

"Then I suggest you wait here while I do what is necessary. Tonight after darkness falls will be our best chance of leaving unseen." He gestured towards a saddlebag under the window. "There is bread and fruit there – I suggest you break your fast while I am gone." He bowed slightly and withdrew, muttering an order to someone outside. They could hear his footsteps as he strode away down the cloister.

Erin hurried over to the door and crouched down to peer underneath it. She swore softly. "There's a sentry outside."

Curse Marten for a liar. It was one thing to remove a guard during the night in an out-of-the-way corner where there were no witnesses, but there were many passers-by here. "Could we break the back window?"

A quick inspection told them not only did it open onto the bustling well yard, but the gap between the mullions and glazing bars was too narrow.

"I'm sorry. I've taken things from bad to worse."

"We're not done yet, my lady."

"If we're questioned, we'll say I killed the guard."

"I'd do it again on the instant, may the Goddess be my witness. He deserved it." Erin prowled round the small chamber, then turned to inspect the fruit, sniffing an apple cautiously before taking a bite and nodding. "We should eat, my lady. This could be the last time in a while we have something that isn't prepared just for us."

"I'm not hungry."

"You need it for the baby, my lady. Here, eat." Erin handed her another apple, then took out her eating knife to cut the bread. She hesitated and put the blade away again, tearing two chunks off the loaf instead.

Alwenna thought she'd kept her secret so cleverly. "When did you guess?"

Erin sat down on the bench, stretching her legs out before her. "Oh, a long time ago. Back at Highkell. My sister took the same way with her first. I never told Vasic, though."

"He set you to spy on me, didn't he?"

Erin nodded. "Didn't learn much of use from me. And neither will this lot, if it comes to it."

"It won't." Alwenna couldn't have said how she knew, she just did. The Goddess had other plans for them. But she could find anything remotely reassuring about that.

CHAPTER ONE HUNDRED

Marten was gone for hours. Alwenna tried to follow Erin's stoical example and spend the time dozing, but she was too much on edge. Every time she closed her eyes that same vision of fire threatened to overwhelm her. Eventually she got to her feet and paced back and forth. The confines of the guest chamber were too tight, too restricting. Goddess, was the fire to consume them both here? She couldn't shake off the conviction they were trapped. Trapped, traduced, and condemned. She was certain.

Alwenna was staring out of the window, wondering again if it might be better to break it and risk recapture than remain here, when the door latch clattered and Marten entered the room. He bristled with energy and purpose.

"Ladies, you are well rested and fed?" His smile was too bright, too determined.

Alwenna folded her arms. "You lied to us."

Marten set one hand over his heart. "Never. I have done what was necessary. The Goddess will watch over you."

Erin jumped up from the bench, anger etched in her face as she reached for her eating knife.

Alwenna caught her by the arm. "No. When the time

comes I'll cut out his lying tongue myself."

"I have no doubt my wife would thank you for such a service, sister, but from what remains of poor Scoular I suspect your fair companion might make a swifter end of me. Please, if you will accompany me, Tresilian is expecting us."

Four soldiers were waiting outside and they stepped in behind them as they walked along the cloister and into the great hall. It was largely empty at this time of day, with only a few servants sweeping the stone floor and cleaning the tables. The air was heavy with the smell of lavender. Motes of dust raised by the servants' brooms hung in the light from the windows along the south side of the hall.

They carried on up the steps to the dais, past the priestess' bench and stopped at the door leading to the panelled chamber beyond. They waited there while the guard made much business of knocking on the door and announcing their arrival to Tresilian, before gesturing to them to enter the room.

Tresilian was seated on a throne-like chair set on the raised dais before the window embrasure. The heavy wooden chair to which Alwenna had been tied was set off to his left-hand side, the leather straps dangling from the arms as if in readiness. Either side of the window stood Curtis and Weaver, neither of whom made any sign of recognition. Beyond Tresilian, in the deep window embrasure, the priestess knelt at the altar table with her back to them, head bent in prayer. Incense burners on either side of the embrasure filled the room with an overpowering scent, while dishes of lavender were ranged along either wall. All this Alwenna noticed as if in a dream. Her eyes were drawn to the ornate dagger lying on the altar table, glinting in the sunlight. Either side of it were two metal bowls, both inscribed with runes – identical to the bowl used to catch her blood.

Two bowls? She glanced at Erin, who was keeping her head lowered and eyes on the ground. One each? One for each arm? One for each throat? No, surely then they'd have need of bigger bowls. The thought was scant comfort.

In front of her Marten made his obeisance in formal court style, omitting the freemerchant gestures he normally used. Sycophant, she thought, and two-faced to the last. She could remember his anger of the day before, even if he and Tresilian preferred not to. That at least had been honest.

"As promised, highness, I bring the fugitives before you." Marten turned and took his place on Alwenna's right-hand side, while Erin stood on her left. He clasped his hands before him and lowered his head in suitably submissive style. Beneath his elaborate court tunic Alwenna could see he wore serviceable travelling garments. Ready to make a swift exit if his plans went awry? Some plan of his own that Alwenna and Erin had overset?

"Dangerous fugitives they must be, to require so many soldiers to keep them in line." Tresilian ran his gaze over Alwenna and the servant girl. "Wife, remove that peasant's garb. It does not become you."

Alwenna tugged the scarf from her head and shook her unbound hair free.

Tresilian's mouth tightened. "I care even less for the way you've styled your hair."

Alwenna raised her chin. "Your court is teeming with vermin, husband. I would sooner make life difficult for them." She was aware of a tiny motion from Marten. Did he presume to warn caution? She glanced his way before returning her attention to Tresilian's face. "I fear my measures to rid myself of them were not extreme enough."

Did she imagine Tresilian smiled?

Behind her one of the soldiers coughed, and Tresilian turned his attention to them. "You four, wait in the great hall until I give you further orders." He watched, frowning, until they'd withdrawn.

The overpowering smell of incense was making Alwenna lightheaded. Absent-mindedly, she let the headscarf slide from her fingers.

The priestess' voice grew louder as she continued to intone her strange, misshapen words before the altar. Alwenna felt as if she should have recognised them. Tresilian seemed to. For a moment he closed his eyes, his attitude reminiscent of one who was lost in meditation. Tresilian opened his eyes, his expression once more dispassionate. She was nothing more than a problem he needed to solve. She might have reasoned with the old Tresilian, the one she knew. This one was a stranger to her, and the time for reasoning long past.

Marten cleared his throat. "Your highness, I have brought the fugitives as I promised I would. You can have no reason to doubt my loyalty. I beg you will now sign the decrees we agreed at Highkell. That is all I ask, then I shall withdraw from court and trouble you no more."

"But Marten, if you withdraw from court you will serve me no more." Tresilian studied the freemerchant. "And you have been inordinately useful."

Marten bowed graciously. "I try my humble best, your highness."

"Unfortunately in the matter of Highkell, your humble

best has not been good enough."

"Highness, I have brought you through death, and you are as strong as you ever were. I have brought you your queen, who is key to the east. Without the support of her people Vasic's situation is untenable."

"It is not enough. I would be stronger than I ever was. You must remove the usurper from Highkell and bring him to me."

"Highness, for that you would need an army. I am no general."

Alwenna watched them argue. Key to the east? Was that all she'd ever been to her husband? She couldn't believe that. She realised the priestess had fallen silent, thank the Goddess. She looked up to find the girl had stood up and was staring straight at her with those colourless grey eyes.

"You mustn't do this. You mustn't." The girl's voice cracked on the final word.

Foolish girl. "I'm doing nothing."

"Nor will you!" The priestess snatched up the dagger from the altar and rushed forward, throwing herself at Alwenna. Alwenna ducked as the gemstones flashed towards her. Marten grabbed Alwenna's arm and pulled her clear, sending her sprawling on the floor when her ankle gave way. He drew his sword as Erin caught hold of the priestess' knife arm, grappling with her. As abruptly as she'd attacked, the priestess went limp and crumpled to the ground, dropping the dagger. It rolled across the floor and came to rest against the foot of the dais, gems bright and vivid.

Curtis ran forward and dragged Erin away from the priestess, pinning his forearm about her throat.

The priestess slumped on the floor, her words muffled

by sobs. "You mustn't do it. The king has been singled out for great honour by the Goddess." She tried to speak with an air of authority, but her voice was that of a frightened child. "You must not fight her will."

"Great honour?" Alwenna pushed herself up to her hands and knees. "All of that died with him in the dungeon at Highkell."

The girl turned her grey eyes to where the dagger had fallen.

Alwenna was closest to it and before she knew what she was doing she'd grabbed it by the hilt. The gemstones flared. "This is the only instrument the Goddess needs." She felt the blood coursing through her veins and that same lightheadedness she'd experienced when Hames died. This was the will of the Goddess, she was sure of it. She'd never been more sure of anything in her life.

The girl stared, wide-eyed. "You mustn't. You mustn't." She leaped to her feet and dashed for the door to the private chambers beyond, diving through it and slamming it shut. The instant later they heard the sound of the bolt being slid across, then the girl's footsteps retreating.

Weaver had moved to Tresilian's side, his sword at the ready. Tresilian seemed frozen halfway through rising from his seat, unable to tear his eyes from Alwenna. Erin struggled, but Curtis now held her arms pinned behind her back.

Marten turned to Tresilian. "Highness. Nothing has changed, let us discuss this calmly."

"Everything has changed." Tresilian's voice was ice. "You have drawn steel in the king's chamber."

"That girl attacked your wife, highness. I sought only to defend her." Marten sheathed his sword, spreading his hands wide.

Ever so slowly Alwenna eased herself up from the floor and backed away from the dais, dagger in hand. If Tresilian summoned the guards who were waiting outside, the three of them were lost. Whose side Marten was on, she no longer knew. He seemed to occupy a side of his own in this strange stalemate.

Knuckles white, Tresilian pushed himself up off the throne. "Give me that blade, Alwenna. It is not for your hand."

"Is it not?" She twisted the knife in her grip, admiring the play of light over the runes and gems. "I think it knows my hand, husband. Do you not?"

"Sister, he is right," Marten broke in. "That blade is cursed. You must not use it in anger."

Such delicate work. They had no craftsmen to equal it now. "It's not anger I feel right now, Marten." The word she would choose was hunger.

But to share that insight with them would be a bad idea.

A very bad idea.

Monstrous.

Another couple of steps and Alwenna was within arm's reach of the door to the great hall. She slid the heavy bolt shut with a snap.

Guessing her intent too late, Tresilian barked a command. "Stop her!"

Erin yelped in protest. A heavy weight crashed against Alwenna's side, knocking her to the ground and driving the breath from her lungs, while the dagger fell from her hand and spun away across the floor. All was confusion, a tangle of limbs as she and Erin scrambled to their feet. Curtis had hurled the servant girl against her. Swords clashed behind them. On the dais? Before Alwenna could turn to see she was hauled bodily upwards and pinned in a crushing grip. A glint of light flashed across her vision, then a blade pressed against her throat.

"Hold hard, freemerchant, or the witch dies!" Curtis bellowed, backing up against the wall while he kept Alwenna between him and the rest of the room.

Marten had leaped onto the dais to confront Tresilian and now fought him and Weaver. The freemerchant's movements were dance-like. He was quicksilver, making the other two appear leaden and slow as he drew Tresilian over to the window. "Look to your conscience, Weaver. You know I'm not the danger here."

Weaver hesitated, glancing towards where Curtis held Alwenna. He lowered his sword and backed away to the edge of the dais, leaving Tresilian to defend himself. The door to the great hall rattled as the guards outside discovered it had been locked.

Behind Weaver, Tresilian and the freemerchant fought on. One of the incense burners toppled with a crash. Erin flung herself at Curtis, scratching at his eyes. He shoved her away with his elbow, the motion making his knife blade dig into Alwenna's flesh. Grim-faced, Weaver jumped down from the dais, and grabbed Erin as she sprang at Curtis a second time. Weaver pushed the girl away to one side, then swung round to smash his sword pommel into Curtis' face. Flinching, Alwenna heard the crunch of bone cracking beneath the impact and something wet and warm spattered against her face. Curtis' grip slackened. Weaver dragged him away from her, pounding his face over and over, continuing long after the man had subsided on the floor. Alwenna stumbled clear and found herself next to the jewelled dagger once more. Numbly, she picked it up.

The guards hammered against the door. Behind Alwenna, from the dais, came a ragged clatter of metal. She spun round. Marten was parrying desperately with a broken sword as Tresilian drove him back against the wall. The freemerchant was her best chance of getting answers to her questions. And she had many questions. She launched herself forward and charged at Tresilian as he raised his sword high and lunged. Heedless of where she placed her feet, Alwenna cannoned against him with no more than a vague hope of knocking him off balance. Tresilian's sword struck the wall with a clatter of steel against stone as Alwenna went sprawling on the floor.

Tresilian grunted and he staggered sideways. He turned to Alwenna, eyes widening as he took another unsteady step, then his legs crumpled and he fell over onto his back. The ornate handle of Vasic's dagger protruded from his ribs on one side, on the other the hilt of Marten's broken sword. Tresilian's feet convulsed and a pool of urine spread over the floor beneath him, creeping along the joints between the floorboards.

CHAPTER ONE HUNDRED & ONE

Alwenna and Marten stared at one another. Marten rubbed the sweat from his forehead and took a deep breath, but for once he seemed to be at a loss for words. Alwenna scrambled to her feet.

The hammering continued at the door but the bolt was still holding. For now. Curtis was slumped across the doorway, barely recognisable and a threat to no one. Weaver jumped up on the dais next to them, kneeling at Tresilian's side. He checked his throat for a pulse. "He's dead. By the Goddess, what have you done?" He glared at Marten. "This man was the saving of me."

"Can you still not believe me? This would never have happened if he'd only kept his word." Marten stooped over the body. "We'll need this dagger." He tugged it from between Tresilian's ribs then hesitated, staring at the blade. The dead king's blood crept along the runes, spreading until it reached the hilt. The gemstones seemed to grow brighter.

Grimacing, Marten wiped the blade clean on Tresilian's clothing, then straightened up and tucked it away in his belt. He glanced at Alwenna. "It's best that I carry it."

The hammering at the door ceased.

Weaver stood up and turned to Alwenna. "Curtis injured you."

Alwenna raised a hand to her throat. Her fingertips came away sticky with blood. "It doesn't hurt."

Weaver leaned closer. "It's only a scratch, thank the Goddess. I thought—"

There was massive crash against the door from the great hall. It shuddered, but the bolt held. They must have been using one of the benches as a battering ram.

Alwenna turned towards it. "What do we do now? Stay? Or run? Can we stop them?"

"Sister, we run as far and as fast as we can." Marten rattled the door to the private chambers, but it was locked fast. He took up the heavy black chair and smashed it against the leaded window. The first blow caused a bulge, the second burst a couple of panes, the third ripped right through the leadwork. He and Weaver set about clearing the shards from the frame.

"He moved." Erin's voice was high and sharp. "The king moved." She stood with her hand pressed to a cut on her forehead. "See, there it is again." She stepped back, pointing.

Tresilian's feet and hands twitched, convulsive at first, but moving with more deliberation until he could clench and unclench his fists. He drew up first one knee and then the other, his coordination improving with each movement. He pressed his hands against the floor and pushed himself to a sitting position, twisting round until his eyes pointed blindly to where Alwenna stood.

Weaver took up position between them. "Get out through the window. Now."

Erin needed no further encouragement and dashed

over to the window. "I'll bring horses." She climbed out through the broken casement and dropped to the ground, sprinting towards the stables.

Alwenna backed away from Tresilian. His impossible, dead gaze chilled her more than anything she'd ever seen. Already he was clambering to his feet. Weaver readied his guard.

Marten swore and grabbed Curtis' sword, jumping back up onto the dais alongside Weaver. "Fire. We need fire to stop him."

The grate was cold, as might be expected on such a warm day. Alwenna turned in desperation and her foot caught one of the censers which had been knocked to the floor during the fight. It had burst open and the embers scattered across the floor. They were already cool. She scrambled across to the other, set a hand on it and discovered it was still hot. She fumbled it open, then realised she needed tinder. Her scarf. Where had she dropped it? She jumped down from the dais, just as a great creaking sound came from the door. They'd be through any minute.

From behind her came grunts and a gasp, then the clash of steel on steel. She risked a glance over her shoulder: Weaver and Marten fought Tresilian, who'd pulled the broken blade from his chest and was parrying their blows with it. Impossible. She scrambled back up to the censer and dragged it over to the window where there were heavy tapestries. She pressed the scarf into the embers and blew gently as she'd watched Weaver. It smouldered for a moment, then died. Hands shaking, she tried again. Behind her came a rending sound as one of the planks forming the door splintered. This time the fire caught and a bright flame sprang from the fabric. Hands shaking, she set it against the fringe of the tapestry. The ancient textile was dry and parched and the fire spread quickly. She pushed the altar table against it and the cloth covering that began to smoulder, then flared. The fire climbed rapidly, devouring the tapestry and racing across the ornate drapery over the window. The wood panelling above it singed and blistered, and smoke billowed up to the ceiling.

The door to the great hall splintered further and shouts from the other side could be heard.

"Get out!" Marten yelled over his shoulder as he and Weaver fought Tresilian away to the edge of the dais. Alwenna clambered into the opening, ducking through it as several priests burst into the room from the private quarters. The sudden rush of air set the flames roaring higher. Weaver spun round to force the priests back, just as Marten propelled Tresilian backwards off the dais. The room was filling with smoke. Alwenna clung there in the window embrasure. She thought she recognised her uncle's scarred face through the smoke before Marten moved to Weaver's side and they pushed the priests back to the doorway.

"I'll hold them here, you go." Weaver shouldered the freemerchant aside. Knocked off balance, Marten staggered towards the window and Weaver planted himself squarely in front of the doorway.

"Weaver, no!" Alwenna shouted, without ever meaning to.

"Just go," he shouted back.

The tapestry beside Alwenna collapsed in a burst of sparks and flying embers and she had to jump away from the window, landing on the cobbles outside. A sword clattered down nearby as Marten dived through after her, his sleeve in flames. He rolled on the ground and Alwenna wrapped her hands in her cloak and beat at the burning fabric. Smoke billowed from the window now, and shouts were going up around the palace.

Marten sat up, coughing. He pushed himself to his feet and retrieved the sword, his eyes on the window.

With a clatter of hooves, three horses charged into the yard. Erin rode the middle one and was leading the other two by halters. "These were all I could get. There're soldiers everywhere."

Alwenna grabbed the halter Erin tossed to her. Marten sheathed his sword and legged her up onto the horse's bare back, then looped the end of the halter round to form makeshift reins.

"What about Weaver? We can't leave him."

"He knows how to look after himself." Marten looped the halter of his own horse round and vaulted on, but he waited, his eyes on the broken window. Thick black smoke poured from the room. From inside there was a sharp cracking sound and a fresh shower of sparks issued from the window, followed by a burst of flames. All three horses spun away from it. Alwenna had to grab the mane to stay seated. Marten brought his horse round in a circle, but now flames roared from the window as the timber dais must have caught alight. He shook his head and turned his horse away. The horses needed no urging to break into a canter and they dashed out through the stable yard.

Everyone there was scrambling for buckets and water. In the confusion no one challenged them. The gates to the palace stood wide open to admit a group of farmers' wagons. They galloped for the gates, their horses' hooves clattering over the cobbles. A single guard at the gateway stepped forward but Marten rode straight for him. Sunlight glanced off the freemerchant's sword and the man fell aside.

A moment later they were free and galloping along the road that led north.

CHAPTER ONE HUNDRED & TWO

They didn't stop and didn't speak until the road had climbed off the plain where the summer palace was situated. There was a cluster of trees by a small stream and they halted there. Alwenna slid from her horse's back, legs almost buckling beneath her as her feet touched the ground. Her face was tight and gritty where tears had been whipped dry by the wind. Erin took her horse's halter and tied it to the tree with the other two. Finally Alwenna turned and looked back along the empty road. A haze hung over the plain, but rising through it was a dark column of smoke, sluggish, belying the intensity of the flames that were devouring the summer palace.

Alwenna's eyes stung. The stench of smoke filled her nostrils again and tickled at her lungs, making her cough. She pushed the vision away, only to find it left her mind, like her heart, desperately empty. She made no objection as Erin led her to the small stream and sat unresisting on the bank as the girl bathed her blistered hands and cleansed the cut on her throat, then tore her own voluminous headscarf in two so Alwenna might also be protected from the sun.

Alwenna sank her hands into the shallow water. It was

clean and pure. It brought her comfort, but showed her nothing of Weaver's fate.

Blisters were forming on Marten's arm where his sleeve had caught fire. Erin helped him remove his tunic so they could bathe his arm in the cold stream. As she did so the dagger slipped from his belt, falling on the ground between him and Alwenna. The stones were dull and lifeless now, the runes barely visible.

"We should leave that thing behind." Alwenna's voice was as dry and cracked as she felt. "Bury it where no one will find it."

Marten winced as the water splashed over his burned skin. "Your instinct is good, but there may be safer places." He straightened up, cautiously rolling his tattered shirt sleeve down over the blisters. "And there is the possibility we may need it again."

"Hasn't it done enough damage?" Alwenna glared at it. Was it her imagination or did the gemstones deepen in colour? Some trick of the sunlight through the trees?

"That's the problem, sister. We may need to draw upon it to undo such damage as we can."

"What could we possibly hope to undo?" The smoke, the flames? Weaver? Tresilian's dead stare? Or Goddess forbid, his father's? Alwenna shivered.

"You saved my life today, sister. Now I would save your soul."

Alwenna's eyes turned to the knife again. The gemstones glinted now. Such a pretty thing.

"We should wrap it up. Bind it up so no one can touch it." Erin's voice startled Alwenna, who looked up guiltily.

Erin hitched her skirt up and took her eating knife to her underskirts, tearing off a long strip which she dropped over the knife, then folded around it. Alwenna followed suit, handing the fabric to Erin, who wrapped the bundle a second time. Marten held out his ragged sleeve and she took the lower portion of that and added it, tying it securely with another strip of petticoat. Then she went to the horses and plucked three hairs from each of their tails, plaiting them and knotting them over the bundle.

"My da always said it was lucky."

As if anything they did now could change what had happened.

They sat there on the riverbank with the innocuous bundle between them. Alwenna's baby wriggled and she finally tore her eyes away from the package, pressing her hand to her abdomen.

"My soul, Marten? Does it need saving?"

"You became kinslayer when you saved me – and you used a cursed blade tainted with your family's blood."

"Is it kinslaying to kill one who has already died?"

Marten shrugged. "In truth, I do not know. The blade already draws you."

Alwenna drew in a deep breath, then spoke carefully. "I'm carrying his child. From... before. Before I was sent from Highkell. Might this curse harm the child?"

Marten's face was grave. "I... It... Our elders will know."

"How will we find them?" How did freemerchants find one another? They could be anywhere across the Peninsula.

"At Scarrow's Deep."

"Where's that?"

"It's the place we freemerchants call home, sister."

"But you're not allowed to hold land."

"You'll not find Scarrow's Deep on any map of the

Peninsular Kingdoms." With a tight smile, Marten picked up the bundle containing the dagger and stowed it inside his tunic.

Alwenna fought the urge to snatch it from him.

"And we don't hold Scarrow's Deep by any royal decree. We scratched it from the bowels of the earth with our bare hands, in a remote corner where no king holds sway."

"Weaver said you had many secrets to hide." She spoke his name without thinking. He might have survived. Maybe if she spoke his name often enough...

"Our people have learned to hide our secrets well, sister. Now we must ride. The sooner we reach Scarrow's Deep, the sooner we can answer your questions."

Alwenna twisted round to look back towards the summer palace before they rode over the crest of the ridge. The column of smoke rose still, higher and higher, dark and bold, climbing through the cloudless sky. Her work this time. She couldn't blame groundwater, or poor foundations. She'd kindled the fire, set the flames, done everything just as Weaver had taught her.

Her monstrous work.

She turned her back and rode after the others.

CHAPTER ONE HUNDRED & THREE

At Highkell, Vasic rose from his sickbed. The room was rank with the stench of stale sweat and vomit. And something else. Smoke? He pushed back the curtains, peering out over the courtyard. He could see no sign of anything burning, no sign of smoke. But the daylight felt good on his face.

He opened the casement, gulping in the fresh air with a vigour he hadn't known in days. He stretched, braced for the pain that would shoot through his limbs and settle beneath his ribs, gnawing at his innards.

Except... the pain had gone. He prodded the area gingerly, again braced for the stabbing sensation, but there was no trace of it. He felt nothing more than the residual stiffness of one who had lain in bed too long.

He summoned a servant. "Bring me hot water. I will bathe. Summon the healer. And my steward after that. And I want food, proper food. Meat. None of that pap you've been bringing me of late." Vasic turned to look out of the window again, out over the gorge across the valley to the wooded hills that were so often shrouded in rain, but now basked in sunshine.

He drew in a long breath, filling his lungs to capacity. He smiled. Life was good.

ACKNOWLEDGMENTS

Thanks must go to my family, for putting up with the ongoing chaos at home that writing a book apparently involves; to my tutors at the Open University for giving me the self-belief to pursue publication; to my fellow students for their friendship and for the collective craziness every November since 2007; to my agent, Sam Copeland, and the teams, past and present, at Angry Robot for their enthusiasm. Especial thanks for early feedback and wisdom from Anouska Huggins, Graeme Talboys and Dave Hutchinson; and to Mike Shevdon for a *blistering* critique of the first 10,000 words back in the earliest days, which helped set me on the right path.

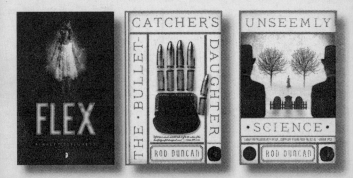